Marsha Barth's book stands out as an in... ...mpassionate and candid journey from ...... ...ing of healing. *THE SHATTERL...* ...ritten with personal knowledge of ι ...h a unique understanding of the hea... ...very reader will learn that, while the ... is not easy and it is not quick, it is possible if we break the silence that has trapped so many in the past. This engaging book will be a valuable resource for all who are committed to the healing process.

~ PA State Representative Mauree Gingrich

Sexual abuse destroys, and how much more when it is perpetrated upon an innocent child. Because of a "little faith" put in Christ Jesus, Marty "was not" and "has not" been destroyed! She is a Victor! "....Though I walk through the Valley of the Shadow of Death I shall fear no Evil." Through Jesus' everlasting power, Marty has overcome! She has been commissioned by our Lord Jesus Christ. She encourages others to walk through the shadows, knowing that the One who suffered unto death will deliver them unto everlasting Life. Thank you Marty for putting your faith in Jesus Christ, hearing God, and coming forward so others may know Him and find healing and peace. *THE SHATTERING II: Breaking the Silence* is a story of a life, enacting Faith to overcome unto Victory!

~ Larry D. Stewart Jr.
Family Preservation and Reunification Specialist

The first right of any child victim is not to have been a victim at all. Marsha Barth's book demonstrates why this is so critical.

~ Andrew Willis
Founder of the STOP ABUSE CAMPAIGN

An important study from the Centers for Disease Control demonstrates that the United States allows one-quarter of our children to be sexually abused before their 18th birthday. This scandal is tolerated because public officials and the general public turn the other way; they can't imagine that per say, normal men and women could commit such heinous acts, discourage children from reporting abuse, and most important, don't believe children. Marsha Barth makes an important contribution by telling her true story in *THE SHATTERING II*. I liked this book a lot. It was really moving for me that Julie went to Hawaii right after her dramatic meetings with her father, as Andrew Willis and I will be going to Hawaii to try to pass the Safe Child Act. Many people turn away when the subject is child sexual abuse, and that is an important part of why it is so prevalent. Marsha's writing makes us care deeply about a frightened and broken girl who becomes a courageous woman. I hope this book can be used to encourage the needed reforms in order to save our children. The author is a woman of faith and reminds us that on earth, God's work must truly be our own.

~ Barry Goldstein
Nationally recognized domestic violence author, speaker and advocate; former attorney representing victims of domestic violence for 30 years; and author of five books including
Scared to Leave, Afraid to Stay: Paths from Family Violence to Safety
and *The Quincy Solution: Stop Domestic Violence and Save $500 Billion*

THE SHATTERING II

THE SHATTERING II

*"If we can be brave enough to enter into the dark
shadows of the unspeakable and pull back the curtains,
we not only reveal the light but we also set the captives
free. It is God's desire to take you from lost to found,
from victim to victor, from death to life."*

Breaking the Silence
MARSHA BARTH

Robert D. Reed Publishers • Bandon, Oregon

Robert D. Reed Publishers
P.O. Box 1992
Bandon, OR 97411
Phone: 541-347-9882; Fax: -9883
E-mail: 4bobreed@msn.com
Website: www.rdrpublishers.com

Editor: Cleone Reed
Cover Designer: Cleone Reed
Book Designer: Susan Leonard

Soft-cover ISBN: 978-1-944279-05-3
eBook ISBN: 978-1-944279-06-0

Library of Congress Control Number: 2017930991

Designed and Formatted in the United States of America

Dedication

To my momma—Whose love guided me, believed in me, corrected me, and assured me that I was so much more…

Acknowledgments

"For we are saved by hope…." I lovingly acknowledge my thread of Hope, my precious heavenly father, whose love for me showed me the love of a true father.

"No greater love than this…." *John 15:13*. "I am my beloved's and my beloved is mine," *Solomon 6:3*. I could have never dreamed in those darkest hours of my life that there was such a "beloved" waiting for me in the next season of my life. To my dearest Mike, my love, my soul mate, my friend; truly you are proof of God's promises fulfilled. You are my heart's beat, the arm that catches me when I slip—the voice that echoes your belief in me. Where was I when God spoke the words—"Yes, this is her beloved." "I will surely do this." I do not know. Yet here I am, safe in your enduring love. Thank you for our life, our family, our foundation, and your endless support, work, and help in bringing this book to fruition. Your tireless effort and encouragement believed in me; your love carried me.

To my dear momma, I will always love you. You saw beyond my brokenness. You may not have known the cause, but you knew my heart, my doubts, and my pain. Your love for me gave me the stability of knowing that "I mattered." I lovingly dedicate this book to you.

To my dear brothers, Donnie, Terry, and Pat; has any sister ever been so blessed to have not one, not two, but three big brothers who believed, fortified, and carried a sister through those dark childhood days? You were my protectors, my mentors, my strength, and my refuge for shelter when I had no one else to turn to. I will be forever twined in the love you gave and continue to give to me.

To my dear Marlene, you bore so much, carried such a load, and yet your love for me came at such a time in my life that it breathed pure hope into my soul. I will always love and hold you in a special part of my heart.

To my "Bucky" who filled a large gap in my heart and loved me as a father, who wiped away my tears and held me to his heart as his daughter. I treasure you.

To all of my family, my precious grandparents, aunts, uncles, cousins, nieces, nephews, and step-sisters, I thank you for the days of sunshine, the good memories, the picnics out at McDonald's Beach, the Sunday dinners, the games of "Wahoo," "Hide and Seek," "Up on the Mountain was a Great Big Bear," baseball games and more. But it is your "love" that resounds in my heart always.

To my steadfast friends and loved ones who stood by me in my childhood, those who stood with me in my adulthood, and to all of you who have taken me under wing and believed in me and know my heart, I truly thank you and lean on your support and prayers.

To my precious children and grandchildren, you are my greatest treasure. You are my ray of light, my laughter, my joy. To my son, Mike Jr., I do not know anyone who has a more sensitive heart for others. You reach to the depths of others' needs and your love is unending. To my daughter Missy (Mike's wife), you are an inspiration. I love you dearly. To my Jen Jen, my precious "baby girl", you are a bright and shining light. Your fearless unseen faith grows deep within and propels you forward in everything that you face. You are our sweetheart. You are so loved. To my precious boys, my grandsons, you are my hope for a better tomorrow, my greatest heritage. My Ethan, you are the steady heart, full of love, our philosopher, and our bright light in the night. My Jadon, you are our professor, organizer, our sure tower, and a true gift of love.

My Colin, you are our beacon of joy, giving us laughter, love, and strength. My Benjamin, you are our quiet confidence, a thinker, and one of the most sensitive and loving of souls. My Isaac, you march to the beat of your own drum, have a smile that could change the world, and you overflow with sweetness. Our baby Matthew, you hold our hearts in your grasp, bring preciousness as the morning light, and are the essence of enduring love. To our sweet baby girl, Savannah Rose, who just joined us, we trust that you will straighten all of our boys out.

My thanks to Robert D. Reed Publishers and staff for all of their labor and work in making this book a success. Thank you for believing in this work and for giving me this opportunity.

Preface

"Our lives should be a beacon so that even after we are gone, our light still helps others to find their way." *(mlb)*

"This little light of mine,
I'm gonna let it shine,
Let it shine, let it shine, let it shine."

This is a song that we sang a long time ago, in the little country church where I grew up, in the hills of Appalachia. How one longs for a glimpse of light to shine through when we are in the midst of our darkest nights. But where do we find the light? Who has escaped the darkness that will dare to come back to shine a light? And what light is bright enough to pierce that darkness?

If we can be brave enough to enter into the dark shadows of the unspeakable and pull back the shades, we not only reveal the light, but we set the captives free. Anytime that truth is hidden, regardless of how painful it is to reveal it, evil will continue. Prevailing truth destroys evil. Prevailing love nurtures the broken and shattered.

Abuse of any kind shatters the spirit and rapes the soul. Abuse rips your hope, your joy, your laughter, your dreams, your worthiness, your value, your peace, and your love. The more one is abused, the more one will desire to be loved. But instead of feeling the love that is craved, the less they are loved, the more anger they will feel—anger at not being loved, anger at being hurt, anger at being trapped, anger from the pain, anger at the next anticipated abuse. Anger rages where love was meant to grow. Anger is chosen as a means to defend, to empower, and to protect. It is as if anger is a volcano which erupts within us and spews forth its hot fire threatening to devour everything in its path, beginning with the very mountain it originated from. Nothing seems to matter but to break free of the pain that is ricocheting within us. While we try to numb the hurt and pain, our mind races helplessly, while the broken and shattered heart lies in a crumpled pile. The mind finally grabs onto anger again, wielding its sword in a different manner now, not to defend or protect, but to join with its partner—rage. Together, anger and rage vent and plummet, caring not who or what is in their path, not even themselves; for their heart still lies broken and shattered, still and lifeless. Fear continues to press anger and rage forward. The broken and shattered do not know what to do and hope is gone.

We were never meant to try to live our lives empowered by anger and rage. We were never meant to live our lives in darkness, under the shroud of fear and shame and guilt and blame, torn asunder by denial, minimization, justification, control, manipulation, and intimidation. We were meant to be set free, to heal from our hurt and pain, to be delivered from anger and rage, and to go from "Victim to Victor." We can heal. Healing is first a choice and after that a journey.

But how does one heal? How can all of the shattered pieces of our life be put back together again? "All of the king's horses and all of the king's men couldn't put Humpty together again."

"For we are saved by hope...." *Romans 8:24.* I remember as a little girl when someone had given me a little cardboard book marker. It had a picture of Jesus at the top, and on the bottom half, a little white cross implanted on a blue velvet shield. The amazing thing was that the cross glowed in the dark. Such a faint light it was, but a beacon to my soul. It was a constant reminder to me throughout my childhood, of a hope that I had found as a little girl in that country church. Without hope, we perish. "Hope is tangible and breathes life and passion into every human soul that will dare to reach out, grab it, and believe." *(mlb)*

"A broken heart and a shattered spirit, He will not refuse." *Psalm 51:17.* God is more than a Humpty Dumpty God. He does more than try to put the pieces back together again. He makes us a new creature in Him. He gives us a new hope that is tangible. He takes away the anger and rage as they are no longer needed to defend, empower, and protect. He restores, creates, and mends the brokenness, until once again the heart is made anew and whole. It beats forth with a new hope, laughter, joy, strength, faith, courage, wisdom, understanding, determination—a victorious heart; a loving heart. Love replaces hate. Courage replaces fear. Hope replaces despair. Understanding and wisdom replace vengeance. Laughter replaces sorrow. There is a new beginning, a new season, a future.

May you be blessed in reading this book. Though it is a sequel, it stands on its own story line. It is my true story of overcoming childhood sexual abuse. It is a story of the power of love, the promise of hope and the inspiration of knowing that what has happened to us does not define who we are.

"Man can only discover new oceans if he has the courage to lose sight of the shore." (*Andre Gide*)

This is my continuing story of knowing the joy of overcoming. Join me on this healing journey. The journey continues....

The Cliff

CHAPTER

1

Julie nervously paced the floor, back and forth. Her mind raced. No matter how hard she tried, she could not organize her thoughts. They bounced around inside her head like ping pong balls, ricocheting one against the other, until Julie thought that her head would burst. *What can I do? What can I do?*

Julie could hear the sound of voices rise from downstairs as the argument escalated. There was no stopping them. Julie had tried and tried countless times before to help settle her dad and step-mom's arguments, but tonight, this would be impossible. Things had gone too far. There was no turning back.

Julie walked quickly to the window and pulled down the blind with a quick jerk. As she let it go, it snapped at the top and continued to spin. Julie reached and unlocked the window, and then with a quick thrust pushed it upward. Dampness had made the wood frame swell as Julie tugged at the window earnestly to get it to open further.

It was late. Julie leaned out the window. She shivered as the cold air rushed past her. Looking up into the sky, tiny snowflakes caught onto her eyelids causing her to blink. The full moon cast its light, brightening the surroundings. The porch roof on the other side of the opened window was covered with a fine dusting of snow. Julie pulled the blind back down and left the jammed window open.

Again, she paced the floor, her hands on her forehead as if to pull some solution to the problem out of her troubled mind. Julie walked to her bedroom door and quietly cracked it open. She had hoped the quiet pause might have meant that the argument was over. She listened intently and then heard Alice say, "I'm leaving Ron. I've only been staying because of Julie, but now, I feel that I've lost her love also. I'm calling my mom to wire me some money. I'm going back to Michigan."

Julie could barely hear her dad's slurred response. "Go. Go. See if I care. You think you'll do better in Michigan?" It became very quiet. Julie could hear Alice pick up the phone receiver and heard her begin to dial.

Tears flooded down Julie's face. She couldn't lose Alice. All of her brothers were grown and had left home. Julie, now seventeen, just couldn't live—in this house—with her dad alone. She felt a wave of panic hit her. *I can't stay here. I just can't. I'd rather die. I'd rather die.*

Julie rushed around the room and looked for her jacket and shoes. She had left both of them downstairs when she had come home from babysitting her cousins earlier that evening. Julie dropped to her knees and looked under the bed for any pair of shoes; however, there were none. All that she could find was an old pair of thin rubber boots that were made to slip over shoes. Julie quickly rummaged through her dresser drawers and found a pair of socks. She pulled on a thin sweater and found her lighter jacket lying on the vanity bench. Quickly, she put on the thin socks and grabbed the pair of boots. The straps had broken long ago. They were much too small but Julie had no choice. She couldn't go downstairs to get her shoes and coat. It would just start the arguing all over again. Julie could see the scenario unfold in her mind as it had in reality so many times before. If she would tell her dad that she was going up to her gramma's house, he would yell, "Get back here young lady!" Alice would try to defend and protect her from her dad, and then he'd start all over again and tear into Alice.

Julie could feel her heart pounding within her chest. If only she had not hurt Alice's feelings. Alice was the dearest of souls. They had never even had a disagreement in the three years that Julie had known her. She couldn't even recall what they had disagreed about this time. All that she knew was that she had hurt her stepmom's feelings and she didn't know how to make it right. And now, Alice was going to leave and Julie wouldn't ever be able to make it right. It would be all her fault, just as when her dad's old girlfriend, Rhonda, had left them.

Julie gave each of the rubber boots a quick tug and felt them slide on one by one. She grabbed the thin jacket and put it on. Once again, she pulled the blind up and felt the cold air hit her face. She straddled the window and then began to climb out. Carefully, she placed one foot onto the icy shingles and tried not to slip as she hoisted the rest of her body onto the roof. With her hands still clutching the window sill, she glanced back into her bedroom. She listened intently to hear if anyone had heard her or if there was any noise at all coming from downstairs. Everything was silent. Julie let go of the window sill and decided to not even try to close the stubborn window. She turned and positioned herself onto the slippery roof. She knew it was late, possibly two o'clock in the morning, as all of the cars across the street at Lindy's Tavern were gone.

Julie sat for a moment on the roof. She pulled her knees to her chest. She looked up at the mountainside that stood before her where her Gramma Emma and Uncle Tom lived. The moonlight shined brightly onto their homes in the distance. Snowflakes melted as they landed upon Julie's warm cheeks. They mixed with the tears which ran down her face. She had to leave. She knew that she could not stay and live with her dad if Alice left. In her confusion, her mind raced. She would have to figure it all out later. The main thing was…where could she go tonight? *Up to Gramma's,* she thought. Gramma was used to her coming up when her dad and stepmom argued.

In all of her seventeen years of excursions, Julie had never attempted to climb out of her window onto the roof of her house and down onto the porch. *I have no choice,* she thought as she eyed the length of the roof and the slippery snow that dusted it.

Julie slowly scooted across the porch roof and tried to feel for the rough shingles to keep herself from sliding. Slowly, she crawled towards the corner of the porch roof. When she made it close to the edge, she grabbed onto the gutter to feel more secure. She knew that it would never hold her if she slipped. She glanced down. The moonlight brightened everything around her. She could see the ground beneath her. It surprised her at how far down it looked. Julie eyed up the corner and turned onto her belly. Slowly, she inched her way to the edge. She let her fingernails dig into the rough shingles. She knew that it would do little good if she started to slide. She felt her legs drape slowly over the roof's edge as she slowly pushed herself down. While lying in place, Julie rested her arms and upper body weight onto the roof. She swung her legs gently below to find the porch post. She wrapped both of her legs firmly around the post and then, ever so slowly, began to slide down the post. Julie let go of the roof with her one hand and then let go of the gutter with the other hand and quickly wrapped both of them tightly around the top of the porch post. Feeling with the tip of her boot as she slid slowly down the post, she finally felt the top of the porch banister. She placed both of her feet firmly onto the banister and then, as if in one quick motion, jumped and tumbled down to the ground and then quickly jumped back up. Julie glanced at the front door and expected it to open up in front of her with all the noise that she had made. To her dismay, she could hear the sound of shouting and knew that the argument had started all over again.

Julie opened the front gate of the fence and shut it quietly. *It wouldn't have made any difference, if she had slammed it shut,* she thought; *no one would have heard it.*

Julie walked up the deserted path. She knew it by heart and had walked it often. Even in the dark, she wasn't afraid. The moonlight was bright and the snow had stopped falling. She crossed the little wooden bridge over the stream and climbed up the steep bank along its narrow path. She then crossed the dirt road and climbed up another steep bank. She hoped that Mr. Sellers' dogs were tied up as she took the shortcut across their yard, past their old outhouse and onto the dirt road that led past her Uncle Tom and Aunt Lisa Sue's house. Julie paused for a moment to get her breath. She turned and looked down into the valley. She could see her house with its faint lights still lit. She turned and looked at her Uncle Tom's house which was pitch black. Julie knew that her aunt and uncle had gone to bed a long time ago. Julie sadly turned and began to walk up the dirt road to her Gramma Emma's house. She tucked her head down from the cold and walked aimlessly up the road. At the top of the hill, Julie paused and looked up at her gramma's house. All the lights were off except for one dim light which Julie knew was her Gramma Emma's bedroom light.

Julie shivered in the cold. A light breeze blew through her hair. Her feet were freezing cold from walking upon the icy snow with only her thin rubber boots. She wished that she could have grabbed her shoes and heavy coat but had thought that she would be okay until she got to her gramma's house.

As Julie approached the house, she imagined how warm it would feel once in bed and under the covers. But now she wasn't sure. Stopping at the front porch, she hesitated. She knew that the front door would be unlocked. Somehow it just didn't seem right to barge into her gramma's house this late at night. Julie guessed that by now, it had to be near three o'clock in the morning. She knew that she'd surely get into trouble with her dad once he found out that she had awakened her gramma in the middle of the night. *I don't know what to do? I just don't know where to go?* Julie turned reluctantly and began to walk up the old worn path that led to the little white house with red shutters. It was their old home. She climbed its few steps and sat on the deserted porch.

Julie began to weep. She gripped the rail in front of her which surrounded the small porch. She and her family had lived here many years ago until she was six years old. This used to be their home, the home where her mom and dad and three brothers had once been a family. Julie remembered that it was on this very porch that her brothers brought home a little cocker spaniel that they said had followed them home from school. They had talked Julie into convincing their parents on letting them keep her. To all of their surprise, their mom and dad had allowed them. They named her Mamie and she became their best friend.

Julie brushed the tears from her cold cheek. She rested her head upon the porch rail as her thoughts raced within her. She looked past the big old blue spruce that towered towards the sky.

In her mind she could see Ronnie, her oldest brother, running up the hill those many years ago when they were just young children. His face was white as a sheet as he had joined her and her brothers Jerry and Matt. His popgun hung limply at his side. "We have to run away!" Ronnie blurted out.

"What's wrong?" Jerry asked as he rushed to Ronnie's side. Both Julie and Matt ran to join them. This was their way. The four of them did everything together. They were inseparable.

"I shot Pap Pap James in the eye with my popgun," Ronnie exclaimed.

"But how did you do that?" Matt asked nervously. He knew that the cork from the old gun had been lost for a long time. "There's no cork to shoot."

"Well, I, I, just pushed the gun down into the mud and when I saw Pap Pap James, I aimed it at him, kind of pretending and then somehow I just pulled the trigger and the mud hit him right in the eye."

"What did you do then?" Julie asked, speaking up for the first time.

"Well, I ran like crazy! That's what I did!" Ronnie answered. "But I gotta run away! You all want to come with me?"

"Sure!" Jerry answered.

"We'll go with you Ronnie," Matt joined in.

Julie just nodded her head in agreement.

All four of them had run up into the woods. Julie remembered hearing her mom and dad calling them to come home for supper but they ignored them. They knew that they were in trouble. They reluctantly returned home when it became dark. And as they had expected, they got a licking with their dad's old Marine Corps belt and were all sent to bed.

A cold breeze suddenly blew, sending shivers through Julie, shaking her out of the thoughts of her childhood. She shifted nervously on the porch. She felt the rough boards beneath her. She loved this old house. Julie couldn't hold back the emotions and began to sob into her folded arms which rested upon the porch rail.

Julie remembered when just a year ago, she had sat on this very porch. Even then, her dad and Alice were having difficulties in their marriage. Julie had felt on that day that her dad had gone too far. He had hurt both Alice's and her brother Matt's feelings. He had accused them both of horrible things. Matt had left home that very day, permanently, and had gone to live with their mom. Julie remembered how, on that day, she had stood up to her dad and told him that she, also, was going to leave home unless he apologized to Matt and Alice and made it right. She didn't know what had gotten into her. She had never confronted her dad in such a way. Julie hated confrontations. She hated to deal with problems. It was so much easier to just push them under the rug and try to forget them when anything bad would happen. This is what she had always done throughout her childhood. But somehow things were changing inside of Julie.

Ever since she had given her heart to God, her life had begun to change in ways that Julie never expected. She had begun to stand up to her dad. She tried to be respectful in the ways that she would confront him, however, without backing down. She couldn't understand why, but at times it seemed a matter of survival for her to take a stand. As difficult as it was and as much as Julie tried to avoid the confrontations, when confronted by her dad, she would not back down. It upset her father terribly. He couldn't tolerate not having control over her. Julie always knew that she would eventually pay a price for standing up to him.

Julie, now sitting on the same porch that she had sat on a year ago, wondered how this could be happening all over again. Julie shook from the cold as she sat quietly, staring aimlessly down at the valley before her. On that day, a year ago, she had run out of the house ignoring her dad's angry screams. He, at first, had practically laughed at her when she had told him that he must apologize. Julie could still remember the incessant smirk on his face, only to see it turn to anger when she defied him by leaving. She was determined to never return home until her dad would make things right with Alice and Matt. On that day, Julie had tried to sort out her thoughts and come to terms with what she had done, much as she was doing right now. These same thoughts were once again racing through her mind as they had so many times in the past. *What have I done and where will I go now?* As back then, there hadn't been much time to think or make a plan.

Julie's dad had followed her on that day a year ago. She remembered sitting on this same porch and watching her dad pull up in the little white Chevy. Rocks sprayed everywhere as he came to a screeching stop in front of her gramma's house. He didn't see her at first. She wanted to jump up and run away and hide. But it was too late. He saw her and approached her angrily, demanding that she come back home. But Julie respectfully refused. "No, Dad," she said calmly, "not until you make it right with Matt and Alice."

She had caught her dad off guard. She could see his expression go from astonishment, to confusion, and then to unmistakable anger. Julie had not wanted to upset her dad. She didn't want to be disrespectful. She hated confrontations. She was so torn inside.

How could it be right to stand up to her dad? As a Christian, she was supposed to honor and obey her father. As her mind spun in confusion that day, her dad approached the porch. Julie sat and watched him approach closer and closer. She looked for his hand to move to his belt waiting for him to unbuckle it, as he had done so often when she was a child, and pull it off in a show of authority for her to come with him. But he only looked at her with a steadfast glare. More than a belt or any words that he had ever spoken, it was this look that had controlled Julie for years.

With one piercing look, he paused to emphasize the point that he was going to make and then spoke. "Then you are no longer a daughter of mine!" He didn't wait for her response or for her to follow him but turned and walked away leaving her all alone. His words had pierced through her heart. She had always wondered if her dad had ever really loved her and her brothers. Julie didn't know what to feel or do when he outwardly disowned her as his daughter.

Julie, once again, sat and cried as she had back then. Julie tried to reflect back, deeply to that day, trying to remember how she could have done anything different. However, once again, there didn't seem to be any answer other than to go forward blindly.

Julie remembered when, on that day, she had gradually pulled herself together and wiped her eyes. She had waited until she thought that no one would know that she had been crying and then went down to her Uncle Tom's house to babysit her cousins while her uncle and Aunt Lisa Sue went bowling for the night. She had tried that whole evening to put her thoughts aside, but they continued to ricochet through her mind. Julie had figured that she would just go to sleep at her Gramma Emma's house that night until she could work out the problems with her dad. She hated to drag her gramma into the problem.

Julie pondered as she recalled that day, and that now a year later she was in the same predicament, except that this time it was worse because it was too late at night to go to her gramma's or her uncle's house. While remembering that day, she had hoped to find the answer that wasn't there a year ago. Julie recalled, later that night after her Uncle Tom and Aunt Lisa had come home, she had gathered her things to leave and it had surprised her when Aunt Lisa had asked her where she was going to stay. Julie had paused and looked at her aunt's face and then glanced over at her uncle who was sitting in the corner chair behind the kitchen table. The realization then hit her that both her aunt and uncle must have heard what had happened between her and her dad earlier. Julie had felt her head spin as she groped for the words to answer her aunt. "I thought I'd go up to Gramma's tonight?" Julie answered softly.

"And then what?" came the kind voice from behind her.

Julie turned to face her uncle to search his face. His kindness to her touched her in such a way that Julie thought she would break down and cry. *Could anyone possibly care about the dilemma that she had gotten herself into?*

Aunt Lisa touched her arm gently in affection and looked deeply into her eyes. "Your uncle and I have talked, Julie, and you can stay with us for a while if you want to."

Julie's mind raced within her. She turned to look at her uncle and then back at her aunt. Emotions rose up within her to the point that she didn't know what to do or think. She was so moved by their compassion that she thought that she would just burst into tears. She reached for the kitchen chair and felt its cold metal frame against her hand. She tried to steady herself as her mind raced to try to organize her thoughts in order to respond to her aunt. But all Julie could concentrate on was the nausea that arose inside her stomach. She thought she was going to be sick and didn't know what to do. Everything began to swim around her and she felt weak as her legs went limp and buckled beneath her.

Julie saw her aunt and uncle leaning over her as she slowly awoke and opened her eyes. She felt the coolness of a cold rag as Aunt Lisa Sue wiped her forehead. Julie tried to get up but her uncle told her to lay still. Gradually, Julie sat up and leaned against the leg of the kitchen table. She felt embarrassed as her aunt and uncle stood by her quietly.

Julie stayed with her aunt and uncle in their little house for a week before she had decided to go back home to keep peace. Julie felt so badly for intruding upon her aunt and uncle even though they had made her feel so welcome. Alice had forgiven her dad though he had never told her that he was sorry. He still believed that his fiery accusations against Alice and Matt were true. He never apologized to Matt. Matt had never returned home after that night and had gone to live permanently with their mom. Julie knew the contention that night had caused within her family. She could only imagine the heat that her uncle had received from her dad for his intervention. And yet, through it all, they had taken a stand for her. Julie would never forget their act of love and kindness.

Julie began to learn that the more she dealt with their family issues, and the more that she confronted them, the more empowered she felt to overcome them. She also knew that the more she confronted her dad, the more problems it would cause in their family, especially when it affected her gramma or aunts and uncles. For that reason, more than ever, she did not want to upset the whole family again tonight as she had the previous year.

Julie lifted her head off the cold porch rail and once again looked down into the valley. The trees blocked her house far in the distance. Even thinking back to the incident last year, it gave her no resolve of what she could or should do tonight. She wondered what was happening with her dad and Alice. *Had Alice gone or would she dare try to stay at their house and wait until morning?* Julie just did not know what to do. *Where can I go? What can I do?* she sobbed as her mind raced. Her body shook with each sob as the cold continued to penetrate to her very soul.

"Nothing matters anymore," Julie whispered out loud. She wiped her eyes and stood up. Shivering from the cold, she rushed off the porch and began to walk up the path that led further up the mountain and into the woods. Julie didn't know where she was going. She had no plan but knew that she couldn't go home. She walked in a daze. Nothing seemed real.

The full moon reflected brightly lighting her way. Julie climbed to the top of the mountain and over the knoll which led down into a little vale where she knew the deer often slept. She crossed over the vale and continued to climb up to the next crest. She knew the way. She knew every turn. Julie veered to the left and not to the right, fully aware of the steep cliff which ran along the side of the mountain, its edge hidden in the darkness. Coming to the crest of the hill, she slid down the other side while half standing and half stooping. There at the cliff's edge, she paused. In the moonlight, Julie could see the silhouette of the treetops far below her and could hear the faint gurgle of the Potomac River as it flowed downstream. In the distance, she could see the town of Grantville, brightly lit as it lay nestled in the valley beneath her.

Julie turned and walked away. She had hiked these woods all of her life with her three older brothers, Ronnie, Jerry, and Matt. Sometimes they would hike all day long in the woods before going home, dirty from head to toe. They had no indoor plumbing in the little white house with red shutters. Their mom would always have their big aluminum tub full of rain water waiting to give them a bath. She would warm the water on the stove and add it to the tub for each one of them as they would climb in. Julie remembered those good times along with the bad times, but the one thing that remained constant through it all was that they always had each other.

Julie shivered as she felt the cold wind penetrate deeper, once again, through her thin layer of clothes. Her heart was pierced with a sorrow that engulfed her. She could hardly bear the loneliness which flooded over her. Her brothers had always protected her, lead her, and helped her. Everything in her life was changing and she felt so all alone.

Julie paused, not sure of which direction she should go. The thought did not even occur to her to turn back. *There was no turning back,* she thought. It had started to snow lightly again. A few snowflakes fell on Julie's eyelids and cheeks. She reached up aimlessly and brushed them aside. She rushed ahead and hurried down the backside of the steep mountain. She knew where she was headed but hadn't walked that way for many years.

Julie walked without giving thought as to where she would eventually end up. She concentrated more upon her footsteps and her clumsy boots than as to where her final destination would be. Suddenly, Julie hit the dirt road beneath her with a slight thud. Her knees buckled as she fell onto the dirt road landing on the palms of her gloveless hands. The road was not much more than a rocky path. Julie paused once again and caught her breath. Shivering from the cold she gently rubbed her hands together trying to warm them. She rubbed her head in frustration as she looked to the right and then to the left for direction. Right would take her to a desolate main highway that led to the small town of Benson. Left would take her back to the main road that went past her home.

I can't go home, Julie thought. By now, surely her dad must have known that she was gone. *I'll be in so much trouble. And with Alice gone...* "No," Julie said softly to herself. "No! I can't go back." Julie quickly crossed the road, then stumbling down a small bank in front of her, Julie's feet landed into the water of a little stream. The coldness pierced through the thin rubber boots and caused her frozen feet to ache in pain. Julie crossed the stream and began the climb up the steep mountainside.

Halfway up the mountainside, she stopped to catch her breath. She was so tired, so very tired. She leaned against a tall oak tree to rest. Julie stood upright and looked up at the mountainside in front of her. She had no more strength to will her legs to go forward. Once again, she leaned against the old oak tree and then slowly let her back slide down its rough bark until she came to rest onto the lightly snow-covered ground. She rested her head against the tree and placed her numb hands into her pockets. Julie felt numb all over, both inside and out. She couldn't shake the cloud of hopelessness that had engulfed her. She began to cry and pray. "Please help me God. Please help me," she repeated the words softly, as tears flowed down her cheeks. Julie felt her eyes grow heavy as she rested against the tree. The cold no longer seemed to bother her, and she was unaware of the effect that the cold was having upon her.

Julie lifted her head slowly and reluctantly at hearing the faint sound of muffled voices. She stirred from her cramped position and rubbed her neck. There were no houses anywhere to be found. So how could she be hearing voices. *Was it voices?* Julie thought, as she sat more upright and pulled her legs up to her chest. She wrapped her arms around her knees and held them tightly.

Julie peered down the mountainside to the deserted dirt road. In the far distance she saw two young men walking with a flashlight. She felt lightheaded, her head was spinning. *Who could it be?* she thought, as she felt fear begin to grip her heart for the first time that night.

Julie strained her head to hear the voices as they echoed up through the dark valley. "Julie," came the faint call of her name. "Julie," came the call again. Julie strained her eyes and tried to focus on the silhouette of figures walking in the moonlight far below her.

"It can't be," Julie said in a whisper through her chapped lips. "It can't be," Julie spoke softly as she began to cry. But it was! It was Jerry and Matt. Julie sat upright as her mind raced. *How could Jerry and Matt know that she was missing? Had her dad gotten in touch with them?* Julie cringed at the thought that the whole family might know that she had run away. *But she hadn't really planned on running away,* she thought. She just didn't know where she should go.

She was ready to run down the mountainside and into her big brothers' arms. She was so glad that they were there. As she started to get up, she stopped short. "I can't," she said to herself. "I can't," she said again as she began to cry. She could see the figures turn around and head back down the road. Everything inside of her cried out, *Get up, go after them, call out to them.* But it was too late. Everything was too late. *They'll take me back to Dad; and Alice is gone; and it's all my fault. I'll be left all alone with him. Everyone will be mad at me for running away and he'll start, he'll start, he'll....* Julie buried her head hopelessly into her lap and cried and cried. She jerked her head up and looked down at the road. She watched the figures and the dim light of the flashlight fade out of sight.

Julie leaned her head once again against the tree. Tears continued to flow out of her eyes even though she didn't have the strength to cry anymore. She felt colder than she could ever remember. She closed her eyes and prayed softly. "I don't know what to do God. I just don't know what to do. Please help me. Please help me."

Julie felt her eyes grow heavy. *"Lo, I am with you always,"* sprang the scripture from her heart which she had read earlier that week in the Bible. *"Let not your heart be troubled, you believe in God; believe also in me."* The words began to flow over Julie in a cloak of comfort. Julie felt an unexplained calm come over her. A peace had settled upon her, quenching her hopeless thoughts while soothing her doubts and fears. She turned her head to get more comfortable and once again laid her cheek against the rough bark of the tree trunk. She barely felt its coarseness upon her cold cheeks. She felt a warmth come over her as she ceased to shiver. She closed her eyes to rest. She felt herself beginning to fall into a deep sleep. It felt so good.

Julie jolted forward and nearly fell to the ground as her head slipped off the tree trunk. It startled her. But once again she laid her head against the big oak.

"*You must get up*," the still small voice of God spoke tenderly to her heart. Julie remained motionless just wanting to rest her eyes for a minute. She began to drift off once again. "*You must go back,*" the voice in her heart spoke firmer. Julie opened her eyes and straightened her back. "*It'll be okay,*" the still small voice assured her. Julie sat quietly not wanting to leave. She didn't want to go back. "*It'll be okay,*" the voice echoed, pushing aside her doubts, fears and questions. "*If you fall asleep here in the cold, you will die.*" At that moment a peace, and an unexplainable calm, seemed to flow over her. Julie tried to stand and grabbed the old oak for support. She steadied her legs and rubbed her eyes. Slowly, she started down the mountainside. She carefully watched her steps lest she would slip and fall. She walked back across the stream, up the bank, and onto the dirt road.

Julie paused, more than a little surprised that she still felt engulfed with such a peace. *Should she go towards home or to Gramma Emma's?* she wondered. Home would be easier and quicker. Going to Gramma Emma's would mean climbing another mountain. Julie wasn't sure if she could do it. The numbness that had prevented her from feeling the cold for a while was gone. The cold now began to pierce through her, as needles, from her hands to her feet.

Julie started up the mountainside. *It was easier to face the mountain than to face her dad,* Julie decided. Slowly, she climbed the mountain, step by step. She cut through the thickets veering off of the normal path. She was thankful for the brightness of the shining moon that lit her way back.

Julie came out at the old 'hollow' road and onto the dirt road that affronted the little white house with red shutters. The overgrown hedges nearly blocked her view of it. She looked at the small house, the red shutters barely visible in the dark. Julie felt a tear run down as it warmed her cold cheek.

She continued down the road to her Gramma Emma's house. She paused there and debated within herself whether she should stop and go in or not. *It didn't seem fair to awaken Gramma Emma this late at night,* Julie thought sadly, and then continued down the road. *I have to go back home,* Julie lamented.

"Lo, I am with you always," the still small voice of God spoke to her heart bringing her the comfort and strength that she needed. It propelled her to go back home.

"Julie?" a voice came through the darkness. "Is that you?" the voice called out a little louder now.

Julie turned quickly. She was surprised to hear her name being called. She looked in the direction that it was coming from. It was Uncle Tom's house.

"Julie?" Aunt Lisa called. She was standing on her porch. "Is that you?"

"Yea, it's me," Julie called softly up to her aunt. Julie felt embarrassed that the whole family must be aware of her situation. Aunt Lisa came running off the porch, down the little path, and over the bank to Julie.

"Are you okay?" Aunt Lisa asked. She put her arm around Julie and directed her to her house.

"Yes," Julie answered soberly.

Lisa looked at the thinly dressed Julie and felt her quivering in her arms' grasp. "Come on Julie," Aunt Lisa urged her on. "Let's get you up to the house and get you warmed up."

Slowly, Julie walked beside her aunt, her head hung down. She dreaded the very thought of facing her dad....

Julie, Matt, Jerry, Ronnie

Chapter

2

How long had it been since that fateful night so long ago? Julie wondered. Suddenly startled, Julie jumped up from the glider that she was sitting upon. "Ouch!" she cried out, while lost in the thoughts of her past. A dead branch had fallen out of the tree above her and hit her on the arm. Julie rubbed her arm softly while tossing the small branch aside as she sat back down onto the glider. She stretched her legs forward and gazed up into the large dawn redwood tree that sprawled above her. Its branches climbed ever upward into the sky. So many years had passed. At times those memories seemed a lifetime ago, and at other times they seemed as if it was yesterday.

Julie couldn't help but think of her past. Her family had just been down for a visit a few weeks before when they had had a large picnic and set off some beautiful fireworks. Everything had changed from those days so long ago; and yet, in some ways with the precious things that they had shared, everything was still the same. During their visit, Julie sat at her dining room table and reminisced with her mom and brothers. She could still read her brothers—their smiles, the glint in their eyes, their whole body language—and Julie knew that they could still read her. She often knew what they were going to say before they would even say it. Julie's sister-in-law had once made the remark, "The four of you can be in a room together and not speak a word and yet somehow one knows that a whole conversation has just gone on between the four of you." It was true. Their love had not only carried them through their childhood, but it was still a constant part of the very fiber that had always held them together.

Julie smiled as she allowed her thoughts to tumble one over another. She marveled at how her life had changed. She never dreamed, on that night so long ago, that her life could change and that she would ever be so happy. She loved her life now: her family, her children, her grandchildren. How could she, Julie, ever feel so much happiness? She could never have thought that God would have ever blessed her with the life that she now lived. No longer did she live in fear and shame, guilt and blame. God had not only brought her through those troubled years but had taken her hand and led her on a healing journey—a journey that, unknown to her at the time, had begun so many years ago with the first time that she had confronted her dad. Her heart was full and it overflowed with thankfulness for the new life that God had bestowed upon her.

Julie blinked her eyes and squinted hard as she looked up into the sun's bright rays. It was unusually warm for a late September day. She sat on the glider and let it gently carry her back and forth. She felt the sun's rays bathe her in its warmth. A gentle breeze blew over Julie. She leaned back into the glider and allowed her thoughts to take her back once again to that troubled night so long ago. Her heart was touched as she remembered how kind and supportive her aunt and uncle had been to her that night. They had eased her fear of facing her dad. Julie closed her eyes and let her mind drift as she remembered that night so vividly...

Julie slowly walked up the worn path with her aunt at her side. The touch of her aunt's arm around her brought her comfort and warmth. The moonlight shined like a flashlight before them, brightly lighting the path. Julie looked down at the path. She knew it by heart. She remembered that just hours before she had run up this same path to babysit her young cousins while Uncle Tom and Aunt Lisa Sue had gone bowling.

Aunt Lisa opened the door and stood back, ushering Julie into the house. Julie felt the warmth of the little kitchen engulf her. She sat down on the kitchen chair that Aunt Lisa had pulled out for her. Julie was little surprised to see her Uncle Tom sitting at the far end of the kitchen table in his favorite chair against the wall. Julie glanced quickly at him and then down at the kitchen table. *What could her uncle possibly be thinking of her right now?* she wondered. *How in the world could Julie have caused so many problems?* Julie wondered if the whole family was aware of her running away. It wasn't as if she had planned to run away. She would have definitely dressed warmer if that had been her original plan. She just didn't know what to do or where to go. Julie thought of how ironic it was that in not wanting to bother anyone she had managed to upset the whole family. She couldn't even imagine how her dad was going to react to what she had done. She remembered how upset he was the last time she had left home.

Julie shivered uncontrollably as the warmth from the kitchen began to warm her cold body. Aunt Lisa brought her a blanket and draped it around her shoulders. Julie took the edge of the blanket and slowly wrapped it tightly around her. She wished that she could just rest her head on the table and go to sleep for a few minutes. Julie heard the quiet clank of the cup onto the saucer as Uncle Tom put his coffee cup down. Aunt Lisa placed a warm cup of tea onto the table in front of Julie. Julie cupped her cold hands around the warm glass allowing the heat to penetrate deeply. She snuggled down into the blanket before looking up slowly across the table at her Uncle Tom. He looked very tired as he sat staring at his coffee cup in deep thought before lifting it and taking one last long drink. Uncle Tom sat the cup down and looked over at Julie. Their eyes met as Julie waited to see his reaction. He gave her a faint smile, more with his eyes than with his mouth. They were kind eyes, full of strength and compassion, so unlike her dad's. Julie couldn't help wonder, as she had so often throughout her lifetime, of how two brothers could be so different—Uncle Tom with his rich blue eyes, her dad with his dark brown. But it was their personalities and demeanor that were the most different. *How could they be so totally different being that they were both raised in the same house?*

"Well," Tom spoke for the first time. He took his hand and ran it through his graying salt and pepper hair which stood straight up uncombed.

But before he could continue, Aunt Lisa spoke up. "Tom, you can't take her back home. She's not up to that right now."

"I know," Tom spoke patiently. "I know," he repeated. He pushed his chair back slowly as its metal legs made a loud rattle. Julie watched his tall thin frame as he stood up. "I'll take her up to Mom's and call Ron from there and let them all know that she's okay."

Them all? Julie repeated the remark in her mind. *Them all,* the thought made her shiver all over again. *What did Uncle Tom mean by "them all"?* Julie's thoughts began to race once again. Aunt Lisa gently placed her hands onto Julie's shoulders. Tenderly, her aunt's hands braced her. Lovingly her aunt's touch calmed her.

"Don't let Ron upset her, Tom!" Lisa spoke softly but deliberately. Tom just gave Lisa a nod and an assuring look that he'd take care of it.

There was something about that look that Julie had grown to know through her years of growing up with her Uncle Tom. It was a confident look, a quiet strength which Julie had seen her uncle follow through with so many times.

Aunt Lisa gave Julie one more quick soft squeeze to her shoulders and then stepped back and helped Julie stand up. She grabbed the blanket that Julie had let drop and wrapped it once again around her shoulders.

Tom opened the door and let Julie go first. Slowly, they began to walk up the path that led to Emma's house. Julie remembered the countless times that she had run back and forth on this same path. Uncle Tom didn't rush her. It was still dark, but Julie knew the path, every incline, every curve. Julie felt the cold as it once again whipped through her thin clothes. The warmth of her aunt's kitchen had just begun to warm her numb body and now everything hurt so intensely—her feet, her hands, even her ears.

"It'll be okay," Uncle Tom spoke softly.

Julie barely heard his words. They touched her heart so much that she thought she might burst into tears. She bit her lower lip tightly to hold them back. She couldn't say a word.

Julie stepped up onto the porch. Uncle Tom opened the screened door and turned the knob on the heavy wooden door. They walked into the dimly lit kitchen. Julie glanced around the small room where all of her life, every Sunday, the whole family—aunts, uncles and cousins—would all come together for dinner at Gramma Emma's. Julie crossed the small kitchen and began to climb the steps to go upstairs. *Let not your heart be troubled,* the still small voice spoke to her heart. Julie felt God's love and peace come over her once again, as she had earlier in the woods. It propelled her forward. Julie paused for a moment at the top of the steps and took a deep breath.

Uncle Tom joined her and went ahead of her into the room where Emma was sitting. Julie followed reluctantly behind him. Julie could only wonder what her gramma's reaction would be. Her gramma had such faith in her. Julie often felt that her gramma had a greater expectation for Julie's life than Julie even had for herself. Gramma Emma believed in her and Julie knew how very much her grandmother loved her. *What would she think of her now?* she wondered. But as Julie's thoughts tumbled forward in her tired mind, it was not facing her gramma that troubled her. Julie hated the confrontations which were facing her; however, it was the thought of confronting her dad that troubled her the most! Julie

entered the room with her head hanging down. She couldn't bear
to look into her Gramma Emma's eyes. Julie flopped down onto
the big old blue velvet chair that sat by the heater vent. She sat
quietly in the chair and tightly wrapped the blanket around her.
She could feel the warm heat coming up from the vent beside her.
She nervously wrung her hands and twitched her feet together.
There was nothing that she could do but wait to see what her
gramma and uncle would do…

The sound of a car horn in the distance startled Julie back to the
present once again. Quickly, she opened her eyes and shifted on
the glider not wanting to get up. That night, so many years ago,
had been a turning point in her life. It was a forerunner of one of
the many times that she would have to face and confront her dad,
the very confrontations that she had felt as a child would destroy
her. Little did she realize then that they were to be the beginnings
of her healing journey.

Julie stirred once again on the glider, stretched her arms and
legs and then sat upright. A gentle breeze blew over her and
filled her with its warmth. It brushed past her, softly tickling her
cheek and then it was gone. She raised her hand slowly and gently
touched her cheek. She gazed aimlessly as she stirred from her past
thoughts and pushed her legs gently causing the glider to go into
motion. Julie rubbed her eyes. The past no longer troubled her as
much as it would often cause her to wonder. There were too many
years, too many issues.

Julie felt a thankfulness engulf her. It wasn't just that her life
was so different now, and it wasn't that she had forgotten her past,
but it was because she had healed from it. It was a long journey.
For so many years she had tried to ignore her past. She had buried
the hurt, the pain, and even the memories. But she found that in
doing all this that it didn't take away any of the hurt, the pain,

or even the memories. God had dealt with Julie's heart. Looking back, she could see that God had been dealing with her since her childhood. God had led her and given her the boldness to face her past, confront her dad, and deal with the pain rather than bury and ignore it. It had been painful to heal, but Julie learned that the God who had brought her out of her sorrow was also able to deliver her from it. Her past did not have to hang onto her like a ball and chain, wearing her down, destroying her hope, crushing her relationships, thrusting discouragement and depression on her with a cloak of despair. She learned that she did not have to put on a smile just to please others but that she could experience a true joy which now radiated from deep within her heart. But first her heart had to heal.

Julie felt a stronger breeze rush past her. She looked up into a sky that was filling with dark gray clouds. The weather was changing. She could feel the changes in temperature. Summer was passing as she felt the ushering in of the fall season. Julie gazed at the site before her. She smiled as she noticed the toys that littered her yard. Tricycles, scooters, balls, and bats laid scattered throughout.

Julie arose to get up and gather all the toys that her grandsons had played with the day before on their visit. She could see in her mind each of their little faces as she had carried the toys out for them. They were her sunshine and they made her heart smile.

Julie placed the last toy into the bin and walked into the house. She smiled once again as she entered through the back door of the house. Blocks and cars and race tracks laid scattered across the floor. She paused before picking them up and walked over to the antique jukebox which sat in the far corner of the room. She pushed the select buttons for the songs that she wanted to hear. Slowly the old machine went into motion, gliding from side to side before mechanically picking the selected record. Julie listened to the song, which began to play softly, and began to hum along as she bent down to pick up the toys.

"Hey, I'll be outside working," Mike called out to Julie over the music that was playing. Julie watched him hurry to the door. He paused and looked at her for a moment as he so often did. "You okay?" he smiled as he looked around at the toys that left a trail throughout the room.

Julie's eyes met his and locked onto his smile—his smile, this smile that was meant for her, a special smile that was hers and hers alone. She looked at the man that she had been married to all of these years and let his smile fill her heart. Even now, all these years later, he could always make her heart smile.

"I don't mind," she said as she nodded at the toys and carried an armful to the toy box. Mike gave her another quick smile and hurried out the door.

Julie put away the last toy truck and walked into the kitchen. She filled a cup with water and placed it into the microwave, heating it as she daydreamed. She then retrieved the cup of hot water and made herself a cup of tea. She stirred the spoon softly in the cup.

A song caught her attention as it played from the next room. Julie smiled as she listened to it. She took her tea, grabbed two cookies, and went into the living room to sit down. As she sat down in the big blue chair, she raised her feet up on the recliner. She took a deep sip of her tea as she looked out the large front windows. Mike was busy pushing a wheelbarrow that was loaded with mulch and rakes.

Julie loved him dearly. He was her soul mate. God had led them together so many years ago. They had raised two wonderful children who were now grown and married and had blessed them with six grandsons. Julie loved the times when they would all get together. She loved the way that all of their laughter would fill the house. It made it the home that they had all grown to love.

Julie smiled as the many memories flowed in her mind. She burst into laughter as the song she was listening to went into the chorus again. She remembered when she used to sing it around the house when her children Mikey and Jenny were small.

"Oh, Mom, that's not a real song," Mikey said one day when she was singing.

"Sure it is," Julie quipped back to him as she continued to sing the song.

"Really?" Jenny asked. "Mom is that for real or did you just make it up?"

"No, we used to sing it all the time when I was growing up with my brothers," Julie answered and then once again blurted out the chorus to the country melody.

Julie smiled as she recalled how they had rolled their eyes at each other, doubting that it could ever be a real song. One day while she was cooking dinner a few months later, she heard them come running down their steps. Both Mikey and Jenny nearly tumbled into the kitchen at the same time.

"Mom!" they both exclaimed in unison, out of breath. "It really is a real song!"

"What are you talking about?" Julie asked laughing. She looked at them with a puzzled look as she stirred the spaghetti. "What song?"

"Wolverton Mountain," they both answered together.

"They were advertising old songs on television," Mikey quipped.

"And it was on the advertisement," Jenny piped in, "just like you sang it."

Julie had burst into laughter then, just as she now laughed, thinking of the happy memory.

On the day when they had purchased the old jukebox for the rec room, Julie knew that she'd have to find that record for their collection.

Julie sat in her chair singing the last chorus of the song. While sipping her tea, she closed her eyes and let her mind fill with the memories from her childhood. She remembered, as young children, standing with her three older brothers, Ronnie, Jerry and Matt, at the microphone, all four of them trying to squeeze together to sing. Julie remembered the one year how they had practiced and practiced their favorite song "Wolverton Mountain" and sang it for the whole family at Gramma Emma's family reunion.

The ringing of the phone interrupted Julie's thoughts. She quickly put her cup down onto the end table and jumped up and ran for the phone. She grabbed the receiver and quickly answered, "Hello." Julie was surprised at the voice on the other end.

"Julie, this is Claire," a sweet voice with a strong southern accent spoke softly.

"Hi, Claire," Julie replied back. Her thoughts raced as she tried to figure out why Claire was calling. She rarely called.

Claire was her dad's third wife. She was such a nice person, a wonderful Christian woman who had been married to her dad for the last 30 years. Claire was different from her dad's second wife Alice, whom Julie had grown up with. But like Alice, she was a wonderful person. Julie could never understand how her dad could marry such nice women and then treat them so badly. The only thing that puzzled Julie even more was how Claire could have ever stayed married to her dad for so long.

Julie had struggled with her dad all of her life. There were so many issues, issues that had laid buried for years…what seemed a lifetime. But they didn't stay buried for Julie. As time passed, Julie had to face these very issues in her life, issues that Julie thought were long over and best forgotten. Through the years, God had shown her that she could be free from her tormented past, but that she first would have to confront it head on. Julie had wrestled with the whole idea. The very thought of being free from the pain of her past, which continually crept up into her life, seemed almost impossible. But to confront it, or to even deal with her past seemed more painful than Julie could ever bear. Slowly, through the years, she would begin to yield to God's tender call as He beckoned her to allow Him to heal her from her past.

Cautiously, she had tried to approach her dad at various times, often with the issues and often with the reality of the God that she had grown to know. Her dad didn't want to deal with either. Julie thought that if only he could know the reality of a God that truly loved him, she was sure then, that he would be sorry for all that he had done to her, and that then her past and his could find a path of peace. Maybe this was selfish, naïve, or even an impossible dream. Selfish, because Julie just wanted closure to her past; naïve, because her dad had no desire to change, deal with their past or even acknowledge what he had done; and impossible, because for years deep in her heart, the sea of anger, hurt and disgust at her dad nearly devoured her hope of him ever changing.

And yet she tried. When any opportunity would arise, she would boldly confront him even if it angered him.

One time, he had said to her, "God doesn't hear me the way He hears you, Julie. He doesn't help me like He helps you."

Quickly, Julie had grabbed the moment and retorted back slowly, but firmly, "He can only help you Dad if you surrender all of you to Him. If you only give Him your hand and your foot is in trouble, He can only help your hand and not the foot. You have to give Him all of you. But he had quickly changed the subject. Julie knew, after the many years of trying, that her dad would often just say things to test her, to see what her answer would be, more so, rather than really wanting to know, or that he would even have a desire to change his ways. He just wanted to see what Julie would say.

"Julie," the voice spoke again. "Are you still there?"

"Yes," Julie answered as her mind tried to tune into what Claire was telling her.

"I wanted to let you know that your dad went to the doctors and that they ran some tests." Julie could hear the slight pause in Claire's voice and then Claire continued to talk and let the words rush out as if wanting to say them before she was unable to. "Julie…your dad has cancer. It's pretty advanced, and the doctor says that it's too far advanced for them to do any treatments. They aren't giving him much time to live."

Julie felt the words smack her. She tried to focus as Claire continued.

"I know things aren't the best between you and your dad, but I wanted to let you know. I'll have more information in a few days and I'll let you know more then."

"Thanks Claire," Julie managed to say as her heart filled with more emotions than she could sort out. "I'll talk to you then," Julie said slowly and then put the phone down. She stood motionless and stared in a daze.

As the many years had passed, from the time of her troubled childhood until the present, she had tried and tried to resolve the issues that stood between her and her dad—issues that had shattered her heart and nearly swallowed her up. It had taken years and years for Julie to heal. It had taken the love of a God, who had become more real to her than life itself, to deal with her past, to heal from the brokenness and strife, and to once again be able to trust and even feel again the very essence of the joy of life. It had been a healing journey with many years of confrontations with this man, her dad. And now, he was going to die.

Instantly, Julie felt that presence that she had grown to love and recognize. It filled her very being and wrapped her in love. Julie took a deep breath and felt tears begin to crease from her eyes. She had already grieved so many years ago the loss of a dad that she had thought never really existed. She had accepted that her dad was not capable of showing love and that somewhere it seemed that he had lost even the very capacity to love. Julie struggled with this…for she had thought that it could not be possible for anyone to lose the capacity to love. But after years and years of trying to understand the man that she knew as "Dad," Julie had sadly come to understand that somehow her dad had lost the capacity to love. She didn't know when, but thought that maybe as a child he had lost his way…maybe by his own father's treatment of him. She remembered one time finding a photo of her dad as a young child. She had held the picture with its pinked edges in her hand. The little boy seemed lost, gone. As she continued to look at the picture and study it, she tried to understand his sad expression. There was no smile and he appeared so serious for such a small child. And then Julie realized what she saw on the little boy's face. It was anger.

Julie sat down and rested her head in her hands. Once again the past surfaced, flowing over her in floods of memories compassing the years of her life. How had Julie escaped such a fate as her dad's? How had her heart not become hardened from the pain and anger as her dad's had? How could it have happened that her capacity to love had not only been kept in tack but that, somehow, she had received a double portion? For Julie it was never about giving love. However, the earnestness of her heart would thrust her forward to give more and more even when she felt that she had no more to give.

Julie allowed the tears to come. They weren't tears of sorrow. They weren't even tears of grief. They were tears of thankfulness— thankfulness to a God who had reached down and rescued her. A God who had not only delivered her from her pain and sorrow as a child, but a God who had healed her from the anger, fear, shame, guilt, and blame. This, and only this, was the reason that she had not hardened her heart as her dad had done. The God who had touched her heart as a child with His mighty love, who had healed her broken heart and mended her shattered spirit, was the One who had loved her then when she was all alone. And now, these many years later, He was engulfing her in His presence. Julie could feel His comfort and strength.

Julie sat quietly as her thoughts settled. She remembered it had been nearly two years ago when God had asked her one day after she prayed, *"Will you go talk to your dad if I lead you to him?"* Julie had instantly reminded God of the last thirty-five years and of how she had tried many times in the past to reach out to her dad. *"But will you go to him if I lead you, if I call you to go and talk to him?"*

Julie felt God's words and love nudge at her heart. She had answered, "God, I will go and talk to him again, if you lead me. But only, only, if I know for sure that it is you."

"I will not lead you to him if he will hurt you again," God's loving voice continued to speak to Julie's heart. Her heart was so touched. She could truly feel the love and protection of her heavenly Father. She felt as if He was standing right next to her... this strong Father vowing that He would never let her dad hurt her again. Here, she felt the love of a true father, a true protector. Somehow Julie knew that His words were true. It had taken her many years to realize that God had never left her when her dad was hurting her when she was a child. It had been her dad's choice to hurt her, not God's. But now, out of her dad's grasp after all of these years, there was a surety from God that He wouldn't even let her go near him if God knew that he had any intent on ever hurting her again.

"God, I will go if, and only if, you lead me to him. I will God," Julie whispered softly, renewing her vow. Julie gently rubbed her eyes. Two years had passed and she hadn't been lead to talk to him. Actually, because of the things that her dad continued to do, Julie was lead further away from him, more than towards him. She thought, that maybe, she wouldn't be lead again to talk to him; and in some ways, it was that thought alone that comforted her heart.

Julie sat and stared in a daze. *Would God lead her to him now?* She took a deep breath and let out a deep sigh.

"Only if you lead me Lord," she prayed softly, "only if you lead me."

Julie wanted to get up and go outside to talk to Mike; however, she sat motionless. She needed time to try to sort it all out. She leaned back into the chair and rested her eyes as her thoughts continued to race through her mind darting from the past to the present and then the present to the past. Once again, her mind drifted back to that night, so long ago, when she had run away....

Julie was surprised that her Gramma Emma had not reprimanded her for running away. Actually, she had said nothing at all to her as Julie and Uncle Tom entered the room. Emma immediately reached for the telephone to call the rest of the family. But Uncle Tom gently took the phone from Emma's hand and rested it back into its holder. Julie nestled down into the blanket that was wrapped up around her and barely lifted her head out of it to see what the two adults were going to do. They talked about the situation, as if Julie wasn't even in the room. Once, Julie saw her Gramma Emma's glance upon her. Her rich blue eyes were filled with compassion which moved Julie's heart near to tears. There was no anger or disappointment in her gramma's eyes, only concern of how to resolve the issue of calling Julie's dad.

"Mom, it's best if you let me call him," Tom spoke up softly with his hand still resting on top of the phone.

"Now Tom…don't go getting Ron upset," Emma cautioned her oldest son.

Tom turned his head and rolled his eyes upward giving Emma an incredulous look as if to say *don't upset him?* He then turned and looked at Julie. Emma also turned and looked at Julie. Julie was touched by both of their looks of compassion. Julie felt the warmth from the heat vent surge through her body. She laid her head down onto the arm of the chair near the vent. She felt herself wanting to drift off to sleep. Tom picked up the phone and began to dial the numbers one by one on the rotary phone. Julie forced herself to stay awake. It wasn't like her Uncle Tom to get involved in their family problems. She knew, by his actions, that he did not agree with the many things that her dad had done; but he always tried to stay out of her dad's business. Somehow tonight was different. Julie could see that it had affected her Uncle Tom differently. Usually quiet and laid back, Julie could see that he was set with a determination to protect her even if it meant confronting and standing up to her dad or Gramma Emma. No one had ever stood up for Julie in this manner, and it impacted her with a sense of value that she had never felt for herself. Uncle Tom really cared for her. Julie listened to her uncle as he spoke softly into the phone. He glanced over at Julie curled up in the chair as he listened to Ron speak on the other end of the phone. Julie could only hear a few words of her uncle's quiet responses.

"Ron, she's here at Mom's," Tom spoke in a low voice into the receiver. "No, I don't think she should come home tonight. Why don't you just let her stay up here? She's almost asleep." There was a quiet pause as Tom listened. "Well, just tell the rest of the family that she's okay and that they can see her tomorrow," Tom insisted. Julie could tell that he was trying not to raise his voice to her dad. Julie turned in the chair. She was so exhausted but felt restless at hearing her uncle refer to *the rest of the family.* Julie's mind raced trying to figure out who was the *rest of the family.*

There was another pause of silence as Tom listened and then with his voice rising, he said, "Well Ron, I'm telling you right now!" He turned to look at Julie before turning his back to her and then once again spoke into the phone. Julie could tell that her uncle was getting upset with her dad. She could see on her gramma's face a look of concern that the two brothers were going to get into it. "I'm telling you right now!" Tom repeated as his voice rose louder, "If you come up here, you better not upset her!" Another long pause, and then Tom said in a more subtle but stronger tone, "I mean it Ron!" Tom thrust the receiver hard into the cradle and turned to look at Emma.

Julie looked at her gramma and uncle as they exchanged glances. She thought that they both looked so tired. Julie looked at her uncle's tired blue eyes. He nervously continued to take his hand through his disheveled grayish hair. Julie still felt badly for all the trouble that she had caused. Her eyes felt so heavy. She couldn't hold them open any longer and without warning fell asleep.

Julie opened her eyes at hearing her dad's voice. She felt a cold chill go through her body though she had been warm for a while. She couldn't begin to imagine how angry her dad would be at her. She knew that it would be the embarrassment that she had caused him before his family, more than her actions that would upset him.

Her dad said nothing to her as they went to leave. Julie observed both Emma and Tom shoot her dad a warning glance. Julie walked slowly down the bank to her dad's car, trying not to slip, feeling her legs wobbly as she walked. Her dad got into the car and shut the door behind him but didn't say a word to Julie. Julie glanced at her dad wanting to know his mood but not wanting to make eye contact. She was surprised to see him sober. His eyes appeared tired, but his face was relaxed, subdued, and there was no anger. Julie had thought, that maybe, he seemed to even look a little bit worried. It puzzled her in part. She wondered if she would ever understand this man who was her father.

Her dad turned to her as he caught her gaze and began to speak. Julie slowly turned her head away. "We looked for you all night," Ron said. Julie had thought she heard his voice crack slightly before he continued. "We found footprints going down to the river's bank but there were none coming back." He spoke slowly and haltingly. Julie turned her head cautiously towards her dad to study his face and to try to understand his words. He seemed concerned for her or was it that he felt somehow responsible for what had happened, or was it just that he was embarrassed by the whole situation. Julie could never be sure of what her dad was thinking. "We didn't know what had happened to you."

Julie wondered about her dad's mention of the word *"we"* along with her uncle previously mentioning *"the rest of the family."* "Who's at the house?" Julie asked hesitantly, speaking to her dad for the first time.

There was a pause and Julie had thought that she possibly shouldn't have asked. "Matt and Jerry are there. They went searching for you earlier. Your Mom and Bucky and even Bob came over."

"Bob?" Julie asked.

"Yes, Bob," Ron replied in an irritated voice.

Julie knew that her dad was not happy that all of the family had been dragged into their situation. Bob was her step-dad, but he and her mom had recently separated. Julie was touched by his concern, however, and more than a little surprised that he had come to help find her.

The last of a fading moonlight fell softly across the road as they drove to their home. It then began to fade completely as the early morning sun had begun to rise. Julie rested her head on the side of the car window and nearly fell asleep. Her dad hadn't mentioned Alice. Julie kept wondering whether she had left or if she would still be there at the house.

Julie opened her eyes as the car came to a stop and her dad pushed the gear into park. She sat motionless and looked straight ahead wanting to avoid her dad's glance, not wanting to upset him. Julie was surprised that he just sat there quietly. He didn't say a word. She heard him take a deep breath and then let out a long sigh before turning off the ignition and opening the car door. Julie opened her door and got out of the car. She slowly followed her dad across the street to their house.

He opened the front door and motioned for Julie to go in first. Julie entered the living room. It was filled with her family. Ethel came running to Julie and threw her arms around her. "Oh Honey!" she said. "We were all so worried!"

"I'm sorry, Mom," Julie said softly.

"No, Honey. It's okay," Ethel continued, with tears running down her cheek. She gently stroked Julie's hair.

Julie looked up as her mom released her from her embrace and saw Alice standing behind Ethel. Ethel stepped back and Alice and Julie reached out to each other and hugged each other tightly. "I'm so sorry, Alice," Julie sobbed into Alice's shoulder as Alice continued to embrace her. "I am so sorry that I hurt your feelings. Please know how much I love you and how much you mean to me."

"I do Honey," Alice whispered back. "I know you do. None of this was your fault."

Julie wiped her eyes on her sleeve as the others gathered around her and hugged her. "We were so worried about you sis," Matt said, his big blue eyes filling with tears. Jerry, no words spoken, could only embrace her tightly, his dark brown eyes full of joy and relief.

As everyone slowly dispersed, Ethel and Alice walked Julie to her room. All three talked for a few moments and then said that they would talk more later. Julie lay quietly and watched her mom and stepmom leave the room. Her mind spun from all that had happened. She wanted to try to sort out her thoughts but her eyes quickly shut as she fell into a deep sleep....

Her life had not always been that way..., Julie thought as she drove home from work collecting her thoughts once again from that night which had happened so long ago. She couldn't get the past off of her mind. *Her whole life had been continual seasons of change. The years with her mom and dad together, their divorce, her dad's abusive girlfriend Rhonda who had lived with Julie and her three brothers for several years, her stepdad Bob and her mom, and then more separations. Everything was so difficult when she was with her dad. The worst of all was the way that he had abused her. Julie didn't know as a child how to escape his abuse. And then, Alice had entered her life when she married Julie's dad. Things at home had changed for a short season. There were good times. And then, as it had happened with her mom and dad, slowly Alice and her dad's marriage had begun to fall completely apart and Julie was caught in the middle of it all. Years later, her dad had married once again, this time to Claire.* Now, after all of these years and with her dad's illness of cancer, it seemed that her past had come rushing back to her in a torrent of memories.

Julie drove into her driveway and pulled quickly up to the house that had become home for Mike and her. She sat quietly in the parked car. She had not heard any further news from Claire, her stepmom. When she spoke with her brothers, they only knew as much as she did.

Julie took a deep breath, reached over the car seat, and grabbed her bag of groceries. She hurried into the house. She was glad that she had been able to leave work early. She had so much that she wanted to get done at home. Julie fumbled for her keys as she balanced the groceries on one knee and unlocked the door. She tossed the keys onto the corner stand and rushed into the kitchen. She hurried to put the groceries away and grabbed a skillet to make supper.

The phone rang. Julie ran to answer it. She hoped that it wasn't work calling her with a problem.

"Hey, Jul," the familiar voice spoke.

"Hi Honey," Julie smiled as she held the phone in one hand and continued cooking supper.

"Did you see how messed up the order was that came in today?" Mike asked.

"Yes, I'll call them and straighten it out tomorrow," Julie answered. "Hey, I'm making your favorite for supper tonight so try to get out of work right at closing, okay?"

"Whatcha making?" Mike asked.

"Not telling," Julie teased.

Julie smiled as she put the phone back. They had been married for over thirty-five years and yet it seemed like yesterday that they had met. Years before, they had both ventured out, left their jobs, and started their own business. It had been difficult at first, but through the years God had truly blessed them with their step of faith. As a family, they worked side by side and saw it grow into a successful business.

"Ouch," Julie said loudly as she burnt herself on the hot oven door. *Slow down,* she told herself as she dabbed her hand with a cold wet rag. Her mind raced with everything that she wanted to get done now that supper was in the oven.

I better check the phone messages, Julie thought to herself as she hurried to the phone. She saw the blinking light on the message machine and stopped abruptly. She hated checking the messages. If they were business calls, she would have to return them and get nothing else done. Julie hesitated and thought that she could possibly check them later.

"Better check them now," Julie said out loud to herself as she let out a deep sigh and reluctantly pushed the button on the machine. The robotic machine spoke haltingly, "One new message." Julie pushed the button again and listened intently. The message was from Claire, her stepmom.

Julie took the portable phone and went to the couch. She sat down and wondered what Claire had to tell her. The message had only said that she should call her back. Julie sat and thought of what she would say to Claire. She fingered the phone in her hand nervously contemplating the conversation. Claire had married her dad after Mike and Julie had married. Claire was totally unaware of any of the childhood issues that Julie and her brothers had experienced with their dad. Julie was always afraid that if Claire knew a lot of the things that her dad had done that she would no longer want to remain married to him. Julie didn't want to burden Claire with their past and upset their marriage. She knew that Claire never quite understood why both Julie and her brothers struggled to visit their dad. And yet, as the years passed, though nothing was said, Julie knew that Claire somehow understood more than people had thought. Maybe it was because of the many years that Claire, too, had been put under her husband's control and sadly experienced the hardships of living with someone who was so difficult.

Julie was just unsure of what part she should play in dealing with her dad's illness. She wanted Claire to know that she would try to be there for her. It wasn't fair that Claire should have to bear the load of this all by herself. However, Julie knew that she was limited in helping. She lived almost four hours away, and her dad and she hardly ever spoke to each other.

Over the years, Julie had continually tried to reach out to her dad. At first, after she was married, she would just pretend that they were all a normal family. She would go in to visit and act as if nothing from her childhood had ever happened. Ronnie, Jerry, and Matt, her three brothers, each dealt with their issues in their own way also. Ronnie kind of just went with the flow; Jerry, pretty much did the same as Julie; however, Matt just couldn't pretend and in his pain he struggled with even visiting his dad. Julie knew that when Matt did visit, it was more for his siblings' sake than for any feelings that he had for their dad.

As time had passed, God dealt with Julie about the issues from her past. Julie tried to push it all aside. She thought that the past was best to stay there. "After all, 'it was under the blood'," she would say to herself, feeling that she had given it to God. But still, her past would come propelling into her present life and smack her in the face. Julie would brush the tears away, try to quench the anger that would rise within her, and then try to block it all out of her mind.

The problem was that it did not go away. It became a stumbling block to her even as she got older. There was no closure or resolve. Julie had felt that she was probably the only one who ever felt this way. She remembered that she used to look at other girls in her class at school and wonder if any of them had suffered with their fathers the way she had with hers. Surely, no normal father would do to their daughter what Julie's father had done to her.

Things began to change when Julie had gone to work for a drug rehabilitation hospital. Her job was to type the patient therapy notes. Julie was stunned as she typed the notes from day to day. In so many, it was as if she was typing her own life's story. *Was it even possible that so many people had suffered the same kind of abuse?* So often, she would come home from work exhausted. She would find herself trembling from the emotional drain of typing the painful therapy notes.

It was then that God began to earnestly talk to Julie about dealing with her past. He explained to her that she could never heal or get over her past or put it behind her until she had confronted it. God showed her that it was time for her to heal. If He was God enough to bring her through her childhood, then He was God enough to heal her from it. She had to deal, to heal, to feel again. She had longed to find "Julie." Somewhere, in her buried past, was that lost little girl. So once again, she had taken the hand of the One who beckoned her and with her hand in His she entered into her past, going back in time, back to even before that night that she had run away, back to those troublesome years so long ago to begin the healing journey....

Dad at four years old

Chapter

3

Julie had just turned thirteen years old. She felt torn between the child that she still was and the young woman that she was becoming. Her brothers were now teenagers. Matt was fourteen, Jerry fifteen, and Ronnie sixteen years old. It had been many years since her mom and dad had divorced when she was eight years old. It had been two years since Rhonda, her dad's abusive live-in girlfriend had moved out. All of her brothers were now in high school.

Julie went out the back door of their summer porch allowing it to slam behind her. She hurried down the sidewalk and peeked through the lattice that covered the crawl space under her house. "Come on girl!" she called out to Mamie. "Come on." The reddish brown cocker spaniel stretched out her legs at the sound of Julie's voice. Mamie slowly crawled out from under the crawl space and trotted over to her. Julie leaned down and buried her head into the dog's fur and hugged Mamie. "You good ole girl," she said as she lovingly patted Mamie.

Julie walked down to the old barn that stood at the end of the sidewalk. Mamie followed slowly behind her. Julie walked behind the barn and sat down onto the crosswalk that bridged the little stream. Mamie joined Julie and sat down beside her. For the longest time, Julie just sat there and scratched Mamie's floppy red ears. She felt so confused. She had wondered if her life would always be so full of changes and confusion. She had to continually adjust to these changes all of her life.

She remembered, so many years ago, when they had just moved to this house. What an exciting time it was when they moved from the small little white house with red shutters, which sat next to her Gramma Emma's house, and into their present home. Julie thought that she would never miss the little house which sat up on the hill with an outhouse and no running water. Julie imagined that life would be happy forever the year that they had moved. She was so excited in that she now had her own bedroom and that the house had running water.

Her cousin Tonya had come to live with them. She had just turned fifteen. Julie was six years old and had fallen in love with Tonya. She treated Julie just like a little sister.

Julie's years had been full of tumult going from one family crisis to another. Her dad refused to quit drinking and arguments became a daily routine in their family's life. Her mom would forgive him over and over again for his affairs and drinking. He would promise to stop, life would be better for a few months, and then he would start all over again. It had all ended when Tonya had become pregnant at sixteen years of age. Tonya had reluctantly told Julie's mom and her Gramma Winnie that the baby was Uncle Ron's. Ron denied it furiously. Ethel did not believe him. She had forgiven his other affairs for many years, but to do this to her niece was something Ethel could not get past. To Ethel's horror, Ron had then tried to convince Ethel that they could raise the child as their own. When all of this failed, Ron had tried to commit suicide. Ethel and the children found him one evening in front of their unlit gas stove with its valve opened wide.

Times were difficult. Ethel moved out of the house. Ethel knew that she could never afford to raise the children without Ron's income. There was no assistance and she hardly made enough money to pay for a studio apartment. She had left the children to live with Ron and brought them to stay with her on the weekends.

Julie thought back then that things couldn't get any worse, until Rhonda had moved in to stay with them. It had happened so gradually. Julie was not prepared for the woman's fiery temper and the physical abuse that she would rail on Julie and her three brothers. When confronted by Ethel, Ron would justify Rhonda's actions in that she was merely correcting the children and that they deserved the correction.

Julie had clung on to her brothers and they had clung on to her. There was a solace with the knowledge that their mom loved them even if she couldn't take them to live with her. Julie had hoped that possibly when her mom married Bob that maybe they would get to go live with her; but Bob had three children, and by then the divorce and custody arrangements had already been established for them. Ethel would see them throughout the week and bring them to stay with her every weekend. The rest of the time they would live with their dad.

Rhonda finally moved out when she couldn't explain to anyone why she had jumped on top of Julie, held her down, and punched her in the face. Julie had wondered for years how Rhonda had ever gotten away with beating her and her brothers simply for the reason that she was angry at their dad.

In part, Julie had gotten past all of this. All of the heartache and changes seemed to be just a process of life that Julie couldn't understand. Her sorrow was eased with the time that she was able to spend with her mom and grandparents and by the love and support that she had with her three big brothers. The thing that Julie struggled with the most was the secret that no one knew, a secret that Julie was never going to tell anyone, not her three big brothers or even her mom. She knew what had happened when Tonya spoke up about what her dad had done to her. No one had believed Tonya. Mostly everyone, except her mom and Gramma Winnie, did not believe that Ron had gotten Tonya pregnant. Everyone said that Tonya was always going from boyfriend to boyfriend and that she had gotten a reputation with the boys. "Surely," they all said, "Tonya had gotten pregnant by one of them and was just blaming Ron." But Julie believed Tonya. Even though Julie was only eight years old at the time, she knew Tonya's heart and she also knew her dad's.

Julie kicked her legs above the little stream that ran beneath the crosswalk. Mamie sat quietly next to her. Julie picked up a small twig. She twirled it in her fingers and then tossed it into the water beneath her. The thing that troubled Julie the most about her life was her dad. She had tried all of her life to understand this man who was her father. She tried to see his heart, look past his mistakes, and blame everything that he did wrong on his drinking. However, nothing could explain to her why he treated her the way he did. Everyone thought that Julie, being the youngest of the four children and the only girl, that she was daddy's little girl. That very thought alone made Julie nauseated in her stomach. She thought, how foolish adults were to see and believe what they wanted to see and believe, even if it wasn't the truth.

Julie couldn't understand why her dad sexually abused her. It had started when she was eight years old, shortly after her mom had moved out of their house and it continued throughout her childhood, even until now. That was why, today, she walked down behind the barn. She wanted to disappear before her dad got out of bed. He was working the night shift now so Julie had been able to escape his assaults at night because most of the time he was working late. Lately though, he had resorted to getting Julie alone when her brothers went to play with the neighborhood boys. He would tell her that she was getting too old to go with her brothers. Julie had found out that the real reason, though, was to keep her at home alone with him. The problem was that he had discovered that he couldn't abuse Julie when she was awake. She would not let him. His only success occurred when she was asleep, when he would slip quietly into her bedroom at night.

Julie shivered and shook as she remembered how through the years she would awaken at night to his abuse. The fear and shame, guilt and blame covered her even now in a shroud of pain and confusion. She felt so dirty. She felt her purity was gone. She felt valueless and powerless. Her only defense was to try and outwit him and fend off his advances.

Julie rested her head into her cupped hands and quietly sobbed. Mamie raised her head and looked at her little friend while licking her elbow. Julie heard a car coming up the dirt alley and quickly wiped away her tears. It was their neighbor. Julie quickly dried her face with her blouse before he approached. She raised her head as he passed, gave a big smile and waved. *No one must know. No one,* Julie thought.

"Julie. Julie," she heard her name being called in the distance. Mamie perked her floppy ears and raised her head. "Julie, where are you?" came the voice, louder now as it came closer. Julie listened intently and jumped to her feet. She was just ready to dart into the back door of the barn when she heard the voice again. It was Ronnie, her oldest brother. She now recognized his voice as he approached closer. *He must have just gotten home from work,* Julie thought, as she ran to the corner of the barn. She almost ran right into him when she rounded the corner at the same time that he did. Ronnie broke into laughter as they almost collided together. "Hey, where you been? I couldn't find you," Ronnie said. "Dad's been looking for you too." Julie's face dropped but then lifted knowing that Ronnie was home and that she now would be safe.

Ronnie put his arm around his little sister's shoulder as they walked up the sidewalk together. Mamie followed slowly behind them. "Are we going over to Mom's tonight?" Julie asked.

"Yea, as soon as Jerry and Matt get home from football practice," Ronnie answered.

Julie ran into the house and slipped up the steps past her dad's bedroom before he could see her. She wanted to avoid him and any questions that he might ask as to where she had been. She hurried into the bathroom to clean up and then went to her bedroom to wait for her mom to pick her up.

She sat on the edge of the bed twitching her feet together, lost in her thoughts. As if things were not bad enough at home, Julie was having a difficult time in school. Lindsey, her classmate, was on a mission to bring her down. The same thing had happened to Julie when she was in third grade. Lindsey had moved away for a few years after that but had just recently moved back. Julie thought that it might be different this time; however, it actually had gotten worse. Julie blamed herself for a lot of it. She had at first teamed in with Lindsey to avoid her wrath. Together they ruled. Then Lindsey turned on her, and by then Julie had alienated herself from all of her old friends. She found herself all alone. None of her classmates would talk to her, mostly because of their fear of Lindsey turning their classmates against them.

Julie wasn't sure if she should tell her mom what had happened at school this week. They were waiting inside for the school bus to come because it was raining. Mr. Sanders had stepped out of the classroom. Lindsey had picked on her the whole day. When she wasn't teasing her, she would just ignore Julie. As much as it hurt, Julie was getting used to the silent treatment. As they all sat and waited for the school bus, Julie continued to try to get her homework done. This way she would be able to ignore the rejection of her classmates with their silence. This had hurt her feelings so much. However, on that day Lindsey was not content with just bullying Julie but took it one step further. Lindsey whispered to her friends and then pointed to Julie. Julie could feel their eyes upon her. They all broke out into laughter at Lindsey's cruel remarks. Julie's desk sat nearby as she continued to do her homework and pretend that she didn't notice. This only angered Lindsey more. She now began to say things about Julie and made fun of her in a louder voice. She'd pause long enough to let the other girls laugh and see if she was affecting Julie, and then she'd say something else a little louder so that she could be sure that Julie heard her. Julie continued to work. She bit her bottom lip to hold back her anger and tears. These were her old friends. She remembered when her mom had warned her that Lindsey was not a nice person and how that someday she would hurt her.

Little did any of the girls know that Mrs. Hornworth was watching from her desk in the next room.

Lindsey continued to persist with her remarks. She glanced back to see if she was getting to Julie. But Julie would not show a response. Finally, Lindsey arose, walked back to Julie's desk and began to tease and taunt her as the group watched and giggled.

Julie continued to ignore her. She had already gotten into trouble a few weeks earlier with Mr. Feldon, her principal. She had never been in trouble at school, except in the second grade when David Weinstein had chased her around the classroom at recess because he had a crush on her. They had actually each received a paddling from their teacher that day. But the situation with Mr. Feldon was a little different being that she was now in seventh grade.

Julie had been waiting at the bus stop for her school bus. Her young cousin was waiting with the other children also. Everyday, Billy Klondrike would pick on Julie's little cousin. He was twice his size. Julie would try to stay out of it. She figured that if she interfered, Billy would just pick on him more when she wasn't around. His mom was on the PTA and was active with the school board. Julie's cousin just tried to ignore him, but Billy wouldn't let up. On this day, Billy had pushed her cousin so hard that he slid down the bank and into the ditch. When he got up and started to climb back, Julie could tell that he was holding back tears and she had seen enough. Billy stood laughing and was getting ready to push him down again. Julie then put her books down and ran over and yelled, "Hey, Billy, you leave him alone!" Billy turned and looked at Julie, sizing her up.

"Make me!" he sneered.

Julie felt all of her suppressed anger rise to the surface. "Make me!?" she repeated his words questioningly. Billy's expression changed immediately. He realized too late that he had underestimated Julie. Julie tore into him. Billy tried to fight back but Julie had years of experience from fighting with her three big brothers. She knocked him down and dragged him through the mud puddle.

"Bus! Bus!" the others called out.

Julie ran to pick up her books and catch the bus. Billy Klondrike ran up the hill to his house. Later that morning, Julie was called into Mr. Feldon's office. Billy's angry mother had called the office. Mr. Feldon yelled at Julie and told her that what she had done was not acceptable. He reached for the wooden paddle to give her a spanking. He didn't even ask Julie to explain her actions. Julie felt terrified. However, she was more afraid of getting in trouble with her dad, when he found out, than the actual spanking she was about to receive from Mr. Feldon. "Mr. Feldon," Julie spoke up hurriedly before he could order her to stand. She could hear her own voice quiver in her nervousness. "Don't you want to know what Billy did?"

Mr. Feldon stopped short. He paused and laid the paddle down onto his desk. "Okay," he said. "What did Billy do?"

"Everyday at the bus stop…everyday," Julie spoke earnestly, "Billy picks on my little cousin. I tried to ignore it thinking that he would surely stop and leave him alone, but he just keeps picking on him. And today, he pushed him so hard that he went tumbling down the bank. And he would have done it again if I didn't stop him." Julie let the words come rushing out. She felt so nervous and didn't know what else to say.

Mr. Feldon just stood there looking at her, not saying a word. The paddle still remained on his desk with his hand resting on it. Julie didn't know what he would do. Finally, he spoke up. "Well, well, I see," he stammered, and then he paused gathering his thoughts. "Go back to your room and don't let this happen again."

Julie couldn't open her mouth to say a word. She just gave him a quick nod and hurried back to her room.

Now, Lindsey was standing at her desk. Julie couldn't get into trouble again with Mr. Feldon. She knew that she was near her breaking point. Then Lindsey let out a remark about her family. "What's wrong, didn't your mom ever teach you anything?"

Julie slammed her book shut, jumped up and faced Lindsey. "Leave me alone! Just leave me alone!" Julie said, her voice rising.

Mrs. Hornworth was still watching from the next room. She had noticed for weeks that the two friends were at odds with each other. She had even asked Julie about it one day. Julie didn't know what to say except to tell her to ask Lindsey. Unknown to Julie, Mrs. Hornworth had stood up from her desk, seeing the commotion, and started to walk over to the classroom. She walked slowly and paused to listen to Lindsey's remarks.

Lindsey turned and flipped her hand in the air at Julie and flung her head back and laughed. She strutted back to her desk while making the sound of a chicken, "Bach, bach, bach bach."

Julie followed Lindsey to her desk. All the girls snickered and laughed enjoying the feud between the two girls. "I'm telling you Lindsey. Just leave me alone!" Julie repeated.

"Make me…you coward," Lindsey hissed at her quietly with a sneer.

Julie felt every fiber in her body tense as her anger exploded. Rather than tear into Lindsey, she grabbed the desk, picked it up at an angle and shook every book out of it onto the floor. Julie turned to go back to her desk with her head hung down. Their classmates watched, looking first at Julie and then at Lindsey's desk. Lindsey's face was etched in anger. She turned to follow Julie but then stopped short and quickly slid back into her desk leaning over to pick up her books.

Julie didn't see what Lindsey saw until she returned to her desk. There stood Mrs. Hornworth with her hands on her hips, staring at both of the two girls. "What in the world are you doing?" she asked Julie.

Julie looked up at Mrs. Hornworth, deeply into her questioning eyes. She searched them for any signs of compassion, but found none. With a boldness, which even surprised Julie, she answered as respectfully as she could, "Why don't you ask Lindsey what she did to me?" Mrs. Hornworth stood looking at Julie and then over at Lindsey. Mrs. Hornworth had watched the scene unfold. She knew that Lindsey had picked the argument. She stood firmly with her arms now crossed and her face etched in sternness. None of the students snickered or laughed as they slowly turned around in their seats. The bus pulled up and quietly one by one they lined up at the door. Julie gathered her things and gave Mrs. Hornworth a slight glance. Mrs. Hornworth nodded at Julie to get in line. Julie was glad that she had not sent her to the principal's office.

The sound of the car horn beeping interrupted Julie's thoughts. She jumped up from her bed and pulled back the blind to peek out. She saw her mom parked across the street and ran down the stairs and out the front door. She ran across the street with her brothers following behind her. Julie waited until later when she was alone with her mom and told her what had happened at school. Her mom sat and told Julie stories of what had happened to her when she was a young girl. The stories encouraged Julie. She sat and looked at her mom. Julie pictured her mom as a little girl, as Ethel spoke. "It was during the depression, Julie. My mom had hardly any money…"

"You mean Gramma Winnie?" Julie interrupted.

"Yes," replied Ethel, "and your Aunt Mary, and I had caught lice. So they shaved all of our hair off."

"All of it?" Julie asked.

"All of it," Ethel answered. "It was cold and in the winter, and we didn't have any coats. The government had given my mom what they call ration coupons to buy us clothes, but they were only good to purchase clothes at the men's clothing store. So the winter coats that she bought us were boys' coats."

"You had to wear boys' coats?" Julie asked. Julie sat intently listening trying to picture her mom and aunt completely bald and wearing boys' coats.

"Yes, and Gramma Winnie gave us money to go to the picture show because she had to work and couldn't afford to pay for a babysitter. During the show, when I had to go to the bathroom and got to the bathroom doors, I didn't know whether I should go into the girls' or the boys' bathroom."

"Why?" asked Julie.

"Because with my head shaved and the boy's coat, I looked more like a boy than a girl," Ethel continued her story, smiling.

"So which bathroom did you use?" Julie asked curiously.

"I went into the boys'," Ethel answered laughing.

"Really?" Julie asked, as she burst out laughing.

Julie was glad that her mom had not yelled at her.

Julie continued to sit, late into the night, talking with her mom. Her siblings had all gone to bed.

"Do you remember the time Mom, when my winter coat was in real bad shape and you told Gramma Winnie that you couldn't afford to get me another one because they had cut back your hours at work?" Julie asked.

"I do," Ethel said smiling at her young daughter. Ethel marveled at how grown-up Julie was becoming. But as she studied Julie when she spoke, she could still see her little girl deep within the blossoming young woman who sat before her.

"I loved that coat Mom," Julie continued. "It was a beige fur coat with beautiful autumn leaves placed throughout it, but it had become very dirty and the fur was matted."

Ethel continued to listen intently to Julie. It touched her heart to hear Julie open up to her and talk. So often Julie would shut herself down and go somewhere deep where Ethel couldn't find her.

"And then, one day, when I went to find my coat, Gramma Winnie found it for me and brought it to me," Julie continued with a big smile. "I couldn't believe it Mom!" Julie paused and spread her arms out to express her feelings. "Gramma Winnie brought my coat to me and it looked brand new! She had washed it in Woolite and dried it. It was absolutely beautiful." Julie ended her story, "I'll never forget that Mom, how much Gramma cared to help me. Gramma Winnie knew how bad the coat was and yet how special it was to me."

Ethel and Julie continued to share stories until Julie thought that she would fall asleep at the table. Julie glanced over at her mom. She studied her kind face. She could see the calluses on her mom's hands from pressing the dozens of dresses at the dress factory where she worked. Julie enjoyed the times that she spent with her mom and brothers. She enjoyed the times with her stepsisters and stepbrother, and Bob her stepfather. Here she was able to feel safe, rest, and laugh. Julie knew that she would have to continue to face her fears and problems with her dad, but for now, she would enjoy this time. She arose and kissed her mom goodnight and went to bed.

As she laid in the stillness, her mind continued to race. She wished that she could tell her mom about her dad. She wished that she could move in with her mom. She knew that her brothers would understand if they knew. But she couldn't imagine living without them.

And even still worse, Julie knew that she could never tell anyone. *Who would ever believe her?* No one ever believed Tonya when she spoke up and told what Julie's dad had done to her. No one ever believed Tina Sellers, who lived below Julie's grandparents, when she told her parents that she had been molested by Julie's Pap Pap James. Julie believed Tina because she knew that her grandfather had molested her also when she was younger. People always wonder why kids don't speak up; but when they do, no one believes them and so often nothing is said or done to confront the person that did it.

Julie knew that if her mom knew what her dad was doing to her, that she would believe her. *But what could her mom do?* Julie knew that her mom had tried to get the family to deal with the situation when her Pap Pap James had sexually abused her when she was only four years old. But everyone said, "Oh, Ethel, you must be mistaken." "She's too little; she must have misunderstood what happened." The family refused to address her grandfather or to even deal with the situation. Ethel was even told by Ron, Julie's own father, to let it go, and so it was pushed under the rug. No one ever wanted to hear such horrible things, talk about it, or even believe that such terrible things like this could really happen. Julie wondered whether it was the issue of sexual abuse that their family couldn't deal with or if it was the shame from the sexual abuse that they didn't want to confront. *Couldn't they look past themselves, about how it would affect them, and see what it had done to her?*

No one would ever believe a kid. *And even if they would believe her,* Julie thought, *What would happen to her and her brothers? Where would they all live if she told? Would they get split up or sent to an orphanage far away?* Their dad had often told them, "If it wasn't for me, no one else would raise you, and where would you go then?" "To an orphanage," he would answer his own question.

What would people think of her if she told? She knew what they had said about Tonya and Tina. *Julie knew how hard her life was now and yet no one knew of her secret, how bad would it be if people knew? How bad would they tease her and shun her at school then? How would she ever bear the guilt and shame of it all? How would anyone ever understand it, when even Julie herself could not understand?* There were no answers, only questions and fears. *Would her dad get sent to jail like her Pap Pap James almost did?* As much as she hated what her dad did to her, she could not bear to be the one to send him to jail. She was afraid that even if he didn't go to jail, that he might try to kill himself again as he had tried to do when she was in the second grade. Julie fell asleep hoping that when she awoke she could find the answers.

Julie had started to go to church with Ronnie at the night services. He had begged her to come with him. She admired all of her big brothers and looked up to them. In Julie's eyes they could do no wrong. She had started going to the night services at church with Ronnie after seeing the change it was making in his life. Julie remembered when they were little how all four of them would walk up to the little church that sat at the top of the hill. Mamie, their little cocker spaniel, would follow them slowly up the winding dirt road that led up the hill. There the little dog would lie down at the church's door and wait for them until the service was over. When Ronnie had asked Julie to come with him to the evening services, Julie couldn't help but remember the time that all four of them, when they were younger, had walked up the aisle of the church together for the altar call. All four of them had asked Jesus to come into their hearts that day. Julie was too young to understand it all then, but she had never forgotten what she had felt in her heart that day. It had changed Julie in such a way that no matter what happened to her in her life, somewhere down deep she knew that there really was a God; and that regardless of what anyone else thought, no matter what Julie herself even thought, she knew that God loved her and that she mattered to Him.

So when Ronnie had asked her to go with him to the evening services, she went with him. And once again, she gave her heart to God anew. She understood more now at age thirteen, as she purposed in her heart that she would never stray away from God again. She asked Him to forgive her of all the wrong that she had done. She hoped that someday her dad would come to know this Jesus who loved them, that he would ask Him to forgive him, and that then he would be sorry for all the things that he had done to her, her brothers, and their family. Then maybe she could forgive him and find the old daddy that she thought she once knew and love him again. She just wanted all of the bad memories to go away and be erased as if they had never happened. But Julie wondered how she or even God could ever erase the horrible memories that tormented her mind.

Julie continued to hope that things would get better in her life, especially since she had renewed her heart to God. But later, when she was back at her home sitting in her bedroom and trying to do her homework, all of her hope would fade. She would sit on the edge of her bed and bury her head into her hands turning it back and forth in an effort to find rest for her troubled mind. Things were not getting better. With her dad's continual abuse and her trouble in school with Lindsey and her classmates, she had no joy or hope; and she didn't know how much longer she could bear her life. Sometimes, she had wished that she would just die and go home to be with her Lord. Once again, as when she was in the fourth grade, she was finding it difficult to concentrate on her schoolwork at home and in school. She lifted her head and wrung her hands nervously together and searched for the answers that just were not there.

Hope seemed to flee from Julie. She gritted her teeth as she felt all of her pain come rushing back upon her in a wave of despair. She clutched her wrists so tightly that her fingernails pierced into them leaving deep purple incisions.

Julie clinched from the pain as the tears came rushing out of her tightly closed eyes and ran down her cheeks. She groaned quietly, holding back the breaking of her spirit.

As she opened her eyes, she saw the purple creases in her wrists. She studied them in her hopelessness as a new thought tumbled into her mind—thoughts she had never entertained as a possible solution to her problems. *It would be so easy,* she thought, as she continued to look at her wrists. *The pain would be over once and for all,* she thought, as she considered the option. The idea seemed worthy of the cost. But then, from deep within her soul, she felt a gentle loving tug.

"*No,*" It said softly but firmly. "*No, Julie. This is not the answer. Know I am with you always, always, always....*"

Julie at thirteen years old

Chapter

4

Julie felt the phone slip from her hand. It startled her and brought her back to the present. Mike had not come home yet from work. She jumped up and ran into the kitchen to check on the meatloaf, stirred the peas, and turned down the oven heat to low. She then glanced at the clock, returned to the living room, and sat down on the couch. Julie picked up the phone once again and quickly dialed the number to her dad's home which she still had memorized from her childhood.

"Hello," came the soft voice at the other end.

"Hi, Claire," Julie answered back. "I just wanted to return your phone call."

"Well, there's not much to tell, Julie, but I wanted to touch base with you as I had promised," Claire said. "They did more tests, and basically they just confirmed what was already suspected. The cancer is pretty advanced, and there is nothing that they can do except to make him comfortable as the pain increases. So far, he is a little uncomfortable but seems okay."

"Have you talked to Jerry, Ronnie, or Matt lately?" Julie asked.

"Yes. I called Jerry after I had called you and told him. He said that he would call Matt and Ronnie," Claire answered.

"Well, I don't know what to say Claire," Julie spoke sadly. "If there is anything that I can do to help you, will you let me know?"

"I will Julie," Claire replied. "Thank you for calling. I'll keep you posted if there is any change."

"Thank you Claire," Julie said softly. "I'll talk to you later."

Julie clicked the phone off with her thumb and laid it aside. She leaned back onto the couch propping her feet up. Mike would be home soon. She would share everything with him. Mike knew her like no one else could. He truly was the love of her life. God had promised her during those rough young years as a child that if she would put Him first in her life that He would give her the desires of her heart. With all of Julie's young ambitions, her greatest dream had been to someday have a real home, a Christian home, a home where her husband would love and adore her, and where she would have her children and raise them in a real family and give them a life that she had always wanted to have.

She remembered the first time that she met Mike. She had gone down to the college chapel with some of her new friends whom she had met at college. They all hoped that maybe they could meet more friends that weren't involved in all of the partying and drugs that seemed to be so rampant on the campus. Here she met Mike. Later they were in several classes together.

In time, often on the weekends, she would run into him at the chapel. Julie couldn't bear staying in her dorm with all of the loud partying and drugs going on and often walked down to the college chapel to get away. It seemed that Mike too had left his dorm for the same reasons. They would sit in the chapel and talk and became good friends in time. Julie loved to sit and listen to him play his music. She was surprised to learn that much of the music that he played was music that he had written. They would sit for hours until the campus partying would die down for the night and then go back to their dorms.

They fell in love. For Julie, it was not only a dream come true but a promise from God fulfilled. By then, Julie was trying to put her past behind her. She was out of the clutches of her dad's abuse, and she tried to forget that it had ever happened to her. But when

Mike and Julie had become serious in their relationship and were talking about marriage, all of her past began to haunt her. She felt that somehow she was deceiving Mike. She wondered, *What would he think of her if he knew her past.* She felt that if Mike knew about her past that he would see her as a totally different person, that he would lose respect for her, and that he would see her as damaged merchandise.

She had never told anyone, not a soul. There was no way that she could tell Mike when she couldn't even tell her brothers or her mom. Julie justified within her heart a million times that it was not necessary to tell him. He loved her for who she was. She couldn't tell him. It would ruin everything. *Wonder if he felt cheated and treated her different? Wonder if his love for her would change?*

How could she ever tell him? And how could she marry him and then someday, if he found out, or if she told him then, what would he think of her? Wouldn't he wonder what else she hadn't told him? Julie had prayed and prayed and wrestled about it in her mind. She knew within her heart that she had to tell Mike; but the fear and shame, guilt and blame held her gripped within their vice. She feared talking about it more than death itself. She would rather die than to expose her shame to anyone, especially to her beloved Mike. *But how could she not tell him?* She had waited a lifetime for him to come into her life. *How could she risk throwing it all away?*

Julie had purposed in her heart that she would tell Mike. She knew that she might lose everything and that his love for her might change. She was aware that his respect and all that he thought of her could change forever. Julie decided that she had to know if anything would change between them if he knew. She had to know before they were married. If it would change their love and their relationship, Julie wanted to know it now and not after they had married. She would wait for the right time and then pray that God would give her the strength that she needed to tell him. She would tell Mike, and then she would never bring it up again.

Often, Mike and Julie would sit inside his car in the parking lot in front of Julie's dorm and talk. It was quieter there and they had more privacy. One evening, as they sat talking and sharing the dreams of their future, Julie felt God nudge her heart. *"Tell him."*

Julie squirmed uneasily as God continued to move on her to open up to Mike. Finally, almost abruptly, Julie interrupted Mike gently. "I have something I have to tell you," she said in a serious tone. She glanced up at Mike, into his deep blue eyes and then looked down again at her hands which she wrung nervously.

Mike turned in his seat to face her. He had noticed her uneasiness all evening. He could see how troubled she was and said, "Jul, is something wrong?"

"No," Julie spoke softly. "It's just…I have to tell you something."

Mike reached out and took Julie's hand. He could feel it trembling beneath his own gentle grasp. "You can tell me anything Julie," he spoke softly.

There was a long pause as they both sat quietly. Mike waited patiently. Julie turned and studied his face. How handsome he was. His rich blue eyes, his light brown hair streaked with highlights of blond. He had a slight dimple in his strong chin bone that accentuated the warm smile that sent Julie's heart to flutter. Mike's eyes met hers and were full of compassion. His love filled her and she wondered how he could love her so much. She felt that surely she could tell him. She began to try to start the conversation, but when she opened her mouth no words came out. She felt her fears grip and bind her. She turned and looked again into Mike's patient and kind eyes.

"It's okay Jul. You can tell me," Mike said and encouraged Julie to empty her heart to him. Mike had never seen Julie so troubled. She was the bubbly one, the one who always assured him that with God everything would turn out alright. They had grown together so deeply as one, and they had grown together in their faith in a God who was real to both of them. "Tell me," Mike said kindly, and so softly, that Julie barely heard him. She turned once more to study the man that she had dared to open her heart to. His eyes were unmoved and were full of such love for her that Julie felt undeserving of it.

"When I was a child," Julie paused and then lowered her head. She struggled with the words. "When I was a child," she started over again. She paused once more and took one more look into Mike's deep loving eyes. She wasn't sure if that love would be there after she told him and she wanted to see it one more time. Julie turned away and looked down at her nervous twitching hands which rested in his, and then she let the words tumble out before she could change her mind. "My dad sexually abused me."

Julie felt a weight inside of her lift. She felt her whole body tremble. She could not believe that she had spoken the words. She didn't have the courage to look into Mike's face. She could not bear to see the love in those eyes vanish. She sat motionless waiting for Mike's reaction.

Julie sat in that moment of silence for a minute before she realized that Mike was still holding her hand. He gently caressed it with his other hand before lovingly clasping her hand between both of his. He spoke no words but his touch said it all. He reached his arm around her and she laid her head upon his chest. There they sat in the quietness. Mike's love and touch comforted her. Somehow, he knew to not say a word. He knew how painful it must be for her to share this with him. He wanted so much to assure her that she need not say anymore.

After a while, he kissed her upon her forehead. Julie looked up into his face. Their eyes met. Julie smiled seeing Mike's eyes full of love for her. His love had not vanished. It had not fled. He wrapped his arms around her as they sat in the quietness together. Julie's heart was overflowed with love, love from a God who had carried her, love from a man who wanted her to be his wife.

Julie treasured that memory. She stretched her legs and looked at the phone that was still at her side. She knew that she should probably call her brothers and talk to them about what Claire had shared with her, but she just wasn't sure whether now was the right time. Her heart and mind raced within her. Her thoughts tumbled from the past to the present. This was her battle. She had wrestled with it all of her life. God was leading her on a healing journey. A journey, that looking back, started the first day that she had truly confronted her dad for the first time….

"Fighting soldiers from the sky,
Fearless men who jump and die,
Men who mean just what they say,
The brave men of the Green Beret."

The song played in the silence of the night. The next record would be Dean Martin singing, "Everybody Loves Somebody Sometime." Julie laid peacefully on her bed as she listened to the music that filled the house. Her dad was at work. He was working the night shift. Julie felt safe. As long as she was with her brothers there was nothing to be afraid of. Julie actually loved the times when she and her brothers were alone at night. She began to sleep so much better now that she didn't have to worry that her dad would come into her room during the night. On the nights that he was off, he would often send them up to Gramma Emma's house so that he could go out.

Julie also suspected that he probably had a new girlfriend. There was one morning, after staying overnight at their Gramma Emma's house, when they had arrived and entered into their home, that their dad came out of his bedroom, closed the door behind him, and told them nicely to be quiet. Julie looked at her brothers with a question in her eyes. They looked at her and then at each other. Their dad usually never closed his bedroom door behind him. He was actually nice when he had told them to be quiet before he turned and went back into his bedroom. They couldn't stop wondering why he hadn't yelled at them. Julie could see the wheels turning in all three of her brothers' eyes. She waited patiently to see what they would say.

"Bet Dad has his new girlfriend in the bedroom," Jerry said in a low whisper with a soft giggle.

Julie laughed quietly at Jerry's remark. Leave it to Jerry to make them laugh. He could always take a serious moment and crack them up.

"I think you're right," Ronnie said with a light laugh, agreeing with his younger brother.

Matt nodded his head in agreement and let out a soft giggle.

A few moments later, Jerry started to laugh again. Matt quickly poked him to be quiet and looked towards their dad's bedroom door to see if it was still closed.

"But look," Jerry whispered.

Ronnie, Matt, and Julie turned and looked at their brother.

Jerry just stood there with an impish grin on his face. "I was looking for my shoes for school but I don't think these are mine." In his hand he held, waving in the air, a woman's petite pair of shoes.

All four of them broke into laughter. Julie ran over to Jerry trying to grab them from him. "Put them back under the couch," she said, her voice breaking again in quiet laughter.

Julie heard the click of the phonograph in the stillness of the night as it moved and released the next record. She smiled as she heard the familiar words of the Dean Martin song. It was her brother Jerry's favorite, and she loved to hear him sing along with it. He would change his voice into a deeper masculine tone as he'd sing the song, putting his own "Dean Martin" twist to the words.

Julie took her pillow and moved to the foot of her bed. She lay down beside the open screened window and let the gentle breeze blow onto her face. She looked up into the dark night and watched, mesmerized by the stars in the sky. Their faint twinkle in the far distance brought her comfort. Periodically, a bright light would streak across the sky, pause and then be followed by another. The beacon light from the airport, on top of the mountainside behind their house, shined its light like a ray of hope in the darkness. Julie watched its rhythmical motion as it began to lull her to sleep.

Julie smiled as she allowed her thoughts to wander once again. Julie was glad when school had finally ended for the summer break. By the end of the school year nothing had changed in her situation with Lindsey and her classmates. The summer was refreshing for her. She enjoyed going on the picnics with her family out at Hanson's Park and cherished the times that she was spending with her mom. She had so much fun with her brothers. Sometimes she hated being the youngest. She knew that soon her brothers would be all grown up and leaving home, one by one. She could not even begin to entertain that thought. She didn't know how she could live without them. They all played such a special part in her life. They had always been there for her. They were her heroes.

Julie hardly noticed the change of the seasons as summer had gradually come to an end, flowing right into autumn, as a new school year began to start. To her surprise and joy, Lindsey did not return to their school. Julie heard that she had moved away. Julie hoped that she would never move back to their area again.

It promised to be a different kind of school year, Julie thought, as she continued to look out of her window and watch the beacon as it continued to circle the night sky. All of her classmates were talking to her as if nothing had ever happened. It was as if the summer had erased it all into oblivion. No one would ever know the relief that she had felt when she walked into the classroom that first day of school. Everyone was talking excitedly about their summer. All of the animosity was gone, faded, as if it was a cloud of fog that had dissipated with the morning light. Sarah, her best friend, met her at the door to their classroom. Their friendship had been renewed over the summer. Sunday after Sunday they sat side by side in Mrs. Nelson's Sunday school classroom and listened to the stories of a Savior who taught love and forgiveness. They vowed afresh to each other that nothing would ever separate their friendship again.

As Mrs. Hornworth called the class to order, Sarah and Julie went to sit down at two of the desks that sat side by side. Sarah smiled over at Julie and said, "I thought ole Mrs. Hornworth was retiring this year."

"Me too," Julie said as she placed her books into her desk. Julie turned to her friend and whispered, "You know Sarah, I don't think that she will ever retire. She's taught so long. She even taught my mom." Sarah let out a soft laughter and nodded in agreement.

The loud click of the record player interrupted Julie's thoughts. Julie knew that the record player had played the last album and clicked off. Stillness now filled the house. Julie turned to get comfortable in her bed as she pulled the cover over her. She brought it up to her chin and snuggled down into its warmth. With Lindsey moving away and her dad working the night shift, Julie was able to rest and return to her old self. She had begun to laugh again. Julie glanced over at the glowing cross attached to the picture of Jesus that she still kept hanging on her wall and then turned back and looked out the window. She watched the beacon from the far hillside shoot a path of light, a circling beam that shined throughout the dark night. *Like rays of hope,* Julie thought, *to all who cannot find their way.* She wondered if her family would ever find their way or if they had ever noticed the ray of hope that shined throughout their dark night. A ray that did not sit on a distant mountainside far away, but rather, one that could direct their path and that was so near to their heart. Julie's eyes began to get heavy and slowly closed. Her heart began to fill with a new hope. *God is answering my prayers,* she thought. She felt a peace engulf her as she rested in the One who was lighting her path, a God who no longer was just a picture on the wall but a reality in her heart.

Picture of Beacon

Chapter

5

Julie couldn't wait to see her mom. She could hear the television blaring from the living room downstairs as she sat at her vanity and brushed her hair. She quickly pinned her hair back tightly with a barrette and turned and ran out of her bedroom door and down the stairway.

She ran to the television and pushed the knob in to turn it off being careful that the little knob didn't fall off into her hand as it so often did. She hurried out the front door and turned to lock it. Quickly, she ran the key to the back summer porch and hid it in the old rusty metal cabinet. Julie then ran back to the front porch and jumped up onto the banister kicking her heels against the shingles as she sat and watched the cars pass; she peered down the road as far as her head could stretch looking for Ronnie's car to cross the rickety wooden bridge.

Ronnie was to pick her up after he finished work to take her to their mom's house. Jerry and Matt would be working at their new jobs at the bowling alley and would join them later. They were pin setters. Julie thought it strange that the bowling alleys in Grantville didn't have automatic pin setters like she had seen on television. More than once, Jerry and Matt would come home with bruises on their shins from not jumping out of the way on time from the flying bowling pins and balls.

Tonight, Julie would so enjoy the time that she was going to spend with her brothers. Julie didn't get to spend as much time with her brothers and often felt alone now that they were all working and driving. Ronnie would graduate this year; the next year Jerry would graduate and then Matt. Life was changing too quickly for Julie. She had wondered if it would ever change in a way that she could settle into it.

Julie glanced at the tavern that sat across the street. She watched the cars pulling in and out of the parking lot and listened to the voices as they drifted across the street. She recognized the slurred enunciations and marveled at the hollowness of a life consumed with alcohol. The drunkenness was a mere facade where pain was covered but never relieved. Only sorrow seemed to perpetrate from beneath its veil.

Julie was glad that her dad wasn't home. There were worse things in her life than loneliness. For a short time, her dad's abuse had let up when he had his girlfriend, but as soon as they broke up it had started again. Slowly, Julie was learning to stand up to her dad, against his attempts to abuse her. She continually thanked God for moving her dad to work the night shift. Most of his attempts were now made while she was awake. Julie was older now. Because of her growing into a young woman, his more frequent encounters had made her life increasingly more difficult. However, because she was older, she was now able to stand up against him. God gave her a strength that she didn't even know that she possessed. Julie had begun to confront her dad more and more when he tried to abuse her. She began to feel empowered and strengthened. She began to feel renewed as she began to reclaim herself.

Julie knew that she had shocked her dad the last time she encountered him, but not as much as he had shocked her. Julie had never dreamed that her dad would try to go to such extremes as he had on that day. She had tried to slip out of the house with Jerry and Matt before her dad could stop her. Jerry and Matt had left a few minutes earlier, and Julie's plan was to wait and then join them. If she would have tried to go with them, her dad would have seen her and stopped her. This way she could be more inconspicuous. As she slipped out of the gate, her dad saw her and ordered her to come back. "You're too old to be hanging out with your brothers and their friends," he said. "Get back in here."

Julie turned and saw her dad at the front screen door. He turned and walked away as she re-entered the gate. Julie turned and went around the corner of the house avoiding going into the house. She leaned on the side of the banister around the corner of the house where her dad couldn't see her from any window or door. Here she would remain until he got tired of waiting for her to come inside and would go to bed to sleep. She would then slip out and go to Sarah and Molly's house. *He couldn't yell at her for that,* she thought.

Shortly though, Julie heard her dad calling her. She tried to ignore him and hoped he would give up. She would rather get yelled at by him later for not answering than to confront him now. But, he continued to call for her. Julie heard him open the squeaky screen door. She knew now that she wouldn't be able to ignore him.

"Julie! You come in here, right now!"

"I don't want to," Julie answered back. "I want to stay outside for a while."

Julie heard her dad come out onto the porch. She stood up and saw him standing in his pajamas.

"You come in right now!" he ordered lowering his voice so that the neighbors wouldn't hear him.

Reluctantly, Julie got up and walked around the corner. She saw her dad go back into the house. She walked around to the front of the house and paused for a moment. She stared at the old gray porch and then glanced back at the iron gate. She wondered, *What would happen if she just ignored him and ran up to her gramma's house?* But such solutions were only temporary and ultimately she would have to come home and then what? *And then what?* she wondered as she entered into the house letting the screen door slam behind her.

She sat down on the couch and tried to pray, but her mind was in such a quandary. Fear gripped her heart. She wanted to cry. She wanted to ask her dad why he treated her this way. She knew that he would only say to her what he had said to her so many other times, "Julie, all fathers have this kind of relationship with their daughters. There's nothing wrong with this."

When Julie was little, she had thought that it was because of her dad's drinking that he abused her, but as she grew older she realized that his advances, like today, were made when he was sober. The drinking only made it easier for him.

Julie sat wrenching her hands and digging her fingernails into her hands. *What could she do? What could she do?* Her thoughts had echoed through her mind until she thought her head would burst. She was no longer a little girl but a young woman, and it terrified her of what her dad might have in mind for her. She felt fear rise within her.

"Come in here," her dad called from his bedroom a few moments later.

"No Dad!" Julie called back. She didn't move.

"I said, come in here right now!" Julie heard his voice rise.

"I want to go outside!" Julie yelled back. She was surprised at the tone of her voice as it rose in anger.

"I said now!" he repeated.

Julie stood up. She felt her anger rise above her fear as she began to walk towards his bedroom. "He can't make me!" she mumbled under her halting breath as her chest rose and fell, mixed with her fear and rage.

Moments later she screamed, "No! No! I won't!" She turned and ran out of the bedroom. She ran out of the front door not even pausing to see or hear if her dad was saying anything. She slammed the door behind her. She ran down the sidewalk and into the old barn. The barn was dark and musty smelling, and Julie hated the eerie feeling that surrounded her. She wondered what would happen if her dad came down to the barn. She quickly ran to the big sliding back door of the frail wooden structure. She slid the stiff door just enough to squeeze through and walked across the small footbridge and sat down. She stared blankly ahead at the neighbor's old chicken coop. She let her mind watch the chickens aimlessly, anything to get her mind off of what had just happened. She marveled at how the chickens walked around clucking as if they didn't have a care in the world. Julie watched them pick at the ground for food as they clucked at one another.

"I don't care, God. I just don't care anymore." Julie sobbed, putting her face into her hands and upon her lap hoping that none of her neighbors would see her. Julie had ceased to care whether or not defying her dad was being disrespectful to him. "God, it can't be wrong to do right," Julie murmured softly as she continued to sob. She found it difficult to catch her breath beneath the sobs. Julie stopped crying for a moment as she heard a twitch in the grass behind her. She quickly lifted her head and turned it slowly around to look to see if it was her dad. She braced herself, getting ready to jump up and run. She then saw a little orange tabby cat run through the high grass and across the stream before darting between the neighbor's hedges. Julie leaned back tightly against the back of the barn door where she wouldn't be seen. She stretched out her legs onto the small bridge in front of her. She sat and watched a large red rooster gather his hens to his side as he protested loudly at a battered white rooster that had tried to approach his brood. Julie stayed there until she was sure that her brothers had returned home. Then and only then did she go back to the house.

The honk of a passing car brought Julie out of her thoughts. Startled, she looked up and leaned forward on the banister to peer down the road towards the bridge to see if Ronnie's car was coming. When she glanced back, she was surprised to see Mason Woodley standing in front of the fence.

"Hey, you're going to break those shingles that you're kicking so hard."

She looked up and stared at the friendly voice. She was a little embarrassed that she had not seen him approach her. "Hi," she said softly as she felt her face begin to blush. Mason was a friend of Ronnie's who had already graduated from high school. Julie knew that he was too old for her, but she couldn't help think that he was one of the cutest guys around. He reminded her of Elvis Presley with his deep brown eyes and dark brown hair combed to the side in a wave. She gave him a broad smile at seeing the twinkle in his eyes. "I'm just waiting for Ronnie to pick me up," she said shyly as Mason continued to smile at her. He was always so kind to her and treated her with the utmost respect.

"Well, there's the ole cuss now," Mason said with his southern twang accenting his words. He straightened up and opened the gate for Julie as she hopped off of the banister.

"Thanks," Julie said softly as they both ran across the street to meet Ronnie.

Julie hopped into Ronnie's car and slid across the front seat. She listened as her brother talked to his old friend and told him of his plans for the future. Julie cringed as the subject of Vietnam came up. It was one thing for her brothers to graduate, but Julie couldn't bear the thought of them going to a war in a country so far away that she still wasn't sure of where it was.

"Hi Sis!" Ronnie turned and smiled at Julie as he pulled out of Lindys Tavern's parking lot. Julie smiled a big smile at her brother as he toppled her hair. "Sorry, I'm late. I had to get some gas."

Julie studied Ronnie, her oldest brother. He was so grown up and handsome. It seemed strange to see him drive. Soon he would graduate. *What would she ever do without him?*

"Hey Julie! Mom made a big pot of spaghetti for us," Ronnie continued. "I stopped there first and told her that I would pick you up. Jerry and Matt are joining us after they get off work." "Jul," Ronnie paused and looked at her. "Julie, did you know that Mom and Bob are not getting along lately?"

"How do you know?" Julie asked. She knew that they had been arguing a lot lately.

Most times, she'd hear her mom say, "Not now, Bob. We'll talk later when the kids go home."

"Mom just kind of gets quieter when they're like this," Ronnie answered. "You know, Jul. They're just having problems."

Julie knew what her brother meant. Lately, she had seen that same sad look on her mom's face that she had remembered seeing those many years ago when her mom had lived with their dad. Julie felt sad. She had grown to love her stepfather and her step-brother and stepsisters. She knew that even in the midst of all the confusion of their blended families that they had grown to love them too. She knew, since Ronnie had been driving, that he would often stop by to see their mom on the way to and from his job.

"What kind of problems?" Julie asked, sounding much older than her fourteen years.

"Well, they don't yell a lot; they just kind of get quiet and say nothing," Ronnie said, shrugging his shoulders as if he didn't know the reasons why.

Julie could smell the spaghetti as soon as she walked thru the basement door which led up to the kitchen. She ran up the steps ahead of Ronnie and into the kitchen that had become as familiar to her as her own home.

Julie sat down at the table. The kitchen was abuzz with all of them talking at once. Julie sat and listened to the idle chatter as her mom scooped out the spaghetti onto each of their plates, one at a time. It made her heart smile, the togetherness, the sound of laughter filling the room.

"Hey, Mom!" Jerry teased. "You gave Ronnie more than me."

"That's because I'm bigger than you," Ronnie teased back.

"But at that rate, you always will be," Jerry said laughing.

"Let's play some 'Wahoo' after we're done eating," Matt suggested as he hurriedly ate his supper.

Julie loved playing the game with her brothers, mom, step-brother, and stepsisters. They moved the marbles across the board trying to be the first one home without getting knocked off and having to start all over again.

After supper was done and the dishes were cleaned up, they sat and laughed while playing the game. After handing everyone sodas, Ethel popped a large pot of popcorn, pouring melted butter all over it before putting it into a large bowl which sat in the middle of the table.

Bob went to lie down and get some sleep before he had to work the night shift. Julie had noticed that he was quieter than normal. It made her sad. She had grown to love Bob. She no longer resented him or blamed him for the breakup of her mom and dad's marriage. He treated them kindly. Julie wondered whether her stepbrother and stepsisters realized how good a dad they really had. Julie had also grown to love them too. She sometimes resented them because she wanted her mom to herself. But she couldn't help feeling guilty for this because they had no mom in their lives. Their mom had left them and never came back; she never sent them a card or ever called them. Julie had learned to share her mom with them as they had grown to become a family.

Julie moved her marble around the board while listening to the laughter that surrounded her. She glanced at her mom and saw her look over to the bedroom where Bob was sleeping and then look away again. Julie saw a sorrow in her mom's eyes that was all too familiar. As a little girl, Julie had seen that same look on her mom's face so many times. It grieved her heart to see her mom unhappy. Julie knew that a lot of the arguing was about all of the kids. Bob felt that Ron should be doing more for his kids. She knew that the financial cost of their mom buying all of their clothes and shoes and school things with her small check had left little for helping out Bob's household. But Julie had heard her mom tell Bob firmly that her kids would not go without the things that they needed. She had told him this before she had married him. Julie, at one time, had seen her mom get upset and tell him, "I don't see your kids going without, Bob!" Julie didn't know what tomorrow would bring.

"Come on Jul, take your turn," Matt said as he gave Julie a quick poke with his elbow.

The phone rang and Ethel ran to get it before it would wake up Bob. "It's for you Julie. It's your dad," Ethel said, as she returned to the kitchen.

Julie frowned and slowly stood up from her seat. Her dad usually didn't call them when they were with her mom. He was always afraid that Bob would answer the phone. Julie hated to leave the fun, and the last thing she wanted to do was to talk to her dad. She knew that he had probably been drinking all night, and that once she would start talking to him, it would be difficult to get off the phone. "Mom, will you take my turn for me?" "No cheating, you guys," Julie said while poking Matt as he pretended to move her marble.

Julie picked up the receiver and said, "Hello." She waited to hear her dad's voice at the other end. There was a long pause and Julie thought that maybe he had hung up.

"Jul---ie," came the slurred enunciation.

Julie cringed. She knew that her dad had been drinking. She knew that when he was drunk he wanted someone to talk to. Julie was used to her dad's long conversations when he was drinking. Over the years it had become a pattern. He would start talking to Julie and her brothers while they were watching television. Usually, they would just let him talk until he finally passed out and slept it off. He would, however, rarely call them at their mom's house.

Julie listened to her dad's mumbled talk and tried to understand his words as her mind drifted back to the kitchen where she heard her brothers' laughter. She wanted to get back to the game. At times like this, she actually felt sorry for her dad. Julie thought it was sad for anyone to be alone, even if they had brought it on themselves.

"Jul---ie. Are you still there?"

"Yes, Dad. I'm listening," Julie answered. "What do you want?"

"Nothing, Julie. Nothing at all," Ron answered abruptly.

"Well, I was in the middle of a game…" Julie started to explain.

"Oh, well, I wouldn't want to take you from your precious ga---me," Ron cut Julie short before she could continue. "Go on. Go on, play your ole game. Don't worry about the old man sitting here all alone."

Julie felt her anger rising within her. It was always like this. Julie knew exactly how the conversation would continue. First, he would talk about how unfair everything and everyone was to him. He would start to pity himself and blame everyone else for his demise. Next, it would be how terrible their mom was for leaving them and how he sacrificed everything to raise them and how that she was living the good life. Julie tried to remain quiet and let him talk hoping that he would get tired and want to go to sleep.

"Never mind, Julie; just never mind. Go back to your game. Don't worry about your dear old dad."

"Dad, why don't you just lie down and go to sleep? We'll be home tomorrow," Julie said slowly, trying to calm her dad down.

"So, now you're telling me what I need to do?" Ron spoke haltingly. "Little miss all grown up now, are we?"

"Dad, I'm just saying…"

"Forget it Julie. Just go back to your game!"

Julie opened her mouth to speak but heard the loud click of the phone as he hung up on her. She put her phone down gently back into the cradle and slowly plopped herself down onto the couch. She rested her elbows on her legs and sunk her head into the palms of her hands. "God, what can I do to help him?" she prayed softly. She felt so bad. She had let her dad down simply because she wanted to play a silly game. *What kind of Christian was she?* And then it hit her. The thought came out of mid-air. *No!* She thought. *No, surely that's impossible. He wouldn't do that!* But no matter how much she tried, she couldn't shake the thought out of her mind.

"Julie," Ethel spoke softly. She stood watching her daughter carefully. "Is something wrong?"

"Mom, I think dad is going to try and hurt himself," Julie said soberly as tears filled her eyes.

"Why would you think that, Julie?" Ethel asked.

"Think what?" Ronnie asked as he entered the room.

"What's going on?" asked Jerry as both he and Matt joined them.

"Julie thinks that your dad is going to try to hurt himself," Ethel replied, repeating Julie's remark.

"Why, Julie?" Jerry asked. "What did he say?"

"He didn't say anything particularly," Julie said, as if in a daze.

"Then, he'll be okay," Matt chimed in.

"Don't worry, Julie," Ronnie said, as he knelt down beside her.

"Yea, Jul, just let him sleep it off," Jerry joined in.

"You know how he gets, Jul," Matt continued.

Ronnie reached down to pull Julie up to join them in the kitchen. "Come on; you're winning."

"No!" Julie spoke up. "No! I know there's something wrong!"

Ronnie looked at Matt and Jerry. They all looked at their mom and then back at Julie. Ethel didn't say a word but studied Julie carefully. This was not like her daughter, to be so sure.

"There's nothing we can do," Jerry said tenderly.

"I'm telling you! If we don't go over and stop him, he's going to commit suicide!" Julie allowed the words to come out of her mouth. They made her tremble as if, by saying them, it would make it happen. "We have to go over there!"

Matt, Jerry, and Ronnie looked at each other and then shrugged their shoulders.

"It's no use," said Ronnie. "She's not going to settle down and leave go of this until we go and check on him."

"We'll ride over and check on him, Jul," Matt said reluctantly.

"I'm going, too!" Julie stated as she stood up.

Ethel went to protest and then let it go. She knew there was no stopping Julie once her mind was made up. "I'll drive," Ethel said, grabbing her keys off of the stand. She raised her hand to stop her sons from protesting. "I'll drive," she repeated. "We'll all go together."

Julie thought it had taken forever to drive the five miles to their house. When they pulled in front of the house, Julie saw that it was pitch dark inside.

"He's probably asleep by now," Jerry said.

"Why don't you just wait in the car," Ronnie said to Julie.

"No, I'm going in with you," Julie answered as she reached for the door handle.

Ethel sat motionless and stared at the house. Memories came back like a torrent causing her to tremble. She remembered a similar night, seven years before when much like this night they had come home to this same house and found it completely dark. The eeriness of that night seemed to creep into the present. That night they had not expected to find Ron passed out at the gas stove. It was then that Tonya, her sixteen-year-old niece, had reluctantly disclosed to Ethel that Ron was the father of her unborn baby. Ron had tried to commit suicide that night and had nearly succeeded. *But why would he do it now? What deep dark secret was he hiding from everyone this time that he was so afraid that everyone would find out?* It made no sense to her.

Ethel shook herself out of her thoughts as one by one her children poured out of the car. She knew that they too remembered that night. "Wait!" she called out as she jumped out of the car and ran after all four of them.

Ronnie had already retrieved the key from the back porch and was at the front door when Ethel joined them. Jerry stood pounding on the door.

Matt put his arm around Julie seeing the horror rise on her face. Julie stood in a daze as Ronnie nervously tried to unlock the door. Julie hated what her dad did. She even felt that at times she had grown to hate him. She felt tremendously guilty for feeling that way. She had always hoped that somewhere in his lost spirit was the dad that she thought she had once known as a little girl. She wanted him to know that Jesus loved him and would forgive him if he would just ask Him to help.

Ronnie pushed the door open with a thrust losing his balance, nearly tumbling in as the door got away from him. Immediately, he ran up the steps, followed by Jerry, Matt, Julie, and Ethel. The smell of putrid gas hung in the air. Julie pushed the button that turned the hall light on. In the dark shadows of the bathroom she saw her dad sprawled out in front of the gas stove. He was unconscious. Matt rushed to his side and picked up his feet. Jerry ran with Ronnie and got under his shoulders. Together the three of them began to carefully carry their dad down the stairs. Ethel ran over to the little gas stove, turned its knob to off, and then ran down the stairs past Julie to call Emma and Tom.

Julie stood frozen while staring in disbelief. She remembered so clearly this same scene from so many years ago. She was only seven when her dad had tried to commit suicide the first time. She didn't understand or know what was happening back then. Now, however, she clearly understood exactly, what was happening. Somehow, she felt it deep inside her soul, even though her dad had made no threatening remarks. Julie's heartbeat raced within her. She could hardly get her breath. Quickly, she gathered herself and ran down the steps two at a time and followed her brothers out the front door.

Julie felt every imaginable emotion rise within her. Tears creased down her face and she didn't even know why. She felt anger at all that her dad had done to her and her brothers. She felt anger at what he had just done. She felt a sorrow for everything that had been lost throughout the years, a sorrow for what her dad had become. Emotions ripped through her and tormented her mind. *Would he die? Could she even feel sorrow if he did?* She wanted to pound her head and knock the thoughts out of her mind. *She didn't want her dad to die. She just wanted her dad to stop abusing her. Is this why he had tried to kill himself?* Julie wondered. *How could Julie ever sort out all that had happened tonight?* Somehow, she felt surely, it must be her fault. *If she would've just taken more time to talk to him. Maybe, she had even wanted it to happen.* Julie shook from the top of her head to the bottom of her feet. All she could do was stand there and watch in a daze. *She didn't want his soul to be lost. She just wanted her old dad back. But did that dad even exist? Was that dad only an imagined image of what Julie had hoped she could have in a dad?*

Julie stood and watched in horror as her brothers all knelt down beside him. They tried to gently shake him but his head just bobbed on the porch like a rag doll. Shortly, Gramma Emma and Uncle Tom came rushing from across the street. Julie's brothers stepped back to let Uncle Tom get to their dad. None of them were sure whether he was alive or dead.

Ethel ran to their side with a cold rag and a glass of water. Julie continued to watch the scene unfold before her. She watched as Gramma Emma began to wipe her dad's face with the cold rag. Julie looked at her gramma's tear-streaked face and then over at her Uncle Tom as he feverishly worked to bring his brother back to consciousness. Julie felt such a sorrow for Gramma Emma. Julie had seen her gramma, through the many years, try and try to help her son. Julie had often heard her dad speak harshly to Gramma Emma so many times. Julie pondered how her dad could continue to hurt so many people that loved him.

Ethel came and stood beside her children. She put her arms around Matt and Julie. Jerry and Ronnie joined them and stood by their side.

Slowly, Ron began to stir. He lifted up his head unable to hold it up as it fell limply from side to side. Tom called for Ronnie to help him and together they sat him up and leaned him up against the porch rail. Shortly, Ron began pushing them away as he became more conscious. He began to speak angrily, in a slurred voice, telling everyone to just leave him alone. He staggered while attempting to get up but slipped and slid back down. When he tried again, Ronnie and Tom helped him to stand up ignoring his protests to not help him. They helped him into the house and sat him down onto the couch. Matt and Jerry ran throughout the house and opened all of the windows and doors to air out the house.

Julie sat on the old chair that was by the space heater. Jerry sat on the chair in front of the window. Matt sat crossed legged on the floor in front of the television set while Ronnie sat on the small red chair with the metal frame. Julie glanced over at them one by one but none of them were looking up. They all sat and stared down aimlessly, lost deep in thought. Julie watched her Uncle Tom and Gramma Emma as they tried to settle her dad down.

Ethel walked over to where Julie was sitting and stood quietly in the corner beside her. Though she was concerned for the man that had fathered her four children, she felt anger rise within her as he recovered. *How could he put her children through this again?* If she had even suspected that Julie's hunches had been right, she would have never allowed her to come with them.

Julie listened as her gramma spoke to her dad. "How could you do this? What in the world were you thinking?" Julie could hardly ever remember seeing her gramma so upset. Julie watched as Emma's words fell on deaf ears, as Ron tried to get up off of the sofa.

Tom reached out and grabbed Ron's shoulder gently but firmly. "Just sit awhile Ron."

Ron, however, shook Tom's hand off his shoulder glaring at his brother while mumbling to him to leave him alone. Julie watched her Uncle Tom. He was a quiet but strong man with a gentle spirit. Julie had rarely seen him interfere with his brother, but she knew that he didn't approve of the things that he continued to do. So often, Julie and her brothers would overhear the adults talking of how they all hoped that Ron would cut back on his drinking and pull his life together, for himself and for his children.

Julie sat wearily, staring at her hands turning them nervously on her lap. She couldn't sort out all of the emotions that were racing through her, so she allowed the only one to arise that strengthened her—anger. *Why, why would he do this?* But in her heart, Julie felt that she had an idea why he had wanted to end his life. He had attempted the same thing when he was afraid of what was going to happen when the truth came out about him and his fathering Tonya's baby. Julie continued to let her thoughts run through her mind as she tried to sort it all out. *Was her dad afraid that she might talk?*

"Ron, I am telling you right now," Emma continued talking. "For the children's sake, you've got to get yourself together."

Julie's heart was endeared by her gramma's words. However, Julie couldn't help but think, *What her gramma didn't realize was that they really weren't any longer children and that their dad had never considered anything for their sake.*

"Fine. Fine, Mom," Ron blurted out as he became more alert.

"Well, Ron, you've got to think about what you're doing to yourself—and these kids," Emma said again, emphasizing her point.

"Alright, Mom!" Ron said, allowing his voice to rise, "Let it go!"

As he attempted to stand up, not realizing his legs were still wobbly, he started to fall back down. Tom reached out to steady him as Ron pushed his arm away. "I'm alright! Just go on home," Ron continued. He steadied himself and then walked towards the kitchen.

Jerry shot Matt a raised eyebrow and then one to Ronnie. Julie also knew what was happening and couldn't believe her eyes. Before her brothers could stop her, Julie jumped up from the chair that she was sitting on and ran into the kitchen pushing past her dad.

Ron had not said a word to any of his children or even acknowledged their presence. Julie knew where her dad was headed. That's why she had run past him to get in front of him.

She flung herself in front of the refrigerator door spreading both of her arms outward across the door.

Her dad looked at her and smiled as if nothing had happened, as if she was six years old again.

"Move out of the way, Julie," he commanded almost laughing at her.

"No!" Julie said defiantly.

"What! You are going to tell me no!" Ron let out a laugh of disbelief.

"I'm not moving!" Julie answered in a tone that she had never used with her dad.

Ronnie, Jerry, and Matt entered the kitchen behind Julie but not in time to stop her. They stood stunned at Julie's stance against their dad. Ethel, Emma, and Tom were all taken aback at Julie's actions and were at a loss for words on how to deal with either Julie or Ron.

Ron looked more than a little surprised at a Julie that he had never seen before. Still, in his confused state, he seemed unsure of how to handle the situation. He hung his head trying to recompose himself as his arms hung limply by his side and his legs wobbled unsteadily.

"You are not going to get another beer!" Julie spoke up as her courage mounted.

"And you are not going to tell me what to do, young lady!" Ron yelled out, his words tumbling out broken and staggered.

"Let him go, Jul," Jerry said kindly to his sister as he ran up to her side. Matt and Ronnie ran up to join them. Matt put his hand gently onto one of Julie's outstretched arms as Jerry took his hand and gently pried Julie's fingers from around the edge of the refrigerator door.

"Come on Sis," Matt spoke lovingly to his sister.

"He'll just try to do it again if we let him drink," Julie said as she broke into tears, letting her anger melt away.

Ronnie took his sister's hand as the three of them lead her into the living room away from their dad. Ethel and Tom followed them and left Emma to talk to Ron.

"You go ahead and go, Ethel. Take the kids," Tom said. Mom and I'll stay until he settles down. Tom raised his hand firmly in a stop motion to Julie and looked kindly into her eyes. "He'll be okay. Go ahead and go with your mom."

Julie looked back once more as she stepped out the front door and saw Emma sitting on a kitchen chair across from her dad who was now sitting on another kitchen chair in the distance. Emma was earnestly leaning forward and talking to her dad. Julie watched sadly as she saw her dad lift the beer can and take a long drink. She wondered if he was even listening to Emma.

Julie walked slowly out of the house, followed by her mom and brothers. She heard the iron gate close behind them as they crossed the street to go to the car. No one said a word on the way back to their mom's house. Julie wondered what would ever happen to her family.

Matt, Julie, Jerry, and Ronnie

Chapter

6

Julie sat in the large auditorium filled with a mixture of emotions as the "Pomp and Circumstance" song ushered in the graduation candidates. She beamed with pride as her brother's name was called and he went up to receive his diploma. In another six months, Ronnie would be eighteen years old; and he had already told the family that the day after his birthday, he was going to enlist into the Marine Corps.

Julie quickly brushed away the tears from her eyes with the back of her hand. Next year, Jerry would be walking down this same aisle; and he had also vowed to follow in Ronnie's footsteps in joining the Marine Corps. Julie was all too aware now of where Vietnam was and what the mention of that name inferred. Cutter's Ford had already buried a few of their own who had fought in a war that no one seemed to understand.

The celebration continued as scholarships and awards were handed out to the honor students. Julie had hoped that someday she would be able to get enough scholarships to go to college. She had determined, with a new fervor, to apply everything that she possessed to get good grades. She knew that the Lord was helping her and that He would lead her if she would let Him. Julie had just completed the eighth grade and would be starting high school in the fall. She was surprised a few weeks ago when Mrs. Hornworth had called her aside and told her to meet with her after class. Mrs. Hornworth had been kind to Julie throughout the entire school year, and it seemed as if she had forgotten the incidents which occurred between Julie and Lindsey the prior year. Julie couldn't help wonder why she wanted to talk to her. She searched her mind for anything that she might have done wrong but couldn't think of a single thing.

"Julie," Mrs. Hornworth spoke softly, as Julie approached her desk after school had ended that day. Mrs. Hornworth stopped grading the English exams and slowly turned to look up at Julie standing beside her desk. Julie glanced down at the desk and saw the red D plus on the paper. She scanned the name and saw that it was Tim Andersen's. Quickly, Julie looked away from the paper and up at Mrs. Hornworth. She did not want her to think that she was being nosy looking at the papers. Julie tried to smile as Mrs. Hornworth scooted her chair away from the desk and leaned back slightly. With her glasses resting on the edge of her nose and hanging from a long gold chain, she looked at Julie inquisitively, paused, and then reached and took off her glasses, letting them fall to her chest. Julie brushed a stray hair behind her ear while placing her arms behind her back to hide her nervous shaking hands. *Why do teachers do this?* Julie thought. *Why do they always keep you in such suspense?*

"Julie," Mrs. Hornworth continued, "did you know that we're having an honors banquet at the end of the school year?"

"No, Mrs. Hornworth," Julie answered as she wondered what this had to do with her. She had never heard of the school ever having an honors banquet. This was usually reserved for high school.

"Well, we're to pick two students who've had high achievements this school year. I have chosen Harry Thomas as one of the students."

Julie understood why she would pick Harry. He was the smartest boy in their class. He had always been the smartest boy in their class ever since first grade. *But why was she telling Julie this and not the whole class,* Julie wondered.

"I have spoken to your other two teachers and they seem very impressed with your achievements. Mrs. Seymour told me that you memorized the whole "Paul Revere's Ride" and quoted it in front of the class. Is that correct?"

Julie felt herself blush and simply nodded yes. She figured that Mrs. Hornworth probably already knew that it was true and that she was actually just being kind to her in letting Julie know that she was aware of this accomplishment. "Your grades have been near straight A's and you are well-liked by all of your classmates."

Julie took a deep breath. *Could she be hearing Mrs. Hornworth correctly? Was this the same teacher that had despised her aunt when she was in her class? Was this the same teacher that had asked her why Rhonda, her dad's girlfriend, was living with them?* Julie was only ten at the time when Mrs. Hornworth had asked her this very question. Julie had been at a loss for an answer. She remembered when she had quickly blurted out the only thing that had come to her mind at the time and replied that Rhonda was their house-keeper. Julie recalled how Ronnie, Jerry, and Matt had rolled with laughter when she told them what she had said to Mrs. Hornworth. *But how could this be the same Mrs. Hornworth that had nailed her in front of the whole class last year when Lindsey and she had argued? And now, this same Mrs. Hornworth, was telling her what a good student she was and that her classmates liked her.* Julie wasn't sure what she was supposed to say. She wasn't even sure why Mrs. Hornworth was telling her all of this.

Julie stood quietly, smiling shyly, allowing Mrs. Hornworth to continue. "Julie I would like to invite you to be the other student to join us at this honors banquet. Would you like to participate?"

Julie tried to answer but found her mouth so dry that it seemed as if her tongue was stuck and wouldn't move. "Yes," she finally answered. "Yes, I would love to participate," Julie answered politely.

"Well, it will be a dressy occasion," Mrs. Hornworth continued, as she gave Julie all of the details and the date of the banquet.

Julie went home and searched in her closet for a dress that she thought would be perfect for the banquet. Someone had given it to her a year before, when, at the time, it was too large. Julie had loved the dress and kept it. When she pulled it out and tried it on, it fit her like it was made for her. It was a beautiful peach chiffon which hung on Julie, accenting all of her features. Her dark hair and eyes brought the dress to life. Her mom bought her a new pair of stockings and shoes. Julie felt just like Cinderella going to the Ball. But nothing had prepared her for the honors that she received that day. It had put a new hope and determination within Julie that maybe, just maybe, she could continue on and excel and get the scholarships that she needed to go to college.

Now sitting in her brother's high school auditorium, just a few weeks after that banquet, Julie watched Ronnie go up to get his diploma. She was so very proud of him. Julie smiled from ear to ear and clapped as loudly as she could as Ronnie left the platform.

Julie watched as they continued to give out the awards to the college bound students. Gramma Winnie sat to her right and Gramma Emma on her left. As if reading Julie's mind, Gramma Winnie leaned over and whispered, "Julie, you can get scholarships and go to college." Julie turned and looked up into her Gramma's kind blue eyes.

"Do you think so Gramma?" Julie asked earnestly.

"I know so!" Winnie replied as she put her arm around Julie and gave her a squeeze.

As they announced the Swadley award, Julie heard another voice speak to her from her left. "Julie, you could get that award," Gramma Emma spoke in a whisper into Julie's ear. Julie turned to her left and looked at her Gramma Emma. Her soft face was encompassed by her silver gray hair which laid in short waves.

Julie was touched by the sincerity and belief that shined in her gramma's eyes.

"I don't know, Gramma," Julie said.

"Yes, Julie. You can. I know you can," Emma stated with a determination set in her eyes as she looked kindly at Julie.

"I'll try Gramma," Julie said with a smile. She marveled at how much both of her grammas loved and believed in her.

Julie applauded loudly one more time as the ceremony ended and she watched Ronnie walk down the aisle with his classmates.

Summer came in with such a rush that Julie hardly had a chance to think of how her life was changing. With all that was happening, Julie couldn't understand why she felt so badly. She knew that Ronnie would be leaving soon for the Marine Corps but had thought that she would at least have him for another six months.

Ronnie came to her one day to talk to her privately. "Julie, I'm going to move out and stay with Mom," he told her.

Julie feared that this might happen one day. Ronnie had mentioned it in passing to Jerry, Matt and her. Their dad was coming down so hard on Ronnie that he had finally had enough. So often, he would make remarks to Ronnie about his going to church and "being religious." Sadly though, when Ronnie had begun to go to work, he pretty much quit going to church. Julie missed him terribly as she continued to go by herself. Jerry and Matt still went with her on Sundays. But Ronnie had let them know that he couldn't bear his dad being on him all the time for no reason and that he thought he might probably have to move out.

Julie remained quiet, looking sadly up at him as he continued, "Come on, Jul, you know how it is here. I'll be leaving soon anyways to go in the Marine Corps. Tell me you understand."

"I understand, Ronnie," Julie answered sadly. "Truly, I do Ronnie. It's just that I'll miss you so much."

"I know," Ronnie said as he reached out and hugged his little sis. She would always be his "little sis." "I'll still see you on the weekends. Besides, I work at nights anyway, so whether I'm at Mom's or here, you still wouldn't see me that much."

Julie, looking up at the big brother who had helped her find her way so many times, gave him a weak smile. "Do Jerry and Matt know?"

"Yea," Ronnie answered.

"Does dad know?" Julie asked looking deeply into Ronnie's eyes.

"He will!" Ronnie answered as he looked afar off.

It was a hot summer. Ronnie moved out shortly after he had told Julie. The house seemed so lonely with Ronnie gone. Jerry and Matt had saved their money together and bought an old 1955 Chevy which they were working on to fix it up and share.

The only relief that Julie had found was that her dad seemed to have found another girlfriend. Julie discussed this possibility with Jerry and Matt one day, shortly before they were to go over to their mom's house for a visit. They, too, had agreed that their dad seemed to be acting as if he had found a new girlfriend. Julie was glad. A sense of relief came over her. She could only hope that she would be nice and that maybe things would get better at home.

It wasn't long before they met her. Her name was Alice. Julie was taken aback by Alice. She had a kindness that just radiated from her smile. Her long jet black hair and high cheek bones accented her beauty. She was much younger than Julie's dad. She seemed more like a big sister to Julie. Alice had no children and readily took Julie and her brothers into her heart.

As the summer passed, Alice slowly moved in. The only thing that made Julie sad about this was that she couldn't bear for such a nice person as Alice to be used by her dad. Julie, however, had seen a change in her dad too. He was nicer and he drank less. Julie could see that he was really trying. He let up on Jerry and Matt and his abuse to her had stopped. Julie wasn't sure if he had let up on Jerry and Matt because Ronnie had moved out or if it was because Alice had moved in, but regardless, he was much nicer and happier. Then one day, just before they had a large picnic at

Hanson's Park, both Alice and Ron let Julie and her brothers know that they had married.

Julie couldn't understand why, with everything changing for the good in her life, that she was having such a difficult time concentrating. Her nerves were shot and she could hardly eat. Worst of all, she had tried to fast. She had heard about this at church and thought that possibly this would help her to get better. But it had actually made her worse. Julie became trapped to the point where she wouldn't allow herself to eat or even drink. She had such a fear of losing God. She felt tormented and couldn't concentrate. Julie felt that she was always failing God and couldn't find peace. She began to lose weight and began to withdraw within herself as she had done in the fourth grade.

No matter how hard she tried, she could not shake what was happening to her. Julie really liked Alice. She knew that God had brought her into her life. Ronnie, Jerry, and Matt liked her too. What made Julie really happy was that even her mom liked Alice. Julie had asked her mom one day how she felt towards Alice. Ethel took Julie's hands into hers and squeezed them tightly. "I like her a lot, Julie."

"She's nothing like Rhonda," Julie reminded Ethel.

Ethel smiled and nodded. Ethel was glad that someone as nice as Alice would be at the house with her children. She had seen how withdrawn Julie had become and was concerned about her. Ethel knew that something was worrying Julie. No matter how much Ethel tried to gently push Julie to open up and talk, she couldn't get her to tell her what was bothering her. She had asked Ron, at numerous times, what was bothering Julie; but he would just reply, "How in the world would I know," and brush it aside. Ethel once before had seen Julie go into this same depressed state when she was in the fourth grade. She had also noticed how Julie lightened up as soon as Alice had moved in to live with them. Tears filled Ethel's eyes—tears of sorrow, in that she couldn't be there for her, and tears of joy in that Julie was happy.

Julie couldn't understand what was happening to her. Julie thought to herself, *Why was she falling apart? Why was she with-drawing from everyone when in her heart she really wanted to be with them?* She felt trapped within her body and she could not understand why.

Ethel continued to ask Julie over and over again what was bothering her. But she couldn't answer her mom because she didn't know the answer. As Julie continued to eat less and less, her clothes began to hang limply upon her frail body. She became ashen and sickly looking. She lost energy and concern about her appearance. She actually didn't seem to want to be attractive. She wasn't ready for womanhood or the changes it was bringing. The only attention she had received as a little girl and young woman had been the negative attention from her dad. The thought of young men being interested in her flattered a part of her and made another part of her cringe, all at the same time. Julie couldn't separate the confusion or sort out her feelings. She had tried to pray, but she began to feel that maybe even God was disappointed with her. She was still tortured by the affects of the abuse. She tried to put it under the rug. Julie told herself that it was over now. *Alice is here. Just forget about it. Pretend it never happened. Don't dwell on it. It wasn't as bad as you think it was.* All of these thoughts pounded the inside of her head until she thought it would split wide open.

She was so afraid to hope. Too many times she had hoped that things would change at home. And now that they were, she was terrified that it wouldn't last, that all of her brothers would leave home, and that one day she would be left alone with her dad. She feared that the abuse would start all over again and that she would lose Alice ultimately, so why even let her heart love her. The fear of everything had so strongly gripped her heart that she felt that she couldn't possibly allow herself to hope. She wanted to accept this new dad, so reminiscent of her earlier childhood memories; however, the fear, shame, guilt, and blame left from his abuse encompassed her. She could not free herself. She couldn't sort it out, and it felt as if it was all consuming her from within. Julie felt, each day, as if she was falling deeper and deeper into a bottomless pit and that there was nothing for her to grab hold onto on the way down. At times, she would just go up to her room and lie down and cry until she fell asleep.

School would be starting soon and the thought of going to high school and being with all the upperclassmen scared her to death. She didn't know any of the teachers or the new kids. Even Sarah and Molly, her best friends, couldn't shake Julie out of her depression. They continued to joke with her; and she would often join in with them, but then she would fall right back into her depression. Julie fell deeper and deeper within her shell and felt so comfortable there that even though at times she wanted to come out, she was finding it easier to stay there. It felt safe there. *No one could hurt her there,* she thought. And yet she found herself sad all the time.

One day, after watching Uncle Tom and Aunt Lisa Sue's children, Julie came home feeling a little happier. She loved the responsibility of watching her cousins, and it made her feel good that her aunt and uncle trusted her.

Julie was glad that she had started watching her cousins. She loved going up to her Uncle Tom and Aunt Lisa Sue's house. She would often run up the path from her Uncle Tom's house and visit her Gramma Emma. Gramma Emma had always been special to her. So often, over and over again, Julie heard her gramma try to help her dad. She would tell him to take better care of them and to stop drinking so much. When he wouldn't listen, she would say, "Send them up here to stay with me Ron."

Julie loved staying at both Gramma Emma's and Gramma Winnie's. They gave her stability, a stability that she treasured. It was the same stability that she had always felt with her mom and her brothers. They all gave her love and hope.

Julie had actually found herself whistling a tune on that day. It was a tune that she had heard Matt whistling the day before. She smiled to herself when she saw Jerry and Matt's '55 Chevy' parked in the Lindy's Tavern parking lot. She was always so glad when her brothers were home.

Julie entered the gate and turned to lock the rusty latch behind her. She stopped at the edge of the porch and looked for Mamie, but she was nowhere to be found. *She must be in her favorite spot under the crawl space trying to keep cool,* Julie thought as she wiped her sweating brow with her hand.

Julie ran to the front door and slowly opened the door. She saw Jerry and Matt sitting and watching television. Alice was in the kitchen cooking supper.

"I can't find Mamie," Julie said out loud as she walked into the kitchen to say hi to Alice. "Smells really good," Julie said as she began to set the table.

After supper Jerry said, "Let's go see if we can find Mamie."

Julie and Matt quickly followed Jerry as he went out the rear kitchen door. They then darted out the screened back summer porch door and down the steps.

"See," Matt said as he ran to the crawl space where Mamie always slept. He put his head against the wooden lattice and looked through it. "I told you that she was okay."

Jerry ran to join Matt. "Yea, Jul. She's there. She's just sleeping."

"She is getting to be pretty old," Matt said.

"Yea, the ole girl is about ten years old now," Jerry added.

Julie continued to look through the lattice as Matt and Jerry turned to go back into the house.

"Come on, girl," Julie called out to Mamie. Mamie didn't move. Julie pushed her head closer to the lattice board as she peered through the cracks. "Come on, Mamie," Julie called out again. She looked at Mamie as the sunlight fell upon Mamie's reddish-brown coat, appearing as checkered blocks from the shadows of the lattice.

Julie saw a fly land on Mamie's eye, but Mamie didn't blink, nor did she move. Julie called out her name again more frantically.

Somehow, she knew. "Matt! Jerry!" she called out to her brothers. She began to sob. "Mamie's not moving. I don't think she's breathing!"

Matt and Jerry came rushing back. Matt quickly ran around the corner of the house and crawled under the crawl space up to Mamie's side. He gently stroked their lifeless friend's fur. A tear ran down his cheek as he sadly peered through the lattice at Jerry and Julie and shook his head.

Jerry and Matt ran to find a box for Mamie. Tears streamed down Julie's cheeks. She knew that Matt and Jerry had left quickly to hide their tears. Julie couldn't believe that their little friend was gone. She continued to sob.

"I'm sorry Julie," spoke a trembling familiar voice.

"Ronnie!" Julie yelled as she turned and threw herself into her big brother's arms.

"Mamie's…" Julie started to say.

"I know," Ronnie said as tears raced down his cheeks. Matt and Jerry told me at the front gate.

"I'm so glad you're here," Julie sobbed as Matt and Jerry joined them.

"I stopped over to get some of my clothes," Ronnie said.

The four of them gathered together and placed Mamie into the box that Matt and Jerry had found. They sat on the back steps and stared down at their little cocker spaniel. Tears ran down all of their cheeks no longer hidden or wiped away.

The screech of the screen door opening behind them caused them all to turn around. There stood their dad. As they turned again to look down at Mamie, Ron sat down on the step behind them, not saying a word. Julie studied her dad before turning once again to her brothers and then to Mamie's lifeless form.

"Where can we bury her?" Matt asked.

"Let's bury her up at Gramma Emma's," Ronnie suggested.

"Up at the little white house with red shutters," Julie added.

"She was always the happiest up there with us," Jerry continued as he sniffed back his tears.

One by one they stood up. Ronnie, Jerry, and Matt each took
a corner of the box and carried it to Ronnie's car. Julie glanced up
at her dad who had sat watching them but had not said a word.
He looked sad as he had his head perched onto his hand. When
he rose to leave and go back inside, Julie could see that there
were tears in his eyes. She stood watching him as he entered the
house. She began to sob as she looked across the street and saw
her brothers loading the box into Ronnie's car. She didn't know
whom she was crying for the most, a dad that she could not know
or understand or her beloved Mamie.

Beloved "Mamie"

Chapter

7

Julie was at a loss. It was no use. She could not pull herself together. She couldn't even think, and worst of all, it didn't seem to matter anymore. She didn't want to feel this way. She was making everyone sad and this burdened her. She tried to read her Bible and pray but she couldn't concentrate. She would read the "Beatitudes" over and over again, but the words would just float by and wouldn't register. She felt that she was failing her mom, her brothers, Alice and especially God.

No matter how hard Ronnie, Jerry, and Matt had tried to reach out to their little sister, she seemed lost. It was as if she would appear for a few hours with them, watch a movie, go for a ride to their mom's, or get an ice cream cone, only to withdraw back into her shell. Ethel became worried. Something had to be done, but Ethel had no idea how to help Julie.

"Please Julie, talk to me," Ethel pleaded one day as Julie sat quietly at her mom's kitchen table. All of her brothers were at work and her stepbrother and stepsisters were upstairs cleaning their bedrooms. "Why won't you tell me what's bothering you?"

Julie, sitting at the table, fidgeted with a pencil that laid there. She spun it around and around as thoughts raced within her. She barely heard her mom's question.

"Julie, answer me," Ethel continued to press her.

Julie just sat there in her own little world. Her mind was so focused on trying to organize her thoughts. She thought that if she could sort them all out, then she would possibly be able to lay down the torment and be normal again, that she could then eat and drink her food normally again without trying to fast, without trying to figure it all out, without worrying that she was failing God and making everyone sad and miserable. *Why couldn't her family understand that she dreamed about being happy, about being normal again?* She wanted to lay it all down, to shake it off and laugh again. *Why couldn't she? What was wrong with her?* Around and around, her thoughts would tumble in her mind, never ceasing, full of torment and failure.

"Julie!" Ethel called out loudly. Julie dropped the pencil that she was spinning. "Answer me!" Ethel cried out, tears coming to her eyes.

"What Mom? What did you say?" Julie asked. Julie looked deeply into her mom's deep blue eyes which were quickly filling with tears.

Ethel was speechless. She didn't know what to say. Apparently, Julie had not even heard a word of what she was saying to her.

Julie started to withdraw again, back into her thoughts. "Julie, please," Ethel pleaded as tears tumbled down her face. "I want to know what is bothering you. I want to know what I can do to help you. Please tell me."

"I'm sorry Mom," Julie answered back. "I don't mean to worry you or make you sad. I don't mean to."

"I just want to know what I can do to help you," Ethel pleaded. She walked over to where Julie was sitting and pulled out the chair next to her and sat down. She took her hand and lovingly brushed back Julie's hair from her face, tucking a curl behind her ear. Julie's head hung low. She raised it slowly and looked deeply into her mom's eyes as she searched her face.

"I love you Mom," Julie spoke softly.

"I know you do Honey," Ethel said as she continued to stroke Julie's hair and quietly began to cry.

"Don't cry Mom," Julie said. "Please don't cry. I'll try harder."

"Honey, I don't want you to try harder. I just want you to tell me what it is that is bothering you. You don't eat or even drink. You're down to eighty pounds. You hardly talk to us, and you won't even watch television or play a game with us without going into your own little world. Is it your religion?"

Julie looked at her mom puzzled. Julie had become very stead-fast in going to church, reading her Bible, and trying to live a Christian life. She had wanted all of her family to come to church and get saved. Her dad had already yelled at her and told her that if she didn't straighten up and quit worrying everyone, that he was going up to that church and find out what was going on and what they were doing to her.

Even Julie knew, in her confused state, that it wasn't her faith that was her problem. Her faith was all that she had. Her faith was her last hope. She was reaching out to grab it on her way down as she went tumbling over a cliff of life that she could not see and find her way back up. It was all of the confusion in her life and how to deal with it that she couldn't understand. This was her problem, not her faith. Julie couldn't sort out her thoughts. She couldn't concentrate or focus. She couldn't forget the abuse and everything that it had uprooted within her. *Why couldn't her dad, of all people, see this?* Surely, he, being the only one who knew what he had done to her, should know more than she did herself, what was tearing her apart. Especially, with the last time that he had abused her before Alice had come to live with them. Julie had just gotten her period and started her cycle. She was thirteen years old and officially a woman now. She felt so grown up. Her mom had gone out and bought her some young lady garments.

But then one night, after her dad had come into her room, she had awakened too late. She pushed him away and the shock of it all had made her heart race within her with such force that she felt it would leap out of her chest. She jumped out of bed and ran to the bathroom. She knew that she had been violated but didn't know what her dad had done to her. She sat on the edge of the tub and hit her head with her fists, pounding herself. *How could I let this happen? Why didn't I wake up? What did he do to me?* Fear gripped her like it never had in her life. *How would she ever know what he had done to her? Wonder if…No!* Julie pushed the thought out of her mind.

She waited for days to see if she would get her period. Finally, one day, she could bear it no more. She approached her dad boldly that morning after she had made his breakfast. "What did you do to me?" Julie spoke up loudly. She no longer cared who heard her. She looked at her dad sternly. But he did not answer her and just gave her an intimidating look as he sat down to eat his eggs. But Julie could see that under his false exterior, she had rattled him. "What did you do to me?" she asked again nearly shouting. She could see her dad try to hide the alarm that was rising as he feared Julie's brothers might hear her yelling. But then, to her dismay, the arrogant look that she had grown so accustomed to seeing on her dad when he would regain control returned.

He looked at her as if her question didn't even faze him. He just picked up his fork and began to eat. When Julie started to speak, he swallowed his bite of egg and slowly motioned his hand upwards to tell her to stop. He turned and looked her square in the eyes. A smirk crossed his face puzzling Julie as she waited to hear what he had to say. Smugly, he then said, "What does it matter? You enjoyed it."

Julie stood frozen in place. She swallowed hard. Her heart raced within her. She felt nauseated. Julie ran from the room up the stairs and into the bathroom. There, she stayed and cried into a towel to muffle her sobs from her brothers. *They must not know*, she thought. *No one must ever know.*

Julie waited earnestly, counting the days for her cycle to begin. She only found relief after it finally came. However, the turmoil had unnerved her and uprooted something within her which sent her spiraling further down the dark abyss that she was in. Try as she might, she could not seem to find her way out.

"Julie," came the tender voice again, "Julie, look at me," Ethel spoke softly.

Julie blinked her eyes and came out of her deep thoughts and looked at her mom.

"Talk to me, please?" Ethel said tenderly.

But Julie sat quietly. *What could she tell her mom?* She could never bear the shame and guilt of telling her mom. The fear and blame of it gripped her mind and heart, as if in an iron vice. *No one will ever know,* she thought. *No one.*

"Julie, if this is what your faith in God does to you, then I never want to know that God," Ethel spoke brokenly. Tears were streaming down Ethel's face.

Julie looked at her mom, deeply into her eyes, searching her face. *No,* she thought. "Please don't say that, Mom. Not you," Julie responded and began to cry. *How could she ever win her mom or any of her family to God if the "God" people thought Julie was serving was destroying her?* The thought shook Julie to her core and it awoke something within her. She couldn't understand or explain it, but somehow, if for her mom's sake alone, she had to show her mom that God was not doing this to her. "Mom, it isn't God's fault," she tried to explain, struggling to find the thoughts and words.

"Then what is it, Julie?" Ethel pleaded.

Julie could see the desperation and love in her mom's eyes. This was the mom who had taught her to pray, to believe in a God that was real, who had sat with her when she was six and helped her do little Bible story quizzes that came in the mail. "Mom, I don't know what's wrong with me. But, I promise you Mom, it isn't God's fault." Julie sat staring earnestly at her mom, making an eye contact that she so rarely did. Her eyes pleaded with her mom to believe her, to not be angry at God and blame Him, and to somehow help her find her way back.

Ethel sat and carefully watched her daughter. She was shocked at the clarity, directness, and earnestness of her words. She caught a glimpse of her old Julie. Ethel brushed the tears off her cheeks and then reached for Julie's hands. She tenderly clasped them between her own and stroked them gently, lovingly. She paused to gather her thoughts and then smiled at Julie. Julie smiled back and a relief came over her at seeing her mom's hope return.

"I have an idea, Julie," Ethel spoke softly as she smiled a broader smile than before. Julie was surprised at the change in her mom. There was a spark in Ethel's eyes that wasn't there before, and her eyes seemed to dance with excitement. Julie continued to listen as she tried to shut down the many thoughts which still continued to ricochet through her mind.

"Why don't you and I go away to Ocean City, Maryland, to the ocean?" Ethel asked, "just you and me?"

Julie looked at her mom, astonished at her questions. She wanted to answer but was confused.

Ethel saw that she had Julie's attention. She was like a fisherman that had hooked a big fish. Ethel got a glance of her lost little girl, and she was not going to let her go. She continued on, quickly explaining. "Didn't you do a report on Florida and Hawaii because you love the ocean so much? Well, we can't go that far, but I have some vacation days coming and a little money and you and I could go to Ocean City."

"But Mom, we can't. It wouldn't be fair to the others. And what will Bob say?" Julie knew that things had only gotten worse between Bob and her mom lately. She had even overheard them talking about getting divorced. Surely, this unexpected trip would not be good for their marriage. Julie didn't want to be the reason that they would finally get divorced.

Ethel was so excited. She had not had this much of a conversation with Julie in weeks. No, she was not going to let this go. She had somehow hit a chord, a connection with her Julie, and she had to follow through. "So would you like to go to the ocean?" Ethel asked her again. Ethel saw a worried look come over Julie's face.

Ethel took her hands and tenderly placed them onto Julie's cheeks. "Look at me, Honey. Come on; go with me to Ocean City. Just you and me. We'll have fun. I'll take care of everything. Everyone will understand. I'll work it all out. Don't worry about anything. Bob and the other kids will understand. It will be okay, I promise." As Ethel's words tumbled out, she watched Julie's expression. She saw the fire come back into those dull eyes and then a smile creased across Julie's face—a smile that she had not seen for some time. "Then it's settled," Ethel said as she reached over and gave Julie a big hug. Slowly, Julie wrapped her arms around her mom's neck. She hung on as if she would never let go. Ethel felt Julie's warm tears drop onto her neck. She didn't know what was happening, but somehow the dam had just broken and Ethel knew that she was getting her Julie back. "We'll have so much fun, Julie! Just wait and see, Honey. Just wait and see."

Julie sat gazing at the blue ocean which sprawled before her. She looked to the horizon as far as she could see where the blue ocean met the blue sky and they became one. She had never seen anything in her life more beautiful. The sound of the ocean's fury pounded against the shore with each breaking wave. The seagulls squawked as they flew through the air dancing in the ocean breeze. It was more beautiful than she had ever imagined, more beautiful than any of the pictures she had seen in the encyclopedia when she had done her reports on Hawaii and Florida. Julie let the warmth of the sun's rays beat down upon her. She was so happy. All of the beauty which encompassed her chased her troubled and tormented thoughts to somewhere where she could not and did not want to find them. She smiled and closed her eyes as the breeze blew her wisps of hair across her face. She could feel the salty ocean mist light upon her cheeks.

Ethel lay on the blanket beside Julie pretending to be resting, watching Julie from the corner of her eye. Seeing her smile again and coming alive made Ethel's heart dance with joy. She knew it would be no easy task convincing Bob that she had had to do this with Julie. She knew that with all that they had between them right now that Bob would not understand. He loved Julie; Ethel was sure of this. He had grown to love her kids as his own. Ironically, the problem of having seven children in a blended family had been the original source of a lot of their trouble in the past, but now it was these very children that were probably keeping them together because of the love that both of them had grown to have for each of their children. It was their other problems, now in their relationship, that needed to be worked out; and Ethel wasn't sure that they could be worked out. So instead of stirring up an argument with Bob before she left, she had simply left Bob a note explaining the situation and said that she had hoped that he would understand that she needed to take this trip with Julie. She would find out, when back home again, whether he did or did not understand; but in either way, Ethel knew that she had done the right thing. She saw it on the many smiles that never ceased to cross Julie's face since they had gotten there. More so, what confirmed it to Ethel was that it wasn't just the smiles on Julie's face but also the way that her eyes had lit up with life. Ethel saw life come back into her little girl, the little girl who was struggling so hard to find her way and become the beautiful woman that was unfolding before her. She found her Julie again; and more importantly, Julie was finding herself.

As the days passed, Ethel found that Julie was opening up more and more and withdrawing less and less. Ethel didn't expect everything to just return to normal. However, this was a beginning. Julie and Ethel walked the boardwalk and together ate ice cream cones. Julie fed the pigeons and the squawking seagulls. Ethel bought her a canvas inflatable raft and Julie floated on it, out into the ocean, unafraid. They hummed and sang songs, and most importantly they talked, not so much about the problems of life but about the simple joys which surrounded them.

Julie couldn't remember when she had ever felt so happy, to have this special time alone with her mom. She was in shock with what her mom had done. Julie could not remember when she had ever felt so loved and so special. She felt a weight break loose from her heart and mind. She began to feel that peace which she had not felt in such a long time. She ceased from trying to answer her unanswered questions. She read her Bible and began to understand for the first time in her life that walking with God was about grace, not works; about love, not failures; about joy, not pain. Something began to change within Julie, and she didn't want to try to figure it out. All she knew was that the beauty of all that surrounded her those days spoke to her heart and reminded her of a heavenly Father who loved her for just whom she was. Whether it be a shattered spirit, a wounded heart, or a troubled mind full of confusion and despair, none of this mattered. All that mattered was that He was a God who loved her, would carry her, heal her, and help her to find her way. *It may take a while,* Julie mused one day as she sat at the ocean with her feet in the water. *How long would it take for those roaring waves to carry each piece of sand out to sea and wash them away? How long will it take an all powerful God to take each of her troubled thoughts from her mind out to a sea of forgetfulness and wash them away?* Julie did not know how long it would take.

But somehow, it didn't seem as important now as to how long it would take, because the greater question had been answered. The question was not how long it would take, but rather, it was the realization that it could be done. Such hope it gave Julie, to know that she could be healed and be made whole, one step at a time.

Julie walked behind the old shed that sat up on the hill behind her Gramma Emma's house. She paused at the horseshoe pegs and bending over slightly, braced her hands onto her knees to catch her breath.

Julie then straightened up, arching her back, as she felt the crisp breeze blowing her hair onto her face. She tucked the loose wisps of hair behind her ear and looked at the trees further up the mountainside. The rich red and yellow leaves of the maple trees' autumn colors blended into a hue of orange in the distance. They stood in stark contrast amidst the tall oaks with their lifeless brown leaves hanging limply on their branches refusing to fall to the ground. Julie walked towards the cliff and paused to enjoy the view below her. She never walked too closely to the edge as her brothers often did. Just glancing down at the river, hundreds of feet below her, would make her knees weak and wobbly.

Julie turned to climb further up the mountainside. She stopped at a small clearing where a humped and mounded pile of shale stood before her. At the far end of the small mound stood a small rugged wooden cross made from two old boards nailed together. Carved roughly on the rough boards were the letters M-A-M-I-E. Julie stood and stared at the letters and then looked down at the ground. She brushed the bigger pieces of shale aside and sat down. "I miss you so much, ole girl," she whispered as she softly patted the mound.

After a few minutes, Julie stood up and brushed the loose stones from her clothes before turning and continuing up the hill. Julie pulled her sweater around her as she walked into the wind. The trees rustled and swayed in majesty above her as the sun beat down onto Julie's neck, filling her with the warmth of its rays.

Julie knew every inch of these woods. She could walk them in the dark or with her eyes closed. She knew every knoll, every thicket, and every thin and rugged trail which she and her brothers had worn through these woods with their many years of adventurous hiking.

Julie paused at the very top. She turned and looked behind her. Far down the mountainside sat their little white house with the red shutters and the little shed a few feet from it. The path to the outhouse had long disappeared. The grass and thickets had been let go and everything was overgrown around the house. The little house looked lost and all alone. Julie bit her lip softly and held back her tears as she continued to look at the house. "It looks so sad," she said aloud to herself. Julie couldn't help feel that all her memories seemed like a dream. It seemed so very long ago that they had all lived there together as a family. She closed her eyes and then slowly opened them. She wondered how different it all could have been. Julie then turned around to face the cliff's edge. The view was magnificent. The whole city of Grantville lay spread beneath her, appearing as a small toy village far in the distance. Julie placed her hand above her squinting eyes as the sun shined brightly. The sky was as blue as the ocean that she had seen earlier that summer. There was not a single cloud in the sky.

Julie turned and started down the gentle slope that sprawled before her. She thought this was the prettiest part of the woods. A little vale parted the path like a small cradle. The forest floor was covered with soft pine needles, and the rich dark soil that lay beneath them gave a fragrance of earth that one only smells in autumn breezes. Rhododendrons grew wild and surrounded the little cove and created a wild hedge where the deer often sought refuge in the heat of the summer.

Julie walked slowly before carefully climbing over the next knoll. She knew to bear sharply to the left as the path now disappeared into openness when she approached what was called "the devil's slide." She climbed around the protruding rocks and carefully down the gentle slope watching that the loose shale didn't cause her to slip. Julie knew that there would be no danger of falling here. The rich soil was speckled with soft green moss and beckoned her to sit down.

Julie sat looking at the steep slide that fanned out beneath her. The slide flowed downward, as gentle sweeps before her, in a gradual decline to the river's edge. Julie let her eyes follow the flow of the river, far beneath her, as it meandered through the foothills at the base of the mountain. As she closed her eyes, Julie sat quietly, leaned back onto her outstretched arms and listened to the robins sing. Upon opening her eyes, she saw several large black ravens swooping down into the cliff's vastness before soaring up once again high into the deep blue sky.

Julie could hear the sound of the rustling river far beneath her as it flowed rapidly downstream. She picked up a large rock and tossed it, watching it roll uncontrollably down the cliff. Slowly at first, the rock propelled itself downhill. Fiercely, it gained momentum, tumbling down the descending slope which swallowed it up in its power and thrust it forward with such force that the rock now skipped and bounced down the remaining summit before plummeting helplessly into the rushing water of the river far below.

Julie tossed another rock down the steep slide and gazed at it aimlessly. She sat in a daze and brushed the dirt gently from her hands. It seemed minutes before she heard the rock's final cur-plunk and then a loud splash as it hit the water below. Julie stretched out her arms once again, relaxing as she leaned back. She closed her eyes, enjoying the quietness of the woods being interrupted only by nature's chorus: an animal running in the distance across the low brush, the birds singing, the squawk of the ravens as they continued to dive and soar, and the chirp of a squirrel as she heard it fleet up the side of a tree. The wind brushed over her in gentle breezes as it soothed Julie's very soul.

Julie allowed her thoughts to run free and then opened her eyes once again. Slowly, she had found her way back. The trip with her mom had become the beginning of a new season. Julie couldn't explain it, nor did she know why, but ever so slowly, her life had come back together. Julie found herself laughing again. Her friendship with Alice, her dad's new wife, was like a healing salve for Julie. Alice's very presence had stopped her dad's abuse. Julie knew that Alice would never know what a profound impact she was playing in Julie's life. Julie had entered into a new season of her life; and slowly, over a period of time, a new energy and hope had entered into her very soul. She knew that no one would understand, even if she would try to explain. Julie didn't know if she could even put it into words to explain it all. Her walk with God had taken on a deeper meaning. There was a greater peace and surety in, that no matter how bad life would get, however helpless she may feel, whatever problems life might present her with, that she might not have any explanation or answers for, that regardless of how hopeless and valueless her life may appear to her at times, that her God would be there for her. He was a presence Who had become real to her, Who rose above her doubts, fears, and failures. Something had changed within her since coming out of her last crisis. Somehow, God had become a reality to her and not a mere religion. He was a much greater God than the God of those small little walls of that precious little church which sat on the hill. His never ending love, mercy, and grace had become so much more real to Julie than just what the simple sermons expressed to her in word or what the people did in deed. For Julie, He had become a living presence within her very soul, and it was this God that had empowered her with a new force to move forward into a path of life which promised to bring her hope and love.

Julie slowly stood up and brushed off the pine needles and stones from her clothes. She walked back down the mountainside with a slight spring in her steps. Again, the wind blew gently across her face, like the breath of God, refreshing her. As she walked back through the woods, she could no longer see the river that raced beneath her at the foot of the mountainside. She couldn't even hear the rustle of its waters. But Julie knew that it was there, ever powerful, ever present, strong, sure, and majestic. And so it was with God. His presence ever present, even if she couldn't always hear His still voice or see His all guiding hand, somehow Julie would never doubt again the reality of a God who loved her, kept her, and brought her out of a dark abyss when she could not find her way.

The Cliff

Chapter

8

How can one not have the courage to face their past but convince them-
selves that they have the courage to face their future? Can we really
believe that we can have more courage to face the things we don't know
than the courage to face the things that we have already lived through?

Julie wondered about this one day as she contemplated what
she should do concerning her current relationship with her dad—
now that he had cancer. The doctors didn't hesitate to make it
clear to the family that he wouldn't live long. Julie talked at length
with all of her brothers. All of these many years later, the issues
between them and their dad still lingered like a dark shadow that
just wouldn't lift from their lives. It was true that they had all gone
on with their lives. They had all married, and all but Ronnie had
children. They had all made a good life for themselves and their
families. All four of them had risen above their circumstances and
had gone on to make something of their lives. No longer were they
bound by the issues of their childhood; however, at times, the dark
shadow would arise out of nowhere like a shroud covering them
with pain and sorrow.

"How can one be free from their past, God?" she asked one
day in prayer as she sat in church. Moving two-hundred miles
away doesn't change the issues. It's only geography. Burying the
past only allows it to resurface at the most inopportune times.
Minimizing or denying it doesn't resolve a single issue. It only

causes the wound to fester, appearing to be healed, and then erupting with a newer and sharper pain than could have ever been imagined. "So what does one do, God?" Julie continued in prayer and pondered it all in her heart.

Through all the many years, Julie had tried to convince herself that what was in the past was in the past. She could even quote scripture for it. "Forgetting those things which are past. I press towards the mark of the high calling." But Julie could not forget, and she didn't like the way that the anger from her past would rise from within her unexpectedly. She didn't like the vehement disdain that couldn't be assuaged by her trying to convince herself that her past was under the blood and that she had forgiven her dad. In part, this was true. She had talked to God many times about her past. During the many years that had passed, God reminded her that she had started on her healing journey. God began to walk her through this healing process. Julie, however, didn't want it to be a journey. She wanted the healing to happen all at once. She didn't want to feel the pain from her past anymore. In time, Julie began to learn that healing was a journey and a process, and that God would walk her through it one step at a time if she would take His hand and follow Him at His pace and not her own.

Following college, Mike and Julie married and moved to New Jersey. They were so in love. Julie never dreamed that her life could be so full and so happy. On Sundays, they would often talk by telephone to their families. But to Julie's dismay, no matter how happy her present was, the past would always, once again, come back. Her dad would often call her when he was drinking. Julie knew it from the first words out of his mouth. She could never forget the slurred speech, the lack of enunciation of his words, and the tone of his voice. All of these were red flags, and they triggered more than a warning to Julie on those days; they would put a chill through her body that would make her shake.

Mike and Julie had only been married about a year when her dad called one evening. She motioned to Mike pointing to the

receiver in her hand, sadly shaking her head. She motioned for
Mike to stay near while she talked with her dad. Julie still did not
like facing her dad alone even when he was sober. She was tired
and could no longer pretend that what had happened to her in her
past did not exist. *How would she ever be able to forgive her dad or
get past her anger if she continued to live in denial or minimize that it
had ever happened to her?* And so, time after time, she would take
the calls. And slowly, ever so slowly, she would begin to have confrontations with her dad. They would often start in the present and
with the flip of a switch, during their conversation, accelerate back
to the past.

This time, her dad started with the same usual small talk. But
Julie learned and Mike had encouraged her to avoid talking to him
when he was drinking. And so for Julie, it had become an ironclad
rule that she would get off of the phone immediately if her dad
was drinking.

"Dad, you've been drinking," Julie responded to his small talk.

"Now, Julie, I don't know what makes you think that?" Ron
stated, trying to maintain his words in a smooth flow.

"Dad, we'll talk another day when you aren't drinking," Julie
remarked emphatically, so as to not leave the door open for debate.

"Now Julie, I only had one beer. How could you tell I was
drinking?" Ron baited her with a question.

"I can tell, Dad. Call me back another time."

"Julie, I just wanted to ask how you and Mike are doing?" he
came back.

Julie thought he sounded sincere and that maybe he wasn't
drinking as much as she had thought. *How could she ever reach him
with God's love if she was too short in her words with him?* "Well,
Dad, we're doing pretty good," Julie weighed her words and his
carefully.

"So how is married life these days?" Ron continued.

"Married life is great, Dad," Julie answered. She glanced over
at Mike, shrugging her shoulders at him, making a questioning

gesture with her one hand as if to ask Mike symbolically, *How she could get off of the phone?*

"No, Julie. I mean, how is married life really?" Ron asked.

This time, Julie distinctly heard his slurred enunciation and realized that he had more to drink than she had thought.

"I told you dad, married life is really great. Hey, I gotta get off now."

"Julie...," the voice came over the phone. The very tone of her dad's voice unnerved her for some reason. She started to interrupt him in an attempt to get off the phone but before she could speak, Ron spoke once again.

"No, Julie, I'm trying to ask you *how--is--married--life, really?*" Ron repeated.

His voice was sinister. It cut through Julie to her very core. She knew what her dad was really asking her and it appalled her that he could even think of such a thing. *As a matter of fact, how could he dare to ask her such a personal question? How dare her dad even hint at asking her intimate details pertaining to her relationship with her husband. How dare him to cheapen their love by bringing it down to his filthy standards.* Julie felt her anger move into rage within a mil-a-second.

"How dare you, Dad!" She then slammed down the phone. Julie broke into tears as Mike asked her what had happened. It was all that Mike could do to not pick the phone back up and call his father-in-law.

"Don't Mike," Julie said softly. "It won't do any good anyway."

"Jul," you need to talk to your mom about all of this," Mike said lovingly, as he put his arm around Julie's shoulder. She leaned her head onto Mike's shoulder and became quiet. "Really, Jul, you have to talk to your mom the next time she visits us. You've got to tell her everything. It's time that you told her what happened to you as a child," Mike continued on slowly.

"But Mike, I can't," Julie implored. "It would break her heart. She'll blame herself for everything: for not knowing, for leaving us with Dad, for not being there."

Mike turned and looked directly into Julie's eyes, locking his onto hers. Julie looked into his rich blue eyes, full of love and compassion for her. "You have to tell her, Jul. You have to let her know. It's time."

So when Ethel visited Julie a few months later, Julie sat and told her mom briefly what had happened to her those many years ago. And as Julie had expected, she saw her mom break down into tears and her spirit rise in an anger towards her dad that she had hardly ever seen in her mom. They talked several times, and as painful and difficult as it was for Julie to speak about it and for her mom to hear, Julie knew that Mike had been right. Julie couldn't get over how the more she exposed the dark secret that had her bound for so many years, the more relief and the more control she felt over her own life. She could feel herself being set free. And the more that she confronted her dad and took back the control of her life from him, the more that she began to heal and feel empowered to overcome her past, for no longer did this dark secret have a hold upon her; no longer. The more Julie revealed it, the less control it held over her. More than a little surprised, Julie realized that the more the secret was exposed, the less fear and shame and guilt and blame she felt.

Through the years, more and more of the hidden dark secret was exposed. One day while talking to her mom, the subject came up once again. Julie's frustration at her dad's continual drinking and his treatment of her brothers had reached an all time high. Ethel began to speak to Julie, first to the woman who Julie was and secondly as the daughter whom she treasured.

"Julie, you need to talk to your brothers about this sometime," Ethel said slowly, being gentle with her words.

"Oh, Mom, I can't. I just can't," Julie said, her voice quivering with uncertainty.

"Just think about it, Julie," Ethel spoke softly not wanting to press Julie. Every time they spoke on this subject, it was all Ethel could do to hold back her tears and to maintain her anger at Ron. She didn't know how she could ever take away the pain that she knew Julie still experienced. She felt that it was all her fault for not being there and for not seeing any of this when Julie was a little girl. *How could she not of suspected it of Ron? She knew what his father had done to Julie. How could she not of suspected this of Ron after he had gotten Tonya pregnant? How could she have been so blind? But it was his own daughter. For that reason alone, how could she have ever thought that he could ever stoop to this level of degradation?*

Julie sensed her mom's quietness as they talked. She knew that her mom was going through these questions in her mind and that she had blamed herself for years.

"Mom, it's not your fault," Julie said kindly.

Ethel remained quiet. She didn't want Julie's consolation or for Julie to justify and excuse her. All she could think and would ever think is that somehow, she should have known. She was the mother. With all the things that Ron had done during their thirteen years of marriage—the affairs, the drinking and the fights—somehow Ethel would have never had thought that Ron was capable of sexually abusing his own daughter. Even with what he had done to Tonya, Ethel surmised that Tonya wasn't his own blood. She wondered how she could have had four children with a man and not known that he was capable of such abuse to his own flesh and blood. Ethel would never excuse herself, no matter how much Julie would try to set her free from the pain that she felt—the pain of knowing what Julie had experienced and the feeling that she alone could have prevented it.

"Mom," Julie said again, "there is no way that you could have ever known. There is nothing you could have done. Even if you had taken us to live with you, I believe Dad would have still abused me when I visited him," she continued. Julie wouldn't give up on reassuring her mom of this fact. She refused to let her mom bear the guilt of what her father, and he alone, had done to her.

And so the conversations would continue from time to time. Julie did think about what her mom had said about talking to her brothers concerning what her dad had done to her. She discussed the matter with Mike and got his opinion. Once again, he fortified Julie with his loving words, "They need to know Julie. It's time that you told them. It will help them to understand what kind of man your dad really was, along with how he affected their lives too."

Julie thought about it for a long time and prayed about it. She didn't want to do it for herself, but she could do it if it would in some way help her brothers. She didn't know how they would react to their dad if they knew. She didn't want to make them hate their dad or break up their relationships with him. But as time had passed, Julie realized that they, like she, did not have a true relationship with their dad. There had been too many years and too many issues and too much neglect and not caring on their dad's part for any of them to have had a true or good relationship with him.

Ronnie struggled with their dad for many reasons. It had been exceptionally difficult for him, because at such a young age, he had found out that Ron was not his biological father. Ron had done so many horrible things to Ronnie over the years that Julie knew that the strained relationship between her dad and him had made Ronnie feel that he was the problem and not their dad. One day, as Julie was talking to Ronnie, trying to encourage him, they began to talk about the past.

"I understand, Julie," Ronnie spoke. "I know that Dad is not my real dad, and maybe that's why he feels the way he does towards me and why he has always treated me the way he does. It's not really his fault that I'm not his blood son."

"But Ronnie," Julie implored, "he knew before he even married Mom, that you weren't his son. He agreed to love you and raise you as his own."

"Yea, Julie, but you can't blame him for not feeling what wasn't there," Ronnie continued.

"Ronnie, none of that matters. Regardless of that, he still should have never done the things he did to you and said the things he said to you," Julie emphatically stated.

"It's different for you, Jul," Ronnie said sadly.

Julie took a deep breath. She had thought that she could assure Ronnie that none of this was his fault, that Dad was Dad, and that whether you were his own or not it wouldn't have made a difference. But the only way that Julie was ever going to be able to show Ronnie this was to tell him why she knew that this was the truth.

"Ronnie," Julie spoke slowly.

"Yea, Sis," Ronnie answered.

"I need to tell you something, and I think you'll understand it all better then."

"No, Sis. You don't have to explain. I get it. Don't worry about it, okay?"

"No, Ronnie. I need to tell you something that I've been meaning to tell you for a while. Please hear me out, okay?" Julie pressed gently.

"Okay, Sis," Ronnie conceded. He loved his little sister. If it made her feel better for him to hear what she had to say, then he would listen.

"Ronnie, I don't want you to get upset about some things and at people when I tell you this, okay?" Julie asked. She felt timid and took a deep breath and whispered a prayer for the courage to continue.

"Okay, Sis. I'll try. Go ahead." Ronnie knew his sister, and he could tell by the tone of her voice that something was gravely bothering her.

"Ronnie, do you remember when I was a little girl after Mom and Dad divorced, and I had a hard time doing my homework and my nerves were real bad?" Julie asked.

"Yea, I do," Ronnie answered, now more intent on what his sister was saying and confused at the direction she was heading.

"And then when I was about twelve or thirteen years old and I lost a lot of weight and went into my shell and was having a hard time the same way again? Remember Mom took me to Ocean City on a trip to try to help me?"

"Yea, Sis, I remember all of that. We were really worried about you; all of us. But then you seemed to snap out of it and got better. We all figured the trip with Mom helped you out a lot. We were glad Mom took you. We never felt bad about that," Ronnie answered. He was still confused and wondered how this connected with his relationship with their dad. He could hear the stress and pain in Julie's voice as she spoke.

"Well Ronnie, there was a reason for me getting so bad. I could never talk about it back then, and I held it all in and there were times when I thought it would destroy me," Julie continued, speaking in broken sentences as she tried to find the right words. Ronnie was only the third person that she had ever shared this secret. Julie paused before continuing.

"I'm listening, Sis," Ronnie said lovingly. "We always wondered why you struggled, but we all were struggling at that time; and we figured it was just from Mom and Dad's divorce and from Rhonda, Dad's girlfriend, beating on us so bad. Were there other reasons too?"

"Yes, Ronnie," Julie answered. "It's just I want you to know Ronnie, that it's not your fault that your relationship is strained with Dad. The problem is with Dad, Ronnie, not us." Julie hurried on before she lost the courage to tell Ronnie. Ronnie remained quiet as Julie continued. "It wasn't just you that Dad couldn't show love. I know at times he tried by giving us a nice Christmas, or listening to a ballgame with you boys; but I also know that Dad could be very cruel, and it wrenches my whole insides when I remember the things that he did to you, and I just can't let you think that it was you when it really was Dad." Julie hurried on, allowing her words to rush out tumbling one over another. "Ronnie, there was something wrong with Dad. I don't know why. Maybe because of Pap Pap James, his dad...I don't know. But Ronnie...most of my life, Dad sexually abused me."

There was complete silence and Julie didn't know what to say. She couldn't say another word. Though she felt another great release in sharing this with her oldest brother, the words had exhausted her in just speaking them. She just wasn't sure what Ronnie's quietness meant. And then, without warning, she heard his sobs.

"Sis, I am so sorry," Ronnie spoke and cried at the same time. "I never knew. I never knew." Ronnie sat shaking his head as if to hope that it wasn't true.

"I know Ronnie," Julie said, "there is no way that you could have known."

"Do Jerry and Matt know?" Ronnie asked in a shocked voice.

"No. I'm going to tell them sometime when I find the right time," Julie answered softly.

"Julie, I'm so mad!" Ronnie interrupted. "I feel like I should do something. I should have known."

"How could you have known, Ronnie? We were kids. We were just little kids. There's no way you could have ever known. Listen Ronnie, the only reason I'm telling you is that you have to know that the problem is not you. There is nothing wrong with you. The problem is Dad's. It doesn't matter if you are his blood or not. Do you see why I'm telling you?"

Ronnie went to hug his sister and answered, "Yea, Sis. I see why you're telling me. But I am so sorry. I'm just so sorry that you went through all of that and I wasn't there for you."

Julie reached out and hugged her brother and sobbed. "But Ronnie, you were there for me," she continued to speak while in their embrace. "And..." she paused as she put her hands kindly onto Ronnie's shoulders and looked him in the eyes. His kind deep brown eyes full of tears met Julie's. Julie continued, "...you were always there for me; Jerry and Matt were too. All three of you were always there for me. You were my heroes. Your love was always there for me. It was one of my only hopes that I always had, your love."

"Thank you Sis," Ronnie said, brushing his tears. He was at such a loss for words.

"We'll talk more again, sometime," Julie said, bringing their conversation to a close.

"But you do see that none of this, or your relationship with Dad, is your fault?"

"I do Sis. I do," Ronnie spoke slowly and gave his sister another big hug. "We'll talk more later. Thanks for telling me."

"I love you big brother!" Julie said softly, and gave Ronnie a big hug.

Julie was glad that she had been able to tell her oldest brother Ronnie. It seemed to help Ronnie put things in perspective, and Julie was glad that she had shared it with him. However, she was in no hurry to tell anyone else.

Julie couldn't understand it, but she had really thought that as more years passed things would get better between her dad and herself and between her dad and her brothers. But as time went on, it seemed that the more the issues were pushed under the rug, the more that they would rise to the surface, not only with herself, but she could also see the tension mounting with her other brothers and their dad, especially with Matt.

After working at the Drug and Alcohol Rehabilitation Center for a while, Julie felt that God was really pressing her to confront her dad. Things had grown so severely strained between her dad and herself that they hardly spoke. Julie felt that if they were ever to have a relationship of any kind then Julie would have to talk with her dad. God was beginning to deal with her heart. *Why can't I just let it go?* Julie would pray and ponder within her heart. *What good can ever come out of it all by talking about it?* Julie and her brothers hardly ever visited their dad these days and the family couldn't understand it. There was much talk amidst the family and questions. "Why don't your kids visit you, Ron?" people would ask. "After all, you're the one who raised them all by yourself? Ethel walked out on them, but they visit her. It just doesn't make sense." The remarks would continue throughout the family grapevine and within their small community.

Julie felt frustrated by it all, and it made her very angry, some-times to the point that she felt very unchristian. "Why can't I get past all of this, God? Why can't it just go away after all of these years?" Julie would ask God in prayer. She would ask Him to help her to understand and to know what to do with all of the pain and anger that she still felt so strongly within her.

"You have to deal, to heal, to feel," God spoke to Julie's heart one day. It was such a simple message, and yet Julie knew that she had not dealt with it, that she had not healed, and that the continual pain, anger, and unforgiveness continued to affect her capacity to feel. And so, when she had asked God what she should do, He answered her. *"You must confront your dad with your past and you need to tell your other two brothers about the sexual abuse because they are also struggling with everything that all of you had gone through as children."*

One day, Ron called Julie. Julie cringed after she said hello and heard her dad's voice at the other end of the phone line. Julie asked her dad to hold a minute. She called up to her children, Mikey and Jenny, telling them that she would be on the phone for a while. Mike was at work. Julie reluctantly went to her bedroom and closed the door. Julie had not told her children about her father, even though she knew they had wondered why they didn't visit him. She wanted to shelter them from the harshness of this world as long as she could.

Julie picked up the phone and once again said, "Hello, Dad."

"I haven't heard from you, Julie," Ron started the conversation.

Julie remained quiet and was at a loss as to what to say to her dad. She whispered a prayer under her breath as to what she should say and how to continue.

But Ron continued the conversation. "You never visit Claire and me when you come in. People ask me why you no longer visit."

Julie could feel the anger begin to rise within her. *So this is really about what people are saying and thinking,* she thought to herself.

"Even Claire feels that maybe it's her fault that you don't visit…that maybe you don't feel at home here," Ron continued.

How could her dad blame Claire? Julie thought angrily. Julie heard the words come out of her mouth before she could check them. "Don't you dare blame her, Dad!" Julie spoke with a boldness that surprised even her.

"Well, Julie, what else could she think?" Ron countered.

Julie felt her spirit begin to calm and that unexplainable peace of God come over her. She said nothing, listening, sorting out, and putting her dad's words in perspective as he continued to talk. Julie tried to figure out what was really behind his underlying message.

"So, why don't you come to visit?" Ron asked, trying to manipulate Julie with guilt as he had done so often in her childhood.

Julie's mind raced trying to find a reason to make an excuse as she had done in the past. She was going to tell him that they had only been in for a few days the last times, and that there had not been enough time to visit. And then, Julie began to feel God's love and strength fortify her as He spoke to her heart, *"It's time to confront your dad. Tell him why you really are not visiting him."*

She could feel the courage mount within her. *No!* she thought to herself. *He would no longer give her the guilt trip. Those days were past, even if he did not know it yet.* "I think you know why I don't come to visit," Julie answered softly but firmly.

Julie heard her dad cough and clear his throat. She knew that he had always done this when he became nervous and whenever he felt that he wasn't in control. She braced herself for his reply.

"What are you talking about?" Ron answered.

A question with a question, Julie thought. *That will not work either.* Julie forced her mind to get ready to counter her dad. "I think we need to talk when I come in," Julie stated matter-of-factly, not leaving it open for debate.

"About what?" Ron continued on, pretending to be ignorant of the topic that Julie was alluding to.

"You know what we need to talk about, Dad," Julie answered. Julie wondered how that her voice was steady, firm, and unwavering as she felt her heart beat rapidly and hard against her chest. "If we are to ever have a relationship, we need to talk about the past. And I don't want to talk alone with you. I think that Matt should be with us."

"Why Matt?" Ron asked. He was taken aback by Julie's confrontation and did not want to broach the subject of their past, so he tried to sidestep the conversation onto Matt.

"I just think it would be good if Matt was with me," Julie answered. She thought that if maybe Matt and she could approach their dad together, then possibly they would be able to begin to make peace and find resolve. Of course, she hadn't asked Matt yet to do this. She wasn't even sure if he would consider doing it with her, but her dad didn't know this. She waited for her dad's reply. Julie couldn't explain the strength that she felt. She felt as if she had just overcome something and yet didn't know what it was that she had overcome. She was no longer intimidated by her dad, and she knew that he could no longer manipulate her. But nothing prepared her for his answer.

"Julie!" The voice came over the phone in a low whisper but harsh in tone and then continued, "Don't start something." Then a distinct pause before he continued, emphasizing every word, "Don't start something that you can't finish!" Ron said, and then hung up.

Julie sat down on the bed. The phone slipped from her hand. She sat there stunned, not believing her dad's words. It shocked her that her dad would actually threaten her. The words rolled over and over again in her mind as she began to cry.

Matt, Ronnie, Julie, Jerry
The Bond of Love~~
(Still one after all these years)

Chapter

9

Julie awoke with a start. The dream had brought her face to face with pure horror. She lay still, trying to calm her racing heart. She could feel her heart pounding fiercely within her chest. She was so tired and had to get up early to go to work with Mike in the morning. She turned over and glanced at the clock. It was 4:30 in the morning.

Julie felt the gentle rhythm of Mike's breathing beside her. His very presence made her feel secure and comforted. Slowly, she began to feel at peace and began to pray. *God what is it with these dreams that I'm continuing to have all the time?* Julie had shared them with Mike, every dream, every detail.

It was a recurring dream. Sometimes, Julie would have a string of them within a few weeks, then a lapse of a few months, and then a string of them again. The thing that amazed Julie was that they were always different and yet always the same.

Julie was always inside a house. Sometimes, it was in the house that they lived in now. At other times, she was inside their old house in New Jersey. Sometimes it was a house that Julie didn't recognize, and sometimes it was her childhood home that had been torn down over thirty years ago. But the dream was always eerily the same. Everything would be normal, happy. Julie was always alone in the house. She would be happily going through the house, and then all of sudden she would approach a door which was cracked open. Sometimes, it was the front door of her home. Sometimes, it was the side entrance to the garage. At other times, it was a basement door in their old New Jersey home. But it was always a door that was barely ajar. The mood of the dream would go from happy and peaceful to full terror. Julie knew in the dream, every time, that when she saw the door ajar, that someone had entered into her house. She knew that it was a man and that he was always alone. She also knew, in the dream, that he was powerful and that his intent wasn't to hurt her, but rather to kill her!

Julie would run to the door and slam it shut and throw the latch. But she could feel "his" presence and she knew that it was too late. He would approach her but she could never see who it was or identify him.

As the dreams proceeded and continued to re-occur, sometimes Julie could see down the basement steps and would see the man's form up to his chest. This only terrified her more and made the presence more real. This is what had happened in her dream tonight. With each dream, she seemed to get closer and closer to confronting something or someone that she dreaded. It terrified her; and even when she awoke, she felt a tremendous fear. She wondered if she would totally confront the man what would happen. *Would he kill her, or would she simply die of fright?* She began to ask God, where was He in her dream. *Why couldn't He just appear and scare the man away? Why couldn't she just pray in the dream and wake up? Why was she having this dream over and over again? What did it all mean?*

Julie prayed into the night, wondering about what it all meant. It was nearly morning before she fell back asleep into a deep rest.

The ringing of the phone slowly penetrated into Julie's deep rest and awakened her. Instinctively, she jumped up to get the phone. When she did, she stumbled and found herself tangled in the covers. Quickly, shaking the covers off, Julie ran to the kitchen and grabbed the phone. She knew by the quietness of the house that Mike had already left for work at their business and had let her rest.

Julie said a quick hello and tried to get her mind on track. Rubbing her head, trying to wake up, she listened intently for the caller to respond.

"Hey Sis, you okay?" came the familiar voice.

"Oh, hi Jerry," Julie answered with a sigh of relief as she collected herself.

"Did I wake you?" Jerry asked.

"Not really. I mean, I should have been up a long time ago. I'm just glad it was you and not someone else," Julie answered with a laugh. She was wide awake now. "What's up Jerry?"

"I just wanted to let you know that I was in to visit Dad," Jerry answered.

"How is he doing?" Julie asked. She pulled out a kitchen chair and sat down. Her dad had been diagnosed with cancer for about a month now. Julie knew that they all had serious issues with their dad, and although all of their issues varied in different ways, they had all been affected by their dad's treatment of them as children. They all dealt with their issues very differently and in their own personal ways, but the camaraderie that they had always shared as children still brought them together, never letting the issues divide them. It was as if they were four separate people, but somehow that bond of love that they shared made them one. And so it was, at this season of their lives, that it seemed that Ronnie and Jerry were able to talk to their dad and to get through to him more than either Matt or she were able to.

"He's not doing good, Sis," Jerry continued speaking sadly.

"I wrote him a letter the other day Jerry, but I haven't heard back," Julie replied.

"I have so many mixed emotions when I visit him," Jerry spoke in a low voice.

"I understand," Julie said softly. "It's good that you visit him, Jerry. He seems to listen to you. Maybe you can reach him."

It was a short conversation, but Julie knew her brother's heart. Not many words were needed. Julie sat and contemplated their conversation.

Julie gave Ronnie and Matt a quick call and updated them on what Jerry had told her. Ronnie had visited their dad too, but not Matt. Julie encouraged Ronnie to continue visiting him. "What did he have to say?" Julie asked Ronnie.

"I don't think he believes that he's as sick as they say he is," Ronnie answered. "I've tried to talk to him a few times about God."

"I hope you can help him, Ronnie," Julie said softly and sincerely.

"Are you coming in to see him?" Ronnie asked hesitantly.

"I don't know, Ronnie. I just don't know yet. If it would help him, I'd come. But I just don't know how he'd receive me," Julie answered. "Remember when Dad had his stroke eight years ago?"

"I remember Julie," Ronnie replied.

"I thought of coming in then, Ronnie," Julie shared, "but he just made it impossible for me to even try."

"I know Jul. He told me then to tell you that you could come to see him if you didn't mention Jesus to him."

"Claire had told me the same thing, Ronnie; and Dad knew that I'd never agree to come see him, or for that matter, would I go anywhere where I was restricted to talk about God. He knew that I wouldn't come to see him, and yet by my not coming, he was able to tell all the family how horrible I was for not visiting him. I had even told Claire that I didn't think it was a good time to try to renew our relationship and that the stress might cause him to have another stroke."

"What did Claire think when you told her that?" Ronnie asked.

"She sadly told me then, whatever was meant to be would be. But I didn't want to be the cause of him having another stroke or maybe even causing him to die. I told Claire that if she needed any help to let me know and that I would come in. Claire told me then that it looked like he was going to pull through everything, but that he would have to do therapy." Julie paused. She felt as confused now, as she did then. "I guess we'll just have to wait and see what happens," Julie said and let out a sigh. "Keep me posted, Ronnie."

"I will, Jul." Ronnie replied and then hung up.

Julie sat in the reclining chair. She knew that all of them were dealing with not only the issues of their dad's pending death but also with the erupting of the past issues of their childhood, which laid so deeply buried within all of them, still unresolved.

She remembered when she had told Matt about their dad sexually abusing her. Julie had tried to tell Matt for the same reason that she had told Ronnie. Several years had passed since she had told Ronnie when, one day, Matt was down visiting Mike and her and the family. Julie and Matt had gone out to eat breakfast when the subject of their dad had come up.

"Matt, do you want to visit him with me when I come in?" Julie asked. She tread the deep waters cautiously with her brother. Julie looked once again into his deep blue eyes. She could still see the Matt of her childhood in those eyes.

"No, Sis!" he answered kindly but firmly.

"I understand," Julie answered back, reaching out and placing her hand onto his.

"You know how it has always been between us, Jul," Matt continued.

"I do," Julie replied softly.

"Dad's just never really liked me," Matt opened up. It surprised Julie a little.

"You know what I think?" Julie stated more than asked and continued. "I think that Dad never got over it when you told Mom that you saw him kissing our cousin Tonya when we were little."

Matt just looked at Julie with a puzzled look on his face. It was too late to turn back. Julie knew that she would have to continue.

She had hoped that she could comfort Matt with this thought, but now it seemed that it had opened up an old scar.

"You don't remember that?" Julie asked.

Matt sat quietly and nodded that he did not. Somehow, Julie had to help Matt see, that like Ronnie, Matt wasn't the problem with their dad. And the only way that she knew how to do this was to explain it all to him.

"Matt, do you remember when our cousin Tonya lived with us and she got pregnant and she said that it was Dad's baby?"

"Yea, Julie; she was only sixteen years old at the time," Matt added sadly. "And we were only what?" Matt asked and then answered his own question. "You were about seven years old and I was eight?"

"Just remember, Matt, you were only eight years old. Well, Dad denied that he had anything to do with Tonya. We didn't understand what was happening or even what it all meant. You told Mom that one night when she was at bingo, that you got up to go to the bathroom and you looked downstairs and that you saw Dad kissing Tonya while they sat on the couch." Julie looked at Matt's sad face.

"I do remember that now," Matt answered.

Julie couldn't leave it there and let Matt think that it was still all his fault. Julie could see that Matt didn't seem to want to acknowledge that he was just a little boy, and that as if somehow he had not said anything that maybe things could have been different. "Matt, you have to know something. I didn't ever want to tell you or upset you, but you have to know."

It was Matt's turn now to look deep into his sister's eyes. He searched them as she had searched his earlier, and he too saw that little sister that he knew so long ago. "What Jul? Tell me."

Julie hung her head. She thought it would be easier this time to talk about it. And it was a little easier each time. But she hated the pain that still erupted within her when she spoke about it. But she couldn't stop now. Matt must know that he did nothing wrong to make his dad not love him. He had to know that it was their dad who had the problem. Slowly, Julie raised her head and looked deeply into Matt's eyes. She still had her hand resting on his. Matt took his other hand and placed it on top of Julie's.

"Matt, shortly after Tonya moved out and Mom and Dad separated, Dad began to…" Julie paused.

Matt gently squeezed his sister's hand in his. "Continue, Julie…"

"Dad began to sexually abuse me and continued to sexually abuse me until I was about fourteen years old and old enough that I could stop him," Julie ended the sentence abruptly and hung her head down.

There was a moment of silence and then Julie looked up slowly. There were tears in Matt's eyes. They were full of love and compassion. "Do Jerry and Ronnie know this?" Matt asked.

"Ronnie does, but Jerry doesn't," Julie answered quietly. She watched as Matt's compassion turned to anger.

"How could he do that to you?" Matt exclaimed. "How could he do that?"

Julie had not anticipated Matt's response. The purpose of telling Matt was for him to see who Dad really was and that Matt had done nothing wrong as a child. Julie didn't want to upset her brother and make him even angrier at their dad. "Matt, I just wanted you to know that Dad is the problem. Not you, not me, not Jerry or Ronnie."

"I never knew, Julie," Matt said sadly, holding Julie's hand now between his.

"I know you never knew," Julie squeezed her brother's hands between hers. "I never told anyone until I met Mike. Then I told Mom, later Ronnie, and now you."

"You need to tell Jerry, too," Matt said lovingly to Julie. "He'd want to know."

"I will, Matt, when the time is right," Julie assured him.

But several years had passed and Julie had not had the opportunity to tell Jerry. Maybe when she could sort it out more, she would call Jerry and talk to him. He was still in the Army. Julie didn't think he needed to have all of this to deal with on top of his responsibilities with the service. She wanted to tell him, but she was still dealing with so much of it herself.

Then things took an unexpected turn, as life so often does. Julie had traveled in to visit the family and to also help Ronnie settle his wife's estate after she had died. They had just settled everything, and Julie could tell how relieved Ronnie was to have it all straight.

"Sis," he said one day. "I saw Dad the other day and he said he just didn't understand why you didn't come to see him."

"Well, he can always ask me that question and I'll tell him," Julie replied.

"I told him, 'Dad, I think you know why she doesn't come to visit you!'" Ronnie said. Julie could hear the anger filter through as Ronnie's voice rose when he spoke.

Julie thought that she would never understand her Dad. One thing, though, that she was learning was that she didn't need to understand it all for God to help her to deal with it. God, more and more, was leading her forward on this healing journey. *"You must deal, to heal, to feel,"* God would speak to her heart. He seemed to fortify her with courage, and little by little she began to feel the shackles of her past begin to drop off.

She remembered just a few years before this, shortly after she had told Matt what had happened to her as a child, that she had run into her dad at the drugstore when she was in for a visit. She found it very awkward. She tried to be kind to her dad and Claire and then politely broke away and hurried to get out of the store. Julie was still surprised at how her dad's very presence, these many years later, still unnerved her.

Before she could get out of the drugstore, she heard her name being called. Her dad had left Claire at the register and followed her. "Wait up, Julie," he called out. "What's your hurry?" he laughed and tried to make as if everything was normal.

Julie stopped short and turned around to face her dad. She quickly gathered her thoughts and whispered a prayer for God to help her to stand her ground. She had to let him know that he no longer had any hold on her. Julie had tried to tell him throughout the years, during their controversial conversations, that Mike knew everything, that there were no secrets anymore. But somehow, Julie felt that her dad had just brushed those remarks aside, that he either didn't believe her or didn't want to believe her.

"I have to go Dad," Julie spoke firmly, looking her dad directly into his eyes.

"Well, why don't you come over and visit while you're in?" Ron questioned Julie.

"Dad, you know why. We've had this conversation before. When you are ready to talk, we'll sit down and talk. But no more pretending," Julie shifted her weight with the bag in her hand. "I have to go."

"Well, if this is about your brother Matt and me not getting along…"

Julie stopped short and looked at her dad incredulously.

"You were younger than him, Julie. Too young to see all the problems," Ron continued, ignoring Julie's questioning look.

"Dad, this has nothing to do with Matt! But first of all, I am only one year younger than him; you surely know this, and second of all, none of the problems you mention ever existed except in your mind."

"Now, Julie," Ron continued on as he tried to patronize Julie.

"Dad, I am not ten years old. I'm fully aware of those situations. I lived through them; remember?"

Ron started to continue, but Julie held up her hand. "No, Dad! Don't! Don't you dare make this about Matt, and don't you dare say anything bad about him. Not now! Not ever! And you know fully well why I don't come to see you." Julie turned and rushed out of the store.

Julie had returned back to her home in Pennsylvania but learned that she had to make one more return trip to help Ronnie with the last of his legal matters. Again, they went to the hearings and everything was worked out. Julie stayed a few extra days to enjoy them with her mom. One morning, when the phone rang, Julie stood in the doorway and watched her mom's face grow saddened as the phone call continued. Ethel then hung up the phone placing it gently back into its cradle.

Ethel turned to Julie and spoke softly, "Tonya died last night in her sleep."

Julie couldn't believe her ears. Her Tonya. The Tonya that had been the only big sister that she had ever known. The Tonya that had come to live with them. Tonya had combed her hair, dressed her, and shared the things that only big sisters can share. Julie loved her now as much as she did then. All the memories of their past seemed to rush through Julie's mind like a river of water that had just burst through a dam. Julie felt her sorrow turn to instant anger as the memories continued to flow by. She hated what her dad had done to Tonya. Julie felt that he alone had ruined Tonya's life, and Julie blamed him for everything. Julie took a deep breath trying to control her emotions. Tears flowed out of the creases of her eyes as Julie stifled back her anger and tried to divert her thoughts. She'd have to sort out her emotions later. She couldn't do it now in front of her mom. It would only upset her. "But, Mom, she's not that old. How did she die?" Julie asked and went to comfort her mom.

"They don't know yet, Julie," Ethel replied. "They think it was a complication with her prescriptions and alcohol."

Julie walked out onto the porch to get some fresh air. *How could this be?* Julie wondered. She had always wanted to sit and talk with Tonya. She knew that Tonya had never gotten over the trauma and complications of getting pregnant by Julie's father. Julie had heard Gramma Winnie talk of Tonya often as she grew up and how that Tonya had blamed herself for breaking up her

Aunt Ethel's family. But Julie knew what her dad was capable of and she never blamed Tonya. Tonya had given birth to her son and raised him by herself with all her love. He was the apple of her eye. She adored him. But she could never get her life on track.

Julie had tried to call Tonya and reconnect with her a few years earlier, one time, when she was in for a visit; but it was only a short conversation on the phone. Julie could tell that her own feelings and love for Tonya had only made it more complicated for Tonya. Julie was a symbol from a past that Tonya had tried to put behind her. Julie's phone call only made life more complex for Tonya; and unwittingly, Julie's very presence opened up Tonya's old wounds. Julie realized that her good memories only triggered sad memories for Tonya and reminded Tonya of an era in her life that was full of pain and sorrow.

Julie sat down on the worn chair on her mom's porch and let the warm breeze brush past her. Tears came down her cheeks. How she had longed to be able to tell Tonya that she loved her, that she never blamed her, and most of all that she had never forgotten her.

It was later that same morning, when to Julie's surprise, her dad had pulled up in front of her mom's porch. Julie had not seen him since they had run into each other at the drugstore. Apparently, he had heard that she was in town, and Julie thought that he was possibly making an attempt to reach out to her. *She never wanted to shut the door to her dad; maybe somehow, someway, she could help him. But why, of all days, did he have to come on the very day that Tonya had died. Surely, he couldn't have heard about Tonya's death already. It wouldn't even be in the newspaper until tomorrow.*

Julie jumped up from the chair and went into the house into the back bedroom. She would have to gather herself and say a prayer before she could face her dad and deal with him. Shortly, she went out into the kitchen where Ethel had poured both Claire and Ron a fresh cup of coffee.

Julie pulled out a heavy metal chair and sat down at the end of the table. She hoped that Matt wouldn't swing by and stop in unexpectedly. She knew that if she wasn't up to dealing with her dad, Matt definitely wouldn't be. Julie just sat and listened to the small talk. Ethel paused and then said slowly, "It will be in the paper tomorrow, but just to let you know, Tonya died this morning."

Julie looked up and studied her dad's face and expression. It had caught him off guard, though Julie knew that wasn't her mom's intent. Julie watched her dad quickly collect himself. He asked how she had died and Ethel explained the best she could with the information that she had been given. Julie glanced at Claire's kind face. She wasn't sure what she knew after all of these years of being married to her dad.

Julie had hesitated many times in confronting her dad in front of Claire. Julie never wanted to ever be made responsible again for any of the breakups of her dad's relationships. Her dad had blamed her when Rhonda and he had broken up. He had used it as a reason and a justification for his continuing to sexually abuse Julie after Rhonda left. The last thing that Julie ever wanted to do was to lay the heavy burden of what her dad had done to her on Claire. Julie was unsure of what her dad had told Claire throughout their years concerning the situation with Tonya.

Julie's eyes darted back and forth as the adults talked. She studied their faces, trying to understand the depth of what laid beyond the conversation. Julie could feel the awkwardness of the moment. Ethel excused herself and went out onto the porch to have a cigarette. Ron said he thought he'd join her and have one too. Claire and Julie continued to talk. Julie liked Claire. She had hoped that through the many years of Claire's marriage with her dad that maybe her dad would finally change. Julie had felt that surely, being given such a nice Christian woman like Claire, her dad would come to know the Lord and see all the pain that he had caused. She felt sure that he'd be sorry and somehow life would be different. But nothing ever had changed with her dad. If anything, the justification, denial, and manipulation just got worse.

Ethel and Ron came back in from the back porch. Julie noticed that her dad seemed a little uneasy and that her mom seemed extremely bothered. Claire and Ron said their goodbyes and quickly departed.

Julie sat and ate her lunch watching her mom carefully as she did the dishes. She knew that her mom was still stunned by Tonya's death, but somehow she knew that something else was bothering her. She saw it on her face when she had come in from the porch with her dad. "What's wrong, Mom?" Julie asked.

Ethel continued to wash the dishes and didn't turn to face Julie. "Nothing," she answered softly.

Julie slowly pushed back her chair and stood up. She went over to her mom where she was doing the dishes. "Mom, what's wrong?" Julie asked again. "Is it about Tonya's death?"

"Nothing's wrong, Julie," Ethel replied once again.

Julie knew her mom. She could understand if Tonya's death had brought the past back to her mom. She also knew that her mom loved Tonya and had never blamed her for her and Ron's failed marriage. So for her mom to say nothing, when Julie knew at the very least that Tonya's death was a factor in itself, something just wasn't right.

Julie put her arm around Ethel's shoulder and turned her towards her. "Mom, what's wrong?"

Julie could now see the tears in Ethel's eyes. And try as she could, Ethel could not hold them back. "Tell me Mom. Tell me what's wrong," Julie pleaded. She led her mom over to a kitchen chair and pulled it out and sat down beside her and waited for her mom to answer.

"It's your dad, Julie. That's all," Ethel stated and then stopped.

"What did he do, Mom?" Julie asked patiently.

Ethel just shook her head and said, "No, Julie. Forget it. Just let it go."

"Mom," Julie spoke up again. "Tell me."

Julie sat nervously and played with a napkin and waited for her mom to answer. "Mom, I won't let this go. You have to tell me."

Ethel took her coffee cup into her hand and took a large drink. Julie could hear her gulp as it appeared to almost get stuck in her throat. She paused and then looked at Julie. *Who was this woman who sat in front of her and where was her little girl that she used to be able to dissuade so easily?*

Julie sat quietly and waited for her mom to talk. Ethel picked up her cup one more time and took a large sip to wash the other one down and then began to speak. "Julie, your dad asked me to come over to his house for 'Freddie'."

Julie sat and stared at her mom puzzled and tried to understand what she was saying.

Ethel continued. "He wanted me to come over when Claire was at work. 'Freddie' was what he called sex when we were married."

Julie was shocked. *How could her dad continue to do the things he did? He was almost seventy years old.* "How dare he come to your house and say these things to you, Mom, especially, and of all days, on the day that Tonya has died!" Julie scooted back the old chair with such a rush that the metal framed chair rumbled across the floor. Julie hurried to the next room and had her hand on the telephone when Ethel joined her.

"That's why I wasn't going to tell you, Julie," Ethel said. "Let it go, Julie. You and I both know how your dad is. It won't change a thing to say anything. It will only make things worse, and it will hurt Claire."

"I get the feeling Claire knows more than people think she does," Julie remarked.

"Let's just let it go," Ethel said gently, giving Julie a big hug.

"I'm going to go into the back bedroom for a while, Mom," Julie said. She then gave Ethel a hug and walked away.

Julie wept, letting her tears flow as she sat on the edge of the bed. This is why she hated to even come in for a visit. She began to pray. "God, I am so angry. I am so very angry. I could just spit dust," Julie said out loud, resorting back to her southern slang. "How can he do this? How do I deal with him? How do I even pray for him, for his soul?" Her anger continued to rise as she spilled more out, "And God, do you want to tell me why this is in my face again. I lived through this. I even forgave my dad, like you told me to. And here I am again, after all of these years, and it's right in my face again." Tears flowed, and the more they came, the more Julie's anger released. She laid back and when her tears finally dried up, her anger was gone. And then, in the stillness, with that ever-present presence that she had grown to so depend upon, she felt Him speak, once again, to her heart. *The reason this is in your face again, is that you have not healed in this part of your heart. I want to heal you, so that I can bring you up higher.*

And then there were more tears. But this time they were not tears of sorrow, but tears of peace, healing tears, comforting tears, tears full of love flowing over her and healing her shattered heart. Julie sat up and reached for her Bible. She opened it up at random and read the scripture from the Old Testament which stood out in the small print. "Do not hold the guilty, guiltless." "Do not hold the guilty, guiltless," Julie read the scripture out loud once again, as if to etch it into her heart.

Later, the next day, Julie and her mom dressed to go to the funeral home for Tonya's viewing. Julie had called Mike and told him what had happened. He told her to stay with her mom until after the funeral.

It had been many years since Julie had seen some of her family. It seemed that they lived in two different worlds. She knew that so many of her cousins and even Tonya's children were unaware of Tonya's younger years living with Julie and her family. They were too young, and many had been born long after Tonya had left their home. They would never know how much she loved Tonya, and she would never be able to tell them. The secret had been buried a long time ago.

Julie thought that she had gathered her thoughts and fortified her heart to go meet her family. She entered into the back seat of the car and let her Aunt Mary get up front with her mom. They pulled into the parking lot of the funeral home.

"Look," said Aunt Mary, "there's your dad and Claire."

Julie turned to look where her aunt was pointing. There was no time to stop the quick eruption of anger that sprang out from deep within Julie's heart. She wanted to clasp her hand over her own mouth to forbid the words that were on the tip of her tongue. She was grateful for a God who was able to stop her tongue from saying what her heart was thinking. She remained silent for a moment as the words ricocheted through her mind. *How could he come? What in the world is he thinking, coming to the funeral home? Did he really think that even forty years later that his presence would be acceptable?* Julie was puzzled about how her dad's mind worked, in that, he could even think that it was acceptable for him to come.

Julie watched as her dad and Claire walked across the parking lot, across the street, and up the stairs to the funeral home. Ethel continued to park her car. Julie thought that maybe her mom was deliberately taking her time parking. She wondered what her mom was thinking. Tonya's death was one thing. Her dad showing up at the funeral home was another. But knowing what her dad had said to her mom the day before, on the porch, was just too much for Julie to filter. Julie was infuriated. It was meant to come out softly, but the force of Julie's words even shocked her as she exclaimed to them, "What in the world is he doing here?!"

Julie saw her Aunt Mary turn around quickly and look at her with shock on her face. Julie stopped there. She knew that no explanation was better than a feeble attempt to try to explain it away. Julie felt her palms sweat and the blood drain from her head. She wondered how she could get out of the car and even walk into that funeral home with her dad there. She didn't trust herself around him. She was afraid that she might tear into him, and she knew that this was neither the time nor the place. Usually, when Julie would feel this much rage she would excuse herself, get away, go into a bathroom or anywhere, and say a quick prayer. However, there was nowhere for her to go.

Her mom and Aunt Mary had already stepped out of the car. Julie reluctantly opened the car door. She moved slowly, gathering her purse, stalling for time. Time to whisper a prayer, *God please help me not to lose it. I have to stay focused on my family. Please help me.*

"Come on, Julie," Ethel gently spoke. Aunt Mary put her arm through Ethel's as the two sisters started to walk towards the funeral home. Julie glanced at her mom, and her mom glanced at her. They both read each other's thoughts through each of their eyes. Julie walked slowly behind them. Aunt Mary didn't say a word.

There were a lot of people standing on the porch that affronted the funeral home, some to take a break from inside, and some to have a cigarette. Julie recognized one of her cousins. She was two years younger than Julie. Julie hadn't seen her in many years. "Mom, I'll be in shortly," Julie called out as Ethel and Mary approached the doors to the funeral home. Julie joined her cousin, who was standing on the porch and welcomed her to join them. Julie continued to try to gather her thoughts about her dad and tried to place them in the back of her mind as she started a conversation with her cousin. It was only then that she realized who was standing right next her. He was a fine young man about eight years younger than Julie. Julie knew who it was right away, even though she had not seen him for nearly thirty years. Her mind raced. There was just too much happening all at once. It was more than her mind could process. Her heart beat heavily within her chest as she tried to calmly talk to her cousin. Julie turned and smiled at the young man who still stood beside her listening to their conversation. Julie could tell that he was unsure of who she was.

"This is Aunt Ethel's daughter," her cousin explained. Julie turned once again to the young man. He smiled at her. It was Tonya's son.

Julie was at a loss for words and let her cousin continue to talk. Julie only half listened as she quietly studied the young man. As she studied his features she noticed the gentleness that belied the great sorrow in his eyes. Julie felt such a strong ache in her heart for him. He had lost his mother, his rock. Julie wanted to take him into her arms and hug him tightly—this cousin who was really her half-brother.

Lost in emotion, Julie retained her composure, so much so that she didn't hear her cousin's words at first. "Julie, there goes your dad and his wife."

Julie turned and saw her dad and Claire, a few feet in back of her, going down the steps of the funeral home. Julie turned to her cousin, who seemed surprised that Julie didn't run after them to say hi. Julie was at a loss for words. She noticed the puzzled expression on Tonya's son's face and the more surprised look on her cousin's as Julie stood still and watched her dad cross the street.

Julie turned back and looked at her cousin, who was awaiting some kind of response or remark of explanation. But Julie had nothing to say. Her mind could usually outrun her emotions while later sorting out her feelings; but for some reason, her mind was on overload and she could not think of anything to say. She hoped that the conversation would pick up where it had left off; but because she had only been half listening, she didn't even know where to pick up the conversation.

Her cousin said nothing in her confusion and seemed to leave it up to Julie to give some kind of explanation. Julie, finally, slowly spoke up, trying to weigh her words. There was no easy explanation to give, nor was this the time or place to even try. "Well, I guess he either didn't see me or didn't want to see me," Julie spoke up. However, the pause continued, and Julie reluctantly finished her sentence, "And either way is okay with me."

The expression on her cousin's face was even more puzzled now. Julie gave her a weak smile. She turned once more and smiled at the young man beside her. She gently touched his arm and said she was so sorry for his loss. She excused herself and walked into the funeral home. She had wondered if she would ever see him again.

Beloved Tonya and Julie

Chapter

10

There were times when Julie didn't know what to do with all of the emotions that would surge through her. Normally, she would do what she had done the majority of her life—push them down, tuck them away, suppress them, and then make her mind up to go on to something else. It really wasn't that difficult to do. With working in their family business sixty or more hours a week, raising the children, taking care of her in-laws, and resolving all of the problems that arose in the business, there was hardly time or energy remaining to think very long on the past anyway.

Julie liked it that way. After all, what would it benefit to go back to the past? Didn't everyone say just forget about the past, get a life, or just plain get over it. Even Christians seemed to have the cliché of saying *"That's all under the blood."* It seemed that we were to just let it all go. *But how do we do this?* Julie wondered.

Julie tried hard and she had done a good job of it too, of shoving it so far down within her, to a place where she thought it wouldn't bother her anymore. If it would have just worked and stayed there it would have been fine. But it didn't.

The past always resurfaced. And when it did, it would catch Julie so off-guard, that she could never be sure of how to handle it.

Julie began to ponder within her heart and search her Bible to try to understand more of how God would want her to deal with the past, a past that always seemed to rise up and haunt her—now, even more so, with the recurring dreams that she continued to have.

One night, she awakened with a start. The dream had terrified her.

She was back in her old home, in her bedroom. She was a little girl. The bed was where it always was, the dresser beside it. She was awake in the dream and was trying to listen keenly to the perceived sound that she thought she heard. She slightly held her breath, as if to quiet her racing heart, and listened again. There it was again, that slow creak and then a soft snap, another creak and then another soft snap. Julie felt terror rise within her. She felt her heart would leap from her chest, and then she saw the door open in the dim light of her bedroom and the shadowy figure entered the room.

"No!" Julie screamed. "No! No! No!"

Julie awoke with the words still upon her lips. Her heart was racing and pounded loudly within her chest. She turned over quickly and faced her sleeping Mike. The sound of his even breathing comforted her as she came back to her present. She laid still and began to pray. Oh that sweet peace that flowed over her, that peace that she had so grown to depend upon.

"It's okay Julie," the still small voice spoke lovingly to her heart. *"It's okay to scream."*

It was only then that Julie realized, for the very first time in her life, that she had never screamed. Through all the years of the abuse, and the terror and fear that would arise within her, she had never screamed or cried out. It was just understood that she must be quiet, and so it was. But now, as she lay quietly in her bed, the words continued to comfort her. *It's okay to scream.*

Julie let the dream roll over in her mind like a movie reel. The creak of the steps and the snap of his knee as her dad crept up the steps that led upstairs to her bedroom. The creak of the door, that ever slightly shut door, that was so symbolic of her other dreams. And yet, as her heart settled, and her eyes began to drift off to sleep, she felt as if she was cradled in the arms of God as He gave her peace and comfort.

It wasn't long after Tonya's funeral that Julie was surprised to get a call from her dad. Her brother Ronnie had talked to her concerning their dad on the phone earlier one day and had told Julie that their dad might call her, but Julie didn't think that he really would.

"Dad asked me why he didn't get an invitation to Mikey's wedding," Ronnie informed Julie that day.

"Just tell him to ask me, Ronnie, so that you don't have to get in the middle of it," Julie replied.

"Well, he asked me to give him Mikey's phone number so that he could call him," Ronnie continued. "Do you want me to give it to him, Sis?"

"No, Ronnie. Don't give it to him." "What do you want me to say if he asks me again?" Ronnie asked.

"Just tell him that I said if he wants Mikey's phone number, that he will have to give me a call and I'll explain," Julie answered.

Julie couldn't remember the last time that her dad had called her but thought it was probably when he had told her to "not start something that she could not finish." Julie had not talked to her dad since Tonya's death.

Julie rushed to grab the phone. She said, "Hello," happily, not knowing who was on the line. Then to her surprise, she heard the rough cough and the clearing of the throat that had always ushered in her dad's voice.

"Hello, Julie." The voice was sober, direct and firm.

Of all days, Julie had company at the house. She motioned to her company that she had to take the call and went into the bedroom and shut the door. Immediately, Julie's mind began to race and her emotions began to rise. She said, "Hello, Dad," keeping her tone even as she whispered a prayer. She was so taken aback, she couldn't even begin to gather her thoughts. *God please help me,* she prayed in her heart. And then a flint of hope, *Maybe he called to talk, to make things right. Always, keep the door open for his soul's sake,* her thoughts and prayer seemed to mesh together all in one as she waited for her dad to say something.

"I talked to your brother," Ron spoke up and then paused.

Julie waited for him to continue speaking, but he didn't.

"And?" Julie asked. She wanted to hear what her dad had to say. She wanted to watch what she said, until she could settle her emotions, gather her thoughts, and whisper another prayer or two under her breath before she would continue.

"Ronnie told me that you wouldn't let him give me Mikey's address or phone number."

Julie knew that voice. She could hear the intimidation and the manipulated undertones. She knew what was coming but she waited once again.

"So?" Ron continued.

"What Dad?" Julie asked.

"So, I can't have the address and phone number of my grandson?" Ron continued.

Julie could hear his tone sharpen. She knew that this conversation was not going the way that her dad had planned. "No, Dad, you can not have his number."

"And why not?" Ron asked sternly.

"Because you are never going to get the opportunity to hurt my children," Julie answered quickly and firmly.

"Well, I think that Mikey is old enough now to make that decision for himself," Ron came right back.

"Yes, he is," Julie agreed, "but not before he has all the facts of why I won't give it to you." Julie's voice was calm but rose in a sternness that surprised Julie herself.

"Well, I would never do anything to hurt him," Ron answered back. His voice was calmer now. Julie knew that if at anytime there would be even a hint of all that her dad had done to her might come forward, he would immediately change his tone and his tactic.

"I can't take that chance," Julie stated matter-of-factly.

"Why?" Ron came back. He was taken off guard. It had been a while since he had talked to Julie, and he didn't like where the conversation was heading. He had thought that he could give Julie the guilt trip and persuade her to not only give him the phone number but also invite him to the wedding.

"Dad, you have hurt everyone who has ever come into your life, and you will not ever get that chance with my family," Julie's answer was direct.

Ron was unsettled and uncomfortable. Julie waited for him to continue. Ron cleared his voice and coughed nervously and then continued. "What do you mean that I have hurt everyone that has been in my life?"

"What you did to me, Dad?" Julie was surprised at how easily the words came out but she was not surprised at the anger that began to erupt inside of her. She prayed once again, and pushed the anger way down into her soul. This was not the time or the place to allow her anger to rule.

There was a silence. She could hear her dad's breath on the other end of the line. Julie continued to pray as she waited, *God give me the words to say, and please help me to get off the phone. God, I've told him so many times that this is no secret anymore. I've told him that I've told Mike, Mom, my brothers. Why does he always seem so surprised and believe that this is still some great secret and that he has some kind of hold over me? Why doesn't he get it?* Julie prayed in her heart. As she waited during the long pause, God answered her, *"Because he doesn't believe you. He thinks you are just saying that. He thinks you would never tell anyone "the secret" and that he still has control over you."*

"Well, Julie, I told you that I was sorry for that," Ron finally answered in a hushed and rushed voice.

"No, Dad, you didn't. I think I'd remember that," Julie responded in an even tone. She could show no weakness, no stammering, no hesitation or she knew that her dad would trample her in the conversation within a minute. She had to stay on guard.

"Well, I only ever did it to you," he spoke in an irritated tone.

"What about Tonya, Dad?" Julie let the words rush forward. "You ruined her life, Dad! You got her pregnant!"

"Everyone did that to Tonya, all her life, no matter where she stayed," Ron retorted back.

Julie knew her dad. She expected the unexpected from him. He had ceased to surprise her anymore, until now. Julie's mouth gaped wide open. She nearly dropped the phone. Her anger rushed up from the depths, from where she had pushed it and was ready to tumble out. *God, I am going to hang up. I have to get off right now or I will say the wrong thing,* Julie prayed. She was too stunned to respond at first.

But God spoke back to Julie immediately. She knew His voice, as He spoke firmly and lovingly. *"Not this time. Not this time. This time you tell him like it is. Do not hold the guilty, guiltless."*

Julie prayed, *I'll say the wrong thing. I'm too angry.*

And then Julie felt that awesome peace as it took her anger and calmed her spirit. A strength came over her and she spoke quickly before Ron could continue.

"So that made it right Dad, what you did to her?" Julie's words came out in a strength that she didn't expect. Her voice did not quiver and there was a boldness which rose within her.

"And what about what you said to Mom when I was in?" Julie retorted back. "How dare you come to her house and ask her to come over for sex! How could you do that to Mom? How could you do that to your wife Claire?"

Now it was Ron's turn to be quiet. He was so taken aback that he couldn't answer.

"And then, of all the nerve to come to the funeral home. How could you do that?" Julie asked.

But Ron couldn't answer Julie's second question because he was still trying to gather his thoughts on the first question. "Do you mean that your mom told you that?" Ron asked in a hushed voice.

"Well, of course, she told me!" Julie answered. "There are no more secrets, Dad," Julie continued on.

Ron stumbled for his words. He had to change the subject or flip it back on Julie somehow. He could not let this conversation continue. He had never heard Julie talk so blatantly and open about this subject. "You, you," Ron stammered, "you make me out to be some kind of monster, Julie," he finished the sentence re-gathering his momentum.

"You are," Julie stated softly. She felt calm and she wanted to remain sensitive. Maybe now her dad would see the destruction of the lives that he had affected. Maybe now his soul could be touched. She paused and waited for his response.

"Anyway," Ron spoke up in a last ditch effort to turn the tables on Julie, "I think that you make more of it than it is."

Julie thought that she would get sick on her stomach. She could not believe what her dad was saying. There was no slurred speech. He was not drunk. He was saying these things and he was as sober as Julie. She had always blamed his drinking on everything, but she had to realize that it was not his drinking at all. It was just the way her dad thought. It was just the way that he was. Julie felt the "surety of God" rise within her. She felt a boldness to not back down. She could not let this remark go unaddressed.

The words came out with such authority that Julie was taken aback at the calmness and confidence that swept over her. "Let me get this straight, Dad," she spoke out and then paused. "You're sorry for what you did to me. But you think that I'm making more of it than it is? Did I get that straight? That's your apology?"

"I told you I was sorry," came Ron's stern remark. He had regained control and he was not going to back down.

"Well, Dad," Julie continued, unmoved by his last statement, "Then this is what we'll do. When you decide to ask God to change your reprobate mind and to give you a conscience that isn't seared with a hot iron, then call me back. Maybe then we can build a bridge and walk over it together. But until then…" Julie paused…, "Good-bye." Julie hung up the phone. She was in a daze. She shook all over, from head to toe. She flopped onto the bed and allowed her tears to flow. The conversation ran through her mind over and over again. *What had just happened?* she wondered. As painful as the conversation was, Julie felt such a peace. She had finally confronted her dad. She had finally quenched all of his justification. Julie felt free as if a large weight had been removed off of her shoulders. Surely now he would have to deal with the truth.

It wasn't long after their son Michael's wedding one day when Julie and Mike were driving home from a trip that Julie said to Mike, "I should call Jerry and wish him a happy birthday. Today is his birthday."

"Go ahead," Mike smiled and nodded as he continued to drive. "You know, you still need to talk to him sometime about your past."

"I know, Mike," Julie replied as she pursed her lips and clenched her teeth giving him a crooked smile. "I just have to find the right time." Julie felt that Jerry was troubled over some things lately. More and more, as time had passed, their childhood would continue to surface. They had talked and reminisced at her son's wedding, but there was no way that Julie was going to bring it up then. And today was Jerry's birthday. At sometime, when Jerry and she were alone, she would talk to him. Jerry was the only one of her brothers that Julie had not told of the abuse.

Julie dialed the phone and listened to the rings—one, two, three. She thought for sure it would go to voice mail, and then she heard that familiar voice. "Hello."

Julie smiled. Jerry still had a little of that southern twang that she so loved to hear in his voice. She could picture him in her mind: those deep brown eyes, his dark hair now brushed with gray on the sides, his strong face and jawbone muscle which would always move when he was bothered.

She remembered the first time that she had seen that jawbone muscle move. He was about ten years old when on one day, Rhonda, their dad's girlfriend, was beating him with the yellow plastic hammer from her son's toy construction set. They had all felt the wrath of Rhonda during those years when she lived with them and their dad. However, never had Julie felt more upset than on that day when she beat Jerry mercilessly. They could never remember what she was even beating him for. They knew that every time Rhonda would get angry at their dad that she would take it out on one of them or all of them. But Jerry was her favorite target, maybe because he looked so much like their dad. Julie could still hear Rhonda's voice as she yelled in rhythm to her hitting him, "So you won't cry! We'll see about that!" as she beat him all the more. Julie watched Jerry's face etched in pain at every swat. She wanted to run over and take that ole hammer and start beating on Rhonda. But all she could do was watch as he tightened his jawbone muscle and it moved back and forth to hold back the tears. He would show her that she, of all people, would never make him cry again.

"Hi, Jerry!" Julie answered back excitedly. "Happy Birthday, Big Brother!"

"Thanks, Sis," Jerry answered. "How you doing?"

Julie noticed that he was more talkative than usual. She nestled down in the car and got comfortable as Mike drove through the night.

They talked for a while about the wedding and their families. Then, as they began to talk about their past, Julie began to feel that twinge in her heart. She needed to tell him. She knew this was the right time, but she still didn't want to tell him on his birthday.

"Hey Sis, I know Dad's difficult and we all have had our problems with him, but what's going on between the two of you?" Jerry asked.

"I just can't visit him, Jerry," Julie answered. She tried to sort out her words.

"You used to visit him some and then you stopped. I don't understand," Jerry continued.

Julie thought and then spoke softly, lovingly to her brother who was such a part of her heart. "Then just ask me about what you don't understand."

"Tell me why. Dad says to me that he doesn't understand why you never visit him when you come in."

"It goes way back, Jerry." Julie paused to gather her thoughts. Mike glanced over and caught the conversation. He reached over and put his hand gently onto Julie's knee. Julie turned to Mike. Their eyes met and held a conversation in the stillness of the moment. Mike's love fortified her and his gentle smile comforted her. He patted her knee gently.

"I never told you. Actually, I never told anyone for a long time, not until I met Mike." Julie paused again.

"You can tell me, Sis," Jerry said softly.

"Well, after Mom and Dad separated…" Julie let her voice trail off.

"Yea, Sis," Jerry said softly.

"Well, Jerry, you know how it was back then and we were so young."

"I know, Sis," Jerry replied in response. He knew that his interjection would help Julie to continue.

"There was so much confusion when Mom and Dad broke up. And then Dad tried to commit suicide and then later we thought that Mom and Dad would get back together again."

"I had always hoped they would," Jerry agreed sadly.

"I think in some ways you took it the hardest, Jerry. You would get so angry at everything and everyone back then."

"I didn't hide it very well, that's for sure," Jerry said with a light chuckle.

"That's because you didn't want anyone to see your hurt, tears, and pain," Julie reflected, "but you didn't mind if they saw your anger."

There was a quiet moment as both Julie and Jerry paused. "Jerry, during that time when things were at their worst...."

"Yes...?" Jerry gently pushed Julie to continue.

"Well, during that time Dad started to sexually abuse me...." Julie paused to collect her thoughts. Jerry was quiet. Julie continued while she could. Each time she spoke of her abuse, it became easier, but never was it easy. "He continued to abuse me up until I was about fourteen years old."

"Jul," came the soft voice from the other end. Julie could hear her brother's voice waiver in the moment. She knew that his pause was to hold back the tears of pain and shock of her words. "I never knew, Sis. You have to believe me. I never knew. I am so sorry." Julie could feel the earnestness of her brother's words. She wanted to reach through the phone and hug him. "None of us knew, Sis."

"You couldn't have known. No one knew," Julie spoke evenly as she let the words come tumbling out.

"Do Ronnie and Matt know about this?" Jerry asked.

"I told them not too long ago," Julie answered. "I was just waiting for the right time to tell you."

"But why didn't you ever tell us?" Jerry asked. His voice was soft, kind, and broken.

Julie could hear the emotion in his voice. "There were so many reasons, Jerry. Mostly the fear and pain of it all. The guilt and the shame. Look at what happened to Tonya when she spoke up. Look how we were picked on and made fun of at school. What would've happened to us had I spoken up. Look at what happened to Tina Sellers when she spoke up about Pap Pap James sexually abusing her."

Jerry was quiet. Julie didn't know what else to say.

"I'm so sorry, Sis," Jerry spoke up. His voice sounded so broken. "I'm just so sorry."

"I know, Brother, but it's okay," Julie replied. "Lately, Dad and I've been having some pretty rough conversations over it and it hasn't been going so good."

"What does he say?" Jerry asked. His voice rose protectively.

Julie hesitated. She knew now the reaction of her other two brothers. She knew that Jerry was upset. She didn't need to see his face. She knew this brother and his heart. Julie couldn't see the need to upset him more.

"Tell me, Jul. What does he have to say about it to you?"

"Well, he just tries to justify and minimize it," Julie answered. She thought it best if they could talk about it another time. She knew that Jerry was upset enough already without hearing more.

"Tell me, Sis," he pressed.

Julie was not going to get into the details of her last conversation with her dad. She hesitated once again. She knew that Jerry's pause was to give her time and she knew that he would not back down until he knew more.

Jerry softly asked again and paused to gather his thoughts. *This was his little sister. The sister he had tried to protect all of his life. How could he have not known? How could he not have saved her or rescued her from her dad's abuse?*

Julie knew her answer would upset her brother.

Julie hesitated and then answered, "He just said, the one time that we talked, 'Don't start something that you can't finish.'"

"Well, when I see him, Jul, I am going to talk to him. I can finish it," Jerry stated.

Julie could hear the anger in his voice towards their dad. "We'll talk more another time, okay?"

"Yea, Jul," Jerry answered soberly.

Julie changed the subject and then soon got off the phone. She turned to Mike and let out a deep sigh and gave him a weak smile. Even in the dark, Julie could see her husband's kind eyes fixed upon her. He gave her a warm smile and gently reached over and took her hand into his as they pulled into their driveway.

"We're home," Mike said to Julie as he gave her hand a tender squeeze.

"We're home," Julie repeated as she looked deeply into his eyes. "We're home."

Dad

Chapter

11

The song played softly. Julie knew the song by heart but studied the words from the songbook. As the congregation sang the familiar words, they seemed to leap from the pages and come to life.

"I come to the garden alone,
While the dew is still on the roses,
And the voice I hear, falling on my ear,
The Son of God discloses.
…And He walks with me,
And He talks with me,
And He tells me I am His own;
And the joy we share as we tarry there,
None other has ever known."

It was her dad's favorite hymn. He had told her that often when she was a child. He had told her that when he died, it was this song that he wanted played at his funeral.

Julie couldn't help but wonder if that would be sooner than later. She had talked with all of her brothers and Claire in the last four weeks. Claire had taken him to the hospital for more tests and to have them make him more comfortable. Jerry had told Julie that when he had gone in to visit their dad that he had told him that the cancer was terminal and that the doctors had said that he didn't have a lot of time to live.

"Sis, I feel bad even visiting him," Jerry said to her one day.

"Why should you feel bad?" Julie asked.

"Because, I don't want you to ever think that by my visiting him that I condone or accept what he did to you."

"I would never think that, Jerry," Julie assured him. "Maybe both Ronnie and you can reach him where Matt and I aren't able to help him. I'm glad that both Ronnie and you visit him," Julie reiterated the remark.

Julie had pondered everything that was happening and she prayed earnestly. "Should I go in to see him, God?" she asked. She remembered how God had asked her, over two years ago, if she would go to visit her dad, if He asked her to. She agreed that she would, but only if God asked her, and Julie felt that He hadn't.

She searched her heart over and over again. She remembered their last phone conversation after Tonya's funeral and before Michael's wedding. She remembered how, afterward, God had dealt with her to forgive her dad.

"But God, I have forgiven him," Julie countered in prayer. Julie knew that though she had actually made a commitment to forgive her dad, she still felt her heart was full of anger towards him. She tried to justify her feelings to allow her heart to be angry. Surely, God wouldn't expect her to not be angry at him. So, she continued to confess forgiveness, yet the anger remained. Julie began to realize that she had it backwards. *How can one truly forgive someone until they understand what forgiveness is and what it is not? And how can one truly forgive someone if you have so much hurt and pain still in your heart? Wasn't it his fault that she had so much hurt and pain?* The hurt and pain had caused so much anger to rage within her heart that she found it difficult to release her true forgiveness, even though she spoke it often in prayer and desired it by faith. She would have to get rid of her anger toward her dad if she was ever to truly forgive him.

As time passed, Julie realized that forgiving her dad did not okay what he did. Even if she truly forgave him, he still had an accountability to God for the wrong that he had done. Julie began to pray that God would help her to understand her pain and anger better and that God would show her how to deal with these issues in her life. There was such a strong feeling to not forgive him because Julie didn't think he deserved to be forgiven for what he had done to her. She felt that if she did forgive him, then she would be expected to have a relationship with him; and in truth, she did not want a relationship with him. And most of all, even if she could forgive him, she didn't want him to know, because for sure, he would think that she was okaying everything that he had ever done to her. So, Julie asked God to give her a vision for his lost soul. Surely, if she could see a vision for his soul being lost forever, then possibly, she could be able to pray for him better.

Julie continued to have the recurring dreams. Each dream that she had would only stir up all of the issues of her past and bring them soaring to the present. … *The door part way open.* … *The villain in the house.* She would awake full of terror, often unable to go back to sleep.

One day, she had the dream once again.

This time it was the side garage door that was ajar. The old fear returned, but she forced herself to go into the garage. As the terror rose within her heart something seemed different this time. There came a sense that she was not in danger…but she still did not like being in the garage. She felt that she had to pursue and check things out. As she went further into the garage she found a little girl sitting inside. The little girl was ragged and dirty. She seemed alone, sad, and broken, but she asked for nothing. She seemed afraid to ask for anything and was content that she at least had a place to stay in the garage. She didn't come to Julie or even ask to come into the house.

The thing that bothered Julie in the dream was that she didn't run to the little girl. She didn't pick her up and hug her. She didn't offer her food or even offer to bring her into the house. Julie noticed that even in the dream itself, this bothered her extremely. *What was wrong with her? It wasn't like her to not feel or show compassion for a child?*

When Julie had awoken, she prayed and asked God to show her what it all meant. And then Julie felt she understood. The little girl was her as a child. Somehow, Julie was content in keeping this little girl locked away. She didn't want to bring her into her present, into her life now. She was fine in the garage. Julie realized that it was time that she dealt with the little lost girl. It was time for her to not be ashamed of her, to love her, comfort her. It was time for Julie to become whole.

Then one night, Julie was awakened by another strange dream. She didn't have to think about what it meant, because now it was clear.

Her dad was in the dream and he had hurt another little girl. The mother had found out, and in the dream the woman was venting her anger towards her dad. Julie wasn't in the dream but just watched it unfold before her. Julie thought the mother might kill her dad, and for some reason this did not make Julie happy. She studied her dad's face as the woman came up to her dad in full force, yelling and ranting at him. Julie was surprised at the look on her dad's face. There was no cockiness, no arrogance. It was as if they had been peeled off and the real face of her dad was left to reveal his brokenness, fear, and shame for all that he had done. Julie could see the very fear of hell itself etched on her dad's face. She had never seen this dad before. The closest resemblance that she could remember was the look that he had on his face after both times that he had tried to commit suicide.

Julie remained in bed and let the dream rerun over and over again in her mind. In the dream she had seen right through her dad's veneer down to the very depths of his broken and shattered soul. Somehow the dream had given her a vision for her dad's lost soul and the hell that he would surely face, for an eternity, if somehow he did not make it right with God.

Julie walked out of the theater with her arm through Mike's. They were both trying to hold back tears. Julie thought the movie "The Passion" was one of the most profound movies of all times in portraying the true love of a Savior. It personified all the love that Julie had grown to know from her God, the God who had carried her all of her life.

Julie knew that it was more than an idea, when later that year God had spoken to her heart to buy the movie "The Passion" and give it to her dad for Christmas. Julie thought, *I can do that, God.* No sooner had she thought that, than the still small voice told her, *"and write your dad a letter and tell him that you forgive him."*

It had been a journey. It had been difficult at times, even unbearable, to deal with her past, but *"in the process of time,"* God had helped her to heal.

She had to first give Him her anger. One day she was so angry. Someone had hurt her feelings so badly. The past came rushing over her, and all of the old hurts that she had laid down so many times just seemed to erupt from nowhere with such a torrent that Julie thought it would sweep away her soul. She felt like giving up on life. She was tired of trying, and dealt with the pain like she had always done. She allowed the anger from all of her pain to sweep over her. It strengthened her, gave her control, and even comforted her. But when the dust settled, the pain remained and she felt the anger consume her.

"Why don't you give Me your anger?" the still small voice spoke to her heart.

"I will," Julie prayed out loud. "But it's not fair, God!"

"I know it's not fair," came the reply, *"but do you want Me to take the anger from you?"*

"Yes," Julie answered, "but what they did...." And Julie repeated the whole incidence over to God in great detail.

There was no condemnation. No commands to get over it. No admonitions to quit self-pitying herself. There was just love and compassion, patience and comfort, and then the same earnest petition, *"Do you want Me to take this anger from you?"*

And then Julie answered. It felt like she had to untie her tongue from her front eye-teeth. "Yes," Julie answered out loud. "Yes, Lord, I do want You to take this anger from my heart."

It all seemed so simple. But in time, as Julie would surrender her pain, hurt, and anger to God, she would feel her heart begin to heal. It took God's love to give her the strength to not only relinquish the anger but to allow Him to take it from her. God showed her that in using anger to survive, it had only become her cloak of comfort. Julie had learned that the more she gave God her hurt, pain, and anger, the easier it was becoming to forgive her dad.

But for Julie to actually write her dad a letter and tell him that she forgave him seemed more than what she was capable of doing. Julie prayed about it. Her greatest stumbling block was that she knew that her dad would take her forgiveness as a license to justify and okay all that he had done. Forgiving him of his past was one thing, but to okay him to think it was acceptable tore Julie asunder.

She sat down to write the letter. *"I will help you write it,"* came the still small voice within her heart. She rolled up each letter into a ball, over and over again and threw them away, until finally the words were there and so was the forgiveness. It really didn't matter what her dad thought. What really mattered was that she had obeyed God; and from choice alone, she felt the greatest peace and freedom from her burdened past that she had ever felt. She began to realize that forgiveness for her dad was really freedom for her.

Julie never heard back from her dad concerning the letter that she had written him. Jerry and Ronnie later did tell her that he had actually gone to see the movie in the theater and that he liked her gift of the movie.

Long after she had sent the movie and letter to her dad for a Christmas present, Julie continued to ponder the words of the song which her dad held dear.

> *"I come to the garden alone,*
> *While the dew is still on the roses,*
> *And the voice I hear, falling on my ear,*
> *The Son of God discloses.*
> *...And He walks with me,*
> *And He talks with me,*
> *And He tells me I am His own;*
> *And the joy we share as we tarry there,*
> *None other has ever known."*

Julie wondered if her dad had ever sought God in the garden alone. She wondered if he had ever heard the voice falling on his ear or felt that God walked with him and talked to him. She wondered if he ever felt that he was God's own. Did he ever hear that still small voice? Did he ever tarry there and share the joy that none other has ever known?

Julie sat at the computer and reviewed the final reservations for her trip. Mike and she had made these arrangements even before her dad had become ill. Julie couldn't believe that they were going to Hawaii. All of her life, she had always wanted to go there. Julie went downstairs and began to pack her suitcase for the trip.

She still had not felt led to visit her dad. She had written him another letter. It was easier this time. It was very similar to the first letter that she had written to him years earlier, urging her dad to make things right with God, telling him that God loved him and that she had forgiven him. But once again she never heard back.

Julie called Claire one evening to see how he was doing. "Julie, he is failing fast. The doctors are trying to adjust his pain meds so that he won't be too dopey, but yet so that he can have relief from the pain."

"Claire, if you thought that it would help, I'd come in," Julie offered.

"Well, I'm sure he'd be glad to see you, Julie," Claire answered back.

Julie knew that Claire was a woman of faith. "I'd come in if it would help his soul," Julie added.

"Well, Julie," Claire paused and then answered, "when I took him to the hospital, he said, 'I'm not a sinner and I'm not going to hell.'"

"I guess that answers my question," Julie said sadly. "I just don't see that there's anything that I can do."

Julie put the phone back into its cradle. She grabbed her sweater and went out the back door. She slowly walked up the path that wound up through the woods behind her house. She remembered when Mike and their son Michael had made the trails and surprised her one year. Julie smiled. *It was Christmas in July that year.* They had made her close her eyes and took her up into the woods and unveiled the cut trails that led throughout the woods.

Julie still loved her walks in the woods to clear her heart and mind. Mike had made a special path in the upper woods just for her that led to a bench where she could sit and think. Julie wrapped the sweater around her tighter in the cool breeze. She turned the corner of the path and saw the picnic tables. She loved the picnic grove and the fire pit. Julie walked over and sat down. She placed her head down into her folded arms that rested on the picnic table and cried, "What am I supposed to do God? What am I supposed to do?"

Julie heard a rustle in the leaves and lifted her head and looked around. A little gray squirrel had darted out of the leaves and was halfway up the tree. Julie laughed at the big nut that he had braced between his teeth. He stopped and looked at Julie. He began to chew on his prize and then seemed to think better of it and rushed back down the tree scurrying away to bury his nut.

Fall was in full color. Julie looked around at the leaves which were scattered throughout the woods. She could see the autumn reds and yellows highlighting the landscape in the distance. The cool breeze blew softly once more and again Julie wrapped her light sweater tightly around her, placing her hands into her pockets. Fall was passing so quickly, and Julie could almost feel the chill of winter in the air.

Julie loved the woods. Here, she could empty herself out and allow her mind to wander as she had so often when a young girl. Nature sang its chorus as Julie listened to the trees blowing softly in the wind, their tops rustling up high. The last of the song birds sang their chorus, as if singing their farewell to another season. The chipmunks fought over an acorn, scolding each other for their right to own it; and then there was the stillness that followed. It filled Julie with a peacefulness that calmed her troubled spirit.

Julie propped her elbows onto the picnic table and rested her head in her cupped hands. Her mind wondered back once again, to those final years growing up.....

Ronnie's Marine picture

Chapter

12

Julie was in the tenth grade and in a few months Matt would graduate. Julie sat Indian-style in the middle of her bed, her legs crossed, her elbows resting on her knees with her hands cupping her face as she sat in wonderment.

She reflected upon how this past school year had been so different from the year prior. No longer did she feel timid or lost among her friends or upper classmates. Somehow, Julie felt that she had awakened into a new season. For one of the first times in her life, she felt alive.

Julie stretched out her legs and scooted up to lean against the headboard of her bed. She grabbed her pillow, hugging it on her lap. Her eyes danced across her room while smiling as she took it all in. The smell of fresh paint still lingered in the room. Julie looked at the walls, which were painted a fresh pale pink, and then to the windows that were dressed with new curtains. She reached down and touched the fresh cotton spread on her bed. Julie loved the way the dainty lavender flowers stood out on the bedspread against the backdrop of white. Julie let her eyes sweep the room again as if to take it all in. Against the wall was a beautiful old desk and chair, and then under the window was a wooden chest, surrounded by her dressers. In the far corner was a little stool with a miniature organ. And underneath all of the furniture was a tweed green carpet that seemed to make the room complete. The extra furniture had filled the room tightly, but Julie felt it was cozy. Julie could not ever remember her room looking so nice. She felt like a princess. Julie smiled to herself as she remembered her mom and Alice working together to make Julie's room anew and fresh. Alice had talked her dad into letting them repaint it; and Ethel had bought the spread, carpet, desk, and chair from an elderly friend that she knew. Her favorite Sunday school teacher had unexpectedly given her the wooden chest, which Julie quickly deemed it to be her "hope" chest, though Matt teased her that it was her "hopeless" chest. Julie kept special things in it that she wanted to save for her future and all the special things that she felt she would want to keep forever.

Somehow, without Julie even knowing how, she had entered into a new season of her life. Alice had brought a new hope to the house and her very presence made it a home. Julie adored her. She treated Julie like a younger sister as much as a daughter. Alice never tried to take Ethel's place in Julie's heart and simply loved Julie. Ethel liked Alice. Surprisingly, the two had become friends. Julie smiled to herself when thinking about this and shook her head gently as if to try to understand it herself. Often, when Ethel came to pick Julie up, if Ron wasn't home, Alice would insist that Ethel come in for a cup of coffee. Ethel wasn't sure about coming in at first, and Julie watched her mom to see if it was still difficult for her to come into this home that was once her own. But too many years had passed, and though at times Julie could see a slight pang in her mom's face, Alice's hospitality and friendship had somehow changed the perspective of the situation. As time passed, the awkwardness faded and the strange friendship had grown.

A loud sound pierced through the silence of the room and startled Julie. "Well, hi Charlie," Julie responded to the loud chirp. "Do you want to come out for a while?" Julie continued talking to the little bird as she sat upright and swung her legs over the edge of the bed. Julie stood up and walked to the far corner of the room where the bird cage stood. She lifted the cage door and reached inside knowing that "Charlie" wouldn't bite her. She pressed her finger up against the little Bee Bee Parrot's chest and waited for him to climb onto her finger. Slowly, Julie pulled him out of the cage and lifted the bird up to her face. It was her Christmas present and the best present that Julie could ever remember receiving.

"Did you think I forgot you?" Julie asked and then stroked the little bird's neck feathers with her other hand. Charlie bent his head and tucked it into his chest feathers and allowed Julie to scratch his head. Shortly, he took his beak and nudged Julie's hand, and then slowly began to walk up her arm until he reached her shoulder. There he lovingly and ever so gently kissed Julie's neck with his beak and then nestled into sitting upon her shoulder.

Julie made herself comfortable once again. She could smell the aroma of the meatloaf that was cooking downstairs as it began to ebb into her room. Everything had changed once again in Julie's life. Ronnie enlisted into the Marine Corps after graduation as he had said that he would do. Jerry had followed the next year in the same footsteps. Jerry had just recently gone to boot camp and shortly thereafter Ronnie had been sent to Vietnam. Julie felt a sorrow in her heart. She closed her eyes and whispered a prayer for her two brothers. She still felt so lost without them. She knew where Vietnam was. She made it a point to watch the nightly news and to learn more about this strange war where her brothers were being sent off to fight. In the last year alone, two young men that were just a little older than Ronnie and Jerry were sent home with only a flag to honor their lives for the sacrifice they had given. Julie brushed away the tears from her eyes.

"Oh God, please, please take care of my brothers. I just couldn't bear it if...." Julie could not say the words.

Julie was so glad that Matt had not planned to go into the Marine Corps. He would graduate this year. Julie knew that he had planned to just try and get a good job and that he was thinking of marrying his girlfriend. Julie was happy for her brother. She wanted him to find some happiness in his life, but she knew that in her heart, she wasn't quite ready to let him go either. Julie mused as she thought of how he also had just settled into the new season of his life.

"Hey, that tickles," Julie said to her little friend as he gently stroked her neck with his beak. Julie put her finger up to his chest as he happily hopped onto it but then clung to her finger when he saw that Julie was going to put him back into his cage. "Come on Charlie. Time to go in." Julie gave him a slight nudge as he reluctantly climbed onto his perch with his little chirp of protest.

Julie walked over to her desk and pulled out the chair. She pushed her schoolbooks to the side and reached for the two letters that rested up against her desk lamp. She fingered them preciously as she began to feel more tears crease from her eyes. She looked at the return addresses. The one was from Paris Island and the other one from Vietnam. Julie had read and reread them over and over again. She pressed them to her heart and held them there and then laid them back onto the desk. She pulled out a pen from her desk drawer and grabbing some paper from her notebook, began to write her letters. "Dear Big Brother,"

"Julie," came a voice from downstairs, "supper is ready," Alice called up.

"I'll be right down," Julie called back. Julie reached for the two letters and grabbed a rubber band that lay upon her desk and wrapped it around them. Slowly, she stood up and walked over to the wooden chest and lifted the lid. There wasn't much in Julie's "hope" chest. She placed these two special letters on a few of her mementos and gently closed the lid.

After dinner, Julie went back upstairs to do her homework. It was Friday evening and she wanted to wait up for Matt to come home from his job. Normally, she would have gone to spend the night with her mom but like so many other things in her life, this had also changed. Ethel and Bob had separated and it looked like they would not get back together again. Julie sat quietly at her desk and fidgeted with her pencil. She found herself lost in thought.

Julie had hoped that both her mom and Bob could work out their differences. As children, they were nearly grown up now and the old pressures of the blended family were no longer problems. Once again, Julie couldn't understand it. She missed her stepsisters and stepbrother. She wondered if she'd ever get to see them again. Just like that, all of a sudden, after six years, they were no longer in her life. Julie's greatest concern, though, was for her mom. To see that same sorrow on her mom's face that she had remembered seeing so many years before when her mom and dad had divorced made Julie's heart ache for her mom. Julie tried to ask Ethel, why Bob and she couldn't try to work it all out, but Ethel would only sadly shake her head. She took Julie's hands into hers and lovingly squeezed them.

Julie studied her mom's face. She saw it etched in pain and her mouth quiver. Julie knew Ethel wanted to explain more to her, but she couldn't speak and hold back the tears at the same time. "It's okay Mom," Julie spoke up. "You, don't have to explain."

Ethel took a deep breath and let out a deep sigh. "You have to know Julie," Ethel paused, trying to gather her thoughts. "Julie, the problems that we couldn't work out in our marriage had nothing really to do with any of you kids, not mine, not his. They were our problems Julie," Ethel spoke softly. "And, Julie, it had nothing to do with me taking you to Ocean City."

Julie felt her mom's hands grasped tightly around her own. She wanted to ask her mom more questions. She wanted to know what would happen to her stepsisters and stepbrother. But it wasn't the time. Julie knew that it was just too painful for her mom to talk about it.

Ethel moved in with the elderly friend that she had bought Julie's furniture from. Ethel paid her a small rent for a room until she could save up enough money for a security deposit for an apartment. Ethel still picked Julie up on Saturdays and Sundays and Julie loved the time that they would spend together, just the two of them. She talked to her mom on the phone often and they met at Gramma Emma's every Tuesday for dinner. Ethel assured Julie that it wouldn't be long until she could get her own place again and Julie could stay with her as they had always done.

Julie felt selfish at the thought of being so happy with Alice, but she was just so glad that Alice had come into her life. *What would Julie have done if her mom and Bob had broken up before Alice had come to live with them? It would have been more than I could have ever borne,* Julie thought soberly to herself. Her dad had quit abusing her since Alice had come to live with them. Julie tried to put the past behind her. She tried to understand this man who was her dad. She tried to look into his heart and see whether he was really changing or whether he would just go back to his old ways. As the thoughts rushed back from her past, Julie felt herself quiver and shake though her room was warm. As much as she wanted to and tried, she knew that she could never trust her dad again. The thoughts made her sad, tumbling over in her mind, quickly bringing her back to a despair that she didn't want to revisit.

Julie abruptly attempted to brush the past aside and turned back to do her homework. But she couldn't concentrate and just sat there flicking her pencil aimlessly from end to end.

Julie was doing well in school and hoped to receive some scholarships to go onto college. She knew that no one on either side of her family had ever gone to college, and it seemed impossible, but she was determined to try her best. She was active in sports, had been elected to the student council, and was well liked by all of her classmates.

With this new season, Julie seemed to blossom. Like a flower, she slowly opened and came out of her depression and the shell that had held her so tightly. No one seemed to understand what had happened to bring Julie out of her depression; and as she became more like her old self, no one asked any questions. Everyone was just so glad that Julie was okay. But Julie knew what had happened. God had given her a new hope.

Somehow, as Julie had made it a point to read her Bible every night and spend time with God, she had begun to learn more about the heart of God. She began to see God differently than the way that people had portrayed Him. She began to experience a love from God that she had never experienced from anyone—to think that God could love her the way that He did knowing all of her dark secrets. *How could He love her so much? How could He care for her and answer her prayers? How could He have lifted her out of that dark pit that was swallowing her up? How could He have brought Alice into her life and stopped the abuse at a time when she had been ready to give up?* This was not the religious God that she had known—a God of rules, damnation, and condemnation—but a God who had become truly real to her and who had showed her His unconditional love.

Julie laid her pencil down and rubbed her tired eyes. She scooted back her chair, stood up, and went to bed to read the Bible. Julie picked up the little black Bible. It wasn't hers. It was Jerry's Bible. She had borrowed it from his room after he had left to go into the service. Julie held the Bible closely to her heart and closed her eyes. Somehow it made her feel close to her brother. She pondered about what he was doing right then and what he was thinking of as he laid in his bunk at boot camp. She wondered about Ronnie and where he was at that exact moment and what he was doing and facing. Julie kept her eyes closed tightly and prayed earnestly for both of her dear brothers. She opened her eyes and opened the old Bible to the New Testament. Julie loved reading the red-lettered words which signified Jesus had spoken them. They spoke such life into her heart and filled her with hope.

There was a soft knock on the door. "It's open," Julie called out. Julie liked the idea that she freely shut her door now and sometimes even locked it, though her dad still seemed bothered by this. He would often knock on her door before he went to bed and say goodnight. Sometimes, he would turn off her light when she had fallen asleep while reading her Bible. Julie wondered if it was the Bible lying in her hands as she slept that stopped him from touching her. Or was it the thought that he would lose Alice or maybe even get caught if he tried. Julie had even pondered that maybe her dad had truly changed. The thought touched her heart and almost beckoned her to trust him and to believe that he had changed. However, the past would come rushing back to her and Julie would find that the very remembrance of the past horrors would still make her shiver inside at the thought of him entering her room without her knowing it while she was asleep. She could not and would not trust him, and never again, would she ever feel safe with him.

To Julie's delight, it was Matt who poked his head through the door. "You still awake?" he asked.

Julie looked at her brother standing in her doorway. His blond hair contrasted with those deep blue eyes.

"Hey, you want to come down and watch some Sherlock Holmes with me?" Matt asked with an impish grin.

"With Basil Rathbone?" Julie asked.

"Yep," Matt answered.

"And you want me to make you a meatloaf sandwich, too; right?" Julie teased.

"Would you?" Matt asked with a big pleading smile on his face.

"Will you do something with me first?" Julie ventured.

"Maybe," Matt answered with his eyebrows shooting up in a questioning way.

"I haven't finished my Bible time yet. But if you'd sing a few songs with me with my organ, I'd be done." Julie smiled at Matt.

Matt smiled back at his young sister. He knew that Julie took her walk with God seriously. He supported her. He had seen how her faith had brought her back to them. He didn't know why Julie had become so broken, and he didn't know how she had come back to being her old self, but all he knew was that he was glad. He knew that Julie clung to him because he was the last of her brothers. But he also wondered if Julie knew that he also clung to her for the same reasons. It had always been the four of them against the world. Matt missed his brothers terribly. He reached out his hand to Julie. "Come on," he said with a feigned look of foreboding.

Julie went to the little organ and sat down and began to play. Matt joined in with her singing the old hymns that they had sung so many years ago at the little country church. Julie loved to hear Matt sing. She looked up at Matt, deeply into his blue eyes. He placed his hand on her shoulder and looked deeply into Julie's eyes. Both teared up and no words were spoken. No words were needed.

Jerry in his Marine uniform

Chapter

13

Julie was so excited to get to school. She grabbed her winter jacket, grabbed her books on the little chair beside the door, and practically jumped into her shoes in one quick movement. She yelled a goodbye to Alice and quickly ran out the front door. She hurried to the bus stop where she met Sarah and Molly.

Julie had been friends with Sarah since they were in first grade together. Molly, Sarah's older sister, was in Matt's class, and had also been Julie's friend for as long as she could remember. She loved being taken under wing, like a younger sister, by Molly and Sarah. They had become inseparable as friends. Julie loved going to their house and visiting them and would often spend the night. They would gather into Molly's room and talk about everything and anything. Sarah and Julie would burst into laughter when Molly would come out of the bathroom, her face caked in white with Noxzema cream. "What?" Molly would ask with an incredulous look on her face, which only made Sarah and Julie laugh all the more.

"You look like a mime," Julie remarked as she and Sarah rolled with laughter.

Sarah and Julie parted ways with Molly when they entered the high school building. As they approached home room, Candy Morris met them. "Hey Sarah, Julie, would you like to have a puppy?"

"A puppy?" Sarah asked. "What in the world are you doing bringing a puppy to school?"

"Donna Martin said that she would love to take him as a pet. I was supposed to meet her and her mother this morning before school started but they didn't show up." Candy let out a deep sigh and then said hopelessly, "and I don't think they're going to show up."

"Wow, you better not let Mr. Jenkins catch you with him!" Sarah said.

Julie pulled back the little blanket that Candy had wrapped around the little puppy to hide him. Instantly, his little head poked out. Julie reached out and tenderly rubbed his ears. "He's so small. What kind of dog is it?"

"He's a Chihuahua," Candy answered.

Sarah saw Candy's eyes light up and gave Julie a gentle poke with her elbow. "We better be getting to class, Julie."

But Julie didn't answer. The dog affectionately licked Julie's hand, and then nudging her with his nose, locked his sad eyes onto Julie's. Julie was already smitten as her eyes met his.

Sarah saw what was happening and gently began to push Julie forward. "Come on, Julie. Don't even think it."

But it was too late. Candy had already laid the bait and was reeling in her fish. "Here, hold him, Julie," Candy ushered as she thrust the little bundle into Julie's arms.

"Oh, Sarah, look. Isn't he just precious?" But before Sarah could answer, Julie turned to Candy and asked, "How big will he get?"

"Not much bigger than he already is," Candy came in for the kill. "And he's already potty trained."

"I'd call him Midget," Julie exclaimed as she leaned down to nestle the little bundle. Without hesitation, the puppy quickly licked Julie across her face. "Isn't he cute, Sarah?"

"Julie, are you crazy? What are you going to do with a dog in school all day, and what if your dad won't let you keep him?"

"I'll call Alice and see what she says. I bet she can talk Dad into it."

Candy was all smiles from ear to ear and appeared as if the burden of the world had been taken off her shoulders. Sarah only sighed and shrugged her shoulders. She knew it would do no good to try to talk Julie out of it. She had known Julie too long. She knew that once she had made her mind up there was no changing it.

Candy started to slowly walk away. "I'll try Candy, but if I can't work it out, you'll have to take him back."

"She probably didn't even hear a word you said," Sarah remarked hopelessly as she glanced first at her friend and then back at Candy who was already halfway down the hall. "So what are you going to do, Julie? It's almost time for the bell to ring?"

"Come on, Sarah. We have to hurry," Julie answered quickly as she wrapped the blanket back over the puppy.

"Here's his box," Sarah said as she followed behind her friend.

Julie darted quickly into the secretary's office. She loved Ms. Moyer, the secretary, but was terrified of Mr. Jenkins, their principal. Mr. Jenkins was an ex-drill-instructor from the Marine Corps whose very presence seemed to keep order in the school. Ms. Moyer had eyes that took you into her heart and a smile that let you know everything would be okay.

Ms. Moyer looked up from her typewriter at Julie and Sarah's appearance. Her dark-rimmed glasses rested gently upon her nose as she peered out over them at the girls. She gave them a broad smile. "How can I help you girls?" she asked warmly.

Sarah looked at Julie, holding back a smile. She was curious to see how her friend was going to talk her way out of this, especially since this was the first time either of them had ever stepped into the office that adjoined the principal's.

"Ah," Julie started nervously. "I wondered if I could use the phone to call home?"

Ms. Moyer could not help but notice the bundle in Julie's arms as it began to wiggle. "Are you sick?" Ms. Moyer asked, knowing full well that Julie was fine.

"Ah, no Ma'am," Julie answered trying harder than ever to keep the bundle still. "It's just…" But it was too late. The puppy had had enough and poked his head from beneath the cover.

Ms. Moyer startled and jumped slightly. She reshifted herself on her chair and looked down for a moment to restrain the laughter she was feeling. She propped her head onto her hand, took her glasses off, and waited for Julie to explain.

Sarah standing there nervously glanced out of the door and down the hallway and then back to the office where the door to Mr. Jenkins' office was closed. Sarah wondered if Mr. Jenkins was already in his office or whether he had not come in yet. Both ideas made Sarah nervous to think what would happen if he walked into this situation. She hoped Julie would hurry up.

Julie took a deep breath. She, too, was as nervous as Sarah and was wondering the same thing.

She let out a sigh and let the words come tumbling out. "Ms. Moyer, Candy Morris brought the dog to school for another girl to take home, but she didn't show up and I thought he was so cute maybe I could take him home; but that would mean that I'd have to keep him here all day because I have no way to get him home but I can't do that until I call my stepmom and ask her if I can keep him; so can I use your phone and can I keep him here just today?" The words tumbled out all in one sentence. Julie hadn't even taken a breath. Sarah looked at her friend incredulously, wondering how she could have spilled out the whole story in just one breath.

Ms. Moyer just sat there, stunned and expressionless. That was the most she had ever heard Julie speak in the two years that she had known her. Lost for words, she reached for the black phone, turned it facing towards Julie, and handed it to her, giving her a big smile.

Julie quickly handed the bundle to Sarah and dialed the number. She knew Alice was home and that her dad was at work. She had hoped that Alice wasn't out in the washroom or outside. The phone rang, once, twice, three times. Julie wondered what in the world she had gotten herself into.

On the fourth ring, Julie heard the familiar voice say, "Hello!"

Sarah stood by and watched trying to contain the puppy that wanted nothing to do with her and insisted on trying to get to Julie. Julie gave Sarah a pleading look to keep the dog settled and quiet. Sarah waited to hear what Julie would say to Alice. Ms. Moyer pretended to go back to her paperwork but listened intently. Neither could believe their ears when Julie rattled off the whole story once again in a single breath. Sarah glanced at Ms. Moyer and saw her turn on her desk chair to hide the laughter she was suppressing. Sarah almost burst out laughing herself but nervously looked down the hallway again. Sarah listened to Julie's part of the conversation and tried to imagine what Alice might be saying to her.

"Alice, do you think that Dad would let me keep him? He's so cute. You'll love him. And he won't get any bigger."

There was a slight pause and then Julie continued. "But I have to decide now; otherwise the girl has to call her mom to get him, and I'm kind of stuck with him now because she went to her classroom."

Another pause and then in a lower voice Julie turned slightly away from Ms. Moyer and continued. "Well, I'm hoping I can keep him with me today until I can bring him home because I know you have no way to come pick him up."

Julie shifted nervously and turned to face Sarah's anxious stare. She listened on the phone as Alice spoke. "You'll do that for me? Do you really think Dad will let me keep him?" Julie asked excitedly. "Alice, thank you. Thank you so much! Wait 'til you see him. You're going to love him." Julie quickly and gently hung up the phone while glancing at Ms. Moyer.

"Well, Julie," Ms. Moyer said. "If you can get the permission of each teacher in each of your classes to let you keep him, then you can try it. But if they won't let you, you'll have to work out another way."

"Thank you Ms. Moyer," Julie said, shooting her a big smile. "Thank you so much."

"Come on Julie," Sarah said nervously. She was sure that their luck was about to run out.

Quickly, both girls hurried out of the office towards their homeroom. The bell rang as they entered into the classroom. Sarah handed Julie her bundle in the box and hurried to her seat leaving Julie to approach their homeroom teacher.

"Say a prayer," Julie whispered to Sarah.

It was the longest day of school that Julie could ever remember. The morning classes went well and all of her teachers agreed. The little puppy slept most of the morning.

Julie showed him to Matt at lunch time. He just chuckled and told her, "Good luck!" After lunch and a few nibbles of Sarah and Julie's lunch and milk, he settled in once again for a puppy nap. He played during Phys. Ed and was made over by all of Julie's classmates.

However, it was the last class that Julie feared the most. It was Mrs. Smith's typing class. Julie knew that she was a strict disciplinarian. She wanted complete silence in her class, and she liked nothing out of the ordinary. Julie wasn't sure whether to be relieved that Mrs. Smith was her last class of the day or if it would have been better if she would've had her class earlier. There was no turning back now.

"What are you going to do?" Sarah asked. "This is going to be the hardest teacher to get permission."

"I know," Julie answered. They had already arrived there early before the bell rang to ask Mrs. Smith before the class began.

The puppy began to whimper. He had had enough of the box

and became restless. "Can you hold him and keep him quiet out here, and I'll go in without him and ask Mrs. Smith?"

Sarah took the box with the puppy and let out a sigh. "I don't know, Julie; he's getting awfully frisky."

"I know," Julie agreed. "We've just got to get through this last class."

"The hardest class," Sarah emphasized, as Julie left her to wrestle with the puppy and went in to talk to Mrs. Smith.

"Well, I really don't think we can do that Julie," Mrs. Smith answered at once, upon Julie's question.

"Please, Mrs. Smith," Julie pleaded. "All of the teachers let me keep him today, and this is my last class."

Mrs. Smith hesitated and then glanced out into the hallway where Sarah stood holding the bundle. Sarah had calmed him down and Mrs. Smith thought that maybe, just this one time. She liked both Julie and Sarah. They were good students and had never asked her for anything. "Well, if you are sure that you can keep him quiet and he won't disturb the class," Mrs. Smith said with a frown of disapproval.

Julie quickly bolted away and met Sarah as she entered the doorway. Promptly, they went to their desks. Julie thought the forty-five minute class would never end. The little puppy refused to settle down and continually tried to climb out of the box. More than once Mrs. Smith had shot her a warning glance.

"We did it!" Julie exclaimed with Sarah as they got off the bus.

Sarah only laughed. "Well, almost," she agreed, as she parted ways with Julie at the bus stop. "Call me and let me know what your dad says."

Julie slowly walked home. Her little friend was asleep in the box and completely exhausted from his day of adventure. Slowly, entering the gate, Julie took a deep breath. Alice had told her on the phone that she would talk her dad into keeping the dog. Julie wondered if she had succeeded as she entered the front door.

❦

Julie was upstairs in her room, sitting at her desk, waiting for her mom to pick her up for the night. She was so excited. Ethel had just moved into a new apartment and Matt was joining them there tonight after work.

Julie heard the gentle scratch on her door and went to open it. "Come on, my little Midget," Julie said, as she reached down and picked up her little dog. Even though he had grown a little, he was still a small dog. She was so surprised when her dad had said that she could keep him. Alice's eyes had met Julie's across the room when her dad had said yes. Julie smiled back and whispered, "Thank you".

Alice had been in their lives for over two years now. It was not as smooth as Julie had thought it would be, but she flourished in the new stability of the home that Alice had made for them. Julie knew that Alice would never know how much her presence and love had affected her life.

Julie heard the voices rise from downstairs. She glanced at the clock on her desk and hoped that she would hear the beep of her mom's horn soon. She knew that her mom wouldn't come over to the house if she saw her dad's car parked at Lindy's Tavern.

Julie hated the times when her dad and Alice would argue. It brought back so many bad memories, and it shook Julie to the very core of her being with the fear of what would happen to her if Alice would ever leave for good. What would she do with her brothers gone and Matt graduating soon? Julie couldn't understand why her dad would roller coaster so much in his relationships. Everything was going so well. They were all so happy. They had driven that summer to Michigan to meet and visit Alice's family. It was a great trip, like a real family.

Shortly, after they had returned, her dad started accusing Alice of wanting to go back home. He would question every letter that she would receive from her mom and sisters, feeling for sure that she would run off to some unknown and non-existent lover that she probably still had back in Michigan. His drinking only escalated and the arguments with it.

Julie thought that she would absolutely die when several times, after threatening to leave her dad, Alice did. She had, at that time, only stayed away for a few days. Julie was terrified the whole time that she was gone. Julie would shut and lock her bedroom door. She would hear the doorknob turn a number of times when her dad had unsuccessfully attempted to come into her bedroom. She was older now. She was no longer the little girl "Julie." She purposed in her heart that he would never touch her again. But the fear of it consumed her.

Julie heard the hard slam of the downstairs bedroom door and the beep of her mom's car horn at the same time. Quickly, she gave her little Midget a hug, which was rewarded by a quick lick of the tongue across her face. She scratched the little dog's ears and hurried out of her bedroom door and down the steps. She paused for a moment at the bedroom door, which Alice had just slammed shut, and knocked on it gently. "I'll see you, Alice," she called out. Julie jerked the front door open and grabbed her coat from the chair. She glanced at her dad who was quietly sitting on the couch and staring down at his beer can. Quickly, she turned before he could say anything to her and ran out of the door.

Alice and Midget

Chapter

14

It was an early spring. The crocuses had bloomed followed by the bright yellow daffodils, and even the tulips and peonies had broken through the ground anxious to usher in a new season. Julie sat on the banister of her front porch and watched for her mom's car to cross the bridge in the distance.

Alice stayed and didn't leave her dad that last time. However, Julie never knew how long Alice would put up with her dad if he didn't change. She had left several times, but she always came back. Julie knew that her dad didn't realize that one day he would push her too far, and then she would leave but would not come back. Julie tried extra hard to let Alice know how much she was loved. She tried to make excuses for her dad and attempted to convince Alice that he really did love her. Julie had even confronted her dad a few times trying hard to not cross a line that was not clearly seen.

"Leave her alone, Dad!" Julie shouted at him one day. He turned to Julie with a stunned look which quickly turned to anger at Julie's defiance.

"You stay out of this, young lady!" he shouted. Alice sadly walked away and went into the kitchen. Julie had watched this beautiful woman, who had brought so much joy into their home, slowly dissolve and disappear. Julie could see the sorrow etched on her face. She knew that brokenness. She had seen it on her mom's face, and she had felt it in her own heart.

If that wasn't enough, her dad had resorted to taking his anger out on Matt. Matt, more than any of them, had always taken the brunt of their dad's anger. Julie recalled the many times that she was confronted with her dad's drunken conversations and how he had tried to convince her that he didn't think Matt was really his son. He felt that Ethel had had an affair on him with another relative. But, Julie thought in many ways, Matt favored their dad more than Jerry. Except for the lighter features of the blond hair and the blue eyes, he had his dad's every feature. But Julie knew that her dad had broken Matt. Maybe in a different way than he had broken her, but all the same he had broken Matt and it crushed Julie's heart.

Julie sniffed her nose and wiped her eyes. She shifted on the banister. She glanced around to make sure that no one saw her brush the tears away. Lately, her dad had taken to really picking on Matt. He accused Matt of insidious things that Julie knew were untrue. Again, she confronted her dad. "Are you crazy? How can you say such things? Leave him alone, Dad!"

After Christmas, her dad had become angry at Matt because he hadn't taken down the Christmas lights on the front porch. Julie felt badly, because she had talked Matt into putting them up. Between school, the weather, work, homework, and his girlfriend, he just hadn't had the chance to take them down. One day, after being dropped off from work, Gramma Emma stopped by and asked Ron if he would drive her up the hill so she wouldn't have to walk home. Matt came running down the steps to leave and go see his girlfriend. "Hi, Gramma," he said as he headed for the front door.

"And where do you think you are going?" Ron asked harshly.

"I'm going out," Matt answered.

"Oh, no you're not!" Ron answered back.

"Dad, I already made plans," Matt answered respectfully. Julie knew that the last thing Matt wanted was to get into an argument with his dad, especially in front of his gramma.

"Well, you aren't going anywhere until you take down those Christmas lights."

"Dad, I'll take them down tomorrow. I can't take them down right now," Matt answered.

"I said you will take them down now!" Ron retorted sternly. Julie knew that now that her dad had made his declaration, there was no way that he would back down in front of their gramma.

"Dad, I can't," Matt said and turned to go toward the front door.

"You stop right there!" Ron demanded as he reached and unhooked his belt and pulled it off in one quick motion.

Julie stood up from her chair. She couldn't believe what she was seeing. Her dad hadn't pulled off his belt to beat them in a long time. They were now grown and usually just pulling privileges or telling them was enough.

Matt stopped dead in his tracks and glared at his dad. His dad was pushing him too far. Matt knew that he was big enough now to not only stop his dad but to put him in his place. However, out of an ill-founded respect, he couldn't bring himself to touch the man who stood before him with the belt drawn in midair.

I said, "You will take those lights down tonight."

Matt's head hung down. Julie could see the sorrow and anger meshed as one. Matt said nothing and started to walk to the door.

"No! Ron, stop that!" Emma cried out, as the belt struck Matt.

Ron shot Emma a look of disdain and raised the belt again.

"No!" Alice cried out, but the belt found its intended mark.

"Stop it, Dad! Stop it right now!" Julie screamed, tears coming down her cheeks.

Matt stopped quickly as the impact of the belt hit him again. He turned and glared at his dad as he faced him head on. His hands were clenched tight, his arms straight, braced in a stance that Julie knew that he would not take another hit.

Ron raised the belt, daring Matt to come at him. Julie leaped between her dad and Matt. She faced her dad directly on. "Stop it

Dad!" She could see in her dad's face that he knew that he had gone too far, but that he also didn't intend to have his pride back down.

"Move, Julie!" he commanded.

"No, Dad. Stop it!" Julie cried out.

"Ron, stop this right now," Emma stepped closer to her son.

"Ron, please," Alice pleaded. "Enough."

But it was too late. It all happened so fast. Julie thought that her dad would put the belt down. She turned from her dad to her brother. "Just go ahead and leave, Matt," she encouraged him. Tenderly she touched his shoulder. And then suddenly she felt the sting of the belt on her back through her blouse. It caused her to jump and her eyes flinched in pain. She turned to glance at her dad and saw Emma and Alice step between her and her dad. They yanked the belt out of his hand, yelling at him and pushed him away.

Matt started to push past Julie to go at his dad. "No, Matt. It's okay; just go. Let it go," Julie said in a low voice. She braced both of Matt's shoulders with her hands to hold him back and to emphasize her point and then she released him and gave him a hug. He hugged her back and glared over her shoulders at their dad and turned and left.

Julie heard the beeping of her mom's horn, surprised that she had not even seen her pull in; she had been so lost in her thoughts. Quickly, she jumped off of the banister and ran to meet her mom. Julie couldn't help notice that her mom seemed to be more like her old self. Every so often, though, when her mom thought that she wasn't looking, Julie would see the shadow of sorrow resting upon her. Usually, when Ethel would be alone in the kitchen drinking a cup of coffee, Julie would see her staring down at her cup in deep thought. It had been almost a year and a half since she had left Bob. It still made Julie sad that they couldn't work things out. She so missed Bob and her step-siblings.

Julie wondered if maybe her mom was seeing someone. She didn't press Ethel for answers but saw a new life in her mom's face as they talked in the car.

"So how is school going, Honey?" Ethel asked. She turned and looked at her little girl who was turning into a beautiful young woman.

"It's going so good, Mom," Julie answered happily.

"Did you ever hear from anyone as to where Lindsey moved?" Ethel asked.

Julie frowned and shook her head and then laughed out loud nervously. "No, Mom, and I hope she never moves back. I heard she was going to a school pretty far away but that we might play them in football this year."

"What will you do when you see her?" Ethel asked.

"Well, I won't ignore her," Julie answered quickly and firmly.

"Good for you, Honey," Ethel said. She marveled at the young woman before her and wondered where the little girl had gone.

Julie looked over at her mom and continued, "But, I won't go looking for her either," Julie said with an impish smile on her face.

"I've got some good news, Mom," Julie said excitedly. She couldn't wait to tell her mom.

"What?" Ethel inquired with a smile and then asked, "Hey, you want an ice cream before we go to the apartment?"

"Sure," Julie answered and continued, "Mom, Mrs. Marshall asked me if I wanted to represent our class at Girl's State Camp this summer. There were only two of us picked out of our class."

Ethel pulled into the dairy and parked the car. She reached over and gave Julie a hug and then cupped her hands around Julie's face. "I am so very proud of you, Julie!"

Julie smiled back. "I've never been to a camp before."

"Oh, it'll be fun," Ethel reassured her. "You won't want to come home."

"I have something to tell you too," Ethel said softly as they ate their ice cream cones. "I have a new friend that I want you to meet," Ethel said slowly. "I know you wanted Bob and me to get back together."

"Mom, I want you to be happy," Julie said. She looked deeply into her mom's blue eyes. The same eyes that she saw when she looked into Matt's. "We're almost grown up now, Mom. I'll be sixteen years old, and Matt's graduating soon. I just want you to be happy, Mom."

Ethel smiled at Julie. She reached over and squeezed her hand and then started the car. "Matt will be off work soon. Let's talk him into playing some Rummy with us," Ethel suggested.

Sixteen years old, Julie thought to herself as she sat at her desk. Charlie chirped in the corner while Midget lay on the carpet near her feet. It was as if the walls of her bedroom had become her home. She loved her bedroom. It had become her own little getaway.

Julie reached across her desk and picked up the letter from Jerry. He was in California now and would soon be sent to Vietnam. She tenderly fingered the letter and pulled it out to read it over again. She then laid the letter down and etched her fingers over the writing as if to feel her brother's presence. But there were no letters from Ronnie. Even Jerry, in his letters to her and to her mom, had asked them about Ronnie. Julie wrote Jerry back and tried to reassure him that Ronnie was okay and that he was probably in an area where he just couldn't write.

Julie had talked at length with her mom at Gramma Winnie's house on Tuesday. "Where is he, Mom?" Julie asked.

"I don't know," Ethel answered sadly.

"I haven't heard from him either," Winnie added, with a worried look on her face.

Julie became engulfed in concern and worry for her brother. Even if it wasn't regularly, Ronnie would always write the three of them in cycles. For none of them to have received a letter disquieted Julie terribly. Julie could see by the look on both her mom's and her gramma's faces that they were very much worried also.

"How long has it been since you got a letter from him?" Ethel asked Winnie.

"Probably about a month," Winnie replied sadly.

"How about you, Julie?" Ethel asked.

"Probably five or six weeks," Julie answered.

"It's been about that for me too," Ethel added. "I'm going to contact the Red Cross this week and see if they can find out any information about him.

Julie tried to steady her voice. She could see the tears in both her mom's and gramma's eyes. "You don't think something happened to him, do you Mom?"

"No," Ethel said, sniffing back her tears.

Winnie stood up and filled the coffee pot with water. She didn't say a word as she added the grounds to the filter and plugged in the pot.

"He'll be okay," Ethel said out loud.

Julie wondered whether her mom was trying to convince them or herself.

Matt's Graduation Picture

Chapter

15

Julie awoke with a start. She heard a slight whimper somewhere beside her. She rubbed her eyes and opened them wide. There beside her bed sitting up in a begging stance was her little Midget. His sad little eyes met Julie's, pleading for her to let him come up onto the bed. Julie felt like she was still half-asleep. Midget had always slept with her and he never sat begging but would always just jump up onto the bed. "Well, come on 'Midg'," Julie said with a puzzled look on her face. But Midget continued to sit in her begging position whimpering. Julie patted the bed and then moved slightly to make room for her little dog to jump up. Suddenly a loud unpleasant chirp startled Julie and stopped her in her movement. Only then did Julie see the reason that Midget was crying and wouldn't jump up onto the bed. "Why you little stinker," Julie laughed as she looked at her parrot Charlie who was comfortably resting on Julie's hip. "How did you get out?" Julie looked at Charlie and then at Midget. Midget placed his feet onto the side of the bed and prepared to jump up but the bird immediately dodged for him with his beak ready to bite. Midget slumped back to the floor and sadly looked at Julie. "Won't that mean birdie let you up onto the bed?" Julie asked with a slight chuckle. Slowly, as she turned in the bed, Charlie two-stepped up her body to Julie's outreached finger. He clung on as Julie lovingly stroked the bird. "Come on," she said as she stood up and walked over to the cage with Charlie hanging on tightly. "Let's see how you got out." Julie could hardly believe the bird had popped the top of his cage off by using his beak like a can opener. Julie reached over the exposed top of the cage and gently put Charlie onto his perch and then popped back on the top of the cage. "You're a naughty little bird today," Julie said and laughed. Charlie chirped back at her and snuggled up to take a nap after successfully taking back his territory from his new rival.

Julie plopped back down on her bed and snuggled under the covers. Midget immediately jumped up and proceeded to kiss and lick Julie ferociously without stopping. Julie scratched his ears and pulled him close to her as he snuggled into Julie's arms claiming back his rightful place.

The sunlight streamed through the curtains casting little prisms that danced across the green carpet and seemed to flicker and flutter like little mystical fairies. Julie glanced out the window without moving so as not to disturb the sleeping Midget. She could see that it was going to be a beautiful day. It appeared that spring had come early and Julie was glad. The weather had been unseasonably warm.

Julie laid in the quietness and listened for a sound, or any noise that might come from downstairs. But everything remained quiet. Too quiet. Julie could never determine what bothered her the most, the loud arguing or the deafening silence. All her life, she knew that both declared a clear battleground.

Julie knew that it was only a matter of time before it would happen. It was just too much for Matt to endure. In the last argument between Matt and her dad, Matt had left home for good. Her dad just wouldn't let up. It was as if he had some point to prove and was determined to prove it no matter what it took or who it hurt. Julie had left home that same day, the day Matt moved out, and had refused to come back unless her dad would make it right with Alice and Matt. Uncle Tom and Aunt Lisa had welcomed her to stay with them. Julie had moved in with them for a week. She knew that her dad would never concede to her demands for him to apologize. Alice had asked her to come back home. Julie was afraid that if she didn't go back that Alice might leave her dad again. She missed Alice. Julie just couldn't bear to see Alice suffer because of her actions. She also didn't want to be a burden on her aunt and uncle by continuing to stay at their home. Even though she had eventually returned to keep the peace, taking a stand against the wrong that her dad had done felt empowering to Julie. Matt promised her that he would stop by and see her and that they'd hang out together over at their mom's apartment on the weekends.

Julie slowly crawled out of the blankets without disturbing her sleeping Midget. She went over and sat down at her desk. Her dad was off today, but it didn't surprise Julie how quiet it was downstairs. Alice and he were hardly talking. As sad as this made Julie, she was glad that Alice had not just given in to her dad as she had always done in the past. Maybe her dad would see with all of them standing up to him that he couldn't treat people the way he did.

Julie rubbed her head trying to erase the headache that was throbbing in her temples. *But wonder if Alice decided to leave for good and to move back to Michigan. What would Julie do without her? How could she live alone with her dad now that Matt had moved out? How could she start in a new school in a different town if she moved in with her mom?* Julie looked down at her desk and stared aimlessly. *I will not stay here if Alice moves out,* Julie vowed to herself. *I won't! I don't know where I will go but I will not stay here!*

Julie pulled out the drawer to her desk, reached inside and grabbed some paper. She began her letter as always, "Dear Big Brother,"....

Jerry was stationed in California now, finishing his training and waiting to be sent to Vietnam. Julie had learned that he wouldn't be sent to Vietnam until Ronnie had returned. She finished writing her letter to Jerry, licked the envelope, and addressed it. Julie remained sitting at her desk, remembering her conversation with her mom a few weeks earlier. She debated whether she should write another letter. A letter to the President!

Ethel had heard from the Red Cross. Ronnie was alive! He was not injured! It had taken the Red Cross several weeks to find Ronnie. There were some problems and at first the details were sketchy. Later, they had learned that Ronnie was being sent to California and would then be released and sent home. As far as Julie had understood, Ronnie was due to return home from Vietnam soon anyway, as his tour was almost up. *But what problems were they talking about?* Julie had wondered at first, but then shrugged it off. It didn't matter what the problems were; all that mattered was that Ronnie was alive and that he would be coming home.

However, as the Red Cross discovered more information, Julie and her mom realized that the problems were serious. Ronnie had not written because mentally he couldn't. He was totally incoherent of the world he was living in. He didn't even know his name or who he was. They were sending home a shell that was once her brother; however, Ronnie was no longer there.

Julie remembered how hard her mom had cried as she told Julie and Gramma Winnie the details of Ronnie's condition.

"Ethel, what can we do? How can we get him help? They can't just send him home this sick?" Winnie asked with tears streaming down her face.

"Mom, we've got to do something," Julie added. They all sat and cried.

After a while, Ethel continued, "The Red Cross told me that there was nothing else that they could do. All I know to do is to write our senators and congressmen."

"Are you going to write to them, Mom?" Julie asked. "Do you think they'll help us get Ronnie some help?"

"I don't know?" Ethel answered sadly.

"I'll write the President then," Julie said emphatically. "He's got to help."

Julie's zeal made Ethel and Winnie smile. "Don't be disappointed if you don't get an answer, Julie," Ethel said as she affectionately patted Julie's hand.

"Well, he has to answer!" Julie replied matter-of-factly. "Ronnie volunteered to go. He wasn't drafted. He was proud to serve his country. All his life, all that he ever wanted and talked about was being a Marine and fighting for freedom. They can't just send him back home like this. They have to get him some medical help. They just have to!"

"I know," Ethel agreed wearily. "I know."

"And what about Jerry?" Julie asked.

"He's already got his orders to go to Vietnam," Ethel answered. "He'll ship out any day now."

"So, Ronnie comes back and they don't want to help him and now they're going to send Jerry over to the same place?" Julie let her voice rise and could not withhold her worry and frustration.

And so with that information, a week later, Ethel had let Julie know that she did write their local senators and congressmen. Julie had wondered, at that time, what she could do to help her brothers.

Julie held the letter in her hand that she had just written to Jerry. She fingered it lovingly and wondered what Jerry was doing and thinking at that very moment. She thought of her beloved Ronnie and wondered what he could possibly be thinking or if he was able to think at all. She stirred in her chair and stretched out her legs under her desk, placing her clamped hands behind her head. She stared up at the ceiling. Julie felt at a loss with what she could do to help her brothers. Her dad had told her that it would be futile for her to write the President and that no one would probably even read a letter written from her, definitely not the President. *But what could she do? She had to try to do something, anything.*

Julie's eyes were fixed upon the small picture which hung above her desk. When they had painted the room, Julie just had to put it back on the wall. It was worn and ragged, but it just meant too much to Julie for her to not hang it back up on her wall. The picture of Jesus—His gentle eyes seemed to search hers. The little cross was still attached to the bottom of it and it still glowed in the dark. The comfort this little token from Sunday school had given her through the years was too precious for her to throw out. It moved her heart.

Julie reached for the Bible that sat on her desk. "Oh, God, please help us. Please help my Ronnie and protect my Jerry," she pleaded out loud. *If only I had a promise from God*, Julie thought. *If I could just know, somehow, that Ronnie was going to be okay.* Julie closed her eyes with the Bible in her hands and opened it up at random. She stared at the page before her and let her eyes fall upon the scripture. She read the verse out loud, "And then Jesus said to Martha, 'thy brother shall rise again.'" Julie read the verse over and over again. It was so sure, so promising, and she knew that it was meant just for her. She would stand on His promise. Martha's brother had died and now Jesus was telling her that he would rise again which was impossible. It looked impossible that Ronnie would ever rise again too; but God was telling her, she knew He was, that Ronnie would rise again.

Immediately, a new hope arose within Julie. She quickly jerked the desk drawer open, grabbed a few pieces of paper and began to write.

"Dear Mr. President,".... And then she added, *"Usually, if a soldier dies, you send them home with a flag. You are sending my brother home and he is alive, but he is dead inside and no one will tell us how we are to get him the help he needs."*

Julie was about to close the letter when the thought of Jerry being in Vietnam came to her heart. She added one last paragraph, *"And my other brother Jerry Clayton has just been sent to Vietnam, and you better not let the same thing happen to him!"*

Julie concluded with a thank you and sealed the envelope. She addressed it simply—The President, White House, Penn Avenue, Washington, D.C. She reached and grabbed two stamps, placing them onto the letters, one to Jerry and one to the President of the United States.

Julie stayed overnight with her mom. Matt came home early from work and hung out with them. They sat and ate dinner together and talked about how much they missed Ronnie and Jerry.

Ronnie was in California being evaluated, while Jerry was now stationed in Vietnam. Julie continually wrote both of them letters. Julie shared her promise from God with Ronnie, "her brother would rise again." She and her mom would continue to receive letters from Jerry, but usually only her mom would get a short note from Ronnie. One day, Julie received a letter from Washington, D.C stating that they had received her letter and that they would review and look into it. Her dad had told her that it was just a form letter that they automatically sent out. But Julie continued to hope that every letter that both she and her mom wrote would help Ronnie get the help that he needed.

Matt and Julie stood up from where they were sitting to call it a night and to go to bed. "You coming to bed, Mom?" Julie asked.

"Not right now," Ethel answered as she poured herself a fresh cup of coffee. "I think Bucky is going to stop by yet." Julie leaned down and gave her mom a kiss on the top of her head.

"Mom told me that she has to work in the morning, so I'll drop you off downtown in the morning to meet Sarah and Molly at the Five and Ten Cent Store, if you're still planning to do that," Matt said to Julie as they left the kitchen.

"Thanks, Matt," Julie answered. "That would be great if you could."

Matt lay down on the couch to go to sleep, while Julie went into her mom's bedroom. She paused at the door and glanced at her mom sitting at the little kitchen table. She sat drinking her coffee, with her head hung low, intensely working the crossword puzzle in the newspaper. For the first time in a long time, Julie thought that she looked happy.

Julie heard a faint knock on the door and watched her mom scoot back her chair to go answer it. Julie quietly closed the bedroom door as she heard Buck come in. His deep voice, though in a whisper, resonated throughout the little apartment.

Julie laid in the bed allowing her thoughts to bounce to and fro, from school to her mom with her new friend Buck, to Matt's pending engagement, to Ronnie's condition, to Jerry in Vietnam, and then to Alice and her dad's relationship. Julie was so tired and just wanted to fall asleep; however, it seemed that her mind just wouldn't settle down. It was as if, somehow, by thinking of it all, Julie thought she would surely find an answer and some resolve.

Julie wanted life to be happy. She wished that for just a period of time that things could remain stable. She hated change. Nothing ever seemed to stay the same. It seemed that life would only allow things to remain the same long enough for her to get used to it and enjoy it; and then without warning, life would yank out the rug of stability as quickly as it could from beneath her.

Julie had sadly hoped that after Matt had moved out of their house, that surely, her dad would quit picking on Alice. But he didn't. Almost every night and after bowling, he would drink; and before they could even get in the front door they were arguing. He constantly accused her of having an affair, which Julie knew was impossible because she was with Alice almost all of the time that her dad wasn't. He had even gotten to the point where he wouldn't allow Julie to go and visit her friends until he returned home from work. He didn't even want Alice to go visit with Aunt Lisa. Julie could see her dad squeezing the very life out of Alice. She had lost weight and her hands shook nervously all of the time from the stress.

Julie heard a deep voice from the kitchen. It was Buck. She couldn't help but like him. He was such a nice man and a hard worker. He rarely drank and if he did, very little. Actually, Julie had never seen him drink. A smile came across Julie's face as she pictured him in her mind with his salt and pepper hair, his kind eyes, and the half stub of a cigar that always hung from his mouth. He had a smile that always made Julie feel the way that she thought a daughter should feel. Warmth radiated from him, and he was so good and kind to her mom. She still missed Bob, her step-father, and her step-siblings; but Julie realized that it was truly over, and she didn't know when or if she would ever get to see them again.

This is what tore Julie up so badly. Every time that she would finally open her heart to someone and let them in, the seasons of life would change, and then they would be gone. Julie tried to build walls around her heart to protect it but God would not let her. His love always tore them down. *"Come unto me, you that are heavy laden, and I will give you rest."* She would read the Bible at night and the Word would keep her heart soft. *"Harden not your heart in the day of provocation."*

Julie turned on her bed and tried to get comfortable. She thought of her brothers and missed them so much. She missed their camaraderie, love, and friendship. Matt talked everyday about getting married. The news, every evening, kept saying that the war in Vietnam would soon be over and that the troops would soon be pulling out; however, even as they would say that, the news footage would show the heated battles. Almost everyday, there was another soldier's name in the obituary of their newspaper. *And then her Ronnie, what would happen to him? How could she get him back?* Amidst it all, the promise would spring from her heart and echo in her mind, *"Thy brother shall rise again."*

Julie took a deep breath, letting out a sigh. She turned on her side and changed her thoughts to a new subject, her birthday. She was going to be sixteen years old. She couldn't believe it. She felt so grown-up. She would be entering the eleventh grade next year. She had her life all planned out. She wanted to get scholarships and go to college and then meet her prince charming, fall in love, get married, and have a Christian home and....Julie fell sound asleep.

The sound of Matt's voice calling her woke her up from a deep sleep. Julie smelled the bacon and eggs that her mom was frying. She knew that Buck had brought the food. She saw the grocery bag in his arms when he had come in the door the night before.

Julie hurriedly got up and dressed and joined Matt and her mom at the little kitchen table. It was a small apartment, but Julie loved it. No matter where her mom had ever lived, it always felt full of warmth and love and like the home that Julie had always remembered from her childhood. Ethel shared with them that she was going to look for a bigger apartment in nearby Benson. Ethel had thought that when Ronnie would be able to come home, it would be nice for her to have a place for him to stay. It would be too much for him to stay at Gramma Winnie's house. Julie thought it was a great idea. Her mom and brother would then be living closer to her. If Ethel could find such an apartment, they would be living in the same town as her high school.

Julie hopped out of Matt's car and waved goodbye. "I'll see you later, Jul," Matt called out as she turned to run into the store to look for Sarah and Molly. It didn't take Julie long to find them.

Shortly, Molly stated that they should really be going.

"Oh..., do we have to go already?" Julie pleaded. She waited for Sarah to join with her in begging Molly to not take them home yet; however, Sarah remained quiet. Julie poked Sarah with her elbow in the ribs to get Sarah to jump in on the conversation. Surprisingly, Sarah just shrugged her shoulders. "Well, let's first at least go over to the Coney Island and get a hot dog and chocolate coke," Julie proposed.

"I can't, Julie," Molly answered.

"No, we gotta get home," Sarah joined in.

"Really? How come?" Julie asked. They always told her what their plans were. But this time they both just shrugged their shoulders.

"I've got to get Dad's car back," Molly seemed to struggle getting the words out, almost as if she was feigning an excuse.

"Yea," Sarah reiterated.

"Okay," Julie said reluctantly. She felt a little disappointed. She had hoped that she could spend the day with Molly and Sarah. The last thing she wanted to do was to go home and walk into the middle of an argument, especially since today was her birthday. That was the other reason Julie felt a little hurt. Neither Molly nor Sarah had even mentioned or said "Happy Birthday" to her.

Molly pulled the large white Ford into an empty slot at Lindy's Tavern. Julie said goodbye and quickly hopped out of the car. "Hey, we'll walk you over," Molly and Sarah called out almost in unison.

"Okay," Julie answered as she shrugged her shoulders. Julie found it strange because they would usually just pull off the shoulder of the road for her to hop out and would never walk over to the house with her.

Maybe I'm just tired today, Julie thought. She couldn't figure out Molly and Sarah's strange behavior.

There was a strange stillness as they approached the front door. Usually, Midget would start barking at the first sound of the clank of the gate.

Julie gave the stuck front door a quick hard push to get it open. As the door fell open, it took Julie with it.

"SURPRISE! SURPRISE! SURPRISE!" The small quiet living room suddenly burst with life and then another round of "SURPRISE! SURPRISE! SURPRISE!"

Julie just stood there in the small room, her hand still on the handle of the door with her mouth wide open. She was speechless. The living room was so full of people; Matt, Ethel, Alice, and about eight of her school friends. It was a surprise birthday party for her. Julie had never in her life had any kind of party. She heard the laughter behind her as Molly and Sarah pushed Julie into the room and shut the door behind them.

Julie couldn't help it. Tears just came rushing out of her eyes. Never in her life had she felt loved by so many people. "Your mom and Alice pulled it all together," Molly explained.

"It was our job to keep you away until 1:00," Sarah explained.

It was a beautiful party. Julie could not even remember when she had ever felt so happy.

Julie, Matt, Ronnie, Jerry

Chapter

16

Julie finished up the last of the dishes, wiped her hands on the dish towel, and draped the damp towel over the side of the kitchen chair. She glanced into the living room where Alice sat quietly crocheting and watching her soap opera. Alice glanced over at Julie and smiled. "You okay?" Alice asked.

"Yea, I think I'll take a little walk outside," Julie answered.

School was out for spring break, and Julie felt anxious and restless. Molly and Sarah were away for the day. Julie was so lost without her brothers. She wondered how life could be so ever-changing—so full of hope at one moment and so full of despair at other times. She knew that a walk would be good for her and would help her to clear her mind.

Julie grabbed the white glass knob of the kitchen door and turned it slowly. She paused as she opened the door and scanned the little kitchen. The kitchen held so many memories of her childhood years. As she closed her eyes, she could hear their childhood voices echo in her mind. She could visualize Jerry and her making Christmas cookies and potato candy. She could hear Ronnie and Matt join them for samples. She could hear their laughter. She glanced at the worn table and chairs and remembered all the times that her brothers had helped her with her homework. She recalled how they would sit at this very table and with a butter knife diligently try to get their money out of their bronze glass piggy bank, in which they together, saved all of their money to buy their Christmas gifts. It was difficult to get the money out of that piggy bank; that's why they always put it in there. It had a triangular piece of glass missing out of its side where somehow one of them had broken it. The hole made it helpful in maneuvering the change when getting it to fall out of the slot at the top of the bank.

Julie recalled how during that four weeks before Christmas, they would make a pact between the four of them to skip their lunches. Lunch was the only one good meal that they could depend on having to eat. Julie wondered now, as she did then, how they ever gave up their lunches. But with each of them skipping their lunch, they could each save $1.25 a week. This times four gave them a total savings of $5.00 a week. In four weeks they were able to save $20.00, and this was just enough for them to buy Christmas presents for their mom and dad and four grandparents. It allotted them about $3.00 apiece per present with tax. Julie smiled to herself as she tried to remember exactly how many bottles of Evening in Paris perfume they had bought for their mom and how many bottles of Old Spice aftershave they had bought for their dad throughout the years.

Julie turned and walked out onto the summer porch. The metal cabinet still sat in the corner where they still hid a spare key. Julie opened the screened door and went down the steps and sat down. She noticed the peonies completely leafed out, full of bud, and ready to bloom. She glanced over at the yard where they had all played every game imaginable, from football to hide and seek. Julie stood up, letting the May sun beat down upon her. It was a beautiful spring day. Julie walked around the corner of the house and paused at the woven lattice. She touched it gently as to capture a memory of long ago of her beloved cocker spaniel, Mamie. Julie followed the sidewalk that wound around the house. She then passed the budding pear tree and circled back to the front porch which was surrounded with lilac and rose bushes. The lilacs were in full bloom. She took a deep breath and then climbed up onto the banister where she could sit and enjoy their fragrance. Julie could see, in her mind's eye, Matt sitting exactly where she was sitting with his feet dangling above the beer cans that they had been using for bowling pins. He was the unofficial pin sitter. She glanced to the end of the long porch where she envisioned Jerry and Ronnie with their softball ready to bowl. They had had some pretty serious bowling tournaments on this porch.

Julie smiled. The memories made her happy, not sad. These were the good times, which had carried them all through the difficult times. And they weren't gone but lived forever in her heart and filled it full of comfort. Those memories kept Jerry and Ronnie so near to her while they were so far away. Somehow, she could just close her eyes and all four of them were together again, and it was good.

Julie leaned against the banister post and sat with her legs outstretched and crossed. Her back was turned in the opposite direction of the traffic from the main road. Julie let her mind skip even further back to the little white house with the red shutters. She could picture all of them together. Her brothers' love filled her heart. As Julie pondered this, words seemed to come to her mind in the form of a poem. *I should write it down,* Julie thought.

With one quick leap, Julie jumped down and ran across the porch to the front door. She hurried into the house and gave Alice a quick smile and then dashed up the steps. Midget followed closely behind her and darted into the bedroom just before she closed her door. Julie pulled her desk chair out and quickly seated herself as she grabbed a pencil and paper and jotted the words down that were tumbling in her mind before she would forget them.

When she was done, she read the words out loud to herself. They brought tears to her eyes, but then...she was ready to roll the paper up and throw it away. *Oh, anyone else would just think it was a corny poem.* Julie paused. *I bet Mom, wouldn't think it was corny,* Julie thought. *I bet Mom would like it.* She picked up a clean sheet of paper and rewrote it neatly. Mother's Day was on Sunday. She would pick some lilacs for her mom and give her the poem that she had written.

Julie was in such a good mood. She ran down the steps and told Alice that she was going to walk up to the post office and see if there were any letters from Jerry or Ronnie.

Julie walked along the country road. Periodically, a car would pass by and she would leave the pavement and walk onto the dirt shoulder. July loved the spring season. There was a fragrance of sweet aromas that filled the air, a mixture of all the flowers that were in bloom meshing into one. The sun beat down upon Julie's face causing her to squint her eyes. The warm gentle breeze blew her hair and seemed to breathe new life into her. Julie entered the post office and picked up her family's mail. Quickly, she leafed past the bills and junk mail in search for a letter. There it was, at the bottom of the pile. A letter from Jerry, and this one was for her. At times, he would write one letter to all of them; however, it was the times when she would receive her very own letter from him that would touch her heart the most.

The letter was too special to open at the post office. Julie hurried out the door and practically ran home. She bolted through the front gate and flung it hard behind her. She heard the loud clank as the latch caught and the gate shut tight. She ran around to the back porch and sat down on the steps. She laid the other mail beside her and took her brother's letter into her hand. She held it to her heart and thanked God. Every time that she received a letter, she knew that Jerry was still alive.

Slowly, she lifted the letter out of the envelope. *"Dear Julie,"* the letter began. *"How are you, my wonderful little sister?"* Julie lit up like a Christmas tree at her brother's words. The letter continued and Julie studied it intently as she read.

"Julie, my C.O. (Commanding Officer) got that letter you wrote to the President. He called me in, and Mart, I read it. I'm glad you think so

much of your brothers, Jul. He said that I should write and let you know that Don was back in the States. I thought I did. But, thanks for doing everything you do, Jul, but you don't have to write to the President of the U.S. to prove how much you love us, Jul."

Julie laughed out loud. She couldn't believe it. They had taken her letter so seriously, even to the point of contacting Jerry's Commanding Officer. Julie continued to read the letter soaking in every word that Jerry wrote. Because of the letter, Jerry was questioned by his Commanding Officer concerning his intent to be there. Jerry had assured him that he had come to serve. Everyone in command had taken the letter very seriously. Julie smiled again, as she read the last paragraph of his letter. *"I'll go now, Jul, but take care and write soon! To me of course (not the President.) Ha! Ha!"*

Julie knew that her brother was touched by her love for him. But she agreed with him that she probably shouldn't write the President again. It made her happy, though, that the President's office had followed through. Surely, if they had taken the time to track down Jerry, then they would be following up on Ronnie's care, too. Julie couldn't wait to show her mom the letter. She jumped up quickly, grabbed the rest of the mail, and hurried into the house to show Alice the letter. She couldn't wait for her dad to see it too.

Julie anxiously waited for her mom to pick her up that evening. She was so excited to show her Jerry's letter. She showed the letter to her dad when he came home from work. Julie could tell that he was not only surprised that the President's office had responded but also that he seemed just happy that we had heard from Jerry. Julie studied her dad's face as he read the newspaper. She wanted so much to try to understand this man who was her father. She felt that he was honestly concerned for Jerry—and Ronnie, too. At times, he could be so nice and even a normal father. But then at other times, the other person would evolve, the man who was mean and heartless, cruel and selfish. *How could she ever figure him out? How could she ever look to him as her dad after all that he had done?* If she could just erase the bad and pretend that it had never happened. If she could just know that he was sorry and would never hurt her again. But no, she could not be convinced into trusting him ever again. The risk was too great. The pain was too devastating. Julie shook inside at the mere remembrance of her past and shoved it out of her mind.

Julie knew the sound of the familiar horn. She quickly gathered her things and ran out the front door. She jumped into the car and slid across the front seat. "Look, Mom!" Julie said excitedly as she tried to catch her breath. "You gotta read this letter from Jerry."

Ethel broke away from her thoughts, turned the car engine off, and quickly took the letter that Julie handed her. Ethel read the letter quickly. She turned to Julie and smiled a big smile. "Looks like you got the President's attention," Ethel remarked with a light laugh.

Julie laughed, too. "I can't believe they tracked down Jerry, Mom."

"Me, too," Ethel agreed as she re-scanned the letter. "Well, if that's what it takes Julie, we'll just keep writing letters to whoever will listen." Ethel neatly folded the letter and carefully placed it back into the envelope. "Let's ride up to Gramma Winnie's and show her and grandpap the letter."

They sat in the small kitchen and talked. Gramma Winnie cut Julie a piece of her fresh homemade bread and spread a whole glob of real butter on it until it melted down the sides of the bread.

"I've some news to tell you, too," Ethel said.

Julie studied her mom's face to determine if it was good or bad news, but she couldn't tell. Julie listened intently while Gramma Winnie pulled up a chair and sat down next to Grampap John as he was eating his supper.

"I received a letter from California, and they said that they are going to give Ronnie an Honorable Medical Discharge. They feel that he is well enough now to come home."

"That's good news. Right, Mom?" Julie asked. She wanted to jump up and down and shout for joy that Ronnie was coming home. But for some reason the joy of the message was being contained by her mom and Julie wasn't sure why.

"It is good news, isn't it Ethel?" Winnie asked.

"Is he really well enough to come home?" Grampap John asked quietly.

"That's my only reservation," Ethel answered back to all three of them.

"When?" Julie asked excitedly. *Thy brother shall rise again.* The words resounded within her heart. *Surely, Ronnie would be okay or they wouldn't send him home yet,* Julie thought.

"Probably in the next week," Ethel answered with her hope and excitement rising. "The only thing is that I haven't found a bigger apartment yet that I can afford."

"Well, he can stay here with us," Winnie said excitedly.

Ethel looked over at John. "Well, of course, he can stay here with us," he reiterated what Winnie had said.

Ethel took a deep sigh and a smile came over her face. For the first time, Julie saw complete joy flood over her mom as if a big weight had been taken off her with the reality that Ronnie was truly coming home.

"We better stop by and tell your dad and Alice on the way back through," Ethel remarked to Julie as they got into the car and waved goodbye to Winnie and John.

"Mom, do you think all the letters that we wrote helped Ronnie and Jerry?" Julie asked.

Ethel smiled and reached over and took Julie's hand. "I do," she answered.

"I know that God gave me that promise for Ronnie, Mom. I just know it," Julie said.

It was evening, before they could share the news with Matt. Julie saw him beam with joy. "Now we just need to get Jerry home safe," Matt spoke in deep thought. Then to lighten the moment, he said, "Why don't you just write the President, Jul, and ask him if Jerry can come home early." Matt then laughed.

It was a day of celebration. Ronnie was coming home. Julie felt more excitement now than at Christmas. She could hardly wait for Ronnie to come home, and she couldn't wait to write Jerry and tell him the good news.

Later Sunday, after church, Ethel stopped by to pick up Julie. It was Mother's Day. Since Ron was at work, Ethel went in and had a cup of coffee with Alice. Julie sat and listened and watched the two women talk together. Julie marveled at the friendship that they had developed and she loved them both dearly.

Julie got up from her chair and went to the refrigerator and pulled out the makeshift vase full of lilacs, where she had placed them to keep them fresh. The old mayonnaise jar was covered with aluminum foil to make it look pretty. Julie handed her mom the flowers and then handed her the poem that she had written earlier in the week. She hadn't shared it with anyone, not even Alice.

Ethel smelled the flowers and placed them on the table. She smiled at Julie and then opened the paper with the poem. In simple print Julie had titled it "My Three Big Brothers." Ethel began to read the poem aloud…

> *"One day when I was very small and lying in my bed.*
> *I woke up very suddenly and saw three peeping heads.*
> *Though one a year, the other two, the oldest only three,*
> *Little did I know right then, they'd take good care of me."*

Ethel paused and glanced up at Julie sitting beside her. She smiled at Julie and began to choke up with tears as she continued to read the poem, her voice fading out as she read the rest quietly to herself. When Ethel finished reading it, she handed it to Alice to read and reached over to hug Julie. Her tears brushed Julie's face. "Thank you, Honey," Ethel said, as she wiped the tears from her eyes. "You'll have to share that with your brothers. They'd like it Jul," Ethel said. Alice handed back the poem to Ethel and she placed it into her purse. Alice reached over and hugged Julie as they stood up to leave.

That evening, after Julie had returned home, Julie sat down at her desk to do her homework. After she finished, she began to write a letter to Jerry. She told him about Ronnie coming home, told him to stay safe and that she was praying for him and that she promised not to write the President anymore. Julie sat quietly at her desk after sealing the letter and thought of the impact that the poem had had on her mom. She knew that it was just a kid's poem and wasn't professional. She knew that others would probably think that it was corny and not even good prose. But the thing that touched Julie for the first time in her life was the knowledge of how powerful the written word can be and how beautiful it can move and touch hearts. Julie hoped that maybe she could improve and become a better writer and that maybe someday she could write something that would truly help others.

Midget sat beside Julie and stretched his legs. He lifted his head, gave Julie a weary look, and stood up and wagged his tail. He placed his front legs onto her and gently scratched at Julie's legs.

"You ready to go to bed?" Julie asked the sleepy puppy. She reached down and picked him up. He kissed her lovingly and then nestled into her arms. Julie laid him onto her bed and climbed under the covers. She scratched the little dog's ears and softly said, "Ronnie's coming home, Midget."

Julie reached for the little black Bible that she kept on her wooden chest. She opened it up to the page where she had placed a book marker. *"Thy brother shall rise again...."* Julie smiled and then, as she continued to read, fell asleep.

Ronnie arrived home ten days later. Julie ran to greet him as he got out of her mom's car. But Ronnie didn't respond. All he could do was turn slightly to Julie and answer in a subdued voice, "Hi, Sis."

Julie tucked her arm through his as they crossed the street to go to their house and visit their dad and Alice. Julie glanced at her mom following slowly behind. Her head was down and Julie could tell that she was deep in thought. As Julie turned to Ronnie to say something, she could see that he was somewhere far away. His eyes were distant and he seemed to be deep in thought. Julie refused to be sad. Her brother was home and he was going to be okay. Julie thought to herself, *He just needs to be at home a while and get used to everything again. Soon, he will forget the war and in a few months Jerry will be coming home, too. Soon they'll all be together again and Ronnie will be fine.*

But it didn't go as Julie had thought it would. Ronnie stayed with Winnie and John while Ethel continued to look for an apartment and save her money for a deposit. Ronnie, however, would sleep most of the day; and when he was awake, he would just sit and stare at the walls. When Julie would try to talk to him, he would just come back for a few moments, answer her questions, and then fade away again.

Summer passed and Ronnie faded further and further away. Ethel made more phone calls and wrote more letters. It was with great reluctance that Ronnie entered into the hospital. It had taken the joint effort of both Ron and Ethel working together to get Ronnie admitted. Julie smothered him with kisses and hugs when she had to say goodbye to him once again. She reminded him of their promise and told him that everything would be okay, that he would get better, and that he would soon be back home with all of them. Ronnie had barely nodded at his sister's words. But as Julie looked deeply into his eyes, ever so slightly and for a moment, their eyes met and Julie saw her old Ronnie. He was gone in a minute, but Julie knew that he was in there; and she knew that God was going to fulfill the promise that He had given her.

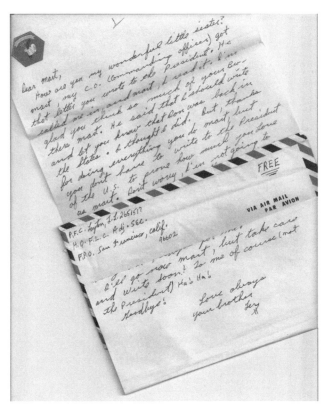

Jerry's letter from Vietnam

Chapter

17

A new school year had started. Julie was so excited to be in her junior year. She loved school and every day there seemed to be new opportunities opening for her.

The elections came for student council, and she was nominated to represent her class. Julie took the appointment seriously. She didn't just want to lead in title, but there was something in her heart that made her want to make a difference. She couldn't explain it, but it was like a fire that kindled within her. Julie was coming out of her shell.

She was surprised when it was announced that for the first time in her high school's history they were going to start an official girl's basketball team. This would be a real team that would compete with other schools, and they would have real uniforms. Julie tried out and became a forerunner on the team. She preferred defense, getting the ball, running with it, and passing it off to their best shooter. It came natural to Julie after years of swiping things from her brothers and running away from them. It didn't bother her not getting the glory of the shot. She knew that Yvonne was the best shooter so why not pass her the ball.

It seemed that everyday something new and exciting was happening in Julie's life. There were the tryouts for the class play. Julie felt really nervous about trying out. She was still so shy about getting up in front of people and really hated being the center of attention. However, she knew that she was good at memorizing; so when she tried out, along with Sarah, they both received parts.

Julie had one of the main leads and found it was more to memorize than she had anticipated. Every night she would study her lines with vigor until she could recite them in her sleep. She studied her lines more than her POD (Problems on Democracy). She figured that she could always make up her grade and ace another test later, but she would die of mortification if she forgot her lines in front of her classmates. She had dreams of forgetting her lines the night of the play. She and Sarah talked about it all the time, and they practiced their lines together while Molly would direct them in their enunciations and acting skills. Sarah played a humorous part, and Julie was so proud of her. She made them all laugh. Julie knew that her classmates had never really seen this side of Sarah. It tickled her for them to see Sarah the way that Julie had always known her. The play was a hit, and Julie felt that she had bonded with her classmates in a new and wonderful way.

One day, Ms. Mitchell had approached Julie in the hallway and asked her to come to her office later that afternoon during her study hall. Julie could hardly eat her lunch and was a nervous wreck. Ms. Mitchell was the school counselor. Julie was terrified of her because she had taught her dad when he was in high school. Her dad more than disliked Ms. Mitchell. Julie knew that he despised her. He blamed her for the reason that he had quit school. She had told him that nothing that he would do in her class would get him a passing grade and that no matter what he did, she would fail him.

Julie knew that Ms. Mitchell was aware of her family history. But for some unknown reason she was extremely nice to Julie. Actually, Julie was as much afraid of Ms. Mitchell because she was nice to her than if she had been mean to her as she was with the other students.

Julie went into Ms. Mitchell's office later that day and sat waiting for her to return. Julie's imagination was all over the place. She just couldn't figure out why Ms. Mitchell would want to see her. Her grades were almost straight A's. She hadn't done anything wrong that she could think of with the exception of possibly carrying on a little in Study Hall, but all the kids did that.

Finally, Ms. Mitchell came into the room and shut the door behind her. This made Julie even more nervous. Julie watched her as she sat down at her desk chair and ruffled through some papers as if Julie wasn't even there. Julie studied Ms. Mitchell, the woman who had so adversely affected her dad. She noticed why both of their personalities could clash very easily. Both seemed to enjoy being in control. Julie looked at the woman's demeanor. She had a rough and almost masculine appearance with her snow white hair, rimmed glasses and her expressionless face. Julie turned restlessly on her chair and tried to conceal her trembling hands by interlocking them.

Ms. Mitchell swiveled in her chair and transformed right before Julie's eyes. She smiled broadly at Julie and made direct eye contact. For the first time, Julie actually noticed gentleness in her eyes. It surprised her. "So, Ms. Clayton, how are you today?" she asked.

Julie wanted to say, "Scared to death," but didn't, and just answered a simple, "I'm fine, Ms. Mitchell."

"You know, I taught your dad in school years ago," Ms. Mitchell continued. Julie thought that maybe she was just trying to find common ground to strike up a conversation, but the very topic only unnerved Julie even more.

Julie just smiled and nodded her head. She was sure that if she opened her mouth to say something that nothing would come out.

"You're a very good student, Julie," Ms. Mitchell continued. Julie felt her face blush. "You are very well-liked by your peers and your teachers."

"Thank you," Julie said. She appreciated Ms. Mitchell's words but was still confused as to why she had called her into the office to tell her this.

"Well, on Thursday of this week, all of the teachers are going to receive a ballot with names on it and are going to mark in who they feel should be placed into the National Honor Society. Julie, you are being nominated as one of the candidates." Ms. Mitchell gave her a big smile revealing her crooked teeth. Julie had never seen her smile so big. She even thought she saw a twinkle in Ms. Mitchell's eyes. "I'm very proud of you, Julie."

Julie was at a loss for words. She was trying to take in all that Ms. Mitchell was telling her. Her words filled Julie with such emotion that she was struggling to respond. Somehow, Ms. Mitchell seemed to understand and just continued to smile at her.

"I think you have a very good chance at being chosen," Ms. Mitchell said.

"Thank you, Ms. Mitchell," Julie finally managed to say. "Thank you so much!"

"Thank your teachers," Ms. Mitchell said, "They're the ones who placed you on the ballot."

Julie left the room and returned to her Study Hall class. All she could think of was that if she did get elected to the National Honor Society, it would surely open doors for her to get scholarships and go to college.

Julie shared every achievement with her mom and Alice. She wrote both Jerry in Vietnam and Ronnie at the hospital and gave Matt all the details. "I knew you could do it, Jul," Matt told her. "You always were the smarter one of all of us."

"But I'm not," Julie answered. "I only succeeded because Ronnie, Jerry, and you always helped me with my homework."

The year seemed to fly by. Matt was due to get married. Jerry was coming home soon. Every evening when Julie watched the news, they reported that they had started to pull out the troops. Kids at school were talking about the war being over and that the boys were coming home. Julie would protest by saying, "They haven't sent 'my' brother home yet!" Julie would study the small television screen and scoot the little red chair closer to watch the news footage. She tried to see if Jerry was in any of the clips. She longed so much to see a glimpse of his face. With each letter, her heart would lift. She knew that as long as she received letters from him that he was alive. Too often, she had heard of young men getting killed one week before they were to come home. Julie also began to receive more letters from Ronnie while he was in the hospital. Most times, he would write their mom and tell her to say hi to all of them for him. However, Julie so treasured receiving her own letters.

"Mom, I think that he's starting to get better. Don't you?" Julie remarked to her mom one day while at her apartment.

"I do, Julie," Ethel replied. "It's just going to take time."

"I can't wait until he gets home," Julie said happily.

"Me too," Ethel agreed with tears in her eyes.

"Don't cry, Mom," Julie tried to comfort her, putting her arms around her. But Ethel just continued to sob.

"Mom, why does life have to change so much?" Julie asked sadly.

"I don't know, Honey," Ethel answered taking a paper towel from the rack and wiping her eyes.

"How come every time you get comfortable and attached to someone, they just change or go away, and then you're left with a gigantic hole in your heart?"

"I don't know," Ethel repeated sadly as she poured herself a cup of coffee.

They sat at the little table waiting for Matt to join them. Julie knew that in just a few weeks that he would be married. Everything was changing once again.

Ethel saw the sad look on her daughter's face. "So what are you thinking, Jul?" Ethel asked. She reached over and took Julie's hands into hers.

"I just miss my brothers," Julie answered.

"Well Julie, you graduate next year, and your life is going to continue to change a whole lot for you, too," Ethel said.

But Julie wondered if Alice and her dad's marriage would even make it until she graduated. Nothing had changed. Her dad would be nice for a month or two, and then he would become more argumentative then ever. He argued with Alice about everything from affairs to groceries. Julie often wondered if it was him that was having the affairs and whether he just didn't want to be tied down to any one woman too long.

Julie felt so selfish wanting to hold onto Alice. *If Alice left, what would she do? Matt was getting married and she could probably move in with her mom then, but it would mean changing schools to a totally different state and school district for her senior year. How could she get her scholarships and compete with other kids in a school that was three times larger than her current school, in a school where no one knew her or her academics? If Alice would just stay until she graduated. But how could she even expect Alice to stay? How cruel it was of her to want Alice to stay and suffer so that her life could be easier. But it wasn't only for that reason that she wanted Alice to stay. It was because she loved Alice. She couldn't imagine never getting to see her again. But one thing for sure…*Julie vowed to herself, *If Alice did leave, Julie refused to stay at the house with her dad, alone, ever again.*

Ethel watched Julie's face as she just sat there quietly thinking. As if reading Julie's mind she asked, "So how are things going with your dad and Alice?"

"The same," Julie answered. She looked over at her mom wondering how she knew that she was thinking about them. "Sometimes they're okay….but when they go bowling and Dad over-drinks, the arguments get pretty bad. I try to break them up and just get Dad to go to bed and sleep it off, but…you know how it is, Mom? So…I just go up to Gramma Emma's house and stay the night when it gets too bad."

"Julie, their marriage isn't for you to fix or referee," Ethel said lovingly.

"I know, Mom, but I just feel so sorry for Alice."

A knock at the door interrupted their conversation. Julie hopped up to let Buck in. She knew if it was Matt, he wouldn't knock.

"Hi Buck!" Julie greeted him as she opened the door. She smiled noticing the stub of the unlit cigar in his mouth. "Let me help you," Julie said, reaching out to take a bag of groceries.

"I brought you one of those good hams that you, Matt, and your mom like," Buck remarked.

Julie carried the groceries to the kitchen as Buck followed her with the other bag. Julie liked Buck. More than once she would catch herself calling him Bucky. She tried not to let him into her heart; however, his love and kindness had penetrated the very walls that Julie had built around it. Julie tried to find a flaw in his veneer. She tried to find a selfish motive for the kind deeds that he did, but try as she could, she couldn't find any. He had no children. He had never been married. Somehow, Julie felt that she and her brothers were becoming a part of his heart, like the children that he had never had. He would make Julie laugh. She began to feel a fatherly love from him. Sometimes though, she would feel confused, that somehow she was being dishonorable to her dad for allowing herself to receive Bucky's fatherly love, but Buck's kindness had won her heart.

Matt dropped by and joined them. Julie's heart began to lift as they talked and laughed together.

Molly pulled off the shoulder of the road, tightly against the gate, at Julie's house. "Ask your dad if you can ride around with Sarah and me tonight and go out to Mason's Barn to get a chili dog." Molly stated.

"I'll be right back," Julie called out to Molly and Sarah as she opened the car door. "I've just got to let him know when I'll be home." It had become a regular routine for the young people from church to ride out to the restaurant, eat, and just cruise around.

Julie hurried into the house. "Boy, I'm glad you came right home," Alice said. Julie watched Alice hurrying around in a frenzy.

"We thought we might have to leave without you, Julie," her dad said, as he quickly rushed around and grabbed his coat.

Julie heard the light toot of Molly's horn. "Go where?" Julie asked. She could see that they weren't arguing and Julie actually thought they looked happy. Things had been going a little better the last few weeks as her dad had let up on his drinking.

Ron and Alice both stopped and looked at each other and then at Julie. "We're driving down to Baltimore to pick up Jerry from the airport!" Alice squealed excitedly.

Julie looked at Alice and then at her dad. She saw the smile and excitement on her dad's face. "Jerry's home?" she asked. "He's home?"

"Yes!" Alice said nodding her head.

"But when? How?" Julie asked. She let out a squeal of delight. "He's home; he's really home?"

"Almost," Ron answered. "He said that he wanted to surprise us but got as far as Baltimore and just couldn't wait to get a bus to come the rest of the way. So he called us."

Julie could see the tears in her dad's eyes. At times like this, he was a real dad. This was the dad that Julie remembered as a little girl. This was the dad that she would get glimpses of from time to time. The glimpses were so far apart that often Julie wondered if she imagined that dad or if he had ever existed. But then, there would come a moment like this and Julie would get a glimpse.

Julie heard the louder, steady beep of Molly's horn honking. "Oh, I have to tell Molly and Sarah; they're waiting outside in their car."

"Go ahead and meet us at the car," Ron said as he went to grab his car keys.

Julie rushed out the front door forgetting to shut it behind her. The cooler air hit her in the face. Tears of joy ran down her face as she ran up to Molly's car and opened the door.

"Hop in," Molly said, and then seeing Julie's tears asked, "What's wrong, Julie?"

Sarah repeated the question before Julie could answer Molly.

"Jerry's home!" Julie squealed. "He's home!"

"Oh my goodness!" Molly squealed back.

"Really!" Sarah exclaimed. "Where?"

"We've got to go down to Baltimore to pick him up. He's waiting for us. He wanted to surprise us but they had no buses leaving for a day and he didn't want to wait any longer."

Julie heard the front door shut. She turned and saw her dad locking the front door. "We're driving down tonight!" Julie squealed once again as she backed away from the car door.

"Call us tomorrow!" Both Molly and Sarah said in unison, as Molly put the car into drive and pulled out.

Bucky and Mom

Chapter

18

Matt was now married. Jerry had met a lovely girl and fallen truly in love. She was so tiny, Julie thought, that you could pick her up and put her in your back pocket. They were engaged and planning their wedding. Julie rejoiced at seeing her brothers find happiness. Now, if only Ronnie could come home permanently. He had been home for a short time again, and he was doing better, but he was still not well enough to stay. For now, it was enough for Julie to have Jerry home, Matt married and happy, and to know that Ronnie was getting better. She had hoped that Ronnie would soon be home for good. She held onto the promise that God had given her, *"Thy brother shall rise again."* It didn't matter about all the idle talk that she had heard by the people in the valley who would rather gossip than hope. It made no difference to Julie. She had heard the town gossip and felt the brunt of it all of her life. Her dad had never helped the situation at all with his reputation and his continual drinking.

Julie recalled, at one time, hearing her dad tell Alice that their neighbor had come over to talk to him. This was really unusual because Julie couldn't remember her dad talking to any of the neighbors.

The neighbor had said, "Ron, you really ought to keep a closer eye on Julie now that she's growing up."

"What do you mean?" Ron had asked, irritated at the neighbor's remark and critique of his parenting.

"Well, I saw her the other night on your front porch kissing a man," the neighbor proudly exclaimed.

"What night was it that you saw her?" Ron asked, amused now at the question.

"Last Friday evening," he answered.

"Last Friday evening Julie was watching Tom's kids," Ron stated firmly.

"Well, I know what I saw," the neighbor continued, insisting on what he had seen.

"What you saw," Ron paused and then stated this time with a little laugh, "…was my wife and me kissing."

"Well," the neighbor stammered, "You should still watch her closely."

The summer had come and gone. Julie had started her twelfth year of school and couldn't believe that she would be graduating this year. Julie was glad that Jerry was still staying with them at their house. He was hardly home between working and dating his girlfriend and planning their marriage. She knew that in a few short months he would marry and move out. But for now, it was still so comforting to walk past her brothers' room and see him lying in his old bed sleeping. It warmed her heart to have him back home. She knew that Ronnie would soon be coming back home. She hoped this time, it would be for good.

The seasons of Julie's life continued to change much more quickly than she could adjust. The joy that had come with Jerry coming home and Ronnie being found had drawn the family together. But it wasn't long until once again, the whole family seemed to come unraveled.

Julie sat on her wooden chest in her bedroom. She reached over and pulled the blind. As it sprang upward, Julie slowly stood up, letting her arm follow it to the top to prevent it from spinning and coming undone. She took her shirt sleeve and wiped the condensation off the window and looked out. It was snowing fiercely. Already, several inches had piled up on the rooftop outside of her window. The parking lot across the street at Lindy's Tavern was nearly empty, not because of the hour but because of the winter storm.

Julie's eyes were fixed on the streetlight across the street. The snow flowed passed the light, each snowflake dancing and rushing past it as if to hurry to its destination. It had a hypnotic effect on Julie, carrying her away to a place where so many thoughts troubled her and so many questions remained unanswered.

Julie blinked and rubbed her eyes and then gazed out the window again. She loved the snow, the way it blanketed everything in the grayness of winter with a sheet of white making everything fresh, pure, and new. Julie loved the stillness that it brought, such a peaceful quiet that seemed to envelop one in its presence.

Julie reached for the window and was going to open it and thought better of the idea. She remembered that the last time that she had opened it a few weeks ago, it had gotten stuck on her. Julie lowered the blind halfway and turned off her bedroom light. She curled into bed, under the covers, and lay mesmerized as she continued to watch the snow fall outside of her window. It was only a few weeks ago that she had run away. Her thoughts rushed through her mind like a movie reel playing back the scene of that night.

As Julie reflected back, she was so glad that it hadn't snowed that night like it was snowing now. There were many things about that night that made Julie thankful. She realized how so many things could have turned out differently that night. Somehow, it had been another turning point in her life and in her walk of faith. She had not planned for any of it to happen. She had learned from that night that no matter what the crisis that would confront her in life, God would always be there with her. All she had to do was reach out and ask for His help. It was the simple prayers in Julie's life that had built her faith the most. The more that she learned about this God that truly loved her and cared for her every need, the more she learned of His heart towards her. He was not this God who stood waiting to condemn and punish us for our failures, but a God who was there to help us to overcome our heartaches and carry us if necessary. He was the solution to our problems and not the cause.

Julie turned in her bed and felt Midget against her feet. Shortly, the little dog was by her side. Even in the darkness, he was able to find Julie's face and give her a quick lick across the mouth. "How do you do that?" Julie asked the Midget. "Come on," Julie continued to talk to her little friend as she pulled back the covers, "Crawl in here and get warm." The Midget snuggled up against Julie. Julie laid back and looked across the room. There on the far wall glowed the little cross in the darkness, as it had most of her childhood, like a ray of hope. Julie smiled and allowed her thoughts to wander. Everyone had been so nice to her after she had come home that night from running away. She was sure that she would have been in a lot of trouble, but somehow, God had worked everything out just like He had told her He would when she was up in the woods. All she had to do was take that step of faith and let God help her.

Julie recalled when Jerry had come to her the next day and sat and talked with her. "You okay, Sis?" he had asked. "We were all so worried about you last night."

"I didn't mean to worry everyone; honest, Jerry," Julie assured him.

"I know, Sis. We all knew that. I think that's what worried us all the most. It was unlike you to do something so radical. What were you afraid of?" Jerry's voice was quiet and tender. He paused and searched her face, looking for an answer.

Julie looked up into her brother's bronze face, still dark from his year of being in Vietnam. Her eyes fixed upon his. He had left home still a teenager but came back a man. Julie reached up and touched his face and felt the coarseness of his rough unshaven face. She smiled at him. How she had longed to pour out the fears which had driven her from her home that night but she couldn't. It brought her too much pain and shame.

"You're not going to believe this," Jerry continued. He took Julie's hand into his, "Dad was really worried about you. We looked everywhere for you. We even walked down alongside the bridge where we found small footprints in the snow. They went right to the river's edge and they didn't come back or lead anywhere else." Jerry became quiet.

Julie studied her brother's face, etched in his love for her. Regardless, of the man who sat beside her, she could still see the little boy that she had always known.

"I didn't know that, Jerry," Julie answered breaking the silence.

"You're just lucky I didn't call the President on you," he said laughing.

Julie laughed too. His love fortified and strengthened her, just as the love of all of her brothers had done so many times when they grew up together.

"Hey, do you remember the time when you and I threw the marbles into a jar on this bed when we were both sick with the measles?" Julie asked Jerry.

Jerry rubbing his knee, answered, "Sure do. Still have a piece of the glass in my knee from when the jar broke and we tried to clean it up so we wouldn't get into trouble."

Things had all worked out on that night, and Alice stayed. Once again, her dad slowed up on his drinking and was nicer to Alice. He was actually nicer to all of them. Maybe he would change for good. Julie was glad that she had had the chance to tell Alice how sorry she was for hurting her feelings. Life puzzled Julie. There never seemed to be any answers to the questions of life; and about the time that you thought you might understand, everything would change once again.

Julie turned once again in bed and pulled the sleeping Midget towards her. She looked out the window one more time. The snow was now several inches high against her window and was continuing to come down heavily. Julie felt her eyes get heavy as she watched the flakes of white float lightly past her window. She then drifted off to sleep.

Jerry had been home now for almost seven months. It didn't seem possible how quickly time had passed. He was due to get married soon. Julie, once again, had such a mixture of emotions. She really liked his fiancé. She was a good match for Jerry and he seemed so happy. There was talk that Ronnie would be coming home soon. Julie could tell that when she received more letters from him that he was doing much better. When he wasn't doing well, his letters would slack off. Matt had settled into married life and would often stop by to see her. She let him know that watching Sherlock Holmes was not the same without him.

One evening, when her mom picked her up for the weekend, Ethel said to her, "I want to show you something, Julie."

Julie turned in her car seat to face her mom. "What Mom?" Julie asked. But Ethel only smiled and looked straight ahead as she drove, avoiding Julie's pleading eyes to tell her.

They meandered around the curves and then passed over the mountain on the winding road that led to Benson where Julie went to high school. "Where are we going?" Julie asked trying to get a clue.

"You'll see," Ethel answered and smiled.

They passed Julie's school and then turned left at the second small side street. Julie saw the little store on the left that a lot of the school kids often went to after school to pick up snacks and a soda. Julie was more than a little surprised when Ethel pulled up in front of it and parked.

"What are we doing here, Mom?" Julie asked.

"Come on," Ethel called out as she opened her car door.

Julie immediately followed her into the store.

"Well, hello there," came the deep familiar voice.

Julie couldn't believe that Buck was standing behind the counter at the register.

"What do you think?" Buck asked.

"I don't know," Julie answered. She didn't know what to think.

Ethel began to explain, "Buck bought the store with a partner, and they're going to run it together."

"Really?" Julie asked.

"So what would you like, Julie?" Buck asked. "A Reese's cup? Some Wise Potato Chips?"

He handed both to Julie and grabbed a soda out of the cooler and popped it open for her. Julie thanked him and gave him a big smile. "I'm so happy for you, Buck!"

Julie watched his jovial face light up as he shared his good news with them. Ethel showed Julie around the store. Julie took it all in as she watched Buck wait on his customers. He was one of the kindest men that Julie had ever met. She didn't trust too many men; but no matter how much she tried not to, she couldn't help feeling Buck's fatherly love. She had thought at first that it was just a ploy to get on her mom's good side, but Julie concluded that pretty much what you saw in Buck was the real thing. He had no facade or veneer to pull off. He was as direct as the noontime sun and as kind as the gentle breezes that blew on a warm summer day. She liked Buck and had grown very fond of him.

"Bring your drink and snacks with you," Ethel said as she ushered Julie towards the door. She gave Buck a wink of the eye and called out, "We'll see you later, Buck."

Buck waved and smiled and then went back to talking to his customers. Julie and Ethel got into the car and drove to the end of the street. Julie waited for her mom to turn right or left but instead she pulled the car up a private driveway that was in front of them. Julie turned and said, "Mom, what are you doing? You can't turn around in someone's driveway."

Ethel turned to Julie and smiled. She then turned off the ignition and opened the car door. "Come on," Ethel said.

Julie was too puzzled and thought it would just be easier and quicker to follow her mom than to ask any more questions. They walked up the rest of the slanted driveway towards the house. Without hesitation, Ethel climbed the steps and then followed the pavement which led around to the back of the house.

"Mom?" Julie called out in an anxious whisper. "What are you doing? Where are we going? You can't just go up to someone's house and…"

But Ethel just turned and smiled at Julie, waving for her to catch up. Then to Julie's surprise, Ethel reached into her handbag and pulled out a key to the back door at which they were standing. Ethel unlocked the door and entered with Julie following closely behind. Julie followed Ethel up the long flight of stairs and then stopped.

Ethel turned to Julie and said to her, "This is our new apartment."

"Really, Mom?" Julie asked. Julie hurried through the apartment. She knew, as everywhere that her mom had lived, that this would be her home too. It didn't matter if she didn't live there every day of the week. Anywhere that her mom had ever lived, since her dad and mom had divorced, had always been home for Julie. Ethel wouldn't have had it any other way.

"It has two bedrooms," Ethel said as she showed Julie the layout.

"Ronnie will have a place to stay when he comes home!" Julie said out loud.

"And you can share the other bedroom with me." Ethel chimed in.

"I like it, Mom! I really do," Julie said, beaming with joy. "I can't believe it's so close to Buck's store and to my school."

"I know," Ethel said excitedly. "It just all seemed to work out at the same time."

"And Ronnie's coming home soon!" Julie exclaimed. "I can stop over after school sometimes and even stay."

"Anytime you want Honey," Ethel said. "Anytime you want." Ethel never wanted to uproot Julie or to ever make anyone feel that she was trying to lull Julie away from the home that she had known all of her life. Ethel just wanted to finally have a place for her children. Ronnie, Jerry, and Matt had all left their home at one time or another to come live with her.

Ronnie and Jerry lived with her and Bob just before they had entered the Marines. Matt also came to live with her after he moved out when things had become so difficult with their dad. Ethel always felt that she had failed her children by not being able to provide them a home with her. At least, she could let them know that whatever she did have, it was theirs also.

Julie ran and hugged her mom. Her mom had never lived this close to Julie. She was so happy. "God is working everything out just in time for Ronnie coming home," Julie said. Ethel only nodded and smiled.

Little did Julie know that God was working more out than she could imagine. Ronnie did come home. He was doing so much better. Little by little, Julie felt that she was getting her Ronnie back. He would sit and talk to her for short periods and join all of them when Jerry and Matt stopped by. The effects of the war still bothered him. It would take time for him to heal. Julie understood this and it was okay. She was just glad that both of her brothers had come home, and that they were all together again.

But things were not good at home. The arguments between Alice and her dad had escalated terribly. One night, Julie heard them both come home late after bowling. Julie could hear her dad's mumbled and sluggish tone as he spoke to Alice. She knew that he was very drunk. She listened carefully. She could hear Alice speaking also. Julie was surprised that for some reason her dad seemed to be in a good mood. At least, he would probably just go to bed and sleep it off. Julie was glad that he was not picking on Alice and that she would not have to get up and referee. She turned over in her bed to get comfortable and to go to sleep.

Then suddenly, Julie heard Alice say loudly, "No, Ron, leave the bird alone." Everyone loved Charlie. Julie had thought it was a good idea for Charlie's cage to be downstairs where he could enjoy more company rather than just be kept in Julie's room.

"Oh, don't worry...he likes me," Ron remarked. "Don't you... ole Charlie boy?" Ron continued.

Julie sat up quickly in her bed and listened. She ran to her door which was partially closed and opened it, trying to hear what was happening. "Please, Dad," she whispered out loud to herself, "just leave him alone." She could hear the rustle of the cage door as her dad tried to figure out how to open it.

"Come...on...Come...on," Ron called to the bird.

"He doesn't want to come out," Alice spoke softly to Ron.

Julie could hear the flutter of Charlie's wings hitting the cage and his loud screeches that he would make when he was unhappy. Julie started to run out of her bedroom door to go downstairs but thought that maybe her dad would just back off. *No use upsetting him or starting an argument,* Julie thought. Julie heard it quiet down and hoped that her dad had given up. She listened to hear what was happening.

"See...he likes...me," Ron stated victoriously as he struggled to get the words out.

And then the silence was broken. Julie heard Alice scream. "Why did you do that?!"

"Because the damn bird bit me!" Ron exclaimed.

Julie ran down the stairs two at a time and was in the kitchen in a second.

"Dad!!!!!" Julie screamed. "What did you do?"

Ron knew that he had gone too far but would not recant or apologize in what he had done. "Well, the damn bird bit me, hard."

Julie crawled under the table and picked up her little Charlie. He lay there with both wings sprawled out on the open floor. Julie wasn't sure if he was dead or alive. She cradled the small bird in her hands and took him to her chest. She could feel her heart race within her. She felt her face flush as her anger rose. Had she not had the small bird in her hands, she thought she would probably be pounding on her dad right then. She shot daggers at her dad and then turned her attention to Charlie. She stroked his little chest and scratched under his little beak. The little bird opened his eyes and began to stir. Julie pulled him closer to her chest while putting a comforting hand on him. She spoke to him softly, "It's okay, Charlie. It's okay." She scratched his feathers where she knew his little ears were and continued to speak to him, cradling him close to her. He nestled into Julie's chest as if for protection and softly nudged Julie with his beak as if to assure her that he was okay.

Now it was Alice's turn to be upset. She was tired of always trying to keep the peace and now seeing that Ron had almost killed Charlie, she spoke up. "How could you have thrown him across the floor like that?" Alice asked, letting her voice rise.

Julie wasn't sure if her dad was too drunk to answer or just knew that he was better off keeping quiet. Seeing the bird was alive, he slowly walked away.

Julie always hoped that things would get better. She longed to find some kind of normalcy in her life. But things only continued to get worse.

They were actually worse than they had ever been. Alice had lost so much weight that Julie was worried about her. Alice's hands shook continually from her nerves being so bad. The thing that saddened Julie the most was the lifelessness that she saw in Alice's eyes. She remembered the laughter and sparkle in those eyes when she had entered into their lives. Now, both were gone. It was as if her dad had extinguished the very essence of life from her soul. Julie would often hear Alice crying in the bedroom or notice her red swollen eyes. She knew that she missed her mom and sisters in Michigan terribly. Ron controlled her as he had tried to control everyone that had ever entered into his life. He controlled her calls to Michigan complaining about how much it cost to call. Julie knew, more than the cost of the call, that he feared that Alice would ask her mom to wire her money so that she could go back home.

Julie thought that her dad would wake up and see what he was going to lose, but he seemed to believe that she would never really leave him. Alice had left him over a half dozen times in the four years that she had lived with them. Sometimes she would stay away for a few weeks at a time at a friend's house. At other times she would stay away for only a few days. But she always came back. Julie felt that her dad had convinced himself, that because she had no family here, and only a few friends, that she needed him and that she would always come back.

Once, Ethel even helped her move out, because Alice had no family or car. Julie couldn't even imagine what the neighbors were saying when they saw this. But for Julie, every time she left, it sent terror through her. Every time Alice left, Julie's heart broke and she cringed at what her dad might try to do. There were a few times when Alice had left that Julie knew he had tried and would've abused her, but either Matt or Jerry was still living there. It was too risky now that they were all older. Matt and Jerry came and left at all hours then. It would be too easy for him to be caught. And Julie knew that, because she had confronted him so boldly the last number of times that he had abused her, he was unsure now, with her being older, that she might speak up. Julie took no chances. During these periods, she shut and locked her door. She made it a point to not be alone with him. She always made sure that she was out of the kitchen after making his breakfast before he came downstairs to eat it, so that he couldn't grope at her. She had learned how to avoid him and she had vowed, now that she was old enough, that she would never allow him to hurt her again and she would never trust him, not ever.

Julie saw it all happening all over again. She was surprised that a few times her dad had crossed the line even with Jerry. He offended Jerry's fiancé one night so badly that Julie thought that Jerry might not ever speak to his dad again. Julie had run after her and tried to tell her to just ignore his remarks. He began to accuse Jerry of the same things that he had of Matt. But Jerry was no longer a little boy or teenager under his dad's control. Jerry was a man, and ever trying to hold respect for this person who was his father, he had firmly put his foot down.

The family continued to unravel. It was fortunate that Jerry's wedding came quickly before he could be thrust more and more into his dad's accusations.

Julie found the house eerily quiet one day when she had come home from school. She was surprised when she had walked into the kitchen to see Alice sitting quietly and drinking her coffee. Alice had grown so quiet.

Julie placed her school books down onto the kitchen table and pulled out a chair to sit down beside Alice. Julie searched Alice's face. She saw her red swollen eyes and guessed that she had been crying all day. Julie had seen that look of despair so often throughout her life. It was like 'déjà vu' all over again. Julie could close her eyes and remember as a child this very same look on her mom's face before Ethel left her dad.

Alice turned slowly towards Julie and looked at her sadly. Julie's eyes fixed on Alice's eyes. No words needed to be said. Alice looked away and down at her coffee cup. She picked it up to take a sip. Julie watched her hand shake radically as she tried to place the cup back down onto the saucer. She reached out and touched Alice's shoulder. She gave it a gentle squeeze and then stroked her long black beautiful hair.

"Is Dad home?" Julie asked.

"Yes," Alice answered, so softly that Julie hardly heard her speak. Julie didn't see his car parked out front and there had been no sign of him since Julie had come home.

"He's in the bedroom," Alice spoke up as if reading Julie's mind. Julie walked to the kitchen doorway and glanced through the living room to the downstairs bedroom door. It was closed.

"What has he done to you?" Julie turned and asked Alice. Julie turned around and started to leave the kitchen and head towards her dad's bedroom door but stopped short hearing Alice's hushed voice. "Julie, don't Honey."

Julie sat back down beside Alice to keep her company. She didn't know what else to do. "Would you like me to cook supper for us, Alice?"

Alice shook her head no and placed her hand on top of Julie's. She looked at her compassionately for a long time as if she was looking at Julie for the last time. She patted Julie's hand gently and then made an effort to take another drink of coffee.

Julie startled as she heard the bedroom door open but not as much as Alice. Julie saw the broken Alice literally jump when she heard the door open. Julie reached over and placed her hand on top of Alice's hand.

She looked up as her dad entered the kitchen. She wondered how her dad could look so drunk this soon after work. Julie kept her hand on Alice's and gave it a gentle squeeze.

"So did she tell you?" Ron's voice broke the silence with a thrust as he raised his voice.

Julie just glared up at her dad and didn't answer him. She didn't look at Alice. She couldn't. She was afraid that if she saw Alice's fear and pain that she might actually tear into her dad. It was too much. He had gone too far. He had always gone too far.

"Well, did she?" Ron pushed forward.

"She doesn't need to tell me anything, Dad," Julie answered just to appease him.

"Oh, she didn't tell you that I came home early today and she wasn't home," Ron grunted out the words as if he had snarled Alice in some great lie.

Julie only continued to glare at her dad and hold Alice's hand tighter, protectively.

"So, I waited and waited and she just comes walking in the house right before I usually get home," Ron continued speaking.

"And did you ask her where she was?" Julie asked. "Not that it matters where she was. She has a right to leave this house, Dad. You keep her locked up like a prisoner. If she stays home, then you still accuse her of having affairs with anyone from Matt to Jerry to the owner of Lindy's Tavern. What does it matter if she went somewhere? Look what you are doing to her?" Julie's voice rose as she spoke and she stood up to face her dad. "Just leave her alone. You're drunk!" Julie couldn't believe the way that she was talking to her dad. She didn't want to be disrespectful, but it was like a time bomb was going off inside of her. Julie didn't know who was more surprised at her words, herself or her dad. She knew that she had crossed the line with her dad, but she didn't care. She just didn't care what he said or even what he did to her. It was as if she couldn't bear it anymore.

Ron just glared at Julie and then, to gain back control, he laughed at her. That smirk of a laugh that Julie knew so well. He brushed off her remarks as if they hadn't even affected him. "She said that she was up at your Aunt Lisa Sue's house all day."

"Well, call Aunt Lisa and ask her!" Julie demanded.

"You know you're going too far, Julie. Don't you dare tell me what to do! Do you think that I would believe either of them?" Ron's slurred words spilled out.

But Julie did not back down. Something had snapped inside of her. She would sort it all out later, but for now she had to continue. "No, Dad. I don't expect you to believe anyone! Not me! Not your sons! Not the family and not Alice or Aunt Lisa! Why would you believe any of us?" Julie felt her face flush as her anger rose.

Then there was a honk of a horn, followed by a longer blast. Julie looked towards the front door. It sounded as if the car was right in front of their house. She paused and listened as the car beeped again. Julie looked at her dad who had flopped down onto the other kitchen chair. There was no sadness or remorse on his face for all the pain that he had caused Alice, only that incessant smirk. Julie looked at him, then to Alice, and then to the front door, as the horn beeped again.

Alice turned and looked sadly at Julie once again and then scooted her chair back to get up. She stumbled and Julie reached out to help her.

"She didn't tell you, did she?" Ron asked slyly.

All of a sudden, Julie was putting the picture together. It hit her like someone had just dropped a ton of bricks onto her. The realization of what was happening actually took Julie's breath away.

"I'm sorry, Julie. I'm so sorry," Alice said. She looked deeply into Julie's eyes. "Please forgive me. I have to leave."

Julie burst into tears and hugged Alice as tightly as she could. Alice hugged her tightly back. Julie whispered in her ear, "I understand, Alice. I do. I love you."

"I love you too, Julie," Alice replied. "My mom is wiring me some money. I'm going back to Michigan. I will always love you, Julie." Alice slowly pulled away and tried to hurry to the front door. She opened the door and motioned to the driver that she was coming. She grabbed the few belongings that she had packed.

Julie started to follow Alice to the door. Julie glanced back once at her dad to see his reaction but he just sat motionless in the chair, disinterested in all that was going on. Julie hurried to the open front door. Alice was on the front porch, handing her things to the driver that had come to help her.

Julie couldn't say a word. It was as if every emotion inside of her froze solid. She couldn't react. She couldn't cry. She couldn't even call out to Alice.

Alice turned one last time and looked at Julie. Tears were streaming down her face. Julie wanted to run into her arms. She knew that Alice wanted to run into hers. But with one final look, they both knew that they couldn't. It was over. Julie knew that this time it was really over. She knew that Alice would not be coming back. Julie stood on the porch and watched as the car began to pull out. Alice had her face thrust into her hands. Julie could see her sobbing. Julie stood and watched the car pull away. She turned and let her eyes follow it down the road, across the bridge, until it rounded the last curve and she could see it no more.

Julie at Gramma Winnie's house

Chapter

19

The words pierced through Julie's heart like a sharp knife. "Julie Anna, you need to come in here!"

Julie turned and saw her dad standing at the front door. Julie took no time to even search his face. She was still in the *I don't care* mood, except that it had escalated. Julie could not think. She could not feel. She could not even react to what had just happened. She felt as if she had just seen someone run over by a truck and didn't know what to do to help them. Julie felt numb, and here was her dad telling her to come in. The words were reminiscent of another time when he had told her to come into the house. They sent terror through her. Julie felt herself shake inside and then a boldness came upon her that she had never felt before.

Julie ran into the house, past her dad, and up the stairs to her bedroom. She shut and locked the door. Quickly, she rummaged through her dresser drawers and pulled out some necessary clothes. She grabbed the pillowcase off of her pillow and threw the clothes into it. She rushed around the room trying to compose herself and pack only what she needed. Julie turned and paused, ever listening to hear if her dad was coming up the steps. She stopped briefly to look at the picture of Jesus on her wall. "Jesus, please help me. I don't know what I am doing."

Julie paused at her bedroom door and listened. All was silent. She got down onto her knees and looked under the door to see whether her dad was standing outside of it. She saw no one. She started to unlock the door and then paused once more to listen. She knelt down to the keyhole of the door and peeked through it. There was no one standing there. She was sure.

Slowly, Julie unlocked the door. She pushed the iron lock ever so softly, so as to not make a sound. She lifted the door slightly as she opened it to make sure it wouldn't squeak. Julie paused outside of her door and glanced towards the bathroom and her brothers' bedroom. She didn't see her dad or hear any noise upstairs. Julie leaned her head towards the stairwell to listen for any sound from downstairs but heard nothing. She tiptoed down the hallway which ran beside her bedroom, ever so softly, and went to the closet to get some dresses. She continued to look back over her shoulder and over the railings on the hallway to make sure that her dad wasn't coming up the stairs. After Julie grabbed a few of her dresses, she wrapped them, hanger and all, around her left arm and grabbed the pillowcase tightly with her hand. She turned and glanced once more down the stairwell before heading back down the hallway.

As Julie approached the landing of the steps she paused once again. She whispered a prayer for God to give her strength to stand up to her dad. She would not stay there, in that house by herself, with her dad, not even for a night. She had vowed to herself a long time ago that if this ever happened, she would leave. She would not stay. Julie didn't want to argue with her dad, nor did she want to push him to the point where he might try to commit suicide again. She did not want to hurt her dad in any way. All she wanted to do was to leave. Julie's thoughts tumbled inside her head as if they were in a tumbler. Julie could only seem to grab a thought here and there. She had to get her books, and she knew that her dad would be waiting to stop her. Her best plan of action was to just get out of the house as quickly as she could. She wouldn't stop to make any phone calls. She would just grab the remainder of her things and go up to her Gramma Emma's house for the night. She would work out the rest tomorrow.

Julie took a deep breath and let out a sigh. She looked down the stair rail to where the couch was to see if her dad was sitting there, but he wasn't. She glanced at his bedroom door. It was open, which meant that he could be in there waiting for her, or possibly not be in there at all. Julie started slowly down the steps. She glanced at the living room as she went down the stairway, but her dad was not there. He was either in the bedroom or in the kitchen. Julie took another deep breath and let it out. She thought that maybe he had left; but until she knew, she had to be on guard. She didn't know what she was going to face. She had never confronted her dad in this manner before. She had never left her home knowing that she would never come back there to live. Julie heard her bird, Charlie, chirp loudly from her bedroom. She saw Midget asleep on the chair in the living room. All of a sudden she began to feel the emotions of leaving her home, the only home that she had ever known.

Julie braced herself at the last step. She didn't think that her dad was in his bedroom or he would've probably come out by now to meet her, hearing the creaking steps, but she prepared herself. Julie stopped dead at the foot of the steps and glanced quickly into her dad's bedroom. He wasn't there. Julie paused and said another prayer. "God, I can't go out there and break down. I have to be strong to face him. Please give me the strength. I'll sort it all out later. I just have to get my things and leave."

Julie turned the corner at the bottom of the steps and walked into the living room. She saw her dad sitting in the kitchen drinking a beer. He saw her immediately and stared right at her. She studied him for a minute to check his demeanor. He seemed to be more subdued, as if he had lost his will to fight. But Julie couldn't be sure. Julie paused and then took a deep breath. She squared her shoulders back and grabbed the clothes in her arms tighter. She felt a strength and a new boldness arise within her.

Julie walked straight into the kitchen. Her dad's eyes had not left her from the time that he had seen her. Julie looked sternly at her dad. She went to quickly gather up her books but made herself do it calmly as if everything was normal. She bit back the tremendous fear that had tried to grip her by quietly uttering another prayer. She said nothing. She could feel her dad's eyes watching every move that she made and waited for him to speak. She knew her dad. She knew that he would say something.

Julie heard the rumble of her dad's chair as she turned with her books flopped on top of her clothes. Her dad had stood up but still seemed subdued.

"So you're leaving, too?" he asked.

Julie looked him straight in the eyes. She could see beneath his veneer the brokenness. She wanted to feel sorry for him. She wanted to show him compassion but she couldn't. She would do nothing that would give him any opportunity to stop her from leaving. She didn't want to be responsible for him trying to commit suicide again. But she could not stay. Julie felt her emotions return and tumble inside of her but she wouldn't yield to any of them.

"Dad, I'm leaving," Julie said calmly but firmly. "I'm going up to Gramma's, so you know where I'm at."

"You don't have to leave, Julie," Ron spoke softly. "I'm not going to do anything to hurt you."

Julie was caught off guard by his gentleness. She had braced herself for the tough dad. "Dad, I'm leaving," she repeated.

She saw her dad's demeanor begin to change. She knew that she had to leave quickly. She turned and walked away.

"Julie!" the voice thundered. "You know that I can…"

Julie turned around abruptly and faced him as he approached her. She broke into his sentence before he could finish and spoke bolder to her dad than she had ever spoken to him in her life. "Dad, I am leaving! I am not coming back home again to live here!"

Ron lifted his hand to order Julie to be quiet, but she continued on. "Don't try to stop me, Dad! There is nothing that you can do or say to stop me!"

Ron began to speak, but Julie cut him off once again. "I mean it, Dad. There is nothing you can do to stop me." She paused and stood her ground, staring directly into his eyes. Giving him the sternest warning glance that she could, her eyes spoke, *If you try to stop me, I will tell what you've done to me all of these years!* Julie felt that she had nothing or everything to lose. *She felt that if she told, she was sure to lose everything—her reputation, self-worth, respect, and maybe her sanity; but if she stayed at that house, she knew that she would lose everything, for she knew that the abuse would start all over again and that it would destroy her.* They stood, staring at each other for a moment, neither budging from their stance. Julie gave her dad one more stern glance and then said, "I'm leaving, Dad." She turned and walked away. She opened the front door by grabbing the knob with two of her fingers while balancing her clothes and books in her arms. She nudged the door shut behind her and left, and then attempted to do the same thing with the iron gate. She managed to open it but left it wide open behind her. She crossed the paved road and walked up the connecting dirt winding road that led her past her Uncle Tom's house and up to her Gramma Emma's house. Julie bit back the tears that were trying to flood her eyes. She could not cry. She could not let herself break down. She felt if she started to cry she might never stop.

Julie entered her gramma's basement kitchen. She was glad that her Pap Pap James was not sitting at the table. Most evenings, he would be sitting there and looking at his plant magazines or playing his records. Julie dumped her clothes and books onto the old Victrola that sat in the corner. Once again, Julie took a deep breath and whispered a prayer. She wanted to talk to her gramma before her dad would call her. She climbed up the steps and entered the living room where her gramma always sat watching television in the evenings on her favorite lounge chair. Pap Pap James was sitting on a large chair in the corner but got up to leave as soon as he saw Julie. "Hi Gramma," Julie said, as she went to sit down onto the couch. Julie wondered if her dad had already called her gramma because it didn't seem like she was even surprised to see her.

"Hi Julie," Gramma Emma replied softly.

Julie waited for her gramma to say more but she remained quiet. Julie was sure now that her dad had already talked to her. Julie could only wonder what he had told her. Julie thought it best to listen to what her gramma already knew before speaking up. But the silence remained. Julie noticed that Perry Mason was on television. This was her gramma's favorite show. Julie leaned back and pretended to watch the show but had no interest as her mind continued to race from everything that had happened. In only two hours, her whole life had changed, and Julie knew that nothing would ever be the same again.

Julie needed to take a walk and sort it all out. She needed to figure out what she was going to do, where she was going to live, but first she had to figure out what to do for tonight. She wanted to call her mom but she couldn't use her gramma's phone and tell her mom what was going on in front of her gramma.

Julie's head throbbed from the headache that had hit her with full force. Try as she would, she couldn't sort out everything in her mind. She sat in utter confusion and just wished that she could go somewhere alone. Julie saw the show end and sat watching the Lucky Strike cigarette commercial.

"What's going on, Julie?" Gramma Emma asked kindly. Emma could have cared less about Perry Mason and had tried to sit and study her granddaughter.

Julie turned to face her gramma. "Can I stay up here tonight, Gramma?" Julie asked.

"Sure you can, Julie. You know you can always stay anytime you want," Emma answered softly. She worried about Julie. Emma thought that Julie appeared as if she was ready to break. She didn't want to upset her or have her run away again. Ron had called her and told her that Julie was coming up, but he had refused to elaborate with Emma about what was going on. "Are they arguing again?" Emma asked.

"Not any more," Julie answered. "It's over."

"Well, it's good they quit arguing," Emma said with a slight sigh of relief. "Just stay here and tomorrow your dad and Alice will probably have it all worked out."

Julie turned and looked at her gramma. There was such a strength and a sweetness to her gramma, which Julie loved so much. Julie realized that Emma did not know what had happened. "No, Gramma, they won't work it out tomorrow," Julie explained. "Alice left Dad. She left him for good, and she's moving back to Michigan."

Emma was taken completely aback. She couldn't believe what she was hearing. "Are you sure, Julie?" she asked.

"Yes, Gramma," Julie answered, as she bit her lower lip to hold back the tears. Julie just had to get away somewhere by herself before her emotions would consume her.

Emma sat upright in her recliner. "Well, what's going to happen?" Emma asked. She didn't really expect Julie to answer but was mostly speaking in the confusion of the moment.

"I don't know," Julie answered. "I left home, Gramma. I'm not going back to live there."

"What do you mean, Julie?" Emma asked, as she noticed the expression of fear that had erupted on Julie's face when she spoke.

"I'm just not going back, Gramma," Julie answered. She felt so weary. She couldn't sort out her thoughts or her words. Her sentences seemed empty because she was so confused and they all seemed to tumble together inside her mind.

"You mean you're not going to live with your dad?" Emma asked.

Why had Julie opened up this door of conversation? She couldn't explain it to her Gramma. She didn't want to explain it to anyone. *Please God, don't let me have to explain why I can't live with my dad. I can't talk about it. I can't tell anyone what he has done to me. I would rather die. Maybe this is why he didn't fight me in leaving. He knows that I will never tell people what he did to me. He thinks that I'll come back. He thinks that Alice will come back. He thinks that he still has everything under control.* Julie's mind raced.

"Julie," Emma's voice was tender and kind, "what do you mean you're not going back to live with your dad? Where will you live? I mean you can stay here, but surely you don't want to have your dad live all alone by himself?"

Julie thought that she would absolutely burst inside if she didn't get away. *She could not answer these questions. She didn't have the answers. The only one thing that she did know for sure was that she would never go back to live with her dad. Julie almost felt angry at her gramma for feeling sorry for her dad. He didn't deserve her compassion after all that he had done to Alice. If he was alone, he deserved to be alone,* Julie thought. She could feel her anger rise and didn't want to speak harshly to her gramma.

Julie could feel her gramma's eyes searching her. Julie lifted her head and met her gramma's gaze. "Gramma, I don't know what I'm going to do yet." The words just tumbled out of Julie's head without even becoming a thought. Julie wasn't even sure of what would tumble out next. "Gramma, thank you for always letting me stay up here, and I appreciate you telling me that I can stay here. I want to call Mom, and I think I'll probably just go live with her until I finish twelfth grade." Julie couldn't believe the words that she was hearing herself speak. *Of course, that was the solution. She could go to live with her mom now. Ethel lived right beside the school. It was all going to be okay. Why hadn't Julie thought of this before?* Julie was so lost in trying to understand her own explanation to her gramma that she hadn't heard what her gramma had asked her next.

"What Gramma?" Julie asked. "I didn't hear you."

"But why would you leave your daddy at a time when he needs you the most? All these years, he's raised you on his own. Why would you leave him now and go to your mother's? You are his only little girl, Julie. I don't think he could handle that now with Alice leaving."

"What, Gramma?" Julie asked. She was trying to wrap herself around what her gramma was saying. Julie was afraid that she would explode. *It wasn't her gramma's fault. She had no idea why Julie couldn't stay there. It would make sense, what she said, if you didn't know the truth of what her dad had done against her and what her mom had done for her.*

"I mean, Julie, I know that your dad didn't treat Alice right. I know that she was a good woman. I tried to tell him over and over again to treat her right. But now that she's gone, surely you won't leave him, too?"

Julie sat staring at her gramma in a daze of confusion. She had no words to answer her. *What could she say to her gramma? "Well, Gramma, Dad molests me and Mom is the only one that's really been there for me even if I did only get to live with her on weekends."*

"Julie, are you okay?" Emma asked. "You're as white as a sheet. Just stay here and we'll work out the rest with your dad tomorrow when you feel better."

Julie could feel the blood drain from her. It was too much. Julie knew that this would happen. She had thought of it many times, but she never thought it would happen this fast; and she never knew it would impact her so hard. She never realized the dilemmas that she would have to deal with or explain.

"No, Gramma," Julie heard herself say softly to Emma. "No, Gramma, I don't want to talk about it tomorrow with Dad. It's over, Gramma. I'm not going back. I'm never going back." Julie felt herself short of breath as her tone rose in determination for her gramma to understand this.

Emma looked at her granddaughter with grave concern. She had never seen her so pale and drawn, not even the night that she had run away. Something was terribly wrong. This was not like Julie to react this way. Emma watched Julie. She had never heard Julie raise her voice to her, not ever. And even though it was not in anger, it was so unlike her.

"Why, Julie?" Emma asked slowly.

Julie could feel her veneer falling off in a million pieces. If she didn't get alone soon, by herself, she felt she would break.

"Why, Julie?" Emma asked again kindly. Emma felt that she had to find out what was bothering Julie so severely. She knew that it was more than just Alice leaving. This was about her father and her relationship. Something was wrong.

Julie bit her lower lip so hard that she thought that it might start to bleed. "Gramma, I don't want to talk about it!"

"Has your dad hurt you?" Emma asked in desperation. "Has he hurt you?"

Julie looked at the pain on her Gramma Emma's face. *How much did she really know about the dark secrets of her family? For the first time in Julie's life, she knew that her gramma knew more than Julie had ever suspected. But it pained Julie to see her gramma suffer. Julie knew what her gramma was really asking her. It was written on her facial expression as much as in her tone of desperation. Julie did not know how to answer her question. She would not answer her question. She would never tell anyone her secret. No one ever needed to know the fear and shame and guilt and blame that Julie carried. It was enough for her to carry the shame of it all without everyone else knowing and putting more shame and blame on her. No, she would not talk about it.* Julie let her determination strengthen her and she said nothing.

"Julie," Emma spoke softly now. "Julie," Emma said again.

Julie looked up at her gramma. It was all that it took. The brokenness on Emma's face melted Julie's heart. She could not bear to see her gramma hurting.

"Has your dad hurt you?" she asked again.

Through all the pain, Julie saw the determination etched on her gramma's face trying to get an answer. Julie believed she had inherited this same determination from Emma. She knew that her gramma would not back down or let it go until she got an answer.

Julie looked sadly at her gramma, deeply into her rich blue eyes. "Gramma, you do not want me to answer that," Julie replied. Quickly, Julie jumped up and ran out the screened door and let it slam behind her. She ran down the steps from the porch and then ran up the dirt path hardly visible through the overgrown brush that led to the little white house with red shutters. She climbed up the broken steps and sat on the little porch that so often had become a place of refuge. Julie laid her head into her folded arms that rested on the porch rail and cried. She began to pray and pour her heart out to God to help her and to give her direction. Everything that was pent up inside of her burst out like a broken dam. Julie stayed there for hours and tried to let her thoughts settle. Tomorrow she would talk to her mom. They would figure it out together. Julie began to calm down. She didn't know why. She felt a sweet presence come over her. She closed her eyes and felt a peace that seemed to carry her. *"Let not your heart be troubled..."* It whispered to her soul. *"Everything will be okay."*

Julie sat and let it comfort her for the longest time. She didn't even search her mind for anymore answers but just rested in this sweet presence. *"Let not your heart be troubled...."*

Julie's Graduation

Chapter

20

Everything had changed in Julie's life. Julie didn't like change, but she had grown used to accepting the many changes that had occurred in her lifetime. No matter how often she had played the scenario through her mind that Alice might leave for good, nothing had prepared her for the full impact of Alice's departure.

Julie had readily, without hesitation, moved in to live with her mom and Ronnie. Neither her dad nor Gramma Emma ever questioned her again on her decision to go live with her mom.

Julie couldn't bring her Charlie or her Midget to live with her. No pets were allowed to live there. It took a while to get a routine established. Julie had her mom run her over to the house to visit and take care of Charlie and Midget after school. If her dad wasn't there she would often get the key that was hidden on the back porch in the old metal cabinet and let herself in.

Her dad wasted no time in getting another girlfriend; however, the relationship didn't last long. He drank so heavily at first that Julie kept her distance. In time, she cautiously opened up to him. She wished her dad no harm. She was glad that he had not tried to kill himself. She would have blamed herself if he had ever tried.

All of these things wore on Julie's heart and tore her apart. She had to walk around the many questions that so many people had asked her concerning why she had left her dad to live with her mom. She began to just say that she wanted to be with Ronnie and her mom. She told them that she missed Alice too much to stay in the house without her. "What about your dad?" people asked. She just answered that there was just nothing that she could do to help him and that she honestly couldn't live with him because of his drinking. So many people made her feel as if she was the worst daughter and Christian in the world. *How could you walk out on your dad after all he sacrificed for you and raised you all by himself?* Those closest to her understood why she had left, and most thought it was due to his drinking. Julie never told anyone, not even her mom or brothers, the real reason why.

Her best friends, Molly and Sarah shocked her when they had found out about Alice leaving and asked her to come live with them. Julie just stood staring at them in shock and surprise.

Molly watched Julie's expression as she stood in stunned silence. "What?" Molly asked her with a big smile.

"You want me to come live with you?" Julie asked.

"Of course we do," Sarah answered her before Molly could.

"And so do Mom and Dad," Molly added.

"Your mom and dad want me to come live with you?" Julie asked. "Why?"

"Because they love you, silly," Sarah answered.

"They actually insisted on us asking you," Molly added.

Julie didn't know what to say. Their love had touched Julie in a way that she had never experienced. Julie would never forget the love that they had offered her.

In time, the curious quit asking their questions. Julie came up with an agreement with her dad. He had begun to make sure that he was at the house once he knew that Julie was stopping by with her mom. Julie knew that this was difficult on her mom. Julie told him that if he wouldn't drink around her, that she would ride the bus back to their house, make him supper, feed the animals, and help him out as long as he would bring her back to her mom's right away. He agreed readily and left Julie alone. Julie was so happy to see her Charlie and Midget whenever she went to the house, and she cried almost every day for the longest time. Julie couldn't wait to get out of the house once she had cooked and cleaned things up. The house seemed to have died from the inside out without her brothers or Alice being there. Julie could not bear the loneliness that she felt while there.

She even felt sorry for her dad, in part. She truly wondered how difficult it must be for him to live there, after all of the years of having all of them live there with him, and now there was no one. Julie prayed for her dad. She hated all that he had done. It caused her to deal with an unbelievably fierce anger. The anger would surge through her whenever she thought about all that he had done to her and to others. However, she was grateful that God had helped her so that she wouldn't hate him. She was glad that God had given her a compassion for him and his soul. She would never excuse, condone or accept what he had done. She would never trust him again. She even sadly felt that she did not love him. But she did care what happened to him and felt sorry for him even though she knew that he had brought it all upon himself.

She never heard from or saw Alice again. She thought of writing to her, of contacting her, but it didn't seem right to be a reminder of pain to her. Julie knew that Alice would always love her, and she knew that she would always love Alice. Nothing would ever change that; but for now, she had to allow Alice to heal and go on with a life that she deserved. Julie had hoped that possibly, some day, she would get to talk to her or see her once again.

Julie poured all of her effort into her schoolwork. She wanted to go to college. She needed to get scholarships. She knew that she had to get financial aide; if not, she would never be able to go to college. She began to fill out applications to different colleges. There wasn't much information available at her school on how to do this so Julie just began by writing letters. She started to receive information back but nothing concerning scholarships. She read pamphlet after pamphlet; however, her dream always ended up at the same place—on the financial page. It was impossible. She wondered if wanting to go to college was just a pipe dream.

Julie walked down the hallway one day with Sarah to go to their last class when the secretary, Ms. Moyer, called to her from her office. "Julie, could you come here a minute?"

Sarah looked at Julie and Julie at her. Both of the girls were puzzled. Sarah nodded that she would meet her in class and gave her an encouraging smile.

Julie walked slowly into the school office. She had never been called aside by Ms. Moyer. Actually, Julie didn't think she had stood in that office since the day she had adopted Midget.

"Sit down, Julie," Ms. Moyer spoke kindly to her.

Julie pulled the chair out and sat down. Ms. Moyer could see her troubled look.

Ms. Moyer gave Julie a broad smile and thought that this would ease Julie's mind. "Mr. Jenkins just wants to talk to you for a few minutes." Ms. Moyer knew by the look on Julie's face that she didn't manage to ease Julie's fears.

Julie sat quietly, wringing her hands nervously. "He just wants to go over a few things with you, dear," Ms. Moyer pressed on. "Nothing serious." Ms. Moyer saw the color come back into Julie's face and smiled at her once again.

Suddenly, the principal's office door swung open wide. Julie looked up as it opened and saw Mr. Jenkins standing at the door. He looked so official that Julie forgot to move.

"Go ahead in, dear," Ms. Moyer spoke again kindly to Julie.

Julie smiled back to her and then to the stoic Mr. Jenkins who was still standing at his door.

"Have a seat," Mr. Jenkins said cordially as Julie entered his office. Mr. Jenkins had usually presented himself as tough in nature, with his authoritative demeanor, he was known by his students strictly as Principal Jenkins. However, Julie found herself surprised by his gentle disposition. She had always been afraid of him, ever since Matt received a licking from him with the paddle for throwing a snowball at the Home-Ec teacher. The only problem with that was Matt hadn't thrown the snowball, Jerry had. But it was Matt who had been caught; and Matt would've never told on his brother. Matt often reminded Jerry that he owed him one. *Wasn't everyone afraid to be sent to the principal's office?* Julie thought to herself as she waited for Mr. Jenkins to speak. Julie hadn't felt this nervous in school since she had been sent to the principal's office back in the seventh grade for beating up Billy Klondrike.

"Well, Julie," Mr. Jenkins said kindly as he took a seat at his desk across from Julie. He reached up, putting on his glasses, and then ruffled through some pages on his desk. "So, how are you today?" he asked trying to ease the obvious nervous Julie.

"I'm fine," Julie answered as she looked up at Mr. Jenkins and gave him a nervous smile.

"Well, I see that you were elected into the National Honor Society last year and you're on the Student Council. Your grades are excellent and you're near the top of your class. You do very well, Julie," Mr. Jenkins commented as he stacked some of the papers together.

"Thank you, sir," Julie answered. She still couldn't help feeling like one of his former soldiers when he was a drill instructor for the Marine Corps, but Julie was taken aback by his kindness and concern.

"So do you have plans to go to college?" he asked.

"I would like to," Julie answered. She began to feel more relaxed with her principal as he continued to speak kindly to her. She still had no idea as to why he had called her into his office. Julie had never heard of him calling any student into his office to discuss their academics, especially if they were good.

"Have you applied anywhere?" Mr. Jenkins asked.

"I've sent out a few applications and am waiting for some replies," Julie spoke openly now. "But mostly, I've just received information from them."

"Do you know if they're accredited colleges, Julie?" he asked.

Julie had no idea at all what Mr. Jenkins meant by accredited. She was at a loss on how to answer his question.

"Well, never mind. Do you have a favorite school of choice?" Mr. Jenkins continued to pursue the discussion.

Julie smiled and looked at Mr. Jenkins. She was so surprised and touched by his genuine interest in her college plans. *How could she never have seen this side of him? Why would he ever care about Julie going to college?* "The truth is, Mr. Jenkins, I can't afford to have a favorite. I would like it to be a Christian school…but, I just want to go to college. I know that I'll need scholarships to be able to go, and I don't know how to begin to try to obtain them."

"Well, you have the grades, Julie," Mr. Jenkins extolled. He shifted in his desk and pushed his glasses up his nose closer to his eyes and rearranged some of the papers on his desk, sifting through them. He pulled out a brochure from under the pile and reached over the desk and handed it to Julie. Julie took the brochure and began to glance through it.

Mr. Jenkins could see Julie's eyes begin to light up as she thumbed through the brochure. "This college is in West Virginia, Julie. It is an accredited institution and it is a Christian college. I thought it might interest you."

Julie took in every word that her principal was sharing with her. She had learned more from him in the last twenty minutes than she had been able to find out in the last year.

"It's about a hundred miles from here, as the crow flies," he joked with Julie. "I do know some people at this college, and I thought that if you were interested, I could possibly look into seeing if we could get you some scholarships and financial aide."

Julie raised her head up from the brochure and looked across the desk at Mr. Jenkins. She didn't know what to say. Her mouth kind of just hung open in surprise. She just stared at him and was at a loss for words.

"My wife and I are going up to Elkins next weekend. You did know that my wife is the principal for Springfield, didn't you?"

Julie regained her composure and just nodded that she did. She shifted in her chair and leaned forward as Mr. Jenkins continued to speak.

"Well, I know that my daughter and you are on the same basketball team together. And I thought that if you were interested, you could come home with her on the bus, spend the night with us, and we could all visit the college together the next day. You could look around and see if it suited you. Afterward, you'll be welcome to come with us and visit some of our friends up that way. We'll bring you home later that evening."

Julie made sure her mouth didn't drop open this time. She smiled from ear to ear at Mr. Jenkins, trying to take in all that he was saying to her. *How could this be possible?*

"Of course, you would have to talk to your parents and get a permission slip."

Julie regained her voice and said, "I don't know what to say, Mr. Jenkins. I know they'll agree to let me come. I am very interested. I can't thank you enough!" Julie was finding it difficult to contain her excitement.

"Well, you think about it and let me know. I'm not sure what aide we can get you, but I'm sure we can get you something." Mr. Jenkins scooted his chair back and went to stand up.

Julie stood up and reached out her hand to shake his. "Thank you, Mr. Jenkins. Thank you so very much!" Julie could hardly hold back the tears of joy that were filling her eyes.

Mr. Jenkins smiled at Julie and reached out and shook her hand. He could see her eyes glisten and dancing with excitement. "You are welcome, Ms. Clayton," he answered. "Ms. Moyer will give you your excuse card for your class on your way out."

Julie marched down the aisle in her white cap and gown with her classmates. Her heart could not smile broader than the smile on her face. This was the moment that she had waited for all of her life. She was graduating and she was going to college. Mr. Jenkins had kept his word on all that he had offered. Julie had visited the college and applied for scholarships and financial aide. Julie received full scholarship. She didn't know how she would ever be able to thank Mr. Jenkins for all that he had done for her.

Julie sat and listened intently to the songs and presentations. Excitement had built as she anticipated receiving her diploma. But she was astonished at the next turn of events. Her principal stepped up to the podium and announced that at this time he would present the scholarships, awards, and honors. First, Julie listened as her classmates received their various rewards. But then to her surprise, she heard her name being called to come forward.

Julie knew that she had received scholarships but didn't know that it would be announced at the ceremony. Julie walked forward as quickly as she could squeezing past her classmates. Her face blushed as she felt humbled by the attention from her principal, Mr. Jenkins, when he announced the full scholarship that she had received. Julie smiled as she shook his hand and turned to leave. The crowd applauded, when to her surprise, Mr. Jenkins continued to hold her hand and began speaking again, "I know of no awards that are available to present to anyone who has completed twelve years of schooling and never missed a single day of attendance, but it seems worthy to honor her for this dedication." To Julie's surprise he had not yet finished his full presentation. He continued holding her hand and spoke once again. "Julie has represented her classmates on the Student Council and is also a member of the National Honor Society. She has represented us as Miss Benson High. And now it is with great pleasure for me to announce that she has been elected by her peers to represent the Benson High School as our representative to the Mineral County Fair to be held in August." Once again, the crowd applauded loudly. Julie nodded a thank you and turned to leave the stage but her principal continued to hold her hand. "Julie, by the choice of her peers, has also been acknowledged as being chosen for the following honors: *Most Likely to Succeed, Best All Around, Friendliest, Most Studious,* and...," Mr. Jenkins paused, to the thunder of the crowd's clapping, *"Most Athletic!"* Julie felt her face turn crimson red as she faced the crowd. Her peers clapped and Julie was touched by the honors that they had bestowed upon her. These were the people that she had shared most of her life with, the good and the bad. Julie turned and left the stage and returned to her seat to await the presentation of the diplomas. "Before we present the diplomas," Mr. Jenkins continued, "Mr. Tindrel has one more award that he would like to present."

Mr. Tindrel stepped up to the podium and began to speak. "On behalf of the Tri-Hi-Y Club we give an award every year to a member of the Senior Class. This award is called *I'm a Third Award.* The Third Award is an award that is given to the senior that has been nominated and elected by our members to possess the following qualities. They must put God first, others second, and themselves third. On behalf of the Tri-Hi-Y Club, we would like to present this award to Miss Julie Anna Clayton!" Julie sat motionless not knowing what to do to accept this great honor. "Miss Clayton," Mr. Tindrel called out as he motioned with an outstretched arm, "would you come and receive this trophy?" Julie arose to the thunderous clapping of her friends and family. She climbed the steps slowly and felt her legs shaking nervously with each step. She approached the podium and took into her hands the trophy that Mr. Tindrel handed her. He gave her a sincere smile as he firmly shook her hand. The award was more than Julie could have ever imagined. She looked out into the audience and her eyes focused upon her family. They were all there clapping the loudest of all. Her brothers beamed with pride and love for the little sister that was their own. Julie looked deeply into her mom's eyes as the tears flowed down her mom's cheeks. The faces of those who loved her had been the best award.

Blessed Wedding Day

Chapter

21

Hope is tangible and breathes life and passion into every human soul that dares to reach out, grab it, and believe. *"From whence comes my help? My help comes from the Lord. He will not suffer my foot to be moved; He that keeps me will not slumber."*

Julie laid her Bible down by her side. She rubbed her eyes, rested her head against the back of the sofa, and closed her eyes, letting the music that Mike was playing on the piano engulf her.

Julie remembered how she had felt her life was over on that day when Alice had left. It had seemed as if all hope was gone. She had felt so lifeless then, that even the slightest breeze could have blown her away.

She never dreamed that God would have her life orchestrated, planned, and full of purpose. He had not suffered her foot to be moved, but had kept her all the days of her life. He had kept every promise to her that He had ever given her. He had been patient and kind, loved her, waited for her, and guided and protected her. Such love had given Julie hope in her darkest hour.

Julie marveled at the joy that had filled her life. She didn't know how she could have been any happier than on the day of her graduation. It seemed that, on that day alone, God had fulfilled a multitude of promises. But little did she know the whole plan He had for her life. When she sat that day in Mr. Jenkins' office, she only saw the promise of God's hand leading her to college. She couldn't envision the fullness of His plan that day. She didn't know that when she would go to this college, the college that she, herself, had not chosen, but God himself, that she would meet the man that God had promised to bring into her life—a promise that He had given to her when she was a mere twelve-year-old child. *"If you put Me first in your life, I will give you the desires of your heart,"* God had whispered to her heart at the peak of her sexual abuse. So often the promises of God are given in our darkest hour and yet fulfilled in the brightest seasons of our life.

Julie sat reminiscing of how she had gone to college, excelled, and there met Mike those many years ago. The music that Mike was playing lulled Julie back to the memories of where she had first met Mike.

So often, on the weekends, the campus would be buzzing with many drug and drinking parties. To escape, she would leave her dorm and go down to the college chapel to find a place of quietness and rest. The college had not been as Christian as Julie had hoped. Upon approaching the chapel one evening, Julie heard the most beautiful music being played. The small chapel stood majestic, with its stained glass walls reflecting the light from the inside, onto the pathway outside in prisms of brilliant colors. Julie paused at the door to wait and listen, lest there was a concert going on inside; but there was a short silence and then the music started to play again. Julie had opened the door and entered quietly. Only then did she see Mike sitting and playing the grand piano in the corner of the chapel. She had previously met him at their chapel services and had been in some of the same classes with him. He had captured her heart from the very beginning. It was at the chapel that they became friends. Here Julie would take her refuge; and here so often, she would find Mike playing the music that he had written. He would beckon her to stay, and she would sit down on the small steps that led down to the grand piano and listen to the heavenly music letting it carry her far away from the campus.

It was here that they sat and talked, sharing their hopes and dreams, getting to know each other, and falling in love.

All these years later, Julie continued to love to sit and listen to him play. It enraptured her heart. Julie thought she would never be happier than on her graduation day, but she was wrong. The day that she walked down the aisle to become Mike's wife had superseded any of her childhood dreams of her wedding day.

The precious things of life are priceless moments that fill our hearts with such joy that they change us forever. And so, Julie walked down the aisle that day and joined the one who God had picked for her those many years before. It was a priceless moment that hung in the form of a promise until the day that it would unfold before her like a beautiful rose on a cool summer day filling her life with its sweet aroma and beauty.

God had not only brought Julie out of the brokenness of her childhood but had taken her on a healing journey and had helped her find *the little girl* that had been lost for so long.

The years had passed and so much had happened. So many things had changed and yet so many things didn't change at all. After Julie and Mike married, Ethel and Buck married. He had become Julie's "Bucky". He had taken her under his wing. Like a little wounded bird, he showed Julie a father's love and helped her to learn to fly.

It was about this same time when her dad had met Claire and married her. Julie was glad that her dad had found a good woman. She had only hoped that he would treat her right and that he would change his life. Julie thought for sure with Claire's influence, love, and endurance that her dad would finally change. But he did not. Julie didn't know how Claire, through all the years, had continued to endure living with her dad, but she did; and Julie admired her for everything that she had done for him.

Julie knew that her dad's health was failing quickly. She thought that she had done all that she could do for him. She didn't hear back concerning the letter that she had written to him. She had hoped that some mention of it to Claire might help her to discern whether she was meant to come in and visit him. But Claire had told her that she had taken all of his mail to him and that he had not mentioned Julie's letter. Julie had no desire to go in to visit her dad and upset him or condemn him as he neared the latter days of his life. She had always prayed through the years that if someone, just one person, could pray with her dad and bind those horrible spirits that Julie felt had held him prisoner all the days of his life, then maybe, just maybe, his heart would be free to feel the presence of the One, Who longed to meet him *In the Garden,* as his favorite song so sweetly spoke of. But would he want to come to the garden and to beckon to the One, Who was calling him to it? It seemed that her dad had made up his mind.

The one thing that Julie knew was that she was not to visit him, unless God would make it clear to her that she should go. It's an amazing thing, that still small voice of God, Who speaks to our hearts. In the last weeks that had passed since her dad had been diagnosed with cancer, Julie thought heavily on what God had asked her two years ago. *"Will you go talk to your dad, if I lead you to him?"* She had wrestled with God about it at first when He had asked her, but then she had conceded that if He would only make it clear to her, she would go. Julie had talked with many of the family during this time. Some thought that it was terrible that she had not gone in to visit her dad. One family member had told her that her dad wanted her to come see him; however, Claire had not mentioned anything about this. When her dad had had a stroke a few years earlier, he had made it very clear to the family, "Tell Julie that she can come to see me, but she cannot talk to me about Jesus!" Claire had told her on the way to the hospital, this last time, that her dad had stated, "I'm not a sinner condemned to Hell." Julie would never allow anyone to put conditions upon her pertaining to her God. She was still unsure of what she should do, so she waited these last weeks and prayed.

"Whatcha thinking?" Mike asked as he sat down beside Julie on the couch. He rested his hand on her leg and looked deeply into her eyes.

"Oh, you know," Julie answered in a soft voice.

"Your dad?" Mike asked.

"Yea," Julie answered and nodded. "I talked to Jerry the other day and to Claire. Jerry tried to get Dad to understand the reality of his situation."

"Did he listen to Jerry?" Mike asked.

"You know Mike, Dad will listen to Jerry probably more than any of us, but he really doesn't listen to anyone," Julie answered. She turned and laid her head onto his shoulder.

"Jul, I would never tell you what to do," Mike said, as he turned and looked compassionately into Julie's eyes. "I know that you're concerned about your dad's soul. But, I'm concerned about you. You may have to face your dad before he dies," Mike continued. He paused for a moment as Julie sat quietly and intently listened to him. "You need to face your *Giant*, Jul," Mike said softly.

Julie sat up and looked at Mike. What he was saying stirred her heart.

"Whatever you decide, know that it's okay for you to go in. I'll take care of everything here. Go in if you need to."

Julie was quiet as she processed more of what was happening in her heart along with what Mike was saying to her. "Mike, I never really thought I'd go in to see him. To be honest, I really didn't want to."

"I know," Mike replied.

"But just now, for the first time, I feel an urgency that I should go in. I haven't felt that this whole time, until you shared with me just now," Julie said. "I don't know why either. Just all of a sudden, I feel that I'm meant to go in."

"You need to face your *Giant*, Jul," Mike repeated kindly. "He may want to talk to you alone."

"Oh, I don't know if I can do that, Mike," Julie said.

"Well, just feel it out as you go. God will lead you." Mike encouraged her. "When do you want to go in?"

"I'll pack and leave tomorrow," Julie answered.

"Are you going to call and tell Claire you're coming?"

"No," Julie answered. "I'm only going to call Mom and ask her if she'll go with me."

It was late the next day before Julie could pull everything together to leave. She caught up on the paperwork and made some phone calls. She and Mike were scheduled to leave on their vacation to Hawaii on Sunday. There wasn't much time to go to West Virginia and get back.

Julie finally started packing. Her mind raced as she hurried to get on the road. *What would she say? Would he even be able to talk to her? How would he react? What would he say to her?* Mike was right. She would be facing her *Giant*.

Julie finished loading the car. She placed her Bible onto the front seat. She would read it later that night and try to see what God would want her to say to her dad. She stopped at the Garden Center, their place of business, to see Mike and say good-bye.

"Be careful," Mike said and kissed her good-bye. "It's going to be okay, Jul," he reassured her.

"I wish you could come with me," Julie remarked.

"Me too," Mike agreed, giving her hand a squeeze. "But somehow, I think you're meant to do this with just you and God."

Julie turned and exited the parking lot and pulled out onto the main highway. Julie knew the way by heart. They had driven back to her home for forty years. Her mind began to settle as she drove. She thought about what Jerry had asked her the other day when they had talked. "I know they just found the cancer a few weeks ago and they don't expect him to die right away; but wonder if he dies while you're in Hawaii, Jul, will you come back for the funeral?"

Julie answered Jerry, "I don't know." She then paused and added, "Jerry, if he would die while I'm gone, then I believe that I'm probably just not meant to be there then."

"Maybe so," replied Jerry. "Maybe so."

Julie rounded the bend on her last country road and turned to get onto the entrance of the interstate. She turned her CD player on low and listened to the music. The music flowed over her and comforted her.

> *"Just a closer walk with thee.*
> *Grant it Jesus is my plea.*
> *Daily walking close to thee.*
> *Let it be, dear Lord, let it be.*
> *I am weak but thou art strong...."*

Julie still enjoyed the old songs the best. Some brought back a lot of memories. *Just a closer walk with thee...,* the song continued with the chorus. This was one of her Gramma Emma's favorites. They had often sung it down at their family reunions.

Julie was glad that the sun was still shining as she hit the bigger mountains. Julie hated driving in the dark and always loved to see the mountains as she drove through them. The mountains before her had changed into a starburst of color with arrays of reds, yellows, and oranges, blending on the trees, filling the mountainsides so brilliantly that they appeared as a kaleidoscope of color. It took Julie's breath away. *It's like driving through a postcard,* Julie thought.

She was soon near her home territory. Memories began to flow over her at every turn in the road. As she climbed one mountain and neared the top, she remembered the family picnics they had shared at its scenic overlook. Every year when the family went to Gramma Emma's reunion, they would all stop at the overlook on the way back to gather and picnic once again. It was a special time, a time when all the aunts, uncles, cousins, grandparents, and brothers were all together. Julie could even remember when her mom was still married to her dad and she would sing with her Uncle Tom at the reunions.

Julie couldn't help but wonder, *what Gramma Emma would think of her dad.* All of Julie's grandparents had been gone for a while now. Julie smiled to herself. She believed her Gramma Emma would have wanted her to try to talk to her dad, to get through to him. Julie could just hear her, as if she was alive today, and would tell him, "Now, Ron, it's time you straightened up. These children need you...." Tears stung Julie's eyes. "What will you have me say, Lord?" Julie whispered out loud. She then heard that still small voice that she recognized so well. *"You must keep your heart and mind on the mission. It is two-fold. One is for your dad's soul; the other is for you, in that, you must 'slay your Giant.'"* Julie's heart focused upon those two points. *"Your Giant is not your dad,"* the gentle voice spoke to her heart. *"The Giant is the evilness that hangs on your dad like a shroud. It is what hangs onto him and what has always tried to destroy you."* Julie had always prayed that someone would be sent to pray for her dad, to bind this evilness; but never in all of her years of praying for her dad, did she ever think that God would send her.

Julie pondered all of this. She marveled how God was leading her to talk to her dad. It had been two years earlier, when God had beckoned her asking, *"Will you go to talk to your Dad if I lead you to?"* Julie remembered how she had wrestled with God over confronting her dad once again. It wasn't until now that Julie knew that this was the time for her to go see him. She now knew the mission, but still not the words. Julie believed that God knew the time and that He knew her dad's heart. God had showed her that He would not lead her to her dad if his heart was too hard and He had promised her that He would not allow her dad to hurt her again. Sick or not, Julie knew that her dad still had the potential to do this greatly.

Promises Fulfilled
Missy, Julie (Marty), Mike, Mike Jr. and Jenny

Chapter

22

Julie awoke, slowly opening her eyes as she lay on her mom's bed. Behind her was a large arched window where Julie looked up gazing at the stars. She rubbed her eyes and then looked more intently. Above her hung the biggest and brightest big dipper that she had ever seen. Julie just stared at it as she continued to awaken. It put her in awe and wonder, the splendor of it, as if it had been put there, at that time, just for her, a kind of symbol of God's power and love.

She continued to lie there and watched the morning break as her emotions raced to and fro, beating against her heart, like mighty ocean waves beating against the shore. She had never thought that one day she would need to face her dad. She had only thought of his soul and the need for him to make it right with God. She had thought of the need for him to make things right with her brothers so that they could heal, but she had never seen the need for her to face her dad. She had thought that God had healed her and that she had forgiven her dad, so she didn't feel that she had any need to see him. It was only when Mike had brought it to her attention that she realized that there was still a need for closure for her, too.

The sun began to shine brightly through the window. Julie sat up and swung her legs over the side of the bed. She placed her face into her hands and began to pray. She lifted her head at the sound of a lone bird singing loudly outside of the bedroom. It sang so clearly, earnestly, sharp, and full of song. Such a strange time of year to hear this, Julie thought, as she reached for her Bible. So many verses had been impressed upon her heart. She wanted to look them up and mark them in case God wanted her to share them with her dad today. Julie knew that she couldn't preach to her dad, and she had no desire to, nor to condemn him. She just wanted God to touch his heart. As Julie read the verses, she felt a new strength and peace flow over her, even in spite of knowing what she was facing, and the not knowing of what she was about to face today.

She began to feel direction as God spoke to her heart: *"Address the issues, but don't make the issues, the issue. Stay focused on the two-fold mission: your dad's soul and confront the spirits that have taunted you all of your life—slay the Giant."*

As Julie finished reading, she felt fortified in God. She pulled out her journal and noted her thoughts to clear her heart and mind. Julie had looked at her journal one day not long ago and was surprised by something she had written. It seemed to impress her just now. For over ten years, she had had the same dream. She knew that she must have had it over fifty times during those years, always different but always the same. The one thing that she noticed was how the dream had evolved. In the beginning she feared for her life. She was always terrorized and always fled and never saw her tormentor. Through the years, she had ceased to run but would venture to the cracked door to confront her attacker. The terror was still there; however, she now wanted to know who the attacker was, and what did he want. On reading the earlier part of her journal it had surprised her how the dream had changed. She no longer slammed the door shut and ran. She no longer confronted the door and paused to see what would happen; but now she opened the door, went down the steps, and confronted the man who stood before her. In the one dream, where she did this, the man stood before her in a stance, ready for her. Julie felt terror and fear but it did not control her. She saw a shovel and a rake in his hands. She thought that he would attack her; but instead, Julie realized that he was poised to defend himself against her. Julie knew that he would never be afraid of her, but she also knew that he would be very afraid of the God who had the power to stop him.

Julie called Mike and talked to him before she left to go to see her dad. He kidded with her a little and then lovingly said, "It'll be okay, Jul. You'll know what to say as you go."

Julie took a few deep breaths as she walked down the hospital hallway beside her mom. Ethel reached over and took her hand and squeezed it. Julie smiled a nervous smile at her mom and let out a sigh as they entered the hospital room.

Ron was awake when they walked in. He looked at both of them as they entered the room. Julie saw his eyes widen, full of surprise as she neared his bed. It surprised Julie that her dad seemed happy to see her. "I didn't think that you would come," he said.

Julie took a seat in a chair on the one side of the bed and let her mom and dad talk. It reminded her of when she was a child hearing the two of them talk. Most of it was small talk. Julie was shocked at how thin and how bad her dad appeared. She wondered, as she looked at this frail and old man, how it could be her dad. He must have wondered the same about her as he turned to her and said, "You're getting old." There was no smile and Julie knew that he wasn't kidding with her. She reminded him of her age and that she wasn't a young girl anymore. He asked her about the family, and Julie simply answered that they were all fine and then didn't say anymore. He went back to talking to her mom and seemed to be totally unaware of her presence. He spoke about his condition, mostly denying the seriousness of the cancer, his heart, and other conditions. He didn't look at Julie and seemed to have a difficult time addressing her.

Julie searched her heart as the emotions flowed over her: her sorrow with this meeting, and the sadness of seeing a broken and feeble old man denying his condition. She felt her heart fill with anger at his total disregard of her as he continued to make small talk with her mom. Julie couldn't play the *let's pretend to be normal* game. She sat quietly and prayed in her heart for direction and that God would take the anger out of her heart. She wondered, *What am I doing here listening to small talk about the hospital food and nurses? Where is the purpose God? What am I supposed to do or say?*

"Wait," the still small voice spoke to her heart. *"Say nothing, just wait. Remember the mission."*

Julie continued to sit and watch the man who was her dad. She tried to sort out her feelings as her past rushed into the present, causing her mind to spin.

"Did you read the letter that Julie sent you?" Ethel asked Ron after a while.

"Yea, I read it, first a little and then more later. It took me a while to read it and understand," Ron explained to Ethel.

Julie wondered if she was even in the room as her dad continued to talk as if she wasn't there. He slowly turned to her after a while. "I was told that you wanted to see me, Dad," Julie ventured, glad that she had some time for her spirit to settle.

"Yes, I did," Ron answered. "I was surprised that I didn't hear from you or get a phone call," he stated mildly.

Julie could see that he was offended. "I was waiting for you to read the letter and see how you would respond to it." Julie looked her dad in the eyes. She girded her heart and mind with the Lord. She was reminded to be kind as well as firm with her dad, to not be sidetracked by his actions or words, nor let her feelings deter her from God's purpose.

"Dad, I know that Jerry was in to visit you."

"Yea, he was here last week," Ron replied.

Julie was surprised at how clear her dad's mind was. He didn't seem as old when he spoke. Eerily, Julie almost felt like she was ten years old again, and her dad a young man. "Jerry told me, Dad, that he explained to you how serious your condition is."

"Yea, he did," Ron answered. "But, what do they know, Julie? They're not always right."

"How do you feel?" Julie asked.

"Well, a little rough," Ron answered.

"Dad, they're not giving you much time," Julie said with concern. She didn't know how her dad would respond.

"I know, that's what Jerry told me, and that's what the doctors are telling me, too."

"Dad, there isn't a lot of time left." Julie hated to be so direct but she knew that her dad was putting his illness under the rug like he had put everything in his life, and there was no other way that Julie could talk to him.

Julie tried to be kind. She glanced over at her mom. Ethel gave her a smile and a nod to continue. "Dad, I came to see you for two reasons." Julie continued, searching every word before she said it. "One was that your soul could be saved and the other is to face my *Giant*."

Ron looked at Julie a little puzzled. Julie bit her lip and looked into her dad's eyes. She could still see the dad of her childhood. She searched his eyes, trying to see which dad she was dealing with and wondering if the dad that she had glimpses of, from time to time, was there. She wondered once again, if that dad even existed. It was so difficult to stay focused with her mind spinning and her emotions ricocheting through her like bullets. "Dad," Julie paused and then gently spoke, "you were my *Giant*."

Ron just looked at Julie. Ethel said nothing. She watched Julie and listened to her speak. Ethel didn't see Julie, the grown-up woman sitting before her, but rather the little girl that she loved so much. She believed in her, and somehow, she knew that Julie would find the words to say.

"Do you have an answer to the letter I wrote you?" Julie asked softly.

She didn't want to miss the door to talk to her dad about his soul. She didn't know if the doctors or nurses would come in at any time and take him for tests. She didn't know if someone might come to visit, and then they would just sit and pretend everything was normal and talk small-talk. Julie was glad that her dad didn't have a roommate. She felt an urgency to talk to him about his soul. She knew that this was going to mean confrontations and uncovering things from under the rug, but it had to be done if her dad's soul was ever going to be saved.

Julie waited for her dad to answer. She knew him. She knew how he thought, how he manipulated, how he would be content just letting Julie talk, if he could avoid answering her. Julie knew that he would be content and more than satisfied if she would just pretend that everything was okay and leave the past where he had put it. But Julie knew that this wouldn't work. She knew that she was walking on thin ice but also knew that she had to continue and felt an urgency to proceed. She knew that her dad fully understood what she was asking him, so she didn't try to explain and waited for his answer.

"Well, Julie," Ron spoke. He cleared his throat and gave a nervous cough. Julie knew this was what he had always done when he would start to feel cornered or that he had lost control. "What makes you think that I don't talk to God?" he asked.

Julie could feel God's presence strengthening her with each sentence. She knew that God was dealing with her dad's heart and she knew that she was headed for a battle. The enemy of his soul had had him bound for a lifetime; there was no way that he was going to let go now. Julie wondered, if maybe, that was why her dad had avoided her at first. That this was why he had sidetracked and just talked to Ethel, because he knew Julie as well as she knew him and he knew that she would not let go.

"Dad, I don't doubt that you talk to God," Julie answered. "I just wonder if you listen to what He says to you."

"How do you know that I haven't made it right with God?" Ron asked. "I pray."

Julie paused. She didn't want this to become an argument. She didn't want this to become a debate. She knew that she had to tread firmly and gently. Julie stood up and reached for the Bible which she had brought with her and then sat back down. She waited for her dad to protest, but he didn't. She knew as a child that her dad read his Marine New Testament, which he kept in the top drawer of his nightstand. Maybe she could break it down better for him so that he could understand. Julie opened up to Romans 10:3 and read the scripture. *"For they being ignorant of God's righteousness and going about to establish their own righteousness have not submitted themselves unto the righteousness of God."* "Dad, you are establishing your own righteousness without submitting yourself to God and this won't work."

"But, how do you know what I've said to God or what I've made right?" her dad queried.

Julie looked down at the pages of her Bible. She wondered if her dad even recognized that this was the Bible that he had bought her for Christmas thirty-eight years ago. She began to read again and wondered if he would tell her to stop. *"If you shall confess with your mouth the Lord Jesus and believe in your heart that God raised him from the dead, you shall be saved." "For it is with the heart man believes unto righteousness, but it is the mouth that makes confession to salvation."* Julie glanced at her dad. He didn't appear tired or weak. Actually, Julie would've smiled except for the seriousness of the moment. She knew, though, that nothing energized her dad more than a debate.

Julie continued, "Dad, you haven't done this. You haven't confessed this. You want to say that everything is alright. You want to establish your own righteousness without submitting yourself to God or confessing that you ever did anything wrong."

"But how can you say that?" Ron countered.

Julie knew that it was going to get sticky and probably heated now. She whispered a prayer under her breath. "Have you admitted to what you did to Tonya?"

Ron just glared at Julie. He knew where she was heading with all of this.

"Have you admitted to what you've done to Ronnie, Jerry, Matt, me and others? Dad, until you admit to God what you've done, you can't be forgiven. You can't just brush it aside like it never happened, just because it happened many years ago. I've told you in the past, if you never make it right with us, you have to make it right with God," Julie spoke seriously yet compassionately. She never knew, with her dad, what he was really thinking.

"What do you mean what I've done to everyone? I haven't done anything to anyone," Ron pressed.

"Dad, what about what you did to Tonya?" Julie asked.

"I don't know about that?" Ron answered.

"Dad, you molested her!" Julie remarked firmly.

"More like the other way around," Ron came back at Julie.

Julie couldn't believe her ears. Why she had thought it would be different this time, she didn't know. She looked Ron in the eye determined to face every spirit of denial, justification, and minimization. "Dad, she was fifteen years old!"

"Fifteen…"

"You got her pregnant!" Julie said in exasperation.

"He wasn't mine," Ron answered back as calmly as if they were talking about the weather.

"You know that for sure? You had a DNA test done?" Julie countered.

"I'm pretty sure," Ron said unabashed.

"You're missing the point, Dad. Whether he was your son or not isn't the point, even though it is an important point. It's that you had sex with her, and that he could have been your son. You denied him as your son and you destroyed Tonya's and her children's lives," Julie said in desperation as she tried to get her dad to see how he had affected Tonya's life.

Ron sat quietly, not so much thinking as wanting Julie to stop. He knew that Julie wouldn't back down.

"What about what you did to Ronnie?" Julie asked.

"What do you mean?" Ron asked.

"You know how you treated him. You know all the things that you did to him throughout the years," Julie answered.

Ron countered her and denied instance after instance that Julie addressed. "When did I do that? I never did that. Who told you that?" he would ask with a rebuttal.

"Dad…besides living there, Ronnie did talk to me!"

"And you believe him?" Ron asked.

"Why wouldn't I believe him?" Julie asked back.

"Well, I don't remember any of that, and I never did anything to Matt," Ron spoke with his voice rising defensively.

"You broke his heart," she emphasized.

"I didn't do anything!"

"You broke his heart as a little boy, more than any of us, over and over again. And although he's a great husband, dad and brother, his heart is still broken."

"I don't think I did any of that," Ron remarked.

"Dad, you said that he wasn't your son."

"No, I said that I wasn't sure."

"No, you told me yourself that you didn't think that he was your son. You even told me whose son you thought he was," Julie continued.

She hated this. She hated bringing up the past. She hated burying and denying the past. She wasn't trying to prove a point. She was just trying to get her dad to see that he had to make these things right with God. "You never treated him like Jerry."

"I always tried to be fair," Ron responded.

"You beat him harder," Julie said softly. "He tried to do more for you than any of us. He waxed your bowling balls, cleaned your car, anything to try to win your love."

"I don't remember that."

"You accused him of having an affair with Alice," Julie said.

When would it click? When would his heart finally get it? Julie wondered.

"Well, I never did anything to Jerry," Ron changed the subject.

"Except make him feel that you didn't love him," Julie countered.

"How can you say that?" Ron asked.

"Because that's how he felt," Julie answered. "He always wondered why you couldn't sign your letters to him in Vietnam, *Love, Dad*. He thought that you just didn't know how to express your love. Can you know how it is for a son to always wonder if their dad loves them?" Julie asked.

"Well, I don't think that I ruined Sandy's life," Ron changed the subject again.

"Dad, she was a broken little girl looking for fatherly love, a man's attention. She knew that if she didn't go along with you, she would have no home. We were her last chance at having a home. She had nowhere else to go to live. You destroyed her."

"I don't think that you remember everything clearly," Ron stated. "Wonder if you're wrong?"

"How am I wrong, Dad?" Julie asked.

She was so tired. She glanced at her mom. Ethel looked as if she was holding back tears, rocking gently in her chair. Again, she nodded to Julie. Julie felt so sad. She knew how painful this must be for her mom, bringing all of this up.

"You ever think that your thoughts might be wrong?" Ron asked again, trying to gain ground.

"Dad, I lived through it! I saw what you did."

"I just don't see it that way," Ron refuted.

"Dad, for better or worse, I remember." Julie felt led to continue. She would have just as soon ended the conversation; however, she knew that she couldn't.

"What about me, Dad?" Julie asked softly. Julie wasn't sure whether she was up to him denying what he had done to her, but she had to continue onto this dreaded ground.

"What do you mean, Julie?" Ron asked as he glanced over at Ethel.

"You know what I mean, Dad," Julie answered. "And Mom knows everything, Dad. Everyone knows. There are no more secrets anymore!"

Ron appeared stunned at first but quickly regained control and just gave Julie a doubtful look while avoiding Ethel's glare. The nurse came in to take some blood. They talked to Ron and tried to explain the seriousness of his illness. Ron countered them and tried to brush it off.

"Mr. Clayton, you need to realize how truly serious your condition is," the nurse said.

Ron turned away from the needle as he felt the pinch. Julie remembered how much her dad had always hated needles and hospitals. She watched the man who had been her father all of her life. Even now, she tried to figure him out.

He began to joke with the nurses and they joked back. They treated him compassionately, and the one nurse took his hand and rubbed it gently. She called him honey and patted his hand kindly. Julie watched the scene unfold in front of her. She watched her dad play the role of the sweet old man. Julie just wondered what the nurses would think if they knew that he was a pedophile, a child molester. Julie stirred in her chair uncomfortably. She had to stay focused.

As soon as the nurses left the room, Ron began to say something to Ethel. Julie knew that he was trying to change the subject and knew that she couldn't stop now.

"So, Dad," Julie interrupted.

Ron turned to face Julie. Julie was waiting for him to tell her that he was tired or that he had had enough. But he didn't say anything.

"What about what you did to me, Dad?" Julie asked slowly.

"I thought we worked all of this out at your Uncle Tom's funeral," he remarked.

"When?" Julie asked. "How?"

"We talked."

"About you molesting me?" Julie asked. "Did I miss that? When did we resolve and talk about those issues? I reached out to you in compassion at the funeral, but we resolved and talked about nothing."

"I told you that if I did anything, that I was sorry?" Ron answered.

Julie wanted to really address the "*if*" part, but instead replied, "No, Dad! I think I would have remembered. You never said that you were sorry, and Dad…," Julie spoke kinder and gentler now. It took all of the Lord that she had to calm her heart and voice and to keep her focused. She looked him straight in the eye and said, "…Dad, I don't need you to say that you're sorry to me; you can, but I don't need you to say it because God has healed me. Dad, I came here to let you know that I forgive you." Julie felt herself get teary-eyed. "But you need to ask God to forgive you. You can't deny, justify, and minimize all of these things. Maybe you did it because of what happened to you. Because of what Pap Pap James did to you."

"He never did anything to me," Ron answered soberly. He looked down and avoided Julie's eyes.

"He never molested you?"

"No."

"What about the others in our family?"

"I didn't say…that he didn't others," Ron answered.

"What about what he did to me, Dad?" Julie asked. There was no more time left. Julie hated that all of this was coming up now. She really didn't imagine that this was the way that this conversation today was going to go. She couldn't stop now. She had to see it through. It was the only way her dad's soul could be saved, and it was the only way she was going to be able to face the *Giant*.

"You told me that he never molested you," Ron remarked, seeming genuinely surprised.

"When did I tell you that?" Julie asked.

"I asked you one time," Ron added.

"No, Dad. And when have we ever talked about any of the molestation?"

Ron said nothing. Julie searched his face to try to understand which dad she was dealing with. She felt, as if, she had dealt today with all the different dads that she had experienced from her childhood.

"I was four years old Dad. The memory isn't as clear as what you did to me, Dad, but he did molest me; and you did nothing, Dad."

"I didn't know," Ron answered without any emotion.

For the first time, Julie heard a voice come from the side of the room. "Ron, I was going to go to the sheriff," Ethel interjected with tears in her eyes.

"I would've killed him," Ron said.

This shook Julie. *Had she heard her dad correctly? He would have killed her grandpap for the very thing that he had done to her all of her life?* Julie didn't know how much longer she could continue this conversation. She appeared strong and steadfast, but inside she was crumbling. It was just too painful.

"I told you, Ron," Ethel said softly but firmly.

"I don't remember that," Ron answered.

"You didn't protect me," Julie added.

"They said that I'd have to go and place a warrant. I had no ride or money," Ethel added.

"And did you offer to help her, Dad? No!" Julie could feel fire rising inside of her. It was the only thing that was propelling her to continue.

"And what about what you did to me all of my life?" Julie asked.

"No, that was wrong," Ron said.

Julie couldn't think fast enough. She couldn't believe that her dad had just admitted that it was wrong. He had never even admitted to what he did. Julie wanted to stop right there and try to digest his words in her heart, but she knew that she couldn't lose momentum or the conversation would be over.

"Why did Pap Pap James do it, Dad?" Julie asked.

"I don't know," Ron answered in a sober voice.

"Why did you do it?" Julie asked sadly.

"I don't know," Ron answered in a low voice.

"But, I never hurt Matt or Ronnie," Ron spoke up attempting to change the subject again.

Julie couldn't go around that mountain again. She was too tired. She simply said, "Yes, Dad. You did hurt all of them in different ways."

There was a slight pause. Julie tried to search her heart to see how God wanted her to use this to draw her dad to repentance. But before she could think, Ron spoke up once again and tried to gain ground.

"I don't think you remember everything right," Ron said sternly.

Julie was so caught off guard by the switch in dads that she was speechless. Everything had changed in a minute. Julie tried to sort her thoughts, check her emotions, and say a quick prayer to stay focused.

"Dad, you think I don't remember it right?" Julie asked astonished. Ron just turned and blankly looked at her. It was written all over his face that he knew that he had crossed the line with Julie. "You think that I don't remember it right?!" Julie asked, astounded as her voice rose in momentum. "Dad, for better or worse, the one thing that I have always had is a good memory. You know that."

Julie hesitated. It was so important for her to run a check on her emotions and thoughts before she proceeded. She didn't want to get caught up in her emotions of the moment. After a slight pause and in a calmer voice she began to speak again. "Then Dad, this is what we'll do. I'll start with the first time that you abused me, and I'll continue through all the times until you are convinced that I remember right. I can tell you where every piece of furniture was placed. I can tell you that Aunt Tassy watched us that night and that you had just come back from taking her home. I can tell you that I was eight years old. You came into my room and I saw that look in your eyes. I don't know why it terrified me, maybe unknowingly because I remembered that same look from Pap Pap James. I don't know." Julie continued talking until she had expounded on the whole account. She had never done this before. It was too painful to go on, but she had to.

"Dad, do you know what that does to an eight-year-old little girl? I wanted to die. You didn't just molest my body; you raped my soul! And this wasn't the only time. You continued to do it over and over again. Do you know that I wanted to commit suicide? I would have Dad. I had the guts. I was just afraid that I might go to Hell."

The air of the hospital room was electrified. Julie didn't know why any of the nurses hadn't come back into the room, but she was glad. She knew that God was giving them this time. She just had to figure out how to use it for good. There was a silence. No one said a word. Not even Julie. She felt as if all the blood had drained out of her. Her head throbbed and she felt weak. She whispered a prayer and let her head hang down. Slowly, she lifted it and looked at her dad. His head was still hung down. He couldn't look at Julie. He had hung his head down shortly after Julie began to tell him of the incident. Julie heard the Holy Spirit talk to her heart, softly, *"Show him compassion."*

Julie moved her arm slowly, without hesitation, and reached and touched her dad's elbow. He jerked, as if in fear, seemingly unsure of what Julie was going to do, and looked right up at her. Their eyes met. Julie saw a glimpse of the dad that she had once seen a long, long time ago. This was the dad that she had so often wondered if he even really existed. There was no cockiness, no arrogance, and no denial.

"Dad," Julie spoke gently with her eyes still fixed on his. "I didn't come here to condemn you. I didn't come here to throw all of your past into your face. I came here because I don't want you to go to Hell." Julie felt her eyes fill with tears, and they flowed down her cheeks as she looked at the broken man beside her.

Julie continued on, "Jesus said that he didn't come into the world to condemn it but to save it."

"I forgive you, Dad. I really do." "Jesus said that if anyone would hurt a child that a millstone should be put around his neck and that he should be cast into the sea. That's what you deserve. Dad, that's what you deserve for what you did to me," Julie sadly explained. "But, Dad, I forgive you of that debt. Now all that you have to do is ask God to forgive you of that debt."

"How do you know that I haven't?" Ron asked the same question that he had asked Julie an hour before.

Julie took a deep breath. She couldn't go around and around this same mountain that her dad was intent on taking her. But she answered him simply, "Because everything that I just shared with you about everyone, you've denied." Julie opened the Bible that was still on her lap to 1 John 2:3-5 and read, *"If we say that we have no sin, we deceive ourselves, and the truth is not in us. If we confess, He is faithful and just to forgive us our sins and cleanse us from all unrighteousness. If we say we have not sinned then we make Him a liar and His word is not in us."*

"When we truly make it right with God, we keep His commandments, Dad. We don't take our sin and try to justify it and make it righteous. If we say that we know God, like you are saying that you do, then we don't deny, justify, or minimize the sins that we have done. We confess them to God. If we say we have no sin, we make God a liar."

Ron was back in form and began to debate with Julie. "Everyone believes in the Bible differently. How do you know that you're right? It all depends upon what you read and how you interpret it."

"Dad," Julie spoke slowly and deliberately. "People, ministers, and religions may disagree, but all Christians agree on the scriptures that I just read you. There is no gray area."

"I don't think the way you do," Ron continued.

Julie wasn't sure of her dad's intent but answered. "But you're being deceived."

"By who?" Ron asked.

"By Satan," Julie answered as quickly as Ron had asked, "because he wants you to go to Hell."

Julie only continued because she felt that her dad was being serious. He wasn't trying to play a game or to quiz and trap her at this point, as he had so often done when she was young. Julie watched her dad's heart swing to denial, to near tears, to frustration and then back to anger.

"I don't want you to go to Hell, Dad. I'm free from all of this, Dad. Satan has no control over me, no power over me." Ron gave Julie a questioning look. "And Dad, you have no control or power over me," Julie stated. The words seemed to gain in power as she spoke them out boldly.

Ron came back with a quick response. "The Bible also says that children are to honor their mother and father."

Julie asked, "What about the rest of what it says?"

"I don't know," he answered puzzled.

Julie picked her Bible up and said, "Dad, that's the problem. You have to know what's in here. This is what sets you free. It says, *'Honor your mother and father in the Lord.'* You were never *in the Lord*, Dad, in what you were doing. Even so, I have honored you or I wouldn't be here right now."

It was time. Julie knew that she couldn't continue to go around in circles. "Dad, I have to leave now. Is there anything that you want to talk to me about before I go?"

"I do, but I want to talk to you alone."

Once again, Julie felt like all the blood had drained out of her. She felt herself shiver in the warm hospital room. She could not, and would not, be alone with her dad. Would he say perverted things? Did he want to say he was sorry? "You can talk to me in front of Mom. She knows everything. There are no secrets," Julie reminded her dad.

Julie asked him again if there was anything else he wanted to talk about, but he said only if they were alone.

Julie repeated, "I can't talk to you alone, Dad."

"Why?" Ron asked.

"Because every time that I've ever been alone with you, you've hurt me," Julie answered.

"I don't try to make a habit of it," Ron came back.

"But you do a good job of it," Julie replied.

Julie wasn't sure of what else to do. Her dad's moods and words were all over the place. Julie was so tired. Maybe it was just best to say good-bye. She had done all that she felt that God had wanted her to do. But somehow, Julie felt as if something was missing, as if she just wasn't quite finished.

She sat for a moment and said nothing. There was a silence in the room that hung like a cloud. No one said anything. And then Julie knew what she had to do. She didn't know why she hadn't thought of it before. Her mind and emotions were bouncing in so many directions; she thought that she probably wouldn't even be able to tell someone her name right now if they asked. Maybe that's why she hadn't thought of it. She knew that her Dad might say no, but it was worth a try.

"Dad, would you like me to pray for you?" Julie asked lovingly and simply.

Ron answered immediately without hesitation to Julie's surprise, "Yes."

Julie reached into her purse and took out a little vial of olive oil. She explained to her dad that the oil represented the Holy Spirit and that the Bible tells us to anoint the person with it when we pray for them. Julie stood up beside her dad's hospital bed. Ethel joined her on the other side. Ron didn't say a word but closed his eyes. Julie began to pray, softly but firmly. Julie had learned a long time ago that it's the faith in the prayer, not the volume of the prayer, which does the work. She prayed openly for her dad's soul to be saved. She asked God to forgive him of his sins. Julie didn't know if her dad was praying or how he was praying, but she had to pray something that she had thought about for many years. She knew that her dad had the power of choice to do the things that he had done. She knew that there was no one else responsible for what he had done but her dad himself. Julie also knew that this is a spiritual world that we live in and how, so often, we overlook the power and the stronghold that it has on us until we are delivered. She began to bind every spirit that she could think of as she prayed for him. She bound the spirit of justification, minimization, denial, perverseness, lust, lying, deceit, anger, and more. She commanded them to go back to the pits of Hell. She continued on, binding the spirits of intimidation and manipulation. Julie had always felt that, maybe, if her dad could be set free from the evilness that had held him bound, that possibly then, he could come to the *"garden alone"*, to a God, where maybe for the first time in his life, he could feel forgiveness and love; a place where his pain could be taken away, a place of salvation, and redemption. And so she prayed until she felt the Spirit had done the work.

Julie was so surprised that her dad had allowed her to pray for him. Julie opened her eyes and looked down at her dad. His eyes were still closed but his face was serious. Julie's hand still rested upon the top of his head. Ron opened his eyes and looked up at Julie. "You will never know how much that meant to me," Ron spoke softly.

Julie looked into his eyes as he spoke. Something had changed in them once again. He said nothing else and looked down. Julie leaned over and kissed the top of his head.

"I have to go, Dad," Julie said softly and sadly.

"Are you coming back?" Ron asked quietly.

"No, Dad," Julie answered. There were too many emotions going through her. She needed to rest. It was time to go. "I might not see you again," she added sadly, yet compassionately.

"Call me," Ron said.

"I probably won't talk to you again, Dad." Julie knew this was the end. They said good-bye to each other.

Ethel left the room first and Julie followed. Julie turned back and glanced at her dad several times as she went to leave the room. The arrogance and cockiness were gone. All Julie saw were remorse and brokenness.

Julie, Matt, Jerry, Ronnie

Chapter

23

Julie gathered her things together and packed her suitcase, preparing to go back home to Pennsylvania. She sat down on the edge of her mom's bed. Her mind had a million thoughts bouncing around inside of it. She stood up and went to look out the sliding doors connected to the bedroom. She pulled back the curtains and stood there, taking in the view. The mountains stood before her, their colors bursting through the light fog which covered the mountainside. The sun began to break through the fog causing the colors to sparkle and glitter—such beauty to welcome in a new day. However, Julie wondered what the day had in store for her.

Julie had spoken to Mike last night, after she had returned to her mom's house and told him everything that had happened. She told him how that her dad had wanted to talk to her alone. There was a slight pause at the other end of the phone and then Mike spoke softly, "Remember when I told you that he might want to see you alone?"

Julie felt surprised and said, "You're right. You did say that. I had forgotten that in the confusion. I just couldn't face him alone, Mike," Julie continued on. "I just couldn't."

"Well, whatever you decide," Mike said lovingly, "Just make sure that you've faced all of your *Giants* before you come home, Honey," he said tenderly.

"Do you think that I should go to see him again?" Julie had asked Mike.

"Whatever, you think that you need to do, Jul," Mike said reassuringly. "You'll know what to do," he said.

Julie had given it much thought and prayed earnestly about it throughout the night. *Surely,* she thought, as she prayed and searched her heart, *she was not meant to go back again to see her dad?* But no matter how much she tried, she could not shake that tug in her heart which said, *"You must go back."*

Wonder if he wanted to talk to her personally about something? Maybe about his dad, or the abuse, or even God? Julie racked her brain trying to figure out what her dad could want to talk to her about in private. She couldn't help it; even after all of these years later, she hated being alone with her dad. She didn't even like talking, one-on-one, to him on the telephone. But she knew that Mike was right. She would go visit him today.

Ron was asleep when Ethel and Julie walked quietly into the room. Julie looked at the sleeping man and her mind filled with the wonder of everything: her past, the present, and even the future all meshing together as one.

Ron began to stir in the bed and woke up. He focused on Ethel and then Julie. He smiled at Julie. It was a kind smile, an unusual smile. He then said kindly, "I didn't think that you would come back. I hoped that you would come back today."

"You said that you wanted to talk to me alone, and I thought that I should come back," Julie explained. Julie just wanted to do what she was supposed to do and then leave. But she didn't know what she was supposed to do. *"Stay focused on the mission,"* came the gentle words to her heart, bringing her focus, strength, and direction. Julie couldn't imagine what else could be done or said in light of all that they had discussed the day before. But she waited as her mom and dad spoke. It seemed so strange to see them talk. It reminded her of many years ago. Julie couldn't help but see past their worn bodies, and saw the mom and dad that she had known as a little girl. It stirred so many emotions and so much sorrow of what could have been. Julie shook herself lightly to refocus.

"You said you wanted to talk to me, Dad," Julie repeated.

Julie could see that he was clear minded. He was comfortable and the meds didn't seem to have any adverse effect on him. Julie was surprised again at how clear minded and alert he was.

Ethel said, "I'm going to go out for awhile and let you two talk."

Julie cringed as her mom turned and slowly walked out. She turned and gave Julie a smile and a reassuring look before she went around the corner.

Ron lay quietly, slightly propped up, but said nothing. Julie sat in silence waiting for her dad to speak, but he said nothing.

"Dad, I just wanted to give you an opportunity to talk to me alone as you had asked me yesterday, but then I have to get on the road and drive back today."

Ron lay there quietly, thinking, but said nothing.

"What did you want to talk with me about?" Julie asked again kindly.

She had no idea of what to expect. She searched his face from the very time she had entered the room, just as she had searched it when she was a child trying to determine which dad she was talking to and what mood was he in. But it was so difficult and she couldn't figure it out. Julie was sure of one thing; it wouldn't take long talking to him to figure it out.

"I just wanted to talk to you one-on-one," Ron answered her after a few moments.

"Okay. What about?" Julie asked softly.

"Just talk," he answered.

Julie listened as he spoke about Claire, her job, his going home, and his care.

Julie listened intently and tried to read between the lines to find any direction that he might be leading her in. She felt like a kid again. Being alone with her dad had always made her feel that way. As her dad talked about the normal things of life, it reminded Julie of how it was when she was a little girl. How, after the times her dad would abuse her, that by the next day her dad would just talk and go on as if nothing had ever happened. She prayed quietly and earnestly for discernment and direction. *I can't do this anymore, God,* she prayed from within. *Just because we talked yesterday, I just can't go on as if nothing happened and now we have a relationship or something,* Julie thought. *I just can't do this,* she prayed.

Julie felt as if her heart and mind were in a whirlwind and she just wanted out; however, she waited. Her dad had always had such a selfish love. His love for others had always consisted of what was in it for him. Every sentence, every word, and action of her dad was weighed in Julie's heart, mind, and spirit. She did not want to judge or condemn him but just wanted to fulfill the purpose and the mission—his soul and her slaying the *Giant*.

Julie asked him once again what he wanted to talk to her about, but he again just brushed it off and made small talk. Julie found it all very exhausting.

Finally, she asked him, "Did you think about what we talked about yesterday?"

He simply answered, "Yes."

The conversation went back and forth. He said, "I talk to God."

Wherein, Julie answered back, "But do you listen to Him, Dad?" Julie thought the conversation was going to fall into the same pattern as the day before. And it did for a while. Her dad would say how he had done nothing wrong to anyone and Julie would reiterate much of the same conversation that they had had the day before.

At one point, Ron had told her, "I can't apologize for something that I don't feel I did."

Julie found herself emotionally exhausted. *Maybe, I should just get on the road,* she thought.

"Dad, you know that I don't lie. If you don't remember anything, believe me when I tell you, everything that I've told you, you did do."

Ron became quiet again and listened to Julie. Julie thought hard for a moment before proceeding and then spoke. "Dad," she said softly, and then paused. He looked at her and listened. "Did you know that when I left home, after Alice left, and went to Gramma Emma's, she figured out why I wouldn't come back to live with you?"

Ron looked despondently at Julie and said, "Yes, I know that she did."

Julie sat there surprised. She wondered if her Gramma Emma had confronted her dad on what she thought he had done to her.

And then Ron said something that Julie didn't think that she would ever hear from her dad. "I want to make peace with you," he said kinder than Julie had thought she had ever heard him speak. Julie wanted to sit and take the words into her heart, but in all honesty she remained on guard, watching her dad's every movement, his facial expressions, looking deep into his eyes to see if he really meant it.

Julie spoke softly and said, "I do forgive you, Dad."

And then there was silence again.

"You didn't do anything wrong to me, so there's nothing for me to forgive you of," he said, with that same kindness in his eyes. Julie had never seen her dad so sincere. She couldn't help it. It rattled her to her bones.

"I know that what I did to you was wrong," he said.

Julie was quiet. She could not have spoken if she wanted to. His words took her breath away.

"I shouldn't have done what I did to you," Ron finished.

"Why did you do it, Dad?" Julie asked sorrowfully.

Ron looked puzzled and sorrowful, "I don't know," he answered very solemnly.

"Did Pap Pap James do it to you?" Julie asked.

"No!!" he answered adamantly.

But Julie thought to herself, in light of the other things that he had denied in the past two days, that she knew were true; that maybe through the many years, he had truly convinced himself that none of those things had ever happened to him.

"Are you sure, Dad?" Julie asked.

"Yes."

"What about the others in the family?" Julie asked cautiously.

When he didn't answer, Julie then asked more specifically about her grandfather, and he answered, no, to some of her questions, and yes to others.

"You sure, Dad?" Julie asked, repeating a question that he seemed unsure of in his answer.

Ron paused and then answered slowly, "Well, no."

As Julie began to ask more questions and started to get closer to the things that he couldn't and wouldn't deny, he would just answer, "I didn't say that." Julie knew that he would answer her this way when he was actually conceding to what Julie was asking, as true, and that he merely wasn't denying the question or the answer, but that he was clarifying that he didn't say that it was true or not. Julie marveled at that about her dad. Some would say that he was just lying, but Julie saw a difference between what he had made himself believe, denying what was true, and the questions that he couldn't deny, knew were true, but did not want to admit. He would simply reply to those questions, "I didn't say that." Julie knew that, in a strange way, he was agreeing that it did happen. On these points, he wouldn't deny the pain that he had seen inflicted on others. It was strange, as if somewhere in her dad's heart, he still cared too much to betray others that he loved, by denying the truth. And yet he could deny the truth concerning his own pain.

"Why did Pap Pap James do it, Dad?" Julie asked him again, longing for understanding.

"I don't know," Ron replied sadly.

Julie had no idea where the conversation was leading or what good it would bring. However, she knew in her heart that it was the right thing for her to proceed. She didn't stop to think that this had been the first time, really in her whole life, that she was actually talking to her dad about this horrible family secret. Julie ventured that no one in her whole family had ever had a conversation concerning it. She thought, that if they possibly would have, even just once had such a conversation, it would have been exposed and stopped. "Why did you do it, Dad?" Julie asked.

Julie watched her dad think about her question and he then said, "Well," and paused. Julie was still on guard. She would study his facial expressions and his body language. She saw no arrogance or cockiness upon his face. He said the words passé, as if it had all made sense to him.

"Well, sometimes fathers and daughters have had relations…"

Julie cut him off before he could finish the sentence. "NO!!! NO!!!" she practically shouted. "Don't! Don't you even try to make it a normal thing!!!" She felt as if she was a little kid again. The small still voice said within her heart, *"Face your Giant, Julie."* "No!! No!!" Julie said as her dad tried to continue talking. Boldly, she said aloud, "That is a perverse spirit and I bind it in Jesus name!" Julie didn't care who heard her, she didn't care if anyone heard her. She had to face her *Giant* at any cost.

But Ron just continued to try to explain how he felt that it was okay.

"I said, NO!" Julie spoke firmly. "I had to listen to this all of my life as a kid. You would tell me every father does this with his daughter. But I don't have to listen to this any longer. I'm not that little girl any more," Julie exclaimed. She looked directly at her dad and he became quiet. She looked past her dad's eyes into his very soul and then said, as if speaking to the evilness that hung over him more than to her dad himself, "You listen to me! You listen to me! You have no power over me! I don't have to listen to this!"

Julie could feel a Holy power arise within her. All fear had left. There wasn't any more shame or fear, just a peace, a power, *Victory*! It was *Giant* slaying time, and Julie was watching the *Giant* fall right before her eyes.

To anyone else it would have seemed extreme, but it wasn't extreme to Julie. There was a quietness that came over the room. Julie sat in the stillness trying to sort it all out and get direction. She never knew what the next moment would bring.

And then Ron broke the silence. "I know that it was wrong. I didn't know it then."

Julie couldn't believe the words that she was hearing. She almost fell over. No matter how hard she would try, she could never prepare herself for her dad's words. Had she heard him correctly today? The conversation had gone from one extreme to the other. At first, and then even now, Julie wasn't sure if anything had changed with her dad. Was he just toying with her, playing another one of his games? But then, Julie heard his earlier words come back to her, "I just want to make peace with you." Julie knew it would take a while for her to sort it all out. She was not excusing her dad for a single thing that he done in his life, to her, nor to others. But she had forgiven him and it had set her free. *Was it possible that by seeing God's love through her that maybe he could now believe that God would still love him, if he confessed to what he had done? Could he possibly understand that he did not have to deny, minimize, or justify all that he had done to receive God's love? Could he finally realize that it was as simple as confessing his wrongs to a God who would forgive him?*

Julie turned to her dad and then at the doorway where her mom had appeared. Julie nodded for her to join them. "Would you like me to pray for you again, Dad?" she asked.

His answer was, "Yes."

Julie then said to him, "You pray too, as I pray."

He nodded and closed his eyes.

Julie began to pray a similar prayer as the day before. She bound every spirit that she could think of that had tortured her dad for all of his life. She bound every spirit that he had entertained and that had vexed his soul. And then, she prayed the sinner's prayer. Simple, powerful. "Forgive me God for all the sins that I have done. I know that you are the Christ, my Savior. I know that you died on the cross to take my sins away. I confess them to you and ask you to forgive me. I ask you to come into my heart and to cleanse me from all unrighteousness, my unrighteousness. Empower me with your Holy Spirit and fill me with your presence." Julie asked God to save his soul and to have mercy on him. She could feel the power of God's presence. She hoped that her dad could feel it too. Julie paused and finished, "In Jesus name. Amen."

Julie leaned down and kissed her dad on the top of his forehead. He looked up into her eyes. His eyes were filled with a sincerity that Julie had never ever seen. He then spoke, and sincerely and softly said, "It meant a lot that you did this. It means a lot to me."

It was time to leave. Ethel spoke to Ron with tears in her eyes. She told him goodbye and slowly walked away. Julie turned and said, "Dad, I'll be away for two weeks." There was a pause and then Julie spoke, "I might not see you again." Julie searched his eyes. She looked for all the things that she was so used to seeing in them. But they were not there. She said goodbye and turned to leave. She glanced back several times on her way out. But each time the look was the same; it never changed. She saw sorrow and remorse in those eyes, as if he had finally realized the pain that he had caused and of the realization of what he had lost throughout the years. She glanced once more as she stepped into the hallway. Their eyes met one more time. Julie smiled a faint smile. *Was it love that she saw in his eyes?* A tear ran down her cheek. She waved her hand in a light motion good-bye to this dad who had been lost so long, a dad whom she had often wondered whether he even really existed. She waved goodbye to the dad that she had found once again and had known so many many years before.

Beautiful Hawaii

Chapter

24

It was a long flight. Julie rested her head against the window of the plane and glanced out. She loved flying. What a different perspective the world seemed from up here. She wondered if this was the way that God saw them. Man thinks that he is so powerful, so high and mighty, so knowledgeable. *What is man?* Julie thought, *Oh Lord, that you are mindful of him?*

Julie was glad for the long flight. She still hadn't had enough time to sort out the last few days. It had only been three days after Julie had returned home when she and Mike flew out on their long awaited trip to Hawaii. The conversations that she had just had with her dad played over and over again in her mind like a movie reel.

Mike glanced up from his magazine and looked over at Julie. "Why don't you rest?" he asked smiling.

"I will," she answered. Julie reached over and took his hand, and then closed her eyes.

Julie stood outside on the balcony which overlooked the sprawling blue ocean. The sun was just beginning to rise from her left. Before her, far in the distance, were the islands of Lanai and Molokai displaying their towering cliff sides. Julie took in a deep breath of the fragrance-filled air of the island. Mike was still asleep. Oh the refreshing.... *How can God create each new day so dynamic?* Julie wondered. *How does He know how to etch the sky in arrays of pink and white as onto a blue canvas?* Julie watched large gray billows of clouds hang motionless, unattached to the sky. They sat near the horizon appearing like distinct mountains of gray puffs, as if they were a permanent fixture, only to pass ever so slowly and fade away behind the morning sun. White puffy clouds covered the tips of Molokai obscuring its peaks and valleys, soft fluffy cotton puffs of white. Molokai stood majestically before her, firm, unmovable, a reflection of the past, a portrait of the present.

The roar of the ocean pounded before her in a constant and perfect rhythm. Its rhythmic waves would rush to the shore with a loud crash and then pause, as if to take a breath, and then rush back to the vast blue waters to grasp the horizon in the distance. The wind blew a fresh breeze, not cool or warm, just soothing as it rustled past Julie, leaving a fine mist upon her face. She watched a couple, far below her, walking hand-in-hand on the beach, though it was only seven o'clock in the morning. The birds sang and fleeted upon the rail of the balcony. Some chattered, as if scolding the others to begin their daily tasks, while others sang a new song, bright and cheery, so carefree and full of life. Here Julie would find rest and comfort. Here she could sort out her thoughts and feelings and be refreshed.

The next few days passed as Julie and Mike found some much needed rest. They talked and walked on the beach, sharing their dreams, remembering their past, and making new memories. These were priceless treasures.

It was early Thursday morning when the phone rang. It was only four-thirty in the morning Hawaiian time, but ten-thirty on the East Coast. When the phone rang again forty-five minutes later, Julie figured it was not a marketing call and rushed to answer it. Half-asleep, she found her phone on the kitchen counter.

Somehow, Julie knew that something was wrong before she even heard the voice begin to speak on the other end of the phone. It was Claire.

"I went to check on him early this morning," Claire said. She paused and then said, "He wasn't breathing."

Julie took in the rest of the conversation and thanked Claire for calling her. Julie felt numb as the news began to register. It wasn't that she was surprised about her dad's death, but rather at how quickly it had happened. She had just spoken to him on those last two days, a week ago to the day. They had sent him home the next day with hospice care.

Julie walked out onto the balcony. She looked at the beauty before her, allowing her thoughts to empty out. *That soon,* is all that she could think. He had talked to her as if there would be many tomorrows. No one would have ever guessed that death would have come so soon. Julie marveled at God's timing and more so at His mercy and grace. She couldn't help think how good God is, as He reaches down and pulls us out of the mire of this life with its strongholds, as sin attempts to grasp its ugly tentacles around us. None of us are immune. We are all born in sin. *"There is none good, no not one,"* the Word says.

Can any of us think that "we" are not so bad? Julie wondered. *Do any of us think that because we are kind and good that we somehow have escaped the dark places of our heart where sin has scarred us? Do we somehow measure our sin in degrees, meting some to be more forgivable than others?* Words of hope sprung into Julie's heart, *"For all have sinned and come short of God's glory. But He is faithful and just to forgive us our sins, if we but confess them to him. For where sin did abound, grace did much more abound."*

It wasn't that her sins were any less than her dad's or anyone else's. It was God's grace that had forgiven her; why shouldn't His mercy and grace save her dad? *"Was He a God whose hand was shortened or His ear too heavy to hear the cry of a lost soul in their final hour?"* The many scriptures ran through her mind and brought her comfort in the wake of the news.

"For I am persuaded, that neither death, nor life, nor angels, nor principalities, nor powers, nor things present, nor things to come, nor height, nor depth, nor any other creature, shall be able to separate us from the love of God, which is in Christ Jesus our Lord."

Julie's heart overflowed with the joy that God had touched her dad. It was not for her to put him in heaven or hell. It was enough for her to be able to place him into the arms of a loving God. Julie marveled at how great the mercy of God was to touch her dad. It wasn't that she felt that she was any more deserving. It was just that the cloud of evil, which had perpetuated over her dad all the days of his life, was so strong, that Julie could only stand in awe at the reality of a God who could touch anyone's heart if they would just hearken to His call. Some would debate that he did not deserve it; others would think it unfair for him to be redeemed after all of the lives that he had shattered; but who can know the heart of God, and more so, who can know the heart of any soul?

Julie turned as she heard the balcony door slide open. It was Mike. He had given her some time to be alone. He joined her now and slid his arms around her. They stood watching the sun rise, the ocean rustling beneath them, the tropical winds brushing past their faces. A new day was born as God had ushered her dad home.

Julie sat on the beach later that day with Mike by her side. She watched the sea birds dive for fish, people walking on the beach, and children playing in the sand. She sat and thought of everything that had happened. More and more, as she talked to the family, she began to see a clearer picture.

Julie had talked to Ronnie, Jerry, Matt, and her mom. They all figured that she wouldn't come back for the funeral.

"I know you told me that if he passed while you were over there, that you probably wouldn't come back for the funeral," Jerry said as they talked that day.

"I would, Jerry. I thought of it. But it just seems that I'm not meant to be there. I have a peace about it."

"I'm glad you went to see him, Jul, before he died," Jerry added, choking up a little.

"Me, too, Jerry," Julie replied. She told Jerry a little about her last conversation with their dad. "I'll tell you more when we get together," she said.

"You know, Jul," Jerry continued, "One of the last times, when I talked to him on the phone a few days ago, he said the strangest thing to me."

"What was that, Jerry?" Julie asked.

Jerry answered softly, "Dad said, 'Jerry, you know that I love you, don't you?'" I told him, "Sure Dad, I know you love me." As he told Julie what had happened, Jerry continued softly, "And then Dad said, 'I love you Jerry.'"

"I'm so glad that he told you that, Jerry. I'm so glad," Julie comforted her brother.

She talked to Ronnie later that morning and asked him if he had visited their dad before he died.

"You know Sis," Ronnie said. "I went to see him yesterday and we talked."

"What about Ronnie?" Julie asked.

"He said, 'Ronnie, Julie says that I did some horrible things to you when you were younger. Did I do these things?'"

"What did you say, Ronnie?" Julie asked.

I said, "What things Dad?" Ronnie continued to share with Julie, "And we talked, Jul, for a long time. Then he said something that I never expected."

"What?" Julie asked.

"He said that he was sorry for everything that he had done to me," Ronnie answered. Julie could hear him sniffle back his tears. "And then he asked me to ask Matt to come and visit him, Jul."

"Really?" Julie asked surprised. "Why?"

"I think, he wanted to apologize to Matt, too," Ronnie answered.

"Did Matt go to see him?" Julie asked.

"No, I was going to tell Matt today. But Dad died before I could tell him. But I'm going to tell him that I believe Dad was going to apologize to him," Ronnie said.

"Do tell him, Ronnie," Julie urged. "It'll mean a lot to Matt."

"I will, Sis. I'm going to see him later today. We're all getting together," Ronnie explained.

"I don't mean this bad," Julie said. "But that's really what I'll miss, Ronnie," Julie sadly remarked.

"What's that Sis?" Ronnie asked.

"Being with the three of you," Julie answered back.

"I know, Jul," Ronnie said. "We all understand, though."

It was later in the day before Julie spoke to her mom and then to Matt. Matt was solemn and extra quiet. "You okay, Matt?" Julie asked.

"Yea, Sis," Matt answered. "I wasn't going to go to the funeral."

Julie bit her lip to not say anything. She knew that Matt was struggling and she understood why he felt that way.

"I talked to Jerry about it," Matt said.

"What did he say?" Julie asked.

"He said, 'Matt, we have to go through this together. We've always gone through everything in our lives together. We have to go through this together too.'"

"I only wish I could be there with my brothers," Julie said, holding back her tears.

"I know, Jul," Matt replied. "But it's probably for the best."

"I figure I can do better working through everything sitting right here by the ocean than I can do sitting at that funeral home," Julie added. "I'm just not up to meeting the towns' people. They would never understand it all," Julie remarked.

"We do, Sis," Matt assured her. "That's all that matters."

"Thanks, Matt," Julie softly answered.

"Julie, did you talk to Ronnie today?" Matt asked.

"Earlier," Julie replied.

"Ronnie told me that Dad wanted to see me before he died," Matt shared Ronnie's words with her.

"He told me that, too," Julie said. She wanted Matt to talk freely without any pressure from her or anyone.

"Ronnie told me that Dad was going to apologize to me," Matt spoke softly.

"I really believe that he was going to Matt," Julie emphasized to Matt as she spoke.

"Something happened to Dad," Julie said briefly. She didn't want to put any more on Matt than he already had on him.

Julie allowed the quietness, which hung between her and Matt, to comfort both of their hearts. No words were said; none were needed.

Julie hurried up from the beach back to her suite. She swiped her key card to enter their room. Mike had left earlier to run a few errands. She was surprised to see him there.

"Hey, what are you doing back?" he asked as he turned and walked towards her.

"I was going to ask you the same thing," Julie answered with a smile.

Mike took her hand and walked her to the dining table. "Mike, they are beautiful," Julie exclaimed as she touched the bouquet of flowers. The bird of paradise stood out from the rest of the flowers bringing the whole bouquet to life. The colors were so vibrant and the aroma so sweet. "They really are beautiful, Mike," Julie said with tears in her eyes.

"There's a lot of red ginger," Mike pointed out, "your favorite."

Julie gave the ginger flower a hard squeeze with her hand causing the flower to release the sweetest smell. She had learned that you can crush the ginger flower in your hand and it will not injure it. It will only cause the flower to release its beautiful aroma. "Kind of like us, huh, Mike?" Julie remarked as she bent down to smell the flower. "The sweetest aroma flows out of us when we're crushed and yet we're not destroyed."

Mike placed his arms around his wife and held her tenderly. Julie rested her head on his shoulder and let his love flow through her, comforting her heart as he held her safely, tightly in his arms. She looked up into his rich blue eyes, full of love and kindness. He leaned down and kissed her gently before releasing her from his embrace.

"I still have to run to the store. I wanted to get you flowers first before they ran out," Mike said. "Do you want to go with me to the store or stay here?" He gave Julie a broad smile and then said, "It's up to you. Whatever you want."

"If it's okay, Mike," Julie said. "I think I'll stay here and take a walk on the beach."

"Sure," Mike answered. "I'll be back soon."

Julie smiled back at him as he left. She closed the door behind him and then walked back over to the bouquet of flowers. She fingered them gently, smelling them once more.

Julie walked back down to the beach. Today was the day of the funeral. Julie let her feet sink into the cool wet sand. She stood and looked out over the mighty waves to the horizon where the dark blue of the ocean met the light blue of the sky. It seemed infinite, as if there was no end, nothing to hold back the great mass of water from flowing over the edge. *How do we grasp the reality of an ocean that comes and stays and then rushes out again only to return? How do we grasp death, its finality? How do we grasp life?* "For it is a vapor that appears for a little while and then it is gone." And then the infinity of eternity. *How do we grasp the reality of eternity? Never ending.*

Julie continued to walk along the water's edge. The ocean beckoned her to come into the water. It rushed and beat against her legs as she stood looking out at the islands in the distance, tugging and pulling on her legs as each new wave rushed out to sea. Puffy white clouds hung on the top of the island of Lanai, encircling it like a crown of glory, causing it to appear majestic and royal.

Julie reached down onto the sand and picked up the bougainvillea flowers which had floated to her on the last wave. She held them in her hand and studied them, their beauty so representative of life. She waited for the next wave to come in and brush past her. She stood and watched the water rush up onto the beach and then glide back mystically, taking with it whatever it could find as it flowed back slowly into the ocean's white froth. It seemed to mesmerize Julie as she watched. She sat down on a large piece of driftwood and picked up another bright bougainvillea flower and held it in her hand. After a while, Julie began to walk back along the shore.

Julie could still remember the last look that she had seen in her dad's eyes when she had left his hospital room only a week before. The sadness of what had been lost, the brokenness of true sorrow, the thankfulness of the peace that they had between them, the gift of forgiveness received, the hope of a better tomorrow, and the knowledge that she knew that this would probably be the last time that they would see each other.

Regardless of the past, it is a powerful emotion to know that you are probably seeing someone for the last time—and yet to be a part of it all, to feel the peace and power of redemption, to end an era and season of Julie's life. Julie let the sound of the waves comfort her and take her thoughts far away. She glanced down at the bougainvillea flowers which she held in her hand. One by one, as each new wave came and went, she gently released a flower into the unknown. She remembered one of the last things that her dad had said to her. *"I want to make peace with you."*

"Good-bye Dad," Julie said as she released the last flower into the mighty wave that rushed past her. She stood and watched the flower as it washed away until it was gone from sight and she could no longer see it. "Good-bye Dad," she said softly again. "May you truly rest. I hope you made it to *The Garden.*"

Hope is tangible and breathes life and passion into every human soul that dares to reach out, grab it, and believe.

Epilogue

I don't know if my dad made it to *The Garden*. I'd like to think that he did. It is enough for me to know that God's love reached down in His mercy to deal with my dad's soul and that I can place him in the hands of a loving, just, and faithful God. There was a great gulf closed for me on those last days as the Lord had me deal with *my Giants* and as He also dealt with a dad who I had once known as a little girl and had lost a long time ago.

It hasn't always been an easy journey, this healing journey that we choose to take. The hills are steep, the curves sharp, and we often feel that surely life is happening all too quickly for us to stay on this path, which leads us to be whole.

It is important for the reader to know that every situation is different. I don't know that any two are the same. We must never minimize the degree of pain and suffering that abuse causes. We must never deny the severity of the devastation that rapes the soul. We must never justify the abuser or excuse him from what he has done. Even as God helps us to forgive them, you must know that there is and always will be an accountability for their choice. There is a reality of the evil that perpetuates through an abuser. No story can paint a picture of solitude in the midst of so much devastation.

Many will not like the ending. And yet, this is the true ending of what had really happened. Some will say, "Your dad didn't deserve to be redeemed, that even hell would have been too good for him." But we do not heal by holding onto this kind of contempt, hurt, and pain. I believe that this God who carried me through those years is a just and fair God. No evil gets past Him. No injustice escapes His wrath. No person is able to fool this God of love and mercy. My dad did not escape the evil that he did; he was delivered from it by a God who knew his heart of hearts. Do you really think that my dad was capable of hiding the truth of his true heart from a God who knows everything? Anytime that truth is hidden, regardless of how painful that truth is, evil will prevail. Prevailing truth destroys evil. Prevailing love nurtures the broken and shattered. God would not have led me to him in those last hours except that He knew the heart of the situation. And for others, their story will end totally different because God knows the heart and searches the deep things of man.

It must be understood that we do not have to remain in our hurt, pain, and anger. We do not have to let our hurt and pain ricochet through us like unleashed bullets that rip our heart and soul asunder on a daily basis. We do not have to try to find ways to sedate or numb this pain with drugs, addictions, alcohol, or self-medication. We do not have to pitch a tent in our past and remain there. However, we must go back and deal with our past if we are to ever heal from the past to be able to feel again. We do not have to stay under a shroud of fear and shame, guilt and blame. They were never ours to bear. They were put upon us by our abuser.

We were never meant to hold onto anger as a mechanism to empower us over our hurt and pain. There is power in anger; it gives us a "feeling" of control; it fuels us with an unbridled strength that "seems" to help us rise above the hurt and pain. But in reality, it is a loaded weapon, which when fired or misfired, causes more irreparable damage to others and to ourselves. Whether we direct it outward to others or inward to ourselves, it will destroy us. How does destruction resolve anything? How does this make us any different than our abuser? *"Vengeance is mine, says the Lord."* *"It is a fearful thing to fall into the hands of a living God."* We can put a cloak of righteousness on our anger and call it anything we want—"righteous indignation," "justice," or pure blunt "payback." We can justify that we have a right to be angry, and we do; but do we hold onto this anger and allow it to become a *"cloak of comfort"* to us? Anger will never heal us from the pain, or deliver us from the anguish that the abuse has caused and refuses to relinquish.

So what do we do? How do we move forward? How can I heal? Can I really heal? How do I start the healing journey? There is One who waits for us to choose what we will do. He stands with His arms outstretched toward us and waits for us to bring to Him the hurt and pain that we feel. This pain is real, and it does not just go away because others think that it should. It does not go away because it happened yesterday or a long time ago. It does not go away by trying to forget about it, burying it, or drinking and drugging it into numbness. It begins to go away the moment in which we choose to give it away and no longer hang on to it. God does not minimize or deny your pain but asks that you give it to Him, that you choose to give Him something, even more—your heart, your life. Sometimes, people are surprised at how difficult this one choice of giving it all away to God really is. To do this, you must begin to realize that God did not forsake you and look the other way. We must know that He is the solution to our problems and not the cause. We must accept that we truly do matter to a God who has always had us *"carved on the palm of His hand."* To choose to do this, we must deal with our past, heal from its pain and dare risk to go forward and allow ourselves to truly feel again. It is by our choice that we begin this healing journey. The truth is—that we can heal! We can become whole. We can truly become alive again and know the joy of life.

I hope that this sequel has answered many of the questions that you may have had. Healing is a journey, and such a worthwhile one. If we can be brave enough to enter into the dark shadows of the unspeakable and pull back the curtain, we not only reveal the light but we also set the captives free. It is God's desire to take you from lost to found, from victim to victor, from death to life.

I have never regretted the choice that I made as a small child in that small country church of giving my life to Jesus. I wish I knew what had ever happened to that cardboard cross and picture of Jesus that glowed in the dark and hung on my wall. The reality of that God had shone through to my heart and given me a hope and promise that someday my life would be different. *"Hope is tangible and breathes life and passion into every human soul that dares to reach out, grab it, and believe."* God never failed from one of those promises, though I failed Him many times. When I could no longer endure, He carried me. When, I failed Him, He forgave me. When, I cried to Him, He heard my cry and wiped my tears away.

I would ask you to reach out and grab that tangible Hope, that simple choice of asking Him to become your Lord and Savior, that simple choice of surrendering your life totally to Him in simple childlike faith. Can it be that simple, you may ask? And the answer is, "Yes."

So many years ago, God gave me a precious song that mentored me.

> *"Something beautiful, something good.*
> *All of my confusions, He understood.*
> *All I had to offer Him was brokenness and strife.*
> *But He made something beautiful out of my life."*

Please know that you are not alone. It is estimated that there are over 60,000,000 survivors of childhood sexual abuse alone. The numbers spiral upwards even more when you include those who have experienced rape, domestic abuse, bullying, and all other types of abuse.

There still remain more stories to tell and questions to answer. I would welcome your input and questions. The journey still continues and there is so much more that needs to be taught regarding how to walk this healing journey and to learn how to overcome. I hope to bring you further reading. Many of you still desire to know more of what had happened after "Julie's" childhood, and I look forward to bringing more of these sequels which reveal the reality of a God who truly still does many miracles— from chasing down criminals, falling in love, losing our son and getting him back, to fighting corporate bureaucracies, and fighting wickedness in high places, all of which reveal the hand of a God who is not only real, but also reveals a victorious God who rises above anything and everything which we may have to face in this life. My husband often says that he could lock me in a closet and trouble would still find me. He would know after sharing the last forty-four years with me. There have always been dragons to slay, victories to win, and joys to share. Today, I am blessed to have my husband of forty-four years, my children, and my grandchildren. They are promises fulfilled. Love shines.

My next book will be more on "The Healing Journey." It will give you more detailed information on how to heal. It will take you through the steps of going from Victim to Victor. It will walk you through the stages of hurt and pain, anger, unforgiveness, and total surrender. I look forward to sharing it with all of you.

I can be contacted at my website: http://marshabarth.com

There you can obtain more help and information.

I would encourage everyone to begin the journey by taking the hand of the One who has always loved you most. He will not fail you. I hope that my story has shown you this truth. In my story, I often mention picking up that worn little Bible that didn't even belong to me, but to my brothers. I didn't have my own Bible until I was about eighteen years old. This was the source, the beacon of promise, the thread of hope that helped me find my way. Please choose it as your main source and seek those who can help you in God's love, spirit, and truth to find your way. I have also listed below a few resources and links that may help you find guidance, counseling, and information. Be blessed. Be happy and know that you can heal. May God's richest love guide you through this process as He walks with you on this healing journey.

Love,
Marty

Blessed Family Today
"Love Shines"

Contact Information

Contact me for speaking engagements, questions and information at:

marshabarth.com

www.facebook.com/The-Shattering-215752548593960/

twitter.com/mbarthmbarth

www.linkedin.com/in/marsha-marty-barth-9865a840

www.youtube.com/channel/UCdegaQc92g8vLHeB7KDJaUw

Contact your local pastor, counselor, or friend:

To report any suspicion of child abuse:

www.childhelp.org/hotline/

The Childhelp National Child Abuse Hotline

1-800-4-A-CHILD (1-800-422-4453)

For information or to get help for sexual abuse; rape, abuse, incest: rainn.org/get-help/national-sexual-assault-hotline or call **800-656-HOPE (4673)**

To get help from domestic abuse:

www.thehotline.org

or call **1-800-799-SAFE (7233) 1-800-787-3224 (TTY)**

To get help for bullying:

www.stopbullying.gov/get-help-now/

Contact the National Suicide Prevention Lifeline:
http://www.suicidepreventionlifeline.org/
or call **1-800-273-TALK (8255)**

Contact the Disaster Distress Helpline:
www.samhsa.gov/find-help/disaster-distress-helpline/
disaster-types/mass-violence
or call **1-800-985-5990** or text **TalkWithUS to 66746**

About the Author

Marsha Lynn Barth was born in the foothills of West Virginia. A businesswoman by profession she ran the family business side by side with her husband Mike in Pennsylvania for nearly twenty-seven years. She is the mother of two children (Mike Jr. and Jennifer) and has seven grandchildren (six boys and one girl), all who keep her busy playing ball and chase.

Marty, as she prefers to be called, is an author, advocate, speaker, and lecturer. She has spoken to college Criminology and Psychology students, to State Social Service forums, to "advocates against child abuse," and to "foster parents." She has spoken at State events to Representatives and Senators and has met with the Governor to advocate for awareness and prevention for the intervention against child sexual abuse. She has done many radio and TV interviews. Marty has been an inspirational speaker for the last twenty years, has worked at an addictions facility, was a regular speaker on Christian Radio, and has visited prisons across the U.S. for the last ten years.

Marty is the author of two books, *The Shattering I* and *The Shattering II*. Both books are powerful inspirational stories of Marty's life of overcoming child sexual abuse. More than another story of victimization, both stories reveal the power of love, the promise of hope, and the inspiration of knowing that what has happened to us does not define who we are. Written in novel form, both stories stand on their own. The first one deals more with the issues of abuse; the second deals more with the healing journey. Both stories are powerful stories that enable the reader to understand abuse from a child's perspective, why they remain silent, and how just one thread of hope can change a life forever. Readers are held in suspense and will find their hearts forever touched by these inspiring stories where they learn about a healing journey, how we can go from lost to found, from death to life, and from victim to victor!

Marty is an avid teacher, speaker and advocate, and is available for speaking events. She draws from her life's experiences and brings forth a message of hope to the broken, hopeless, abused and shattered—to let others know that they do matter—so that every soul may know the reality of a God who truly loves and cares for them and all of their heartfelt hopes and dreams. She wants others to understand that they can heal, and that healing is a journey that will lead them to God's heart and purpose for their lives—"their happiness and salvation."

Contact Marsha Barth for speaking and teaching
engagements, for her studies on "Victim to Victor,
The Healing Journey, The Pathway to Healing and more
studies and information, at the following:

marshabarth.com
www.facebook.com/The-Shattering-215752548593960/
twitter.com/mbarthmbarth
www.linkedin.com/in/marsha-marty-barth-9865a840
www.youtube.com/channel/UCdegaQc92g8vLHeB7KDJaUw

Books by Marsha (Marty) Barth

"The Shattering I"
"The Shattering II"
Coming soon— "The Healing Journey"

Path to Healing

Emotional		Physical
	HURT *(no choice)*	
ABUSED	⬇	ABUSED
	PAIN *(no choice)*	
VICTIM	⬇	VICTIM
	BROKENESS/ANGER *(no choice)*	
SURVIVOR	⬇	SURVIVOR
	ANGER SPIRIT *(choice)*	
REVENGER	⬇	OVERCOME
	UNFORGIVENESS/FORGIVENESS *(choice)*	
RETALIATER	⬇	CONQUEROR
	HURT/HELP *(choice)*	
ABUSER	⬇	VICTOR
	CONTROL/SURRENDER *(choice)*	
DEATH		LIFE

From Victim to Victor

"If the Son therefore shall make you free, you shall be free indeed." *John 8:36*